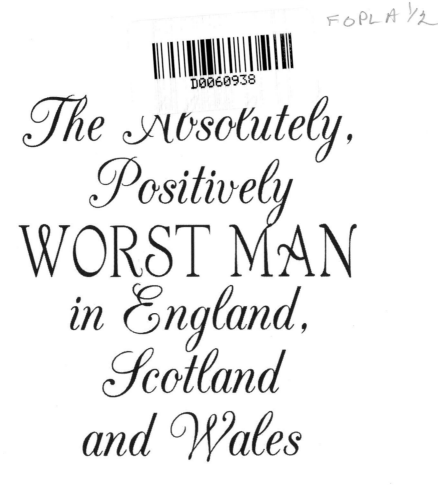

The Absolutely, Positively WORST MAN in England, Scotland and Wales

ANNE STUART

Impeccably Demure Press

I

IT STARTED in a card room at a gentlemen's club on St. James Street in London on a sultry spring night. The heat was oppressive, a positive freak of nature, and while most members of this most august establishment remained starched and sweating, the two disgraced reprobates in the private room had shed neckcloths and coats while they continued their night of gaming and drinking.

Mr. Bowdoin, the manager of the club, a man who terrified green young lordlings and elderly members alike, had only hesitated at the door for a moment. Their dress was an affront to the establishment, but no one could see them, and Adderley had been known to kill a man for less provocation than a complaint about his attire. In fact, he was always a disaster in a world where clothes meant everything, and it was none of Bowdoin's business. He closed the door quietly behind him and walked on, praying God that they left by the back door, or, failing that, after everyone else had finally deserted the place. Neither of the men even noticed he'd been there.

"I'm getting married, y'know," George said.

Christopher St. James Constant, third Earl of Adderley, the absolutely, positively worst man in all of England, Scotland, Ireland, and Wales, slowly lifted his gaze from his cards to view his partner in debauchery in the wavering candlelight. Sir George Latherby, baronet, was not a prepossessing sight, even when sober, and being drunk, which he very definitely was, did not improve matters. The pouches in his soft face turned pink, the malice in his eyes shone forth, and his plump lips relaxed into an expression not unlike a dyspeptic hake.

"Again? My condolences to the bride," the worst man in England murmured. He could drink any man under the table, but Latherby had the merit of holding out the longest, and it was still undecided who would be fleecing whom that night. "Who is the poor woman?"

Latherby chuckled, unoffended. "No one you know, you ripe bastard. She ain't seen out of good company, and you ain't seen in it."

"So true," Christopher, better known as Kit, said lazily. "I'm a lucky man. I rather thought you weren't allowed in much higher gatherings than I am—how did you happen to meet this paragon of womanhood?"

"What makes you think she's a paragon?" Latherby demanded, tossing a card down with a casual air.

Kit wasn't fooled. Even when he was on the edge of passing out, Latherby was sharper in his cards than the most talented player, and he cheated almost as well as Kit did. He could respect that. Ignoring the card, he dealt Latherby another from the bottom of the deck. "She must be magnificent to have lured you into wedlock."

"She's plain and quiet and disgraced."

"Well, obviously she's disgraced—otherwise, why would she accept your offer? The question is, why did you make that offer in the first place?" He'd lowered his gaze to his cards again, seemingly distracted, acutely aware of Latherby's slightest twitch.

His drinking partner slammed his glass down on the table with an excess of good will and beamed at him. "Why in the world should you ask? There's only one possible reason."

"She's wealthy," Kit said lazily. "Obviously. And of low morals despite her plain and quiet appearance, no doubt, if she managed to get ruined."

Latherby made a derisive noise that sounded vaguely like breaking wind. "Much you know. The Honorable Miss Bryony

Marton is as pure as the driven snow. It's her ramshackle father that's the problem. With her upbringing, not to mention her patriarch, no other man would have her."

"Bryony Marton? I don't believe I know the family, and I usually know most disgraceful people in, or out of, society."

Latherby shrugged. "Stands to reason. They're from the Lake District and the scandal was mostly kept out of town. He was the Earl of Doncaster—old, old name. Apparently, Doncaster had a particular affection for one of his neighbors, and the man's wife took exception to it."

"Doncaster's wife?"

Latherby chortled. "No, the wife of the neighbor. Apparently she thought her husband should be in her bed, not with another man. She shot Doncaster when she caught them. Of course, they hushed it up at the time, and Doncaster conveniently took months to die of a septic infection, and he expired on the continent, but you know how rumors spread."

"And tell me why I should be interested in this?"

"You asked," Latherby pointed out fairly.

"I assume it was mainly about her father's estate."

Latherby shook his head, then stilled for a moment as if the gesture had managed to rattle his brain. An impossibility, Kit thought. Whatever brain he had was thoroughly pickled in alcohol—it would only slosh. "Her father was destitute, the estate left to a distant relative with a religious bent. The heir had the manor house in the Lake District burned down. But the girl had an aunt, Doncaster's wife's sister, who married a Croesus. She left everything to the girl once she's married, but the chit's not accepted into the best company with such a cloud on her name."

"I imagine not. Society has absolutely no sense of humor. How did you happen to get your greedy hands on her?"

"Ranelagh!" Latherby said triumphantly. "Nothing like a pleasure garden for being indiscreet. She was there with her cousins, I was wearing my puce with the silver lacing, and I dazzled her."

Kit surveyed his companion's slovenly form and had his doubts.

"So you decided to pursue her once you learned that she was a wealthy orphan?"

Latherby tried to roll his eyes, meeting with minimal success due to the number of bottles he'd downed that night. "Of course not. I compromised her. Easiest thing in the world. Got her lost in the woods and Bob's your uncle. She lives with her cousins, but the family had been trying to get rid of her—they've got two daughters who have made their debut, and the presence of Miss Marton was making life extremely difficult. People could scarcely send invitations to the girls and exclude Miss Marton, but no one wants her around. Rather like the skeleton at the feast, don't you know? This works out well for everyone, and I only had to promise to give her second cousin James a quarter of her exceedingly plump income."

Kit raised an eyebrow. "That sounds uncharacteristically generous of you, George."

"I didn't say I was going to, I merely said I agreed to. Once we're married, there's not much they can do about it without making their own precarious position worse. No, I intend to have every last penny and enjoy it immensely. It should keep me in style for at least two years, perhaps a little more."

"And after that?" It was no more than idle curiosity—Latherby had no more scruples than he did.

His friend shrugged, disposing of another seemingly random care. "Then I'll get rid of her in one way or another. Perhaps take her on a trip to the continent and lose her in the Alps or something. Needs find means."

Kit thought of the plain, quiet Miss Marton with not the slightest sympathy. Knowing Latherby, she'd be better off dead. "And what if this blissful union produces children?"

The look of dismay on Latherby's face was comical. "Lord, I hadn't thought of that. Hadn't thought of bedding her, in truth. She's ugly as sin with hideous red hair and spots all over her face, and she'd be stiff as a board and cry all the time." He thought for a moment. "I suppose an heir wouldn't be a terrible idea. M'great aunt could raise the brat."

"Ah, the joys of fatherhood," Kit said.

"Better go see the sawbones then," Latherby mused. "I've got the pox again and the mercury treatment didn't work last time. Wouldn't want the brat born diseased. I'd have to drown him."

"It might be a girl."

"Definitely drown her," Latherby said carelessly. "You'll stand up with me, of course." It wasn't a question.

Kit lifted his lazy lids. "At the birth, the drowning, or the wedding?"

"The wedding, you idiot. Maybe the other two if I need you."

Kit looked at his companion, the second worst man in England, and smiled his singularly beautiful smile, the one that always took people off guard. "It would be my honor," he said, placing his final card on the table, the one that had been hidden behind the fall of lace at his wrists. "And I believe you're already spending your bride purse."

Latherby blinked. "Cheater," he said amiably enough. "I don't suppose you'd wait till after I tie the knot to make good on my debts?" He stared at Kit blearily. "No, I suppose not."

"I find it's always best to settle one's debts of honor immediately. That way there can be no misunderstandings about intentions."

Latherby didn't make the mistake of underestimating his opponent's good will. "Of course," he said, hurriedly. "We are marrying quite quickly. They've already read the banns the first time. I expect a quiet ceremony in a couple of weeks."

"And you really think I'd be willing to wait that long?" Kit's voice was silken, and Latherby began to sweat. "That's hardly been our arrangement."

"Wouldn't think of it, old man!" he said hastily. "I...er...just hadn't paid attention to the wager. I'm a little short this month. Had to come up with something impressive for my fiancée's ring. It was damned expensive for paste. And I'm not going to get a penny more until we tie the knot."

"Then I expect a trip to Scotland is in order. I'd rather hate to skewer you, old friend. Very few men have the stamina for excess that you do. And who else comes even close to matching my acts of villainy?"

Latherby looked pathetically pleased at the encomium. "We'll head to Gretna tomorrow, I promise. I'll call on you the moment I get back, with your money and a suitable recompense for your wait. Say, an additional ten percent."

"I believe you will owe me double. And you won't be calling on me—I have every intention of accompanying you. Town has grown so boring. I plan to enjoy your honeymoon as much as you will."

For once, he'd managed to silence Latherby. He opened and closed his fish-like mouth once, twice, then nodded.

Kit smiled faintly. His restless ennui had changed on the turn of a card. Kidnapping a proper bride was just the thing to keep him amused for a day or so, and thoroughly in keeping with his dastardly reputation, a thing of which he was inordinately proud. When he tired of the adventure, he'd abandon Latherby and go in search of further sensation. For now, at least, he had something entertaining to accomplish.

Of course Latherby would accede to his wishes—he always did. This would provide only a small relief from the crushing boredom that was his life, but he accepted it well enough. If things began to lag, he could always torture Latherby a bit, to spice things up. Weeping virgins were not his favorite thing, but he knew how to deal with that as well.

With a weary sigh, he rose, tipping over his empty wine bottle. "I'll be ready by nine in the morning."

"Good God, Kit, it's half past two already. There's no way I can get in to see my fiancée and lure her away in less than eight hours. Be reasonable."

"Nine," he repeated. "Be ready."

§

THE HONOURABLE MISS Bryony Marton sat curled up on the window seat in the nursery, staring out over the rooftops of Mayfair in the early morning haze and plotting her escape. She'd managed to open one of the windows on the previous warm day—her cousin Maryanne kept all the ones on the lower floors tightly closed, considering fresh air to be hazardous to one's health. Given the stink of London streets, Maryanne might have the right of it, but it was preferable to suffocating to death in this persistent heat.

Then again, this house felt like an airless mausoleum even in the dead of winter—there was no warm breeze or icy blast that could blow life into it. And two years was more than long enough. Bryony was leaving, as soon as she could come up with a reliable plan.

It was her own foolish fault that she'd agreed to marry Sir George Latherby. When she and Cecilia had run across the cheerful, clearly harmless dandy in the pleasure gardens of Ranelagh two weeks ago, she hadn't worried for a moment when her cousin disappeared with a good-looking soldier. Cecilia was always skating on the edge of disaster, and Bryony was used to rescuing her, covering for her, keeping her on a relatively safe path. Sir George's offer to keep her company seemed harmless enough, and when Cecilia's absence grew to a worrisome length, he'd done the gentlemanly thing and offered to accompany her in search of her errant cousin.

She was lacking in self-preservation, perhaps, but she was far from stupid. Another woman might believe the excuse that he'd gotten lost, he was dreadfully sorry, he couldn't understand how it could have happened, he'd do the right thing, of course, and offer for her. She'd simply looked at him, her expression blank as Maryanne had screeched and Cousin James had bellowed and let them arrange her future with surprising accord. She would marry the man with whom she'd spent too many hours in the thick woods at Ranelagh, and she would be off her cousin's hands. Her untouchable fortune would be the property of the absurdly dressed, decidedly dissolute gentleman who'd compromised her. One could hardly say ruined, since the sour old gossips had already seen to that, and in truth, Bryony failed to see how her standing could descend any lower. No one but Cecilia wanted to be in her company anyway—if she'd been compromised, it would make little difference—but no one was interested in hearing her opinion, everyone shouting over her excitedly, and she'd given in.

She'd actually considered going through with it—with a husband, she'd have a home of her own, babies, and, given Sir George's disgraceful reputation, she probably wouldn't have to deal with him very much at all. But as the banns were read and the time grew nearer, she knew marriage was no escape for her, but simply another prison, and now she had two people to escape from, her fiancée and her cousin. Damn it.

She savored the curse, then said it out loud. "Damn it," was quiet and firm in the nursery, but immensely satisfying.

"What are you damning, coz?" came Cecilia's cheerful voice. "Not me, I hope."

Bryony jumped, startled. "What are you doing up so early?"

Cecilia climbed onto the window seat beside her and took the cup of tea out of her hand. She made a face at it. "Why in the world can't you put more sugar in your tea?" she demanded, nonetheless draining it. "This tastes awful."

Bryony took the empty cup away. "Because I'm sweet enough as I am?" she suggested. "Besides, this was ostensibly for me."

Cecilia dismissed that. "Everyone knows I'm always drinking your tea. They should make adjustments."

"I don't like a lot of sugar."

"But you wouldn't mind having just the teensiest bit more, for my sake?" Cecilia said winningly. "Where's the pot?"

"Over on the table, but it's empty. I've been up since dawn."

Cecilia pouted. "'Oh, churl, drunk all and left no friendly drop to help me after?'" she declaimed, having once performed the death scene from Romeo and Juliet to the boisterous acclaim of her friends and family, and Bryony laughed.

"I dare you to plunge a dagger into your heart," she said.

"Eww, no! I wouldn't have the nerve. If I were Juliet, I'd throw myself off a cliff or something. Much tidier."

"If I were Juliet, I'd step over Romeo's body and get myself out of Verona, posthaste. Anyone who hatches such a hare-brained scheme deserves what they get," Bryony said, ever practical.

"But it was Friar Laurence who came up with the idea, and he's still around at the end, looking guilty as sin."

Bryony hid her surprise. Cecilia was not known for her acute literary criticism, but she'd remembered that much. At some point, she'd have to remind herself not to underestimate her flighty cousin. "So he is. Which just goes to show you should think twice before you trust a man, even a priest."

Cecilia giggled. "Don't let Mama hear you say that. She says women are intellectually inferior creatures who exist to soothe men with their womanly attractions."

Bryony glanced down at her plump body. "Not all of us," she said wryly. "And your mother is an idiot." The words were out before she could stop them, and she slapped a hand over her mouth. "Pay no attention to me, cousin. I'm out of sorts today. Cousin Maryanne is a lovely woman..."

"My mother *is* an idiot," Cecilia said cheerfully. "And you're never out of sorts. It's your father's influence, isn't it? My mother says he was a terrible man, dragging you all around the world, to the most inappropriate places, living a scandalous life. It's no wonder you're..." Belatedly, Cecilia's tact reasserted itself. "That is, you're a bit..."

"Odd?" Bryony supplied good-naturedly. Defending her free-thinking father was a lost cause. She simply had to mourn him in silence. "Doubtless. What are you doing up so early, anyway? You usually sleep hours later. Or didn't you go to bed last night?"

"I woke up and couldn't get back to sleep, so I thought I may as well get up." Her nervous fingers pleated the skirt of the simple day dress she was wearing. "I was worried about you."

Bryony blinked. "You were? Why ever for?"

"It's my fault you have to marry Latherby," she said unhappily. "If I hadn't gone off with the lieutenant, then you wouldn't have been compromised, when I was the one who misbehaved. If anyone is forced into a bad marriage, it should be me."

"Who says I'm being forced?" Bryony said carefully. While she loved Cecilia, she had no delusions about her cousin's ability to keep a secret. If she knew Bryony was planning to leave, she'd either let something drop accidentally or beg to be taken along. "And why should the marriage be bad? Yes, it's hardly a love match, but that's much better. He's not interested in me, and I don't care for him. He's a social creature, I like the country. I doubt we'll be forced to spend much time together."

Cecilia did not look convinced. "If you went out in society more often, you'd know about Latherby's reputation. He's not accepted most places."

"Neither am I."

"There are unsavory rumors about the man...."

"There are unsavory rumors about my father, all of them true, and I adored him. Society loves to gossip, cousin, and most of it is lies. I'm not worried." Because she wasn't going through with it, but she could hardly tell Cecilia, who was eying her out of troubled, china-blue eyes.

"He's friends with the worst man in all of England."

That surprised a laugh out of Bryony. "Someone actually has that title? What an achievement!"

"You may laugh all you want, but I'm serious. I'm talking about Adderley, the Inconstant." She uttered the name in hushed, dreadful tones, as if articulating it might summon the devil.

"And who's Adderley?" It was a prosaic question, and Cecilia didn't hide her affront.

"Who's Adderley? Christopher St. James Constant, the earl of Adderley? You have to have heard stories!"

Bryony shook her head, secretly amused at Cecilia's melodrama. "I'm afraid not. And he's an earl?"

"It's an Irish title." Cecilia sniffed in disdain.

"So the devil is Irish?"

"Oh, he's not that bad," Cecilia said grudgingly.

Bryony surveyed her. "He's the worst man in the world, but at least he's not Irish? That hardly makes sense, CeeCee. What have you got against the Irish?"

"Don't be absurd. You know what I mean."

"Not really." Of course, Bryony knew her cousin's prejudices, inherited directly from her small-minded mother, and arguing was a waste of time. She wouldn't have bothered with Sylvia or Maryanne, but Cecilia wasn't nearly as shallow and silly as she tried to appear. If she actually considered all her preconceived notions, she might see things more fairly.

Cecilia pushed off from the window seat. "Don't lecture me..."

Her protest died suddenly at the unexpected sound. No one ever came up to the fourth floor nursery with that heavy a tread—at the most it was one of the upstairs maids...

The door was thrust open, and Bryony's mouth dropped in utter astonishment, as Cecilia let out a little shriek of dismay. Two huge men filled the doorway, with kerchiefs over their faces, muscling their way into the room.

"Which one, Neddie?" one of them said to the other, ignoring the two women for a moment. If Cecilia had any sense, she might speed around them to the door—she was a great deal closer, and Bryony could distract them. But Cecilia was frozen, her blue eyes wide with shock, and she wasn't going anywhere.

"Dunno, Bill. He only says there's a female up here, and we're to bring her out to the carriage with no fuss. He didn't say nuffink about a second one."

Bill scratched his head. "You think it's the spotted one or the pretty one? Gots to be the pretty one, don'tcha fink? The old one's probably her companion, and she'd just get in the way."

"Mebbe," Ned said thoughtfully. "But I ain't sure. What if he wants the other one? Once one of them disappears, there'll be no way to get back and get the right one."

Bill heaved a heavy sigh. "So we's got to take 'em both, Ned?"

"Don't see no other way about it, Bill."

Bryony's initial shock had faded, and this was turning into a comic nightmare. How had these men even managed to get into the house, for heaven's sake? And who wanted whom?

"I suggest you gentlemen leave the way you arrived, immediately," she said in a cool, stern voice, not moving. "You clearly don't know what you're doing, and I have little doubt that you've chosen the wrong house for your evil deeds."

"She's a governess, all right," said one of them. "But she may be right."

"No, she's not, you idiot! His carriage is in the mews, right behind this house. And it can't be her—she's a starched-up one if ever I heard her, probably some kind of chaperone. Normal wimmen don't talk like that. Grab the girl."

Bill didn't move. "I don't know, Ned. I think the spotty one is the one they want."

"They?" Bryony echoed. "Who are you talking about? What the devil do you want?" *Run, Cecilia, run! Go get help.*

Cecilia simply stood there, her expression blank with fright, and she shivered as both men turned to survey her.

Bryony was off the bench the moment they turned their backs, and she grabbed the nearest thing she could find. It was a hobby horse, the long stick in her hand, the molting head of the pretend beast looking sideways with the eye that was coming out along with the stuffing. She rushed the first one, whacking him solidly on the head, as she yelled, "Run, Cecilia!"

Old Dobbin's head went flying, the stick broke, and the man closest to Cecilia grabbed her, smashed a handkerchief over her face as she struggled, and a moment later, she went limp.

The other man, Ned, she thought it was, had an aggrieved expression on his face as he rubbed his head. "You oughtn't to have done that, miss. We don't mean you no harm—we's just doing our job."

The other man had already tossed Cecilia's limp body over his shoulder, and panic sliced through Bryony. "Leave her alone, damn you! Set her down!" She'd lost her weapon; now her only defense was the heavy volume of Herodotus she'd been reading and a teacup.

"Never you mind, miss," the first man said sternly. "You just behave yourself and you won't come to any harm."

A quiet moan came from Cecilia's limp figure, and Bryony panicked. "Take me instead," she said impulsively, moving forward.

She had no idea where the third man had come from, she only knew a strong arm slid around her waist, drawing her back against a big, unseen body, and a voice murmured in her ear. "Oh, we're taking you both, my precious," he said, and a handkerchief was mashed over her nose and throat, making all her struggles useless. The more she fought, the tighter he held her, and she could do nothing to resist the sudden lassitude that closed down over her like a heavy blanket. As the mists grew thicker, she was aware of three things: Cecilia's limp form, her own helpless fury, and the odd sensation of the man behind her, his hard, warm body pressed against hers as he restrained her, overpowered her, and it had to be whatever filthy drug infused the rag that was crushed over her mouth, but as consciousness receded, Bryony sank back against him gratefully, giving herself over to the darkness that beckoned, giving herself over to him.

2

LATHERBY WAS sound asleep in one corner of the capacious carriage, his mouth open, snoring loudly, when Kit dumped his burden onto the opposite seat. The pretty one was a puddle of pastel muslin on the carriage floor, and she was bound and gagged by the incompetent who'd taken her. He climbed in after his burden, tapped the roof, and the carriage took off with an ungraceful lurch. Kit sighed. He despised breaking in new servants, almost as much as he despised riding in a carriage he wasn't driving, but men seldom lasted long in his employ. He'd had no choice but to let Latherby's inept henchman Coombs place his clumsy hands on the reins of the travelling coach he seldom used.

Even without their unexpected bonus, they would have been too cramped in Latherby's small landau, and while Kit was perfectly capable of ignoring discomforts, he preferred not to, and he'd provided his own carriage. They had a long trip ahead of them, complete with not one but two unhappy females, and he was damned if he was going to suffer. At least his large frame would be marginally more comfortable in his own carriage, and he might even sleep some of the time. He couldn't remember the last time he'd slept.

Latherby made a pig-like, snuffling noise, settling deeper into sleep, and he was drooling slightly. Shifting from that unprepossessing sight, Kit glanced down at the bundle of femininity on the floor. She was very pretty despite the dirty rag that covered half her face. She had bright gold hair, and he knew without a doubt that she'd have dazed, china-blue eyes and the intellect of a peahen. He could only hope she wasn't as noisy.

Her gown was disarrayed, exposing a great deal of one shapely leg, and beneath the virginal fabric her breasts were small and high, the way he liked them. If he grew too bored, he could always convince her to provide marginal entertainment on their trip north, provided Latherby didn't decide to become provincial about his dewy bride. It really didn't matter which one bedded her—Latherby was less driven by the needs of the flesh than Kit was—and assuming they both ended up having her, it wouldn't matter who might father the upcoming brat. Given Latherby's frequent bouts of the French disease, something Kit had so far managed to avoid, the offspring would doubtless be healthier if he sprang from Kit's loins. Which reminded him—he'd definitely have her before Latherby did. He preferred his women pox-free.

Glancing out the window, he watched the city come to life, the streets slowly filling, carts and riders blocking his travelling carriage. Coombs might be ham-handed, but he'd taken his instructions to heart—no one was to get in the way of their progress out of town, and he was proving up to the task, leaving upturned wagons, shrieking horses, and angry curses in their inexorable wake. Well done. Kit turned his back to the window to take one more look at the night's entertainment, stretching out his long legs, when something bumped his side.

He'd almost forgotten about her. He glanced at the woman and cursed abruptly. The damned female's eyes were open and she was looking at him.

Calm, steady eyes, and in the shadowy confines of the carriage he couldn't be sure what color they were, with no tears, no fury, just curiosity, and before he could stop her, she struggled to sit up on the seat next to him, pulling her disarranged clothes about her. Christ, he thought sourly. She was addlewitted.

Another woman would have come at him with claws bared, and he waited, prepared, but she simply shook out her skirts and then turned to look up at him. "I believe you've made a mistake."

Her voice startled him. It was low, pleasing, and completely calm. For a moment, his boredom and annoyance vanished—he was still half-drunk and easily entertained. "Have I?" he countered in an equally civil voice.

She glanced across the way at Latherby's bulk, then down at the girl at their feet, who was, mercifully, still unconscious. "I think you chose the wrong house."

They might have been discussing the weather, and for the first time in what seemed like centuries, Kit felt a stir of interest. "I don't believe I did."

She looked at Latherby again, a critical glint in her eye. "Well, perhaps not, but I cannot imagine what you would want with either of us."

"Your imagination needs encouragement." He took a long, slow look at her. This was Latherby's gorgon bride, with flame red hair instead of snakes. It was dressed neatly, tucked at the back of her neck, but there was no missing the outrageous color. Her face was covered with freckles—little splashes of gold flecks across her cheek-bones, her nose, her high forehead. He had a suspicion her entire, rounded body would be covered with them.

She had a gorgeous mouth. He hadn't expected it, in that freck-led, calm face, but beneath her unremarkable nose was the mouth of a courtesan. Even with his nascent headache, he found that mouth fetching as he thought of all the wicked things it could do to him.

How very odd! He hadn't had a cockstand in weeks, and now this plump little wren was disturbing his ennui-enforced chastity, far more than her companion. His little innocent had no idea, which made his thoughts even more arousing.

"Do you work for Sir George?" she asked.

"You offend me," he said mildly enough. "Do I look like the sort of man Latherby would hire?"

It was, perhaps, a mistake. Those eyes swept over him, slow, assessing, and he realized they were a forest green, startling in her unremarkable face. Her gaze slid down his long legs, up his strong torso to his dark hair that had come out of its queue hours ago, ignoring his lap and the hands he'd draped over himself. It was an odd sensation, as if he found himself being stripped naked by those eyes, even though there was nothing in the slightest bit flirtatious about her.

"No, I suppose not," she said finally, leaning back against the squabs. Her dress had ripped at the neckline—just a small tear, and it looked as if a bruise was forming by that luscious mouth. He would have been too rough when he'd slammed his drug-soaked handkerchief across her face. "Then I expect you're probably the Earl of Adderley."

Score one for the quiet wren. "Your expectations are not misplaced. I presume you're the young lady's duenna? Poor cousin, or something?" He knew exactly who she was, but he was in no hurry to admit it.

"Cousin," she agreed, moving toward the girl's unconscious body as if to help her. He clamped his hand down on her wrist and pulled her back, and that curious gaze met his once again. "I simply wanted to get her onto the seat."

"She can stay where she is. Latherby is not the best after he's been carousing, and I doubt she'd appreciate being covered in spew. She's asleep—it won't make any difference to her."

"If I may just pull her dress down..." she began, but he shook his head.

"I enjoy looking at her legs. Now if you wanted to pull the skirts higher I might agree to that."

She didn't react to that provocation. "I'll leave her be," she said, leaning back. He was still gripping her arm, not gently, but he didn't feel like releasing her. She had silken skin, as most ladies did, but there was an unexpected strength beneath. He glanced down, noticing the trail of freckles on her wrist. She'd have them on her breasts, he thought, momentarily entertained. Perhaps even the insides of her thighs.

She was wise enough not to struggle, though he might have enjoyed it. The stronger she was, the more force he would have to exert, and it would while away a short part of their endless journey.

He didn't waste time on regrets, and at two in the morning, this had seemed like an excellent idea. In the unseasonably humid warmth of a late spring morning, he had his doubts. He could be sleeping off the prodigious amounts he'd had to drink, then prepare himself for another night of doing exactly the same thing. Night after night after night. He'd thought this would at least shake things up a bit. He'd forgotten how damned long it took to get to Scotland in such a comfortable, lumbering coach.

He ought to bang on the roof and order Coombs to stop, let him off. Latherby could continue with his bartered bride and her companion. Or he could ease Latherby's way and take the unconscious companion with him, leaving her on the streets to find her way home. She looked like a pretty little thing from her position on the floor. She looked like every other pretty young lady—boring.

But, in truth, he was much more interested in stealing the woman beside him and showing her exactly what she could do with that unexpectedly sinful mouth.

"Why are you looking at me like that?" she asked, far too calm considering the situation, and his interest increased. "I'm aware that I'm completely rumpled, but being abducted doesn't lead to exceptional grooming, and that's no fault but yours. Would you care to tell me exactly why you have carted us off?"

He was absently rubbing his thumb over the tender skin on the inside of her wrist, tracing the line of freckles, watching as color bloomed on her serene face. "We had nothing else to do, and it seemed like an entertaining idea at the time."

The heat faded, to his regret. She tugged, very gently, at her wrist, and he decided to let her go. For now. "But why both of us? I imagine Sir George had some odd desire to claim his bride two weeks before the marriage vows, but bringing both of us seems a bit excessive."

"Those two idiots that Latherby hired couldn't figure out which of you was the bride," he said lazily. "The obvious answer was to take both of you."

"Obvious," she echoed, and he couldn't read the tone in her voice. Then again, he didn't much care. "And have you figured out which is the bride? It doesn't appear that Sir George has been awake enough to clarify matters."

He leaned back against the rich velvet squabs of his sinfully expensive coach. He'd won it from a puffed-up gentleman with more money than wits, and he'd proceeded to divest him of the former with no more than the slightest slip of the wrist as the cards fell. "At first glance, one would assume Sir George had been wise enough to compromise the beauty who lies at our feet," he said in a meditative voice. "She's pretty enough, and Latherby likes his pleasures of the flesh. He'd be unlikely to tie himself to an antidote even for money. But I'm having my doubts."

"Oh, surely that's too harsh," she said pleasantly. "I wouldn't say I'm an antidote. I'm plain, not ugly."

She was startling him again, and he wasn't sure if he liked that. Boredom had become so pervasive in his life that it had almost grown comfortable. To be lured out of it, particularly by a "plain" slip of a girl, might require too much energy.

"I stand corrected. He would be unlikely to marry a plain woman." He was watching her closely, but his words brought absolutely no reaction from her.

"He might not prefer to, but he's hardly the most eligible bachelor on the market," she pointed out. "His title is new, he's fairly unprepossessing, he needs an heiress, and his reputation is dreadful. Why, he spends time with the appalling Earl of Adderley."

"Well done," he said with a faint laugh. "But on the other hand, there's you. Not, as you pointed out, an actual antidote, but you're not in your first youth, you're covered with spots that are clearly unresponsive to milk poultices, and it appears you have a distressing tendency to speak frankly. Latherby likes his women silent and submissive and rich."

"Oh, I can be silent and submissive, but since we've gotten on intimate terms so quickly, I decided to dispense with formality. Kidnapping has a way of cutting through society's strictures. And I'm very adaptable."

"That, at least, is true." He didn't trust that adaptability. For all her seeming acceptance of the situation, he doubted she'd miss the first opportunity to try to escape. "I'll happily list the reasons I doubt you're the blushing bride. For one thing, if you're an heiress, you would have been snapped up in your first season. Men needing wealthy wives far outnumber the supply, and given the delightful spots that cover your face, you would probably take the first respectable man who offered for you."

She blinked, and he counted that a small triumph. "Perhaps I've been in mourning," she suggested. "This might be my first year in society."

"You're not in society," he said flatly. "At least, not in the first tier. You dress too badly."

She glanced down at her plain stuff gown, three years out of style and patched. "There could still be reasons."

"She's the one wearing the gaudy engagement ring, not you. Whoever had a ring of that size and value would never let it off her hand."

"It's paste," she pointed out.

Another point in her favor, he silently acknowledged. "Yes, but a young woman wouldn't know that. Most of all," he continued, "beneath that impeccably demure demeanor, you're not the dullwit I was mistaken in thinking you were when I first carted you off. I don't think you'd be fool enough to let a fumbler like Latherby trap you."

This time she did blush, not just around the edges of that freckled face, and he congratulated himself. It required effort, which was something he seldom expended, but she could be jarred.

"An interesting conclusion," she said after a moment, and another man might not have noticed that he'd managed to get beneath her calm regard. "You have yet to tell me why you carried off the bride and her cousin and where you're going. Scotland, I presume. Unless Sir George has changed his mind and simply wants to dispense with the whole idea of marriage and the woman with it." She glanced at Latherby's sleeping bulk. "I don't believe he cares much for the sanctity of human life."

"Neither do I."

She nodded, accepting the statement. "No, I expect you don't. Would you consider telling me if we're heading toward a rushed marriage or a darker fate? I do dislike uncertainty."

"Deal with it," he responded.

She glanced down at the girl on the floor. "If I can convince you I'm the bride, would you consider stopping the coach and letting my cousin out? We're not quite at the edge of the city and I'm certain she could find her way home. She's smarter than she appears."

"No one appears brilliant if they're unconscious and trussed up on the floor of a carriage. Though that's another point in your favor. If she's not an idiot, then she'd be unlikely to allow Latherby to compromise her. With her looks, she could do much better."

She nodded, accepting the unspoken conclusion that she, however, could not. "Then why not let her go?"

The heat was invading the carriage as they rumbled toward the city limits, and he realized with surprise that she smelled delicious. Like soap and warm skin and a sort of freshness redolent of the spring air and the beckoning countryside. Odd, how that familiar/unfamiliar scent affected him. He'd grown so used to the stink of London, the overpowering smell of scent that covered both men and women to hide their aversion to bathing, that he barely noticed such things. He could smell her, and he liked it. "Her clothes are much more expensive than yours, negating the idea that you're the heiress. And bedding a pretty woman is more enjoyable than fucking a plain one."

She blinked at the word, and he wondered if she'd ever heard it before. She didn't ask him what it meant, which was a shame, but if he grew bored, he could always demonstrate.

And that's when it struck him that he wasn't bored. Christopher St. James Constant, the Earl of Adderley, was taking an interest in something other than gaming and drink. Who would have thought it possible?

She eyed him critically. "I never thought that the Great Inconstant would be so finicky. I've been told men, children, and animals were often the object of your attentions."

Humor left him, but he gave her a lazy smile. "I do draw the line at children," he said. "And chickens," he added as an afterthought.

"I'm prettier than a chicken."

Lord, she was a dangerous woman! If only she were a man, he could enjoy her deceptive wit. "So you are," he said. "But there's no need to convince me. I have every intention of having you."

And that, of all things, shocked her. Her luscious mouth dropped open in astonishment, and her eyes were wide with surprise. She composed herself so quickly that if he'd started his daily drinking, he might not have noticed, but he considered her reaction a singular triumph.

"The stories must be true," she said lightly. "You really are mad. Stick to the chickens." She glanced out the windows, and he saw the resolve form before she turned back. "Let her go. Please."

It was what he wanted. She was begging him, all semblance of amused calm gone. She continued, "I'm the bride—she was taken by accident, and her parents will raise a huge fuss. No one will care much that I'm gone, but if Cecilia disappears, there'll be hell to pay. They'll send the Bow Street Runners after you. You won't make it even halfway to the border."

"I'm quite familiar with hell, and I seldom pay for my misdeeds. And while you've held your own quite well so far, you just lost your only advantage. You'd do anything for that girl. All I have to do is threaten her, and you'll behave."

"Why would you care?" There was real desperation in her voice as they passed through the city gates, and he knew a twinge of disappointment. She was going to turn into a weeping, whining creature after all.

"The noblest reason of all," he said, giving her his most winning smile. "I'm bored."

THE MAN WAS THE DEVIL. Not like a devil, not a ne'er do well, not a cad. He was Satan, evil personified, and it was all she could do to keep her calm expression. He was going to destroy them all, maybe even kill them, because he was *bored*. And there was not a damned thing she could do about it.

Glancing at the angelic beauty of the impossibly corrupt man beside her, she knew they were in real danger. He was the worst man in England—he had no morals, no scruples, no empathy, no human emotions at all, unless they were bad ones, and for a short period of time, her calm reaction had surprised him, dragging him out of what she suspected was a very bad hangover. Now, like a stray bullet, it had ricocheted and struck her, not her enemy.

He was watching her from beneath heavy-lidded eyes, but she had no doubt he'd taken her measure quite thoroughly. Indeed, he'd gone out of his way to verify her own worst suspicions about herself —spotty, boring, an utter waste of time. He'd been trying to get a rise out of her—she'd known that clearly enough. She'd known more about him than he ever would suspect from such a worthless dab of a girl.

She knew he was spoiled, ruthless, and a sybarite. A total nihilist,

sort of girl, more's the pity. Don't know if she's even worth the very plump settlement that comes with her. Money isn't everything, and a man's got to think of his own comfort, don't he?"

His friend lowered his head, the bloodstained handkerchief still pressed against his face. "Money brings a great deal of comfort, my friend," he observed in a slightly muffled voice. "If you're not man enough to take her, then I certainly am."

Latherby looked like he was about to argue when he seemed to realize he didn't even want what they were fighting over. He laughed, incredulous. "You mean you want to marry her?"

Adderley's laugh sounded almost cheerful. "Good God, no! I don't need her money, and that's the only thing she has to offer."

Bryony didn't flinch with the blow. Cecilia was moving, making a soft, whimpering noise behind the rough gag they'd tied around her face, and Bryony immediately stripped it off, pushing the hair out of her cousin's face as Cecilia's eyes opened.

"Are you all right, dearest?" she said softly, reaching for Cecilia's bound wrists and working her way through the tangled knots. Cecilia blinked up at her, disoriented.

"What...?" she began in a cracked voice, but before Bryony could answer, she felt two strong hands under her arms and she was unceremoniously pulled away and deposited on the seat next to Latherby, who simply eyed her blearily from his place in the corner.

"I don't believe I gave you permission to untie her," Adderley said in a lazy voice.

She didn't want to look at him, but she had no choice. He appeared as relaxed as ever, even as he held an extravagantly laced handkerchief to his face. She'd somehow managed to catch him on his etched cheekbone, and she glanced guiltily at her hands. The plain garnet signet ring that had belonged to her father had obviously done the damage, and she clenched her hands together.

"That's right, you virago," he said peaceably enough. "You've managed to mar my angelic countenance with that ring of yours. I believe I ought to relieve you of it."

Before she realized what she was doing she'd cowered back in the corner of the carriage, her beringed hand trapped beneath her other arm, pressed against her breasts. "You aren't going to touch it."

"You can give me the ring, or I can take it," he said pleasantly. "It makes no difference to me, but you wouldn't like it."

Her erstwhile fiancé decided to enter the conversation. "I'd give it to him if I were you," he offered. "He wouldn't hesitate to chop off your finger, and you've got enough going against you as it is."

She turned to him, all her carefully contained fury bubbling forth. "Oh, surely not." Her voice was like acid. "I'll have the protection of your name, Sir George. The number of fingers on my hand will have little relevance when I'm your dutiful wife."

The man chuckled. "You haven't had a chance to instruct her in how useful fingers can be, Kit?"

"I'd be more than happy to. Lift your skirts, darling." The impotent rage inside her built to a point where she felt light-headed. She could see the knife on the inside of his elegant coat, a concealed weapon that no gentleman would carry, and whether she wanted to believe he'd actually maim her, she wasn't going to take the chance. Maybe if she could get him to pull her back onto his lap, to continue to demonstrate his horrifying depredations, she could reach that knife and plunge it into his throat, and if she was hanged for murdering a peer, it would be worth it.

"Are you visualizing my bloody death, my pet?" he murmured, easily guessing what was going through her mind. "Much more dangerous men and women than you have tried. Only the good die young."

Cecilia stirred again, fighting at the loosened bonds. "Bryony?" she said weakly, struggling to sit up but unable to with the ropes still binding her. "What's happened? Where are we? I'm frightened." She burst into muffled tears, and Adderley let out a world-weary sigh.

"Nothing I despise more than a weeping female," he remarked, pulling the knife from its sheath and toying with it, gazing past it at Bryony's still figure. "Particularly virgins."

"You've had more than your share of 'em," Latherby said with a bray of laughter. "Why in God's name did you bring her, by the way?

Granted, she's much prettier than m'bride, but she'll be ruined, and her parents will raise a hell of a fuss."

"Maybe you should marry her instead. What you lose in the counting room, you'd gain in the bedroom."

Bryony ignored their conversation, surreptitiously trying to move close to Cecilia, but no sooner had she leaned down then she was pushed back by Adderley's hard, bloodstained hands.

"You're very disobedient," he purred. "I like that in a woman. But if you hit me again, I promise that I'll hit you back."

"Then let me go to her."

He considered her for a moment, his eyes running over her like a caress. Which was absurd—no one wanted to caress her. "Say please."

She didn't hesitate. "Please."

He released her, and she immediately sank down on the floor next to Cecilia, cradling her weeping body in her lap. Cecilia's distress came before any dreams of revenge. She would have to bide her time.

But she was going to kill the Earl of Adderley, she promised herself, and she was going to dance in his blood.

❧

KIT LEANED BACK and surveyed the speckled female at his feet. She was hard-headed, and he looked forward to the battle he intended to enjoy for the next few days.

She interested him, unlikely as that was. He'd never met such a calm, self-possessed female in his life, one so innocent and yet with the aura of having seen and done it all. He had no doubt that she was a virgin—his tongue in her mouth had shocked her right before she softened into it, and he knew he'd been on the verge of getting her to kiss him back.

No, she made no sense, and unfortunately, he found that irresistible. She would be a pariah in society, with those golden freckles splashed across her face, but he found them perversely erotic. Where else did she have them?

She was holding her cousin, soothing those tangled blond curls, so different from her own flame-colored hair, scraped back on her skull so tightly she must have a constant headache. She cared very much for the girl, and he leaned back lazily, considering how best to use this information to his advantage.

He ought to want the pretty one, the simple one. He should take her on the floor of the carriage, but that seemed both clumsy and damned uncomfortable. He liked soft mattresses and women bringing him to climax, rather than the other way around. But right then, all the willing, talented women paled, and he was in very real need of something different. Very different, with flame-red hair, dusted with gold.

They made a pretty picture, the two of them at his booted feet. The perfect, boring English rose, wide blue eyes filled with tears, being comforted by her older, wiser cousin. It was damned perverse of him to want the wrong one, but then, he'd always gloried in his perversities. He'd hardly find predictability a desirable trait.

She seemed to have forgotten all about his carefully contrived dark menace as she comforted her cousin. Odd, there was something appealing about the soft, nurturing sounds she made. It was a shame she'd never have children—she would be a good mother. A sight better than the harridan who raised him, who had screamed into his face with spittle flying.

He shook his head to clear the despised memory. It was a weakness, and he despised weakness, vulnerability. Perhaps that was why he was fascinated by George's fiancée—in the most dire of circumstances, she'd remained calm, almost phlegmatic. He wondered if she'd remain so when he got beneath her skirts.

It made no sense that he'd want her, but want her he did, quite intensely.

And he had every intention of taking her.

They stopped only once to change horses, to allow the men to stretch their legs and the women to stay locked in the carriage. One of the maids from the inn brought them food and a pot to take care of their needs, and Bryony would have begged for help, made a leap for freedom, but the menacing driver by the door was casually picking his nails with a very large knife, and she had no idea what he might do with it if she tried something. She would have taken the chance if it had only been her, but both the tavern maid, barely more than a child, and Cecilia were nearer at hand, and she refused to endanger them. Besides, she hadn't had time to come up with a plan. They'd have to stop again, and if she couldn't get help the next time, there would be still another chance. There was no hurry.

Cecilia was famished, eyeing the food with the first interest she'd evinced since she'd woken up, and Bryony ignored her own growling stomach as she passed her the bread and cheese, the cold mutton, and the dried apple tart. The girl hadn't brought much—bare sustenance—and Cecilia managed her first half smile as she polished off the last crumb of tart.

"I must say I was starving," she said with a sigh, looking around for something else to eat. Cecilia was one of those wretchedly lucky women with a prodigious appetite and the apparent inability to gain weight—all the sweets in the world couldn't change her reed-slim body, whereas even looking at something more substantial than a meringue made Bryony's clothes too tight. Of course, she wasn't wearing her own clothes—those had worn out long ago, and Cousin Maryanne had made the inspired decision to pass along the late governess's wardrobe rather than spend their own money to outfit her.

The governess had died unexpectedly, and wearing a dead woman's dowdy dresses had been depressing. Miss Tompkins had been a thin woman, and Maryanne's solution had been to have the upstairs maid lace Bryony more tightly, cutting off her breath and appetite. She'd grown used to the discomfort, but had learned to her regret to avoid most of the foods she would have loved to eat or suffer the consequences. It was just as well she'd given Cecilia all the food—it was uncomfortable enough as it was.

Cecilia was a smart, sweet, lovely girl, but with Maryanne as an example, there was no way she was going to grow up thoughtful and observant. She probably would have snatched a piece of bread from a starving beggar if they allowed her to, and she would have contented herself with the belief that they hadn't really wanted it. She accepted Bryony's share of the food as her due, and Bryony had simply smiled ruefully. She wasn't going to starve, and if there was a chance in Hades that her clothes would be a little looser, it was worth the discomfort. She could easily go without a few more meals as well—it wasn't going to kill her. And she'd have to learn to be frugal once she was on her own—the diamonds wouldn't support her forever.

She was about to reassure the unworried Cecilia when a shadow darkened the small window in the doorway, and a moment later, Adderley swung his large body into the carriage, settling down on the seat once more and eyeing them. He glanced at the empty basket beside Cecilia, at her flushed face and the scattering of crumbs on her day dress, and then he turned that enigmatic gaze on Bryony, taking everything in. There was no way he could know she'd given up her food, and for that matter, why should he care? If Cecilia was a bit self-absorbed, it was nothing compared to the terrible man sitting across from them.

A moment later, the carriage shifted again beneath Latherby's weight, and their party was complete. Her fiancé smelled strongly of drink—odd, she hadn't noticed that about Adderley, and without a word, Sir George settled back into his corner, taking up half the seat to leave the women sharing the other half, settled his hands over his rounded stomach, closed his eyes, and began to snore.

Before she could stop herself, Bryony turned her gaze on Adderley. He was watching her, but he was silent as well. He reached across the carriage and took the empty basket with the china plates that bore not a trace of a crumb and tossed it out the window with a resounding crash. His eyes then bored into Bryony's, as if daring her to say something,

But Bryony simply ignored him. He had clearly expected some sort of reaction from her, one she refused to give, though why the man would even care what she thought was a mystery. She looked anywhere near him after what he'd done to her, with that shocking, open-mouthed kiss. She couldn't risk him doing it again.

"Come here." The purr was gone, replaced by steel, and she jerked, startled. Cecilia didn't wake up, but it was enough to stir her, and she pushed Bryony back to lay her head on the wide seat, leaving Bryony barely enough room to breathe. Adderley must be able to see in the dark, because his strong hand gripped her upper arm and pulled her across the dark expanse between the seats, setting her on the seat beside him, while Cecilia immediately filled the space she left.

Bryony bit back her protest, and she didn't make the mistake of trying to squirm away, at least not immediately. He preferred resistance to cooperation—that was obvious, and she had to walk a fine line between them both. She sat completely still, every muscle in her body rigid, waiting for him to move.

But he seemed to have forgotten all about her. Her eyes were growing used to the darkness, and she allowed herself a brief glance up, but his head was back against the luxurious squabs and his eyes were closed. She didn't dare lower her guard, but as the minutes grew and he made no move, she felt her muscles begin to relax. Unfortunately, that allowed the chill to penetrate once more, and a stray shiver danced across her body, one she clamped down on almost before it started.

But there was one inescapable fact. The man beside her must truly be the Devil, because his body blazed like hellfire, warmth coming off him in waves. For a moment, she wondered if he was fevered, something that would explain his behavior. But nothing else had suggested he was sick, and indeed, there was a calculating calm to his threats and actions. He must simply be one of those people whose body ran hotter than most. And before she could stop it, she shivered again.

"Tiresome," the supposedly sleeping man said, and he put those hands on her again, and she steeled herself against his onslaught.

There was none. He simply pulled her against him, set her head on his shoulder and wrapped his cloak around them both. She tried to push away, but he caught her wrists in one hand and dropped them into his lap, holding them against that intimate part of him, something she never could have imagined touching. "I'm tired," he drawled, "and not interested in a wrestling match. Settle down or I'll unfasten my breeches."

She immediately stilled, and he laughed softly. "That scared you into compliance, did it? Cocks are not what you need to fear, it's the man attached to them. Now lie still and go to sleep, or I'll demonstrate."

She didn't move, she could barely breathe. Cock? What an odd word for a body part. All she could think of was a rooster, strutting in the barnyard of her family home, lording it over the hens, attacking the dogs and humans who happened to displease them. Was his *cock* a weapon? He was treating it as such.

But he'd lost interest in her once more, and she had no choice but to absorb the feelings, his strong arm around her shoulders, the cloak covering them both like a blanket, the fiery heat of him pouring into her bones, filling her with warmth and an absurd feeling of well-being. Which was ridiculous, and she fought against the seductive feeling, willing to set them at war again.

"Why are you being kind to me?" she said in a fierce, hushed voice. "I know who and what you are."

"I doubt it." His instant response belied any belief that he might have fallen asleep again. "And if you think I'm being kind, you must be mad, which makes you even more interesting. I assure you, my poppet, I am never kind."

The mocking term of endearment was more unsettling than it should be. It had been so long since anyone had used a pet name for her that this seemed a travesty, and he only used it because he very obviously didn't know her name, knew absolutely nothing about her except that she was engaged to his drinking companion. But some tiny, hidden part of her wanted that term, that affection to be real. From another man, of course, never this one. But she'd so missed tenderness.

Something that had been left out of this evil man's makeup. "I am not your poppet," she said with exacting calm. "I am not *your* anything. You don't even know my name. I'm not even sure my former fiancée knows it."

"Former?" he echoed. "Never tell me I've interfered with such a love match."

She tried to summon some ounce of fight, some quick comeback, but he was so warm, when she was always so cold. If he were serious, he could seduce her with that warmth alone, but it was all a joke to him. So she said nothing at all, as her muscles relaxed into his loose embrace, her face pressed against his chest, his heartbeat solid and steady beneath her. Ridiculous, she thought hazily. The man had no heart.

She couldn't afford to sleep—it would strip her of all her defenses, when she was trapped with this dangerous man. She forced herself to lift her head away from his chest, but a moment later it was pushed back with a not ungentle hand, and she gave up the ghost. She slept.

*

THE HONORABLE MISS BRYONY MARTON was nestled against him quite comfortably, which surprised Kit. He didn't like to be touched if he couldn't control it, and even the thought of sleeping against whatever nubile body had provided him his release was distasteful. He wasn't surprised that he'd ordered her from the opposite bench to join him—he liked making her do what she didn't want to. But why had his body relaxed against hers?

In truth, she was a peaceful creature when she was quiet. Her soft, round body wasn't precisely pillowy, but there was a certain comfort about her, almost a coziness that reminded him of his nanny when he was very young. As far as he remembered, said nanny, in her eighties, hadn't elicited junior cockstands like this woman had, but he wouldn't be surprised. He'd always been a perverse little bastard.

It wasn't worth questioning. He took what he liked, enjoyed it, and things like morality, decency, and legality were of no concern. If he found the feel of her body wrapped in his to be unexpectedly pleasant, then so be it. He took pleasure wherever he found it.

As she'd drifted into a deeper sleep, she'd curled up against him, her unconscious mind mistakenly thinking he was a provider of comfort and safety. He would have laughed, but he didn't want to wake her. Sparring with her had proven entertaining, but he needed silence, stillness for at least part of the day or night or else he'd really go mad. He was well on the way to that eventual conclusion to his misbegotten life, but he felt no need to hasten it. Not as long as there were intriguing morsels like the speckled robin tucked up against his breast.

He leaned back, taking her with him, and stared out into the darkness. Latherby was snoring noisily, and the silly creature they'd brought was lost in sleep on the opposite seat. Neither of them mattered—if they grew any more tiresome, he'd leave them at the next post stop. For now, he could ignore them and concentrate on the Honourable Miss Bryony Marton. There was a fierce little creature hiding beneath that bland exterior, and he would drag her out, expose her, and probably destroy her in the process.

He liked destruction, but not necessarily in the case of women, who were outmatched in the first place by law and biology. If she were as interesting as he suspected, as he, perish the thought, even hoped, then she might survive his attentions. Anything was possible.

Hope wasn't part of his lexicon. Pleasure, pain, deceit, and delight. There was a chance, slight, but a chance, that she could provide all of that. More likely, she was simply a slightly stupid, placid creature without the imagination to realize how dangerous he was, and when she realized it, she'd dissolve into quavering witlessness, rendering her a dead bore.

He closed his eyes. His senses were acute—he could smell the pungent tang of Latherby's unwashed body, the light floral of the sleeping chit overlaying it. But mostly the clean, warm skin of the woman beside him washed those away. He could smell the trace of a flowery soap on her flesh, in her unfashionable hair, and he considered moving his head down, breathing her in.

He was far too indolent to make the effort. He simply accepted the fact that she smelled clean and pleasant. And that he would do his best to dirty her.

BRYONY HAD ONE NATURAL GIFT, in her opinion. She had been raised as a proper young lady, and she could use watercolors to paint indifferent landscapes, sing on pitch but with little style, play the pianoforte with only a few mistakes, sew adequately, and even manage innocuously polite conversation when called upon. She could bake—but ladies weren't supposed to be proficient in a kitchen, the place she'd gone to in her lonely life for companionship, comfort, solace.

But there was one thing she did quite magnificently, and that was sleep. Once she was solidly in the arms of Morpheus there was little that could dislodge her, not servants pounding at her door, not Cecilia bouncing impatiently on her bed, not crashing thunderstorms or screaming fights or...anything. It was a gift, and it kept her sane.

So it was with only marginal surprise that she woke up in the middle of the day, bright sunlight all around her, lying in a wickedly comfortable bed, no longer imprisoned in that stylish coach.

She was lying on her stomach when her eyes opened, and she lay still, unmoving, taking in the sensations that flowed through her. The mattress beneath her, the smell of freshly laundered sheets.

Someone had opened the window a crack, and even after last night's chill, the unseasonable warmth continued. There was no traffic noise, only birdsong, telling her she was in the countryside. But where?

She could see her hand and arm splayed out on the bed beside her face, see part of what appeared to be a pleasant room, with soft colors and ruffles, and beside a chaise sat a table with a tray of tea on top of it. Tea, she thought longingly, about to stir herself, when realization slapped her in the face.

Her arm was bare. She had a coverlet over her, but that fresh air coming in through the window was wafting across her shoulders, across uncovered skin. And there were two cups beside the teapot.

Panic curled in her stomach. She had to be wrong. She was alone, her body felt no different.

The mattress shifted slightly, though she hadn't moved, and a strong, bare arm reached past to pick something from the bedside table. Her father's ring lay on the table, the one that had cut his face when she slapped him. The trinket was tiny in the strong, elegant male hand, and there was no doubt whose hand that was, whose body lay next to her, closer now than when she was asleep, and even though she'd moved nothing more than her eyelids, he knew she was awake.

"Don't bother pretending," Adderley said lazily. "Your body betrays you."

She kept her mouth stubbornly closed, her eyes as well. He couldn't prove she was awake—as long as she kept her eyes closed she didn't have to face the horrifying possibilities....

His body moved up against her beneath the covers, and her last ounce of composure vanished. It was all bare, hot skin pressed against her equally nude body, and she moved so fast she ended up the floor. Fortunately, she'd held on to the sheets as she'd tumbled, and she covered herself as best she could.

Unfortunately, it left her companion with no covering at all. Not that he seemed to mind—he sat up on the bed, looking down at her ignominious position with no curiosity whatsoever. "Do you always wake up so energetically?" he inquired in that lazy drawl he affected. "I'll have to see we have padding surrounding any bed we share."

Bryony prided herself on her level head and ability to adapt to new situations, but at that moment, she was not only speechless but oddly on the verge of tears. She dropped her head on her knees in silent misery, and she heard the shift of the mattress and knew he had gotten up.

"Look at me." It wasn't a request. He must have walked around the bed—his voice was far too close for her peace of mind.

Of course she refused, keeping her head down, her eyes squeezed shut, her jaw rigid with the effort not to cry.

"Look at me." There was a thread of steel in his voice now, and he wasn't going to take no for an answer. Too bad. She squeezed her eyes tighter still.

His hand on her jaw was hard, rough, forcing her head up. "You won't win this battle," he said in a softer voice. "You may as well avoid a wrestling match—it wouldn't go well for you." He tightened his grip, and her eyes opened to meet his, more an automatic response than any measured decision on her part. He was close, and her eyes looked directly into his, with that strange color, the ring of black around the golden irises. There was no humanity in his gaze, no tenderness, no sympathy. Not even lust, not that she'd expected it. There was only boredom.

She still didn't say a word, but he nodded, pulling back to look down at her. "That's better."

She wanted to slam her eyes shut again, but she didn't dare. He was naked. Completely, unapologetically stark naked, and unmistakably aroused. Or at least that's what she assumed was the problem with his male member.

It wasn't as if she hadn't seen one before. She'd seen boys swimming, she'd seen men bathing in the river, she'd even had a man thrust his naked, engorged penis into her hand, and it had taken years for her to rid herself of the memory of that soft-hard flesh, pulsing in her unwilling hand. She'd been unable to break free, much as she'd wanted—the man was a friend of her father's—and she had no one to complain to, but she'd developed a deep dislike of men's naked bodies from that moment on, when she was eleven years old and sitting by herself in the rose garden and the man—

"Close your eyes again," he said in a deceptively pleasant voice, "and you would despise the consequences."

It wasn't an empty threat, even though he released his hold on her jaw. She stayed where she was, huddled on the floor as he moved back, her body a tight mass of nerves, but if she rose on unsteady feet, she'd be too close to him. She wanted to curl in on herself, but she didn't dare, so she simply waited, watching him.

His almost impossible beauty extended beyond his face. Her father had taken her to the continent when she was fifteen, and they'd spent weeks in Italy, clambering among the ruins, wandering through ancient cities, dozing in the sun in a seaside villa, and, looking back, she knew she'd been at her happiest.

But during their travels, she'd fallen in love with a marble statue of David, outside the Duomo, awed by the breathtaking perfection of his marble body. Adderley's body held the same beauty, the same cold impermeability, and oddly enough, she felt her panic begin to drain.

Bryony considered herself to be an eminently sensible woman, and it had been years since she'd wasted time fussing about things she couldn't change. If she had to be ruined, the circumstances could have been worse. Her seducer was almost celestially beautiful, and she'd been lucky enough to sleep through the whole degrading experience, which seemed to have left no unpleasant after-effects. Hard to believe, when you considered the size of his...thing...that she wasn't crippled. The glorious sculpture failed to have such a grotesquely large appendage, but perhaps Adderley was deformed, and he had to abduct bed partners. Her knowledge of the specifics of the sex act were vague—it wasn't often the topic of conversation at social gatherings. Maybe the entire swollen growth hadn't entered her completely.... She supposed she could ask him.

"It's a cock," he said flatly.

"I beg your pardon?" She'd been staring at it, she realized, and thanked God that she didn't blush easily.

"That part of my anatomy that you seem to find so fascinating.

There are many other names—rod, penis, John Thomas, pig sticker..."

"Pig sticker?" she said faintly.

He continued his litany as her eyes glazed over.

She composed her face in placid lines. Her only defense was to pretend she was unmoved by his shocking behavior. "Very entertaining," she murmured, "but unnecessary. I don't think the subject will come up again."

"Oh, it will most definitely come up again," he said softly.

If she didn't know better she'd think she'd amused him. "Why?"

"Why what?"

"Why should the subject of your pig sticker come up again?" Bryony said. "You've already ravished me, and if I ever had any illusions about my desirability, you've done an excellent job of stripping them from me. There's no reason for you to bother with me again."

Now he was definitely interested, and she wanted to bite her tongue. Maybe it was her inadvertent use of the term "stripping," but how was she to know?

"Let me understand you," he said, lazily reaching for his drawers, though how he was going to cram that thing inside a pair of tight-fitting breeches was beyond her comprehension. "What do you think happened last night?"

She didn't hesitate. "You stripped off my clothes and debased me while I slept and I couldn't stop you," she said frankly.

"You couldn't stop me if you were wide awake."

There, confirmation, if she had any doubts. Not that she had, of course.

"And what was your most horrid memory of my debauch?" he continued, picking up his breeches, and apparently the thing was flexible, since he simply pushed it down and fastened the front placket. She could see the outline of it quite clearly, but she had no idea if that was unusual. She'd never once concentrated her gaze on that part of a man's body.

"I told you, I was asleep," she said with some asperity. "I don't remember anything about it." Too late, she realized her mistake.

"Would you believe me if I told you that you were still as chaste as you were before we met?"

She jerked up her head, startled. "Come to think of it, seduction would seem unlikely given your stated opinion of my appearance."

"What stated opinion of your appearance? I find you quite fetching," he said in a bored voice that belied his words.

She could hardly repeat his earlier ones, when he'd essentially called her an antidote. It shouldn't have mattered enough for her to remember. Besides, she'd always been told that when it came to lovemaking, men were notoriously nondiscriminating. "Then why am I naked? Maybe it was so dark you didn't care that I have freckles."

"It's not the pox, you know. They're charming," he said flatly.

She wanted to hit him. She tried to concentrate on her body for a moment, to see if she felt different, but he was too distracting, too infuriating.

"Besides," he added, "I see very well in the dark."

"So you didn't molest me?"

"I'll leave that up to you to figure out. Clearly, if I did, I'll have to do a better job when I'm in the mood to repeat the performance."

Bryony made certain her face was stony. "That's highly unlikely, given your judgment of my lack of charm. Why waste all that demonic beauty on me?"

He froze in the act of reaching for his shirt, staring at her in sudden amazement. And then he did the very last thing she would've expected—he threw back his head and laughed. "Demonic beauty?" he echoed. "You'd best watch it, poppet. You might end up proving to be far too interesting."

He pulled the shirt over his head and headed, barefoot, for the door. "I'll have someone bring you a bath to wash away the excesses of last night, and someone will doubtless bring something to eat."

The thought of two such glorious treats was almost enough to put her in a better frame of mind, but she controlled her enthusiasm, merely nodding graciously. She needed to be adult about this entire, awkward, messy business. What was done could not be undone.

The door closed behind him, and she scrambled back onto the bed, bringing the covers with her. She waited until she was certain he wouldn't return, then lifted the sheet to take a cautious look at her newly deflowered body.

It looked the same. No marks of passion, no bites or scratches or visible excess of lust. Not even, thank God, many of the cursed freckles. The sun brought them out, and she was hardly likely to expose her entire body to it, but there was still a dusting on the upper part of her chest, on her forearms, on her shoulders. Just enough to render her hideous.

But he hadn't flat-out denied it, and she could think of no other reason she'd be naked and in bed with him. If he were interested in a celibate night, he would have slept elsewhere.

She reached her hand down between her legs, but nothing felt different. Surely there'd be some sign of his presence? She didn't *feel* different, exactly, though in the last twenty-four hours, she'd been kidnapped, kissed, stripped naked, and had her first good look at a...cock. At least the grown-up male version of one. It was no wonder she felt at sixes and sevens.

Adderley must have deflowered her and then gone promptly to sleep. Very efficient, no wasted pets or caresses. Why bother, when she hadn't been awake to notice? In fact, why bother in the first place, since her own opinion on the matter had been inconsequential? Once more, she could thank the gods of sleep, Tutu in ancient Egypt, Somnus for the Romans, Hypnos for the Greeks. She had a particular fondness for the old civilizations, and she wondered if the Vikings had a god of sleep as well. Probably not—they were too busy fighting to take a nap. If she didn't sleep like the dead, she would have had to endure the whole degrading episode, and he wasn't the kind of man to give one fig about her feelings in the matter.

And she had to look at it more reasonably. If she was totally ruined, she'd be a pariah, shut out of her cousin's house, shut out of society, with no one trying to control her. She had just enough money for a small cottage in the country with enough space for her books. In fact, this was possibly the best day of her life, and she didn't even have to remember the whole, degrading experience. Done and over, she reminded herself, and despite his veiled threats, there was absolutely no reason for him to bother again.

The steaming bath almost distracted her. Once the servants left, she slid into the warm, scented water with a sigh of delight, leaning her head back against the copper rim.

Odd that she wasn't feeling more traumatized. The very idea of the sex act had made her ill, the memory of her father's friend with that disgusting swollen object pushing against her. For some reason, the sight of Adderley's far more impressive...cock, he had called it, left her relatively unfazed, and even the thought that he'd laid between her legs, touched her there, put her emotions in a jumble. She was no longer a virgin, and a beautiful man had wanted her. For shameful things, of course, but she'd never had a man look at her twice since she'd returned to England, and obviously Adderley had managed to persevere past her freckles, even if he denied it. The thought was curiously cheering.

She sank under the water, holding her breath, and emerged moments later feeling reborn. She now had nothing to protect— there was nothing to stop her from fighting the battles she had so far carefully avoided.

She simply had to make sure Christopher Constant, the Earl of Adderley, didn't attempt to do to Cecilia what he had done to her.

⁊⁊

IT WASN'T as if Cecilia could sleep. She paced the small, plain room she'd been allotted, probably a servant's room with its utilitarian furnishings and bed linens. The rough sheets were scratchy against her delicate skin, the small space was stuffy with trapped heat, and the window wouldn't open. She'd slept long hours in the carriage, only to be awakened abruptly by the coachman, just long enough to see the large man disappear into the house with her sleeping cousin in his arms. She'd lurched toward him, trying to stop him, but the coachman had halted her, putting his rough, grubby hands on her, and before she could do anything, she found herself hurried into the same house, into this miserable little room, with no sign of Bryony.

She'd be perfectly all right—of that, Cecilia had no doubt. What man would bother with Bryony, spotty, plain, on-the-shelf Bryony with her common sense, when Cecilia was in the room. She wasn't precisely vain—she'd simply been praised for her beauty for her entire life. It was her one advantage—she wasn't clever like Bryony, and bravery was not considered a desirable trait in a young woman. She could flirt like a champion, dance like a nymph, sing like a nightingale. In other words, she was worthless for anything but an ornament. If someone was going to be compromised, then it was definitely going to be her, and she could only hope she wasn't too big a baby about it.

Even if she was ruined, she might still make a decent marriage, though not as high as her mother had hoped. Dukes would be out of the question, likewise viscounts and earls. The best she could probably hope for was a baron. Considering that she never had any say in the matter, it didn't bother her overmuch. Finding her a husband was her parents' business, and her preferences were of no importance. Her mother was the one who cared about titles.

There was a light mist falling, and she had no idea what time it was. She wanted Bryony; she wanted her own bed. She had absolutely no idea why these men had taken them, but she had recognized the sodden man with the food-stained waistcoat as Bryony's fool of a fiancé. Not that he was a fool for wanting Bryony, she thought staunchly. Bryony deserved the best of everything, but most men were too shallow to appreciate her.

If that was Latherby, then she knew who the tall, terrifying god was, the man who'd taken Bryony away from her. Adderley, the Inconstant. Some girls might be blinded by his undeniably beautiful face, but she was much more sensible than that. She might consider an affair with him after she was married and finished with popping out babies—it was de rigeur for the women of her acquaintance, and he'd certainly be a fitting foil to her golden beauty. But even then, she might have her doubts—he looked very uncomfortable.

She wanted a staid, stolid, unimaginative husband and an equally traditional lover. She preferred an even tenor in her life, with her own needs comfortably in the center of everything, and there was little doubt she could have her pick—her father was already contemplating a number of offers.

She had no interest in a man like their kidnapper, no matter how handsome he was.

They had brought her a tray with an almost indecent amount of food on it—she eyed it warily when the shifty- looking manservant delivered it, wondering whose company she would have to tolerate. There was always the chance that Bryony would be returned to her, but the heaps of food were even more than was usually offered to two genteel ladies. People must think they survived on air alone.

It took a moment to realize there was only one teacup. All this glorious food was hers, and she could happily devour it all.

She hesitated for a moment. Her mother's strictures on the small, ladylike portions that were proper still lingered in her head, as well as the warning that she must never put on weight. Her purpose in this world was to be pretty, and to barter that prettiness for a fat settlement from a wealthy husband. If she did anything to jeopardize her only asset, she would betray her loving family. That asset was currently on shaky ground and starving herself wouldn't really help.

She looked at the tray a moment longer, wondering if she were capable of turning her back on the eggs and gammon, the cinnamon rolls and hot chocolate and stewed apples and...

There was barely a crumb left when she got through, and it was a wonder she didn't feel sick from everything she'd devoured. But she didn't—she felt happily, almost decadently sated, ready to face the world head-on and rescue Bryony from the monster's clutches.

No one came to retrieve the tray, and she once more began to stalk around the tiny room, trying to tamp down her worry. At one point, she dragged the spindly chair over to the high-set window to peer out, and she almost fell off it in shock. She'd assumed they were in some sort of wayside inn, but instead of stables, all she could see were vast, overgrown parklands. The sun was hazy, and her room had become suffocating. Dropping down, she headed for the door to bang on it, determined to demand her freedom. It was then she noticed that the blessed thing was slightly ajar—they'd hadn't locked it after they brought her food, and she'd been too caught up in her ravenous appetites to notice.

She pushed the door open, warily, certain someone was about to pounce, but the hall was deserted. If she hadn't been put in servants' quarters, they weren't much better. It was clearly meant for governesses and poor relatives, which meant that neither of the two men would be anywhere around to stop her, and Bryony would be nearby.

She called out her name, softly at first, but there was no reassuring response. Steeling herself, Cecilia moved down the corridor, cautiously opening doors, but it appeared as if none of the rooms had been occupied in months, if not years. Holland covers draped the furniture, and there was a thick layer of dust on every exposed surface.

When Cecilia reached the final staircase, she hesitated. She could only assume Bryony was in the actual servants' quarters, but whether those were up in the attics, as usual, or below stairs was beyond her.

She decided to head up. She could hear sounds in the distance, voices, but she couldn't identify them, and her most pressing task was to find her poor cousin. Bryony must be terrified, in need of comfort, and Cecilia soldiered on, determined to find her.

She might have missed her entirely if it weren't for the noise. The next floor clearly belonged to the family—one glance at the wide, well-appointed corridor with its slightly threadbare carpeting, and she knew they wouldn't be keeping imprisoned spinsters here.

But her sharp ears picked up the sound of a familiar voice and relief coursed through her. She began to run.

Only one door was ajar in the broad hallway, and she pushed inside and halted, momentarily frozen. Bryony was sitting by a window, her long red hair tangled down her back, her body wrapped in nothing but what appeared to be a sheet, a piece of toast in her hand, in conversation with a maid, and she looked up in surprise at her interloper, relief crossing her face.

"Cecilia!" she cried, rising from the window seat, her sheet clutched to her clearly naked body. "I was worried about you!"

"I'm here to rescue you," Cecilia announced bravely. The last of her façade crumpled, and before she could stop herself she burst into tears, flinging herself into Bryony's comforting arms.

PETER BARNES SHIFTED on the coach seat, his temper at a low boil. He was crammed into place by a plump banker on one side and a burly tradesman on the other, and the passengers on the opposite seat of the mail coach were eyeing him with suspicion. They had every reason not to trust him—as soon as anyone moved, he was going to claim a seat by the window, and he'd damned well piss his pants before he gave it up again.

When it came to the crowded mail coach on an unnaturally warm spring day, there was no such thing as squeamishness. He'd eat the wizened old grandmother clinging to the corner so fiercely before he'd go in search of food.

It was war, and he was a born fighter.

He had no way out of this particular assignment. As a member of the Bow Street Magistrate's Court, he took orders like anyone else. He was an expert thief taker, a keeper of the peace, and a solver of crimes. What he was not, however, was someone who went chasing after a pair of runaway females. A job was a job, and the officers of Bow Street, better known as runners, had a reputation to uphold. Eating a grandmother might put a dent in that hard-earned fame, but Peter knew he could talk his way out of it. He was adept at getting out of the trickiest situations, and he was ruthless, a right bastard in fact as well as in nature.

Some stupid chit had run off, taking another with her, and he was supposed to find them and return them home, all without anyone the wiser. One of the girls was a beauty, definitely a marketable commodity in any number of situations, and the other one was disposable. The parents insisted the girls had been kidnapped, but Peter had his doubts. There was no sign of forced entry, and the parents had neither the money nor the social standing to suggest ransom was a goal. In fact, if he'd had to live with those two sour-faced, starched-up, nip-farthings, then he would've run off by the age of twelve.

Of course, he wasn't ruling out any possibility. The pretty one could have been snatched off the street and sold to the highest bidder. But there was no reason her plain companion would have been taken as well, and the parents insisted they'd been abducted from a fourth-floor nursery.

His opinion of that cock and bull story was obscene enough to give himself a moment's entertainment, but it quickly subsided. This was a case for a newcomer, one of those bright young lads who were always showing up at courthouse they counted as headquarters. Peter had been with Bow Street for years, concentrating on more important cases, but he'd made the mistake of insulting his superior, and that hadn't gone over too well.

In fact, he'd sucker-punched Eldon, which had quickly turned into a brawl, because everyone else had hated Eldon as well and were glad of the chance to prove it, and when the fists had stopped flying, Captain Cleghorne had a broken nose and a bad attitude and Peter had been identified as the instigator.

So, while the rest of them got to concentrate on the more important things, he was stuck hunting down two hare-brained girls who'd obviously run off with the wrong men.

They were all welcome to each other as far as he was concerned. The parents had made it more than clear that it was only the pretty one who needed to come back. He couldn't even expect a decent tip from the gratified parents when he completed the job—they were clearly of a miserly bent.

Which was fine with him. There was a part of him who hated taking handouts, a stubborn, angry side that he kept under control. After all, money was money, and he made sure he used his *pourboires* fittingly, in the nearest tavern.

The banker next to him farted, and Peter almost reached for his knife. He could have handled this much better if he'd been given a horse and expenses, but the mail coach was the best he could do

The sooner he finished this job, the sooner he could return to his rightful place among the runners, dealing with things that mattered.

The runaways had been easy enough to track. Peter had taken the North coach—the idiots were doubtless heading for Gretna Green, and at each overlong stop, he'd questioned staff at the coaching inns to find that a huge black travelling coach had come through earlier. Two ladies stayed out of sight in the carriage while the horses were changed, the coachman making all the arrangements, but no one could give him a good description of the gentleman. Just that it was a very fancy coach, which should put the parents' minds at ease. They had no problem selling their daughter as long as the price was right.

Ah, but women of that class were idiots, and marriage might have nothing to do with it. In which case, the sooner he found them and brought them back, the better.

His current situation was putting him in a thoroughly bad mood. He couldn't lean back—his shoulders were too broad to fit with the other passengers taking up space, and his long legs were cramped. He was going to find the missing girls and drag them back to London whether they liked it or not, and then he might be able to concentrate on what was important.

Which included never riding in a damned mail coach again, no matter what his orders.

6

BRYONY PUT her arms around Cecilia's sobbing figure, automatically tossing her lovely piece of toast aside and barely managing to keep the sheet around her. Cecilia was weeping so brokenheartedly, Bryony's worst fears took over. She had no idea what gentlemen were capable of, but if Adderley had deflowered Cecilia as well in the space of last night...

"I was so frightened!" Cecilia wailed, and Bryony's hold tightened. "I was all alone, and you weren't anywhere, and I thought one of those men was going to rape me, and my mother would probably toss me out on the sidewalk so I didn't ruin Sylvia's chances, and you were sleeping in luxury where I was trapped all alone in a servant's room..." The indignation was clear through the tears. "Where were you?" The demand was more accusatory than pathetic, and Bryony let a trace of amusement slide beneath her reasonable gloom.

Cecilia was still unsullied, thank God. Bryony intended to make sure she stayed that way, even if it came to plunging the knife she'd filched from the breakfast tray into Adderley's nonexistent heart.

"Right here, dearest," she replied with her customary lack of drama. "I'm afraid I wasn't in any position to come after you." She hated to envision exactly what kind of position she'd been in while she slept the sleep of the dead. She controlled her instinctive shudder. Unconsciousness had been a blessing, even if she felt just a little bit of curiosity about the whole mysterious procedure.

Cecilia sat up, her easy tears already gone as she looked around her. "Your room is much nicer than mine. Why?" And then she spied Bryony's breakfast tray, still laden with toast and jam, and pounced. Bryony watched her help herself to the remaining food as she considered how much to tell her.

On the one hand, she didn't want Cecilia to become any more upset—she was fond of theatrics, and she'd probably suffer noisily over Bryony's predicament. On the other hand, Bryony managed to survive difficult situations by being practical and honest, and Cecilia would need to keep her guard up. If Adderley had considered despoiling her to be worth his time, how much more tempting would Cecilia be?

"I...er...wasn't alone," she said.

Cecilia kept eating. "Who else is here? Have they kidnapped a whole raft of girls for their wicked purposes?"

"No, dear," she said calmly. "I shared a bed with our kidnapper."

It took a moment for the words to sink in. Cecilia's perfect mouth dropped open, her cheerful blue eyes widened, as she slowly took in Bryony's clearly nude body beneath the sheet.

"No!" she gasped in horror.

Here we go, Bryony thought. She tried a casual shrug. "I'm afraid so. Not that I had any say in the matter, but at least I don't remember much of it." *Any of it*, she amended mentally.

"Why not?" At least Cecilia hadn't dissolved into stormy tears again. In fact, if Bryony didn't know better, she'd say her younger cousin was looking faintly disgruntled.

"Because I slept through the whole sorry business! You know I can sleep through anything."

"Even that?" Cecilia's voice was filled with absolute horror.

"Apparently. When I awoke this morning, I was naked, he was naked, and the deed had been done."

Cecilia narrowed her eyes. "How can you be sure? Just because he was naked doesn't mean he had his way with you. Forgive my plain-speaking, Bree, but gentlemen are notoriously shallow, and you have yet to find someone who really appreciates your finer qualities. After all, everyone can't be a beauty. And we both know Latherby fancies your income, not you."

It was a good thing Bryony didn't need outside validation of her own worth, or between Adderley's murmured barbs and Cecilia's deadly tact, she would be ready to throw herself into the Thames. Except, she suspected, they were very far from the Thames indeed. "It's possible," she said, not in the mood to argue her own unworthiness.

"And besides, why would he bother with you when I am at his mercy?" Cecilia persisted, clearly puzzled.

"Of course," Bryony agreed, seemingly unruffled. But inside a rebellious thought came unbidden. *Because he didn't want you, Cee Cee. He wanted me.*

Absurd.

"How do you feel?" Cecilia went on, seemingly finished with summing up Bryony's inadequacies. "Do you feel ravished?"

"Could we perhaps not talk about this? I find it just a bit distressing."

"You can't just pretend it didn't happen!" Cecilia insisted.

"Why not? I don't feel different, and I can't imagine any reason why he might want to repeat the...er...performance."

"Of course he wouldn't! But if he really did bed you, then there could be consequences. Babies! If that's true, even Latherby won't have you."

"Well, that's no problem, since I have no intention of having him."

Cecilia's shock was palpable. "You have to! Even without such a monumental stain on your reputation, you couldn't do any better. If he's still willing to have you, you should fall on your knees in gratitude."

Bryony resisted a snort. "You sound like your mother," she pointed out gently. "And Latherby is the reason we're in this mess in the first place. I have no intention of marrying a man who decides to kidnap his fiancée and then stands by while his best friend beds her."

Cecilia looked as if she'd like to come up with another objection, but words failed her, and Bryony breathed a silent sigh of relief. "I don't think my matrimonial future is our greatest concern at this point," she pointed out. "We need to concentrate on getting out of here. Wherever here might be."

"I know as much as you," Cecilia said, taking the last piece of toast, "but it doesn't look like there's anywhere we can go for help. We seem to be in the middle of nowhere."

Bryony nodded, rising to her feet and tying the sheet more firmly under her arms. There was far too much of her skin on view—all those blasted freckles, and without the use of Cecilia's maid to tame her newly washed hair, it was turning into a wild red tangle that only called attention to it. The ginger color was bad enough when confined to a simple knot at the base of her neck, but now it was a defiant flag of warning.

"First," she announced in practical tones, "I need to find clothes. Mine disappeared during the night, though our kidnapper possessed fresh garments."

Cecilia had always been easily distracted, and she jumped at that before Bryony could finish her thoughts. "He really was naked? I thought gentlemen simply lifted their nightshirts, and Lily McDonough's widowed cousin told her that with an affair, they didn't even remove their pants, they just shove them out of the way."

"He was starkers," Bryony said flatly. "I saw far more than I wanted to see."

Cecilia's eyes widened. "Really? You saw *it*? What did it look like? Was it absolutely revolting?"

It was the very last thing that Bryony wanted to think about, but there was no avoiding it. "I didn't pay any attention to it." It was a lie, a needless one, but she stuck to it. "And it doesn't matter—you and I aren't going to be around it anymore. We're escaping. I don't expect Adderley is the kind of man who will simply send us home—we need to fend for ourselves."

She pushed the door open and peered out. The idea of traipsing down the hallway wrapped in a sheet was unsettling, particularly if she ran into Adderley. Not that she had a choice.

Cecilia squared her shoulders, and Bryony recognize that gleam in her eyes. Cecilia reveled in melodrama, adored amateur theatrics, and had an abiding love of fairytales. She was clearly seeing herself as a heroine, a cross between Boudicca and Joan of Arc, and as long as Cecilia viewed this as a vast adventure, she'd be fine. Bryony had her wits about her, and clearly even being kidnapped and ruined couldn't crush her *sangfroid*. She ought to be more missish, but she'd never managed to get that behavior quite right. Just as well—she was their only hope, and missishness would get them nowhere. She would do what she had to—get them safely home if she had to find a pistol and shoot Adderley along the way.

It would be a shame—Adderley was such a pretty man, but she couldn't afford to be sentimental. He could just be grateful she wasn't worried about avenging her presumably lost honor.

The hallway was deserted. Bryony tugged the sheet higher under her arms. There had been absolutely no sign of her discarded clothes, not even her shift, and she needed to address her priorities.

First, she had to find something to wear. She could hardly manage to face off with their kidnappers if she was wrapped in a dratted sheet. Holding her clothes together in front of her would ruin the calm exterior she knew she had to project.

Cecilia was following her in full warrior mode, and Bryony had to bite back a reluctant laugh. It would serve Adderley right if he landed with two difficult females.

They moved toward the stairs. The house wasn't vast—more of a small country manor, and it clearly hadn't been occupied in a long time. That, or the owners were particularly slovenly. If it had been up to her, she would have brought this house into decent shape in no time—it really could be quite lovely. But that wasn't any of her business, she reminded herself, as she ran her fingers through the dust on the carved banister. What she needed was escape, and to never see this place again.

She needn't have worried about running into Adderley—in their procession from the bedroom down the flights to the main salon and dining rooms, then down to the library and estate office, there hadn't been a soul in sight. No servant had come that way either—the recently unsettled dust made her want to choke. Cecilia was accompanying their journey with a litany of complaints and guileless observations, prattle that finally ceased when they reached the kitchens on the lower floor and they met with the unblinking gazes of three women and two men, clearly the servants of this squalor.

None of them rose.

The youngest one, the maid who'd brought her breakfast, had been friendly, but at the moment, she simply looked cowed, under the thumb of her disapproving elders. Disapproving of what, Bryony wondered. And then realized she was standing barefoot, witch-red hair flowing down her back, clad only in a sheet.

She straightened her back. "Obviously, we find ourselves in a great deal of difficulty." She aimed for a tone between friendly and confident, though she couldn't tell how well she succeeded. "We've been kidnapped by the two men who brought us here, and we need help. I...can't find any clothes or shoes, and we need a carriage, horses, and a driver."

"Happen there ain't no carriage," the grizzled older man announced, eyeing her. "No driver either. No horses."

She tried to hide her reaction to that last, salutary blow. "Then we'll simply have to use Lord Adderley's."

"Who?"

"Lord Adderley," she repeated patiently. "The man who brought us here. Your master." *Were they all slow-witted?*

"Dunno the man." The grizzled man seemed to have been appointed their spokesman. "This house belonged to the Pevensey family for generations."

There was a small gasp from Cecilia at the name, but Bryony didn't turn to look. "Well, that's none of our concern. We'd like to vacate the premises as soon as possible."

"Haven't you heard me? There's no carriage, no horses, no Lord Adderley or whoever he is. They've left."

"Left?" Bryony didn't know whether to be relieved or stricken. They'd been brought here, wherever here was, and abandoned without a second thought. "We need to leave," she said, hearing the note of desperation creep into her voice.

"Door's not locked," said the grizzled man.

Redheads were famous for their tempers, but anyone who thought about her, and there weren't many, would insist that Bryony was the exception to the rule. She never lost her temper, never displayed emotion, presumably never even felt a passionate response to anything. They would be wrong, but Bryony had trained herself so carefully that she barely felt the spurt of anger before she automatically damped it down.

Suddenly, she was pushed out of the way, and instead of a martial Joan of Arc, Cecilia was now Queen Elizabeth. "Right," she said in a cold, biting voice. "You will find Miss Marton something to wear—shoes, hat, everything, and it will be of the best quality. You there," she addressed the younger man, not much more than a boy, who immediately rose to his feet, his back straightening. "You will walk to the nearest village and hire us as large and comfortable a carriage as you can find." She turned her attention to the women.

Their roles were clear even to Bryony, who in her peripatetic upbringing had never run a household. The young, friendly one was a maid of all work—scullery, upstairs, anywhere she was needed, and the large woman with the apron covering her vast proportions was the cook who was clearly enamored of her own creations. In between sat an older woman, thin, contemptuous, her face in a polite sneer. She had to be the housekeeper, for all that she clearly didn't bother fulfilling her duties in this abandoned house. She had the real power.

"You," Cecilia snapped with all the haughtiness of her pampered upbringing, "You appear to be capable enough to find something appropriate for Miss Marton. Get to it."

The housekeeper didn't move. "I'm more than capable. I just don't choose to."

"Miss Marton is the daughter of the late Earl of Doncaster, and I am the daughter of Sir James Elliston. We have been treated very badly, but we are far from powerless. We will leave this place, properly attired, with or without your help, but if you wish for a decent life and future employment then you'd best remember your station! My father has a great deal of influence and a very bad temper, and if he were to hear how rudely you've treated his daughter and cousin, the consequences would not be pleasant. For you."

The woman paled, but she wasn't one to cave easily. She rose with all her dignity and nodded like a queen herself. "I imagine I can find something appropriate. It will be out of fashion, of course." Immediately, Bryony revised her impression of the woman's station. Only a lady's maid could be that supercilious. "There should be something that will fit...*her*."

That contemptuous term was tossed her way, and Bryony suppressed her grin. She was perfectly happy being a "her" for the time being. As if her near nudity wasn't enough, they would all know she shared a bed with Adderley, and she wasn't paying their wages. She wondered who was.

"'She' is the Honorable Bryony Marton," Cecilia snapped, "and you'd best treat her with proper respect. Go!"

The young man had already scrambled away, the younger maid had jumped to her feet at Cecilia's first command, and even the grizzled man looked daunted. "Now see here, young lady," he began in a weak bluster, but Cecilia overrode him.

"You're a disgrace," Cecilia announced in her steely voice. "This house has gone to rack and ruin, and you're sitting there like the lord of the manor. I'm sure if you simply open your eyes, you'll find work to do. Get to it!"

He moved faster than the superior maid, and a moment later, they were alone in the kitchen with only the young girl and stolid cook, who'd calmly risen at some point. "Seeley's not a bad man," she observed, "but he's lazy as sin and a hard man to take in hand. You got him going faster 'n I ever could."

"You're the cook?" Cecilia questioned.

"I am."

"Make me some toast and bacon!" She thought for a moment. "And something sweet. Does the household have coffee?"

"Aye, miss. We've got coffee, and I just baked a tart with the first strawberries and fresh cream from the dairy. Shouldn't be wasted on that other lot, except for Betsey."

"Jimmy's a good lad," the young girl protested, clearly an admirer.

"Aye, we'll save him a piece as well," she said comfortably, moving toward the worktable.

"Lovely," Cecilia breathed, Queen Elizabeth departing. "I'll have tea, Miss Marton will have coffee, and we'll eat as soon as she's properly dressed. I assume that scrawny creature can be trusted?"

The cook laughed. "That'll be Miss Blench, or so she insists on being called, and she's most likely to do her job once she knows there's no choice. That young girl there is Betsey, the best little worker in the country and more, but there's just too much house for a young thing like her. And I'm Mrs. Seeley."

Bryony blinked, relaxing enough to no longer be a spectator to Cecilia mustering the troops. "That man is your husband?"

Mrs. Seeley grinned. "And a more worthless piece of humanity as I've ever met. I've tried to keep him in line, but most times it's just easier to let it go, and that'll never change, even if the king himself were to visit. Sometimes I wonder why I keep him around."

"You said he was good in bed," Betsey piped up ingenuously, but the cook simply laughed.

"Aye, there's that, begging your pardon, young misses. I'll put the kettle on. Betsey, show them into the little yellow salon. It's a bit cleaner than the rest of the house, and it's warm enough to open the doors to the garden."

Cecilia had wandered over to a row of cabinets to poke among the food, and Bryony wanted to laugh. She only wished she found food as comforting as Cecilia did. Then again, Cecilia never gained an ounce, and Bryony knew she'd quickly rival the mountainous cook if she ate even half of what Cecilia did. "Mrs. Seeley, who owns this house?"

She shrugged. "I really can't say, miss. As Seeley told you, it was in the Pevensey family for generations, the young fribble who inherited it never visited, and we heard he'd killed himself a few weeks ago after losing everything on a wager. Your guess is as good as mine, but it seems like the gentleman who showed up last night is our new master. Adderley, did you say his name was?"

She had no doubts as to who fleeced the doomed young man of

everything he owned and then stood by while he put a period to his existence. "He's not a good man," she warned her.

"Few enough are," Mrs. Seeley returned, "but they have their uses."

He's good in bed, Betsey had innocently quoted, and Bryony didn't want to think about the cook's surly husband in that situation. It was bad enough remembering Adderley with his perfectly sculpted body, his ironic gaze, his barbed tongue.

She needed to remember that there was a good chance they'd never see him, or Sir George, again. Such a cheering thought ought to brighten her outlook, but for some perverse reason she found it...annoying. That was one emotion she would release from its tight confines, and she wasn't going to worry about her mixed reactions to his disappearance. It really would be much better if she were never to see him again.

But what if she was with child? Cecilia's warning words had hit her in the chest and lingered there, burning. Not with pain, but unexpected happiness. She'd never even thought of children, at least, in anything but the most abstract terms. Now that there was a real possibility, inside her body, she could feel the excitement building. It would require careful planning—a trip to the continent with Cecilia's aid, a return home with the orphaned child of a nonexistent relative, but it could be done, and if Adderley knew he wouldn't care. And he wasn't going to know.

"What's that cat-got-the-canary grin on your face?" Cecilia demanded, coming up beside her.

Mrs. Seeley had gone straight to work, and already the divine scent of coffee was spreading its magic through the kitchen air, mixed with the smell of bacon cooking—two of the best aromas in the world. They were already free of their abductors, they had a solid plan for a return to London, and she was going to have a baby.

It was a huge leap from losing her virginity to becoming a mother, but she indulged herself. All this drama might eventually turn out for the best, particularly if she were going to end up with a precious baby and no one to contradict her. If Adderley found out he'd simply dismiss it, let it go with a laugh, wouldn't he? She had no idea about the ins and outs of the Ton, but he was too young to be in dire need of an heir, and besides, she was going to have a girl, with lovely blond ringlets and not a trace of red.

She looked at Cecilia. "I'm smiling because I'm happy. The bad parts are over, we should be back home within another day or so, none the worse for wear, and..." she put her hand on her stomach beneath the sheet, "...I'm going to have a baby, I just know it. What's not to smile about?"

Cecilia was giving her a doubtful look. "I don't think you can tell just yet," she said. "You don't get pregnant every time you do it, or so my maid told me."

"The pregnant one your mother turned off."

Cecilia nodded. "She explained a lot of things to me. And if you're pregnant, what are you going to do about it? If I can find Abigail, I could get the name of a barber down near Harley Street, but she says he's a butcher, and she wasn't going there again, said she was keeping it." Cecilia's face clouded up. "I don't want you to die, Bryony."

"The lass won't die," Mrs. Seeley offered, having eavesdropped. "We'll take care of her here, and she'll be just fine. Our new master, if that's who he is, doesn't have to know anything about it if she doesn't want him to."

Bryony looked at her in grateful surprise. The woman was far too observant, but the offer of help was as kind as it was unexpected. And impossible.

Before she could say anything, though, the cook continued, "However, your friend is right, it's early days yet. You won't know until your courses come."

But Bryony already knew. She'd been deflowered and impregnated last night, no matter what Adderley said, and all she could remember was the sight of Adderley's beautiful, nude body, the feel of all that warm flesh up against her back, the odd smile that occasionally warmed his golden eyes. Her baby girl wouldn't look anything like him, thank God. By the time the babe was born, she had every intention of completely forgetting his existence.

"Come along now." Cecilia put her arm through Bryony's, tugging at her. "And stop daydreaming. Let's go find the yellow parlor and someone will bring us tea and coffee."

There was only one thing better that a sweet, angelic newborn baby girl, and that was coffee. Shaking herself out of her reverie, she sighed, letting Cecilia tug her in Betsey's wake. There'd be time enough for dreaming later on.

7

LATHERBY WAS ALREADY DROOLING SLIGHTLY, and Kit looked away in disgust. The private room in the Cock and Crown had seen better days, but they had a decent cellar, and Latherby had drunk himself into a stupor in record time. Of course, he'd already had a head start from the night before—Latherby was never completely sober and moving from slightly addled to puddled wreck was always a speedy journey.

Kit leaned back in the chair, looking out the windows into the sunlit morning, or was it afternoon by now? Anything was better than looking at Latherby. The sun shone with idiotic brightness, the countryside was a lush spring green, and doubtless the air was fresh and clean. It was hell.

He was a creature of darkness and decay, the night, and all its minions. He didn't belong in this simpering pastoral setting. He'd had every intention of dragging Latherby back to London, albeit at a more reasonable pace than they'd left it, but for some unfathomable reason, they had yet to leave.

Latherby had wanted a drink, of course, but it would have been simple enough to take a case of wine in the carriage to keep him quiet. Kit should have so ordered—the sooner he escaped this sunny sweetness, the better, and yet he'd stayed.

"What's wrong?" Latherby mumbled. "You look like someone took a shit in your beer."

"Thank you for that lovely picture," Kit drawled. "In fact, I'm thinking about your fiancée."

Latherby blinked. "Why? I don't."

"I suspect she's not going to be your fiancée for much longer, so you don't have to worry."

"Wasn't worried," Latherby said, filling his glass once more, upending the bottle. He tossed it toward the massive fireplace, missed, of course, so it simply rolled across the uneven floor back to his feet, clinking against the other discarded bottles. "And she'll marry me. Can't do any better." He was mumbling, but Kit had no trouble understanding him.

"You think not?"

Latherby's snort was even more unattractive. "She's ugly, Kit. Covered in those orange spots, hair like a crazy woman, and now you've ruined her. She has no choice."

Kit thought about the splash of golden freckles across her cheeks, the unbound mass of flame-red hair rippling down her back. "You underestimate her."

Latherby made an attempt at a shrug. "I can't be bothered to think about her at all. But then, all cats are gray in the dark. A quim is a quim. I don't suppose she was any good, was she? I can't say I'm looking forward to the marriage bed."

Kit's eyes drifted over Latherby's unprepossessing figure. The rash on his hands had spread, and there were sores in the creases of his bulbous face. No amount of mercury was going to cure him now, nor would it help his intended. It was none of his business, of course, but there was still his unsatisfied curiosity. Unsatisfied body as well.

He'd had every intention of taking her once he carried her to bed. He'd stripped off her clothes himself, dismissing the nervous maid who'd been hovering. He'd been yanking at his own breeches— he was hard and ready and she'd been arousing him since he'd first sat beside her in that bloody coach. It mattered not that she appeared to be sound asleep—his cock would wake her up quite smartly.

The candle flames had danced across her body, and he paused in the midst of shoving his breeches down his legs. He was always in search of new sensations, new discoveries, and the woman lying on the bed was at least that.

She was lushly, gloriously built, which in itself was an anomaly. He didn't think much of the women he bedded—they all had breasts and cunts and bums and mouths to suck him, and apart from stimulating himself, he paid little attention to their differences, but he knew he'd never seen anyone quite like the Honorable Miss Marton. Her breasts were plump with dark rose nipples, and the bright flame hair between her legs matched her untamed mane. She was all rounded softness, when it seemed to him he'd preferred thin women with bodies like young boys, though he'd never been terribly interested in that variation, either boys or men.

The woman lying stretched out on the bed had the body of a magnificent courtesan, dusted with gold, gold everywhere, as if she were of an exotic race from some faraway land. What society had deemed unsightly was instead infinitely arousing to a dissolute creature like him, and he had no intention of rushing the pleasure. There were few too things that interested him anymore.

He finished stripping off his clothes, then moved to stretch out at the foot of the bed, watching her, considering all the different ways he could enjoy her. One of the things he enjoyed most with reluctant women was making them come. The unfortunate side effect of that malicious pleasure was that they then had a tendency to follow him around, after their novelty had worn off, which was always quite quickly.

His eyes moved along the lines of her body like a caress, the rounded hip, the graceful leg, the tempting red curls. She would lose her fascination just as quickly as the others, unfortunately, but for the moment, he was entranced, and he wasn't going to squander his rare moment of real interest.

In his lifelong pursuit of pleasure, he had become adept at wringing the most from a situation. He could vent his instant, powerful lust on her and go on to look for other gratification, or he could take his time, tease her and himself along, to make the final release so much more pleasurable.

He reached down for his cock, stroking it lightly. It felt like years since he'd found anything that had taken his fancy, and as a dedicated sybarite, he'd be a fool to rush it. He let his eyes wander along her skin in concert with his hand on his erection, vaguely aware that he seemed to be harder, more sensitive than he could remember, like he was young and fresh and unjaded. He never had been, but the throbbing in his hand felt new, his boredom gone. He pressed his leg against hers as he stroked himself, pulling, so hard, and she was so soft, and he wanted—

His cock erupted, semen spattering in his hand, on one of her legs, and he was so shocked his hand stilled, and yet his climax still continued to pump forth, until he lay back on the bed with a groan. What the hell?

His sleeping damsel let out a soft, whisper of a snore, and he laughed weakly. There was something very wrong with him, to be overwrought by an unexceptional woman. He needed to find a whore with freckles.

After a moment he rose, moving to the washstand to clean himself off before glancing back at her. There was a splash of his release on her thigh, but he had no intention of washing it off her. He liked the idea he had marked her, like an animal with his scent.

He was still hard, another anomaly, and he moved over to the bed. It wasn't that she was a dangerous woman—his problems were his own, caused by the doldrums he'd been floundering in for what seemed like years. He didn't like not having iron control of his flesh, and a wiser man would walk away. He was not the man to choose wisdom over sensation.

He stretched out on the bed beside her, suddenly, unaccountably tired. He should find somewhere else to sleep, he thought. He never shared his bed.

But they'd been travelling hell-bent all day, and he couldn't be bothered looking for an alternative. His rules were his own—he could break them as well as everyone else's rules.

Exhaustion washed over him, aided by his powerful release, and he began to drift. The scent of her, sweet and floral, mixing with the powerful smell of sex in the room, was somehow as soothing as it was arousing. He was half asleep when he reached for her, and he knew it was wrong, but impulse and exhaustion overpowered common sense, and he was never one to resist his instincts. He would finish with her in the morning. Tucking all that soft, speckled warmth against him, he'd slept.

He shifted in his seat, reaching for his glass of wine, then letting his hand drop. To his surprise and annoyance, she'd put paid to his evil plans the next morning. The very clever, incredibly naïve Miss Marton believed she'd been ravished, and the thought was so delicious, it had charmed him. He'd told her the truth and she hadn't believed him. She would learn just what true ravishment entailed soon enough.

He glanced at George, who'd happily dissolved into a state of torpor, unaffected by Kit's abstraction. Kit had a tendency to ignore him, and George was just as happy with the situation. He would prattle drunkenly, laughing at his own *bon mots,* and Kit let it all fade into the background.

Bryony Marton had had the ability to shock him, when he thought he'd lost that capacity long ago. He'd planned on enjoying a little bit more of her in the morning, but her blithe assumption that she'd been ravished was irresistible. He knew virgins of a certain class were woefully ignorant of how these things worked, but that she thought she could emerge from coitus with no sign on her body, in her body, astounded him.

He opened his mouth to regale George with the entertaining story and shut it again without a word. George was mumbling below his breath, and he wasn't worthy of such a choice jest.

He wanted to wipe that self-possessed expression off her dappled face, and the thought was delightful. He could see her eyes widen as he pushed inside her. The simple fact of the matter was that he had a big cock—he'd had both adoration and complaints from various partners. He couldn't remember the last time he'd had a virgin—perhaps never. She wasn't going to like it. At first.

He would make certain the complaints disappeared. He had no qualms about the dispensing and receiving of pain, but hurting someone was intrinsically boring. He simply didn't care enough to bother.

There was no denying that the feel of a rapturous cunt squeezing him was one of the few sensations that never bored. Lately, even that hadn't seemed worth the effort, but his freckled hostage had changed things.

He knew the simple science of dealing with women. You treated a whore like a duchess and a duchess like a whore—it never failed. He found he could make a woman do anything he wanted, no matter how perverse, as long as he'd manipulated them properly.

He tossed off the glass of wine and leaned back. While there was unsettled business with his unflappable captive, he was in no hurry to follow through. No matter how very different she was, it would take more than a freckled virago to inspire him to make much of an effort.

That was another thing. Miss Marton, despite her circumstances, seemed blissfully free of the fabled temper ascribed to redheads. No matter how he goaded her, she hadn't snapped. Either she was too dense to recognize his malice, or she simply didn't care, which was extraordinary. He was more than adept at destroying anyone verbally, and yet she'd been impervious.

Which mattered not one whit. If he exerted himself, he could crush her without lifting a finger, but lately, he'd been totally uninterested in absolutely everything. She was surprisingly entertaining, but not enough to inspire him to go to any trouble.

Still, she was there, like a plump hen ready for slaughter. And he was going to have to do something about Pevensey's damned house. Kit had known it would be more trouble than it was worth when that drunken idiot had put it against an indifferent hand of piquet. The young man had been a nuisance all season—a drunken braggart who'd had the nerve to intrude onto Kit's solitude, and he deserved what he got. The fact that he had killed a tavern wench and covered it up was no particular problem for Kit. Nothing ever escaped his notice, and when he'd heard about it, he'd simply shrugged.

Of course, compared to Kit he was an absolute saint, though as far as he could remember, he'd never killed a woman during clumsy sex, or during inspired sex, for that matter. He'd taken a mild pleasure in stripping the young man of his house, his stable, what was left of his already decimated inheritance, and anything else he could think of, and he'd only shrugged when he heard that Pevensey had put a bullet in his brain as soon as he was sober enough to hold a gun to his head. He wouldn't have thought the miserable wretch had that much resolve.

In the meantime, there was the problem of Pevensey's ramshackle estate to deal with. Perhaps he'd been too hasty dragging George off as soon as he'd staggered downstairs. They'd only gotten as far as the neighboring town before George's thirst overcame him, and they'd been sitting there for the better part of the day, laying waste to the landlord's cellars. It would only be logical to go back and come to a decision while they were still so close. Maybe set a torch to it and watch it burn with an unholy light, because everything about him was unholy.

With luck, the two women would already be gone. His erstwhile, still-virginal bedpartner was possessed of a most unfeminine *sangfroid* —she would scarcely sit around waiting to be rescued. His redhead would have found a carriage somewhere and they'd be off, posing no problem to his peace of mind. Not that she could have in the first place, of course. If he ever thought of her again, if he ever decided to further his exploration of such a charming anomaly, he could do so at his leisure in the next few months. There was no place she could hide that he couldn't find her. If he wanted to.

"Wake up, George," he said loudly, and George raised his head from the table where he'd rested it.

George blinked. "Need to get on the road, do we?"

"We're going back."

That caught his attention. "Why?" he said plaintively. "That place is miserable, damp, and cold and I swear the bed had bugs in it. Besides, those women are there!" he added in tones of deep loathing.

Any bugs residing in George's bed had probably arrived there along with George, but Kit wasn't interested in pointing that out.

"The women will be gone by now," he said, not believing it for one moment.

"I doubt we'll be that lucky," George said gloomily.

"You may certainly remain here." His tone was deceptively gracious. "You can use the time to figure out how to repay your wager. I would find it tedious to have to kill you—you wouldn't provide much sport."

George blinked owlishly, and Kit suppressed a sigh. In truth, killing George was simply not worth the effort.

"I'd forgotten about that," George said, lying through his very bad teeth.

"I hadn't. A debt is a debt, George. I'll be needing repayment soon, so you'd best come up with something."

"I don't suppose my bran-faced fiancée would do?" George said glumly.

Kit gave him his dazzling smile. "My dear George, I already have her."

8

THE OPPRESSIVE, unnatural, Godforsaken heat beat down on Peter's head as he plodded down the country road, and he was too bad-tempered to curse. What kind of heathen nonsense was going on— that was no English sun beating down overhead. It was barely May, and even in August, he had to wear warm underclothes when he was working. This kind of sultry warmth was unnatural.

He'd already stripped off his leather jacket and wool waistcoat, and he'd started rolling up his sleeves, when a rustle of noise in the brush beside the road made him freeze. He was a city creature, born not far from Seven Dials, raised in the slightly more refined area of Marylebone. He'd called Aloysius Barnes "father" though there was no legal tie—merely the affection of an eternally befuddled, kind-hearted scientist and his housekeeper for the grubby boy they'd found trying to pilfer the silverware late one night. He had no idea who his real father was, but there was no way he could have been even half the man Aloysius was, and he could barely remember his mother. He'd been Jimmy Bunyon then, but Aloysius had christened him Peter, telling him he was a sturdy rock beneath the chaos of his young life. Of course, the christening had been theoretical, and he'd always wondered why his father had named him after a biblical character, given that the old man considered himself a Philosophical Unbeliever, and Peter had grown up highly suspicious of anything resembling organized religion, following his father's doctrine. His father believed God resided in the goodness of humans and acts of kindness, and he lived his life accordingly, the best example of a good man.

Peter fell short of that example, time and time again, but that didn't mean he wouldn't try. He hadn't seen much evidence of goodness in his fellow man, and most acts of kindness came with a price. His brilliant father was an innocent, eternally looking for the best in people. Peter had given that futile quest up long ago. He had two missions in life: to keep the laws, and to ensure that his father had everything he needed.

That was an added reason Peter was infuriated by being banished to this rich green hellhole. Aloysius was getting older and frailer by the day, and Betty, his devoted housekeeper, wasn't much younger. When he was in the city he stopped by every day, just to keep an eye on them, and he worried when he was out of touch. He could thank his nemesis Eldon for this. If he hadn't been such an arsehole, then Peter wouldn't have had to hit him, and instead of trudging through the thick tree tunnels in this rural horror he'd be keeping the peace in London, not chasing down a couple of flighty women.

A loud shriek broke through his abstraction, and he jumped, automatically reaching for his knife. A huge crow wheeled overhead, screaming his disapproval, and if Peter had had his gun he would have shot him, just to express his opinion of the countryside and the weather and the world in general.

Trudging onward, he kept up a low-voiced grumble of displeasure. On top of everything else, he was certain this was a wild-goose chase. The village of West Hansbury was remote and destitute—the only great home in the district had been left to rack and ruin, the tenant farms abandoned, and yet one of the stablehands at the coach's last stop had insisted that one of the mysterious gentlemen had asked him where Pevensey Hall was. Peter would have been tempted to ignore that, if he hadn't remembered that the scion of that family had recently lost everything in a rigged card game and then blown his brains out, thanks to the worst man in England, the one known as the Inconstant. Personally, he thought that was a totally unfitting nickname—the earl of Adderley was steadfast in his pursuit of debauchery.

And Christopher Constant happened to fit the description of the mysterious gentleman. There were few men in this world that could be described as completely bad, and Peter had seen the worst the London slums had to offer. Adderley wouldn't have blinked at the thought of abducting two proper young ladies, and Peter had no choice but to follow that one hopeful piece of information to its conclusion.

He'd been happy enough to leave the coach and its malodorous occupants, all of whom viewed his departure with relief. Not that he'd been a difficult companion, but it left them with more room in their cramped confines, and he could almost hear the collective sigh as he grabbed his satchel and departed.

Since then, he'd taken a ride in a farm wagon, and a pony cart, and a conveyance transporting kegs of beer to the local pub, leaving him to trudge the last four miles on foot. And his boots weren't made for long walks in the country.

He let out a disgusted, pent-up breath. He would check the abandoned house, ask a few questions of the inhabitants of that small area, and then somehow find his way back to the village and the mail coach to continue his journey north. The mail ran as close to clockwork as anything could, and they were faster, cleaner and more reliable than the public coach, even if they squeezed six passengers where only four could sit. He would have given anything to abandon his duty and head back to London, but it simply wasn't in his nature. There was no way the runaways were going to stop short of Gretna Green, and this was just putting him farther behind....

The shriek this time was louder, and Peter swore. He was going to break that damned crow's neck! The creatures always unnerved him, making him think of death, and he was...

It came again, and he realize these calls were different, more desperate, and it was most definitely not the raucous caw of a crow. It was the cry of a human, a female, thick with tears.

He turned his head, waiting in utter silence for the sound to come again. It had seemed to originate in the field to the left, a large, untended tangle surrounded by a stone wall. He was deaf in one ear, thanks to a blow from a thief taker when he'd been very young, scrambling on the streets to survive, and he couldn't be positive where the sound had come from.

The damned birds kept chattering, the wind soughed through the trees, and in the far distance he could hear the bark of a dog. And then it came again, desperate, and he recognized the word in that tear-thickened voice. *Help.*

Without a moment's hesitation, he dropped his small satchel and bounded over the stone wall, a noble knight in tarnished armor off to rescue a damsel fair. If there was any justice in the world, it would be the missing heiress, but after years in the business, he'd learned that justice held very little sway.

He halted, looking around him, trying to filter through the noisy birdcall to find that desperate plea. Whoever had been crying for help was silent now, and for a moment, he wondered if English country birds could mimic human language the way of colorful, exotic birds he'd seen in Astley's Circus.

And then it came again, fainter now, and with his damned hearing, he couldn't tell if the woman was getting weaker or moving farther away. He could only rely on his instincts, but they'd kept him alive in the most dangerous of circumstances, and he had no choice but to count on them again.

The thick, overgrown field barely slowed him down, the brush catching at him with greedy thorns, but he ignored their entreaties, moving toward the edge of the pasture, into the deep woods that ringed it.

He slowed his mindless run, listening for the voice, but whoever she was, she'd stopped calling out, and once again his instincts were his only weapon as he moved, as quickly as he could, through the thick underbrush that reminded him of nothing so much as a tangle of snakes on a murderous goddess's head. It felt like an emerald tomb around him, one of Dante's nine circles of hell, and when he returned to London, he was going to burn his bottle-green jacket and his sage-green breeches.

The sun was still searingly bright overhead, but the thick trees provided a respite that Peter reluctantly acknowledged. If he'd had to run after the missing girl in the bright sun, he might have thought twice about enacting the knight errant.

But in fact, no one was trying to murder the damsel in distress. He'd finally caught the sound of her noisy sobs, which were ongoing, grating, and completely helpful, leading him straight to the edge of a rushing stream, more forest on the opposite side, and a narrow strip of land in the midst of all that gushing water, a much bedraggled female crouched in the center of it, weeping.

He stopped, surveying the situation. The rushing water and the dramatic sobs were drowning out any sound he might have made, and the girl had her face buried in her hands as her shoulders shook.

Gorgeous blond hair, he noted absently, since he was a man above all else. She was small—perhaps still a child, which made the way he was thinking about her hair uncomfortable—but at least she'd be light enough if he had to carry her out of there, and he suspected he would have to. She was wearing something rose-colored, good quality even though it was stained and torn and muddy. Observing such trivial details was a useful part of his job. Even with her face hidden behind all that silky, leaf-tangled hair, he could immediately assess that she was upper class, very young, and melodramatic. Her sobs were better suited to weeping over a slain lover than simply being stuck in the middle of a rushing stream.

He took a few steps closer, not trying to muffle his sounds, but she was too caught up in her misery to notice. The two sides of the stream were lively, bubbling, but they were only about a foot or so deep, not enough to offer any real danger. Clearly, the young woman was even more of a city child than he was, or she'd simply lift up her petticoats and wade across.

He dropped down on the bank, resting his hands on his knees, watching her for any more informative details. And then he drawled, "Are you going to sit there all day sobbing, or are you going to do something about the situation?"

Her head jerked up, the beautiful hair tumbling away from her face, and he had two immediate thoughts. One, relief that it wasn't a child stirring his lazily lascivious interest, and two, profound irritation. She *would* have to be beautiful, with her heart-shaped face, her glistening blue eyes, her sweet, full mouth. She still looked beautiful after minutes or longer of sobbing, no mean feat.

Beautiful women were the very devil, and he avoided them like the plague they were. Give him a plain, sweet woman any day. Women who'd been given the gift of beauty seemed to feel that the world, and men in particular, owed them even more for a trick of nature, and this bedraggled female, with her creamy skin and beautiful eyes, looked to be monumentally annoying.

At least she'd stopped crying. "Who are you?" she demanded, her voice husky from tears, but still, undeniably, upper class. That sealed it—she was going to be a problem.

"Apparently your knight in shining armor," he said. "How did you end up there?"

He could see the doubt playing in her eyes, the instinctive hauteur that was ingrained in seemingly all of her exalted class. "I don't believe we've met," she said coolly, as if she hadn't been bawling her eyes out moments before.

He threw back his head and laughed, really laughed. "You want to sit there in the mud until someone comes along to make formal introductions, or do you want to get home and change out of those muddy clothes?" For just a moment, the thought of what lay beneath those clothes hit him, but mentally, he swatted it away.

She assessed him, and he simply sat there as she tried to make sense of him. He knew what he looked like. He was a tallish man, deceptively lean, but he was more than capable of besting a man with five stone on him. Some women had found him handsome, some had not, and he didn't worry about it. The women he bedded weren't picky about such matters. In fact, some people might mistake him for a harmless young man, always misguessing his actual age, and he'd used that to his advantage more than once.

She wasn't looking impressed. "You look safe enough," she said eventually, showing her monumentally flawed judgment. He was one of the least safe people she would ever run into during her pampered life, but he wasn't in the mood to demonstrate.

"An absolute lamb," he agreed, and her eyes narrowed in doubt for a moment, and then she sighed.

"Can you help me?" she said.

"Depends," he replied. "How did you get there in the first place?"

"I was going for a walk, but this entire area is unfamiliar, and I must have gotten turned around. When I tried to go back I couldn't find my way, and I got trapped here until someone rescued me."

"And here I am." He didn't bother to hide the irony in his voice, any more than he tried to disguise his city accent. It wasn't the money that separated the classes, he thought lazily, his eyes moving over her like a caressing hand. It wasn't birth or education or lineage. It was their voices. He suspected she'd never talked like an equal to someone born within the sound of Bow Bells.

Though she wasn't really talking to him like an equal, more an uncomfortably classless inconvenience that didn't belong anywhere. That was him, all right.

"I would appreciate the help," she said carefully, not meeting his gaze. "If you could get word to my cousin up at..." she paused, looking momentarily confused. Peter didn't give a toss—he had no intention of traipsing off at her bidding. He had no intention of letting her out of his sight.

His temper had definitely improved despite the heat of the unnatural sun trying to find him through the thick, leafy treetops. For once, luck had been on his side, and if that wasn't one of the missing girls he'd eat his hat.

He'd kicked off his shoes and stockings, but since she was doing her best to stare past his left shoulder she hadn't noticed. "No," he said flatly. And he stepped into the icy cold stream.

❦

CECILIA SQUEAKED IN SURPRISE. Was the man mad, walking straight into that raging torrent, courting death? He was far too pert—it would serve him right to be dragged under, but such a shame, because even in her current disastrous circumstances, she could tell he was an extremely good-looking man.

His shoulders were much broader than the men of her acquaintance, though perhaps that was an illusion since he wore no jacket. She couldn't remember ever seeing a gentleman in his shirtsleeves, even her father, though of course, this was clearly no gentleman splashing toward her like a child through a shallow puddle. Her mother would say he was dreadfully common, and Cecilia could scarcely disagree, but who could argue with a face like that—strong-jawed, high forehead, the kind of wide, generous mouth that Cecilia had always envisioned when she'd daydreamed about kissing. Not that she'd ever want to kiss a man like this, but still...

He'd reached the spit of land, emerging from the water to stand in front of her, and she swallowed nervously. He was huge, not just in the shoulders but in the length of his body, the strength in his arms. "Well?" he said.

She glanced around her nervously. "Well, what?"

He let out a deliberately bored, exasperated sound, and then, to her absolute shock and horror, slid an arm around her derriere and scooped her up in those very strong arms.

She was able to shut off her instinctive scream, but just barely, and there was nowhere to look but at his face as he descended into the stream once more, with her held firmly in his arms. Against his hard chest. If he were anyone else, she would have dropped her head down on his shoulder and moaned in embarrassment and a flurry of other, confusing feelings, but if it were anyone else, she wouldn't be having this kind of reaction.

And she most surely was. Her body felt hot, tingly, especially where it touched his, and his chest was solid and warm, and all she wanted to do was snuggle closer, bury her face in his shoulder, feel his lips in her hair, on her cheek, her mouth...

Which was both dangerous and bordering on insanity. "Put me down!" she said imperiously, shutting out her perilous melting.

"Certainly." Without a word he released her, her feet and skirts splashing in the icy water, and she shrieked. "Stop being a baby!" he grumbled. "The water's barely a foot deep here, and it's just a few steps to the other side."

Her skirts were floating on the rushing water, billowing around her knees, and fury danced through her. "You...you...cad!" It was the best she could come up with—she'd heard other, less socially acceptable phrases for a man like that, but a lady shouldn't lower herself to use such language.

He made the grave mistake of laughing, and enough was enough. She reached out to slap him across his grinning face and slipped on a slimy stone beneath her waterlogged slipper, going down so fast she didn't have time to grab on to him to stop her ignominious descent.

Her posterior had barely touched the streambed when he dragged her upright, his hands under her armpits, pulling her up to wobble precariously on her unsteady legs. With a sigh, he bent down, threw her over his shoulder and marched out of the stream.

He dropped her down with unflattering haste, and this time made no move to help her when she sank down on the patchy ground. She wanted to cry. She wanted to kick her heels in a childish tantrum. She satisfied herself with pulling off her sodden slipper and throwing it at his head.

The fool laughed again. She threw the other, then looked around for something else to pitch at him, but rocks were a little too dangerous, so she had to content herself with glaring. Her rage only grew as she watched him return to a pile of rags by the riverbank and start pulling on his discarded stockings. Her own stockings were destroyed, and she yanked them off, throwing them at him, when cold realization struck her. She was now barefoot, her feet exposed to a man's eyes, and she could just imagine her mother's screechings. Showing an ankle was bad enough, exposing the entirety of her bare feet was beyond the pale.

Quickly, she yanked down her soaking skirts, trying to cover her feet, but the wet cloth was turning the patchy dirt to mud, a disaster for her pretty pink dress.

He'd finished with his sturdy shoes, then glanced over at her. "You're not going to be able to walk like that," he observed.

"I have no intention of walking anywhere They will come to look for me, and they'll make arrangements for my return to..." *To what*, she thought. And for that matter, who were *they*? The few remaining servants at the house were unlikely to do anything for anybody.

"Who are *they*?" Her unwelcome rescuer said, as if he could read her mind, and she had to shake off her reaction.

"They are the servants and my family," she said haughtily.

"Your family is in London, Miss Elliston. And if a ramshackle creature like the late Thornton Pevensey kept a staff at his ancestral home, then he wouldn't have had to blow his brains out over his gambling losses."

She doubted that she'd managed to disguise her shock at the sound of her own name—Bryony had told her she had a completely transparent countenance, and Cecilia had believed her. She'd never gotten away with lies when she was young, and she never dared play cards for pin money. But she could try.

She straightened her back. "And how, pray tell, do you happen to know my name?"

"And how, *pray tell*, could you think you could run off with a man and think no one would do something? I've been tasked with finding you and your cousin and returning you to the loving bosom of your family."

She summoned up as much hauteur as she could manage, thinking of Queen Charlotte and Bryony's late aunt as perfect examples, and looked down her nose at him, no mean feat when he was standing over her. "You're not doing such a great job so far."

She'd been hoping to annoy him, and she did see a momentary tightening of that firm jaw, and then he grinned again. "Well, it seems you weren't such a priority for Bow Street, and my budgeted expenses don't call for much comfort. I'll be returning you by way of the mail coach."

"A public coach!" She no longer tried to hide her dismay. "Don't be absurd!" She narrowed her eyes as she looked up at him. "And you don't look like any Bow Street Runner I've ever seen. Why should I believe you?"

"And you've met so many in your short time on this earth? Clearly you've lived a more dangerous life than I would have thought. I'm a runner all right, though I usually have better things to do than chase after silly young females, and Bow Street is on a tight budget when it comes to the less criminal of their activities. You don't strike me as particularly dangerous, so a public coach it is. Or I can leave you behind if you intend on ruining your reputation. I was told not to exert myself overmuch."

"You're just trying to anger me," she said shrewdly, refusing to believe such shabby treatment.

He shook his head. "I do that simply by breathing, I expect. Your parents either don't have the money to rescue you or they're unwilling to expend it on you, which, now that we've met, doesn't surprise me in the least. So it was left to the public forces, Bow Street, to rescue you from a fate worse than death, and you have me as your Galahad."

In fact, no one had been the slightest bit interested in offering her a fate worse than death, she thought a little mulishly. For some reason, it was Bryony who'd been compromised, which made no sense at all, and while she wouldn't have wanted *that man*, or anyone she could think of to do something so intimate and degrading and disgusting, she would have thought that at least they should want to.

"Galahad," she said, savoring the word. "I'll call you Gal."

Oh, he didn't like that one, and she mentally put a tally mark on her side. "If you must call me by a name, it's Barnes. Peter Barnes."

"Oh, I was hoping it would be something much more entertaining, like Bosomworth, or Bottomley." She sighed happily. "Perhaps I'll simply refer to you as 'my hero' if I need to. Since you apparently think of yourself as such."

Was that a growl she heard? How delicious. Her smile broadened as she felt her confidence return. Who was she to be cowed by this common little man? Except that he wasn't little, and he was, in fact, most uncommon. Unable to resist, she pressed it.

"So if you're planning on forcing me to use public transportation, how do you intend to get me there? And what are you going to do about Bryony?"

"Who?"

"My cousin. The reason why Adderley and his repulsive little friend carried us off."

He raised a dark eyebrow. "She's worth even less trouble, according to my orders. Why would Adderley want her? Is she that pretty? That wealthy?"

"Neither. I'm much prettier than she is, and her fortune is respectable, but not astonishing. I expect the Inconstant has a great deal more money. In fact, it's incomprehensible that he would choose her to share his bed."

"You sound peeved, Miss Prettier-than-my-cousin. Cheer up— I'm sure he'd be willing to ruin you if you asked him. But you'll have to be nicer to him than you are to me," he added, deliberately annoying her.

There were far too many offensive things in that speech for her to know where to start. She had to content herself with an icy glare.

"If you're going to assist us in getting home, then I'm sure my parents will show their appreciation," she said stiffly, clambering to her feet, her wet, clammy clothes clinging to her most unpleasantly. "Shall we go?"

His survey was long, slow, insulting, starting at her shockingly bare feet, up her skirts, lingering for just a moment at her chest and then moving up to her face and hair. She couldn't help it—she glanced down and realized there were...*points* sticking out on her chest, on her...breasts. Hard, definite points. She may as well call them what they were—her mother wasn't around to slap her for improper language. Her nipples were hard, obvious through the wet, clinging fabric, and she immediately flung her arms around her body, hiding the disgraceful things.

Again that rumble of laughter, and this time she would have slapped him if she dared take her covering arms down. Before she realized what he was doing he'd picked up her sodden shoes and limp stockings.

She took a reluctant step toward him. "I need those..."

"No, you don't. They're falling apart. A family that can't afford to buy decent shoes for their child is hardly likely to provide worthwhile gratitude on the order I'd expect." He tossed them—no, he heaved them—back into the water and she watched with despair as they sank.

"How am I supposed to walk to the house?" she demanded. "It's half a mile down the road, and it's so rocky it hurt through my slippers."

"Easy," he said, and before she knew what he intended he'd scooped her up again, over his shoulder once more, his strong bones digging into her stomach, and he started back toward the road with what seemed to be an unerring sense of direction.

She kicked, of course. She drummed her fists on his back, but he seemed impervious. She screamed every imprecation she could think of, even the ones she should never say, and his voice drifted back to her.

"Somebody ought to wash your mouth out with soap." And he slapped her across her backside.

Enough was enough. After her final howl of rage, she manage to latch her hands onto his sides, despite the bobbing, and she pulled herself close enough to sink her teeth into his side, hard.

He let out a shocked yelp of pain, abruptly loosening her, and she slid off him in one graceful swoop and, without a moment of hesitation, took off toward the beckoning forest, ignoring the twigs and rocks beneath her feet.

❧ 9 ❧

Bryony was in the garden, draping her clothes across the over-grown hedges. It was so hot and humid that she had her doubts about them drying, but she could only hope.

They'd found them, her plain, boring clothes, in a dust bin, and she'd managed to get the friendly upstairs maid, Betsey, to wash them as best she could. They were still torn, but Bryony could take care of that when they were dry enough, and they were a great deal better than her current attire.

The last woman who'd lived in this house, who'd left her clothes perfectly preserved in a clothes press, had been here a long time ago, and she'd been no blushing virgin. Not that Bryony liked to think of herself as blushing, and heaven knows that since last night she was presumably no longer a virgin, but with her pale skin and freckles, any sort of emotion colored her face.

Of the colorful dresses they'd found, the one she wore was the least shocking. It was in the style of the last generation—tiny waist, voluminous skirts, and a décolletage so extreme she was afraid her breasts would pop over the top. Of course, there was no suitable underclothing left, no corset or pannier cage or anything of the sort, but the previous owner had been short, so that the dress merely

skimmed the floor without its whalebone support, instead of trip-
ping her up. The bodice was tight enough that she could only pray it
would serve as its own corset, and she had a tendency to cross one
arm across her torso to rest above her bosom, holding the gown in
place.

To top it all off, it was yellow, a terrible color for someone with
her flame-red hair. She'd never worn yellow in her life, not even in
happier times when she'd travelled around Europe with her father,
and this had to be a total disaster. A glance in a mirror had been
surprising—along with her scarcely-contained hair, she looked like a
wanton. A pretty wanton. If it weren't for her freckles, that was. If
she didn't know better, she'd think the dress was actually flattering,
but it was an indisputable rule of fashion that redheads could never
wear yellow.

She needed her own clothes to remind herself of her life and who
she really was, and she poked at the full brown skirt lying across the
top of the bush, as if that would make things go faster, rather like
pushing a rasher of bacon in a pan. Her clothes weren't baking, and
she turned away in disgust.

One good thing about the skimpy gown and the one simple petticoat she wore—they were cooler than her usual layers. The heat had
become even more oppressive, if such a thing were possible, and if
she could have found enough pins to put her hair up, she would have
been a great deal cooler. Occasionally, she could hear a distant
rumble of thunder, but she wasn't worried. England didn't seem to
get the wild storms that were prevalent in the southern part of
Europe, and those distant warnings were no more than that, a lot of
sound and fury, signifying nothing.

Speaking of *Macbeth*, she'd also discovered the saving grace to
this debacle. There was a library. Granted, it was covered with dust,
and some of the books were worm-eaten and crumbled with age, but
most of it was in fine shape, including a translation of Herodotus
into French, which would keep her busy for hours, if not days. While
Cecilia enjoyed her walk, Bryony could curl up in the dusty library
and read to her heart's content.

The boy should be back eventually with a suitable carriage and horses. They were safe enough there, now that Adderley and her fiancé had departed, so that she should feel comfortable spending a second night there. In fact, with Betsey's help, she'd managed to get the entire staff into at least a semblance of cleaning, with one small salon just off the library benefitting the most. It must have belonged to the lady of the house—the walls were shredded pink damask, the chaise comfortable enough for swooning or simply eating chocolates, and if it had been hers, she would have ripped down the damask, left the light oak paneling exposed, replaced the moth-eaten rug and scrubbed the tall windows, opening them to let in the light.

But it wasn't hers, and all she could do was imagine what it could be. It was peculiar—having grown up in a nomad's existence, she'd never become attached to any particular building or place, and the suffocating confines of Cousin James's bland residence only served to increase her indifference. But each well-proportioned room of this wreck of a house made her think of ways to make it habitable, even beautiful. Herodotus in French was just the thing to banish such schoolgirl fantasies.

Oddly enough, she had no desire to move. She'd never thought of herself as much of an outdoor person—she preferred being immured with her books if she wasn't travelling, and those wonderful travels had ended when her father died. When she was little, she'd imagined the perfect life—travels all over the place, with a not-too-big house in the country in England to come home to. This ramshackle house would do nicely.

Not that travel, or this house, were in her future. She'd learned to tone down her expectations to the confines of a thick book, and most of the time that sufficed. Her life's goal was modest—a small cottage in the country, with books and chickens and peace of mind. Surely that wasn't too much to ask.

It was odd—during all those years of travel, no one had been horrified by the spots on her face and arms. She'd spent hours in the sun, which only seemed to increase them, and no milk bath or chemical treatment had the ability to fade them. She'd never realized how unsightly they were to English sensibilities—she'd always rather liked the little flecks that dotted her pale skin. But not in England. Here, she was better off isolated.

She stirred her clothes once more. The heavy dark stuff of her dress was still sodden, but her milky white pantalets were showing signs of promise, and her chemise was improving. Even her simple shift seemed to be drying in the thick, humid air. If they weren't done by the time the boy was back with the carriage, she'd simply put the damp clothes on—she couldn't imagine travelling back to London in this skimpy dress with absolutely nothing on underneath.

Cecilia had been shocked at her lack of underclothing. Bryony had been a bit shocked herself, but there was something undeniably enticing about it. She felt light and free and a little bit wicked. The touch of the beautiful dress against her bare skin was just the slightest bit unsettling in a not-unpleasant way, and while she knew she should have all those layers, she simply didn't care.

A low rumble in the distance, and she tilted her head up to squint into the sky. Not that she could see the sun, she thought. In England you could never see the sun—the best you could hope for was a sullen glow behind a deep haze. She missed the sun of Italy and Egypt and Spain, the Greek Isles. And yet there was something about the feel of the breeze, the rich, earthy scent of the air with the slightest hint of the flowers that the English so loved, that called to her.

Sinking down on one of the marble benches in the small, enclosed garden, she closed her eyes, breathing in the air, opening herself to the sensations, the faint rustle of the leaves on this still, torpid day, the distant trace of horses, something baking in the kitchen, and her empty stomach rumbled even as she slowly relaxed. She could hear the distant voices of the uncooperative servants, the nearby crunch of boots on a gravel pathway—

Her eyes flew open to find the Prince of Darkness himself, returned from hell or wherever he'd gone to, towering over her, a distant, unreadable expression on his face. Her kidnapper, her seducer, her tormenter, her complete nemesis.

She didn't move a muscle other than her eyelids as she stared up at him in silent wonder. She'd never seen him in full daylight, only in the cramped carriage and their shared bedroom where she'd been in too much shock to take proper notice. He was Lucifer, the most compelling of the angels, fallen from grace. He was the David, perfectly proportioned, ravishingly beautiful.

But he was no boy saint. He said nothing, simply looking down at her with that distant expression, and for the moment, she'd lost her voice. She'd never been one to admit defeat so easily, and she pulled herself together.

"To what do we owe the pleasure of your return, Lord Adderley?" she inquired in a dulcet voice, pulling herself together. "I assumed you had gone on to continue your pillaging ways."

Odd, how he smiled without smiling. "You mistake me for a pirate, my dear."

She hated that false term of affection, but she refused to show it. "Aren't you one?"

"Oh, lord, no!" he said, moving past her to the boxwood where her lacy pantalets resided. "I couldn't be bothered." To her absolute horror he touched her underclothes, ran one long, elegant finger up the split in the drawers, and she felt her body warming and tightening.

"Please take your hands off my clothing," she said, trying to hide her instinctive squirm of restlessness. "It is completely inappropriate." She couldn't, however, keep the strain from her voice.

This time, more of his smile appeared. "And what made you think I was ever appropriate?" His eyes slid over her as though they were his elegant hands, and she squirmed again. "And what a charming dress you have on. Are you wearing anything at all beneath it? I can see the shadow of your delicious nipples just beneath that shockingly low neckline. Babies will suck on them at some point in your life, but I think I prefer to suck on them now. Lower your dress."

There was a phrase she loved, one that she'd only used in a select few places, but it was out of her mouth before she could stop it. Fortunately it was also in Arabic. "Be buggered by a camel," she said sharply, enjoying it.

"Oh, I don't think so. It sounds painful. Perhaps we could bargain down to a donkey, or even a wolf, if we can change continents. I want to be able to walk afterward."

She knew she turned bright red, always unattractive with her coloring. Not, of course, that she was worried about being unattractive to this man. How in the world did he understand Arabic? And his graphic response shocked her—she'd never thought of the insult in particularly specific terms.

He let out a small, laugh-like sound at her expression. "I speak many languages, my pet. I have a gift for them. Maybe this night when I take you, I'll only speak Danish. No, not erotic enough. Perhaps Spanish. *I want to lick between your legs.*" That last part was in Spanish, but unfortunately, Bryony had the same gift for languages, and she stared at him in shock.

"Why...?" She stopped, not wanting an answer.

"Because I want to," he answered, and she braced herself, but he seemed in no particular hurry, wandering over to her worn chemise and fingering it. It had no decoration on it whatsoever, no lace or fine needlework. In fact, it was one of her inherited pieces from the dead governess and she'd always hated the rough feel of it against her skin.

Apparently Satan...er...Adderley agreed. He lifted it off the boxwood, made a disapproving sound, and ripped it in half. He turned and looked at her over his shoulder. "I suppose I should have waited and ripped that off you, but it offends my eyes. I prefer elegance and beauty."

She couldn't help it, she actually snorted, and normally she'd be mortified at the sound that had escaped her. Mortification had been passed long ago. "Then what, pray tell, are you doing, bothering with me?" she demanded.

He didn't even look back at her as he wandered over to the next bush and her modest shift. At least this had a row of needlework across the high bodice, one that she had put there with more enthusiasm than skill, but apparently it wasn't enough for Adderley's refined tastes. That was ripped in half and tossed on the ground next to her shift. "Don't fish for compliments, poppet. It's beneath you."

For a moment she was speechless. Was the man blind as well as morally bereft?

"And don't look so worried," he added, reaching for the ugly brown dress. *Rip.* In all honesty, she was glad to see it go, but she was still too befuddled by Adderley's words to think clearly. "If I want you in clothes, I'll buy them for you."

Bryony had the sudden, irrational desire to scream. He was confusing her with his lies of attraction, and she just wanted to shut him and everyone else out of her mind. She bit her lip, and with a great deal of effort, she summoned up what she hoped was her best smile.

"I don't understand why you've returned, my lord," she said in a deceptively weak voice. "Surely you accomplished what you set out to do."

"And what is that, my pet?"

She would not blush again. "Me."

"Oh, you weren't my only interest. There's your money as well."

She raised her eyebrows in the haughtiest expression she could manage. "But you're rich as Croesus, if you'll pardon me speaking so plainly."

"You may always speak plainly to me, my love. And one can never be too wealthy or too decadent."

She despised his endearments, but she was going to get her question answered. Perhaps an unexpected moment of conscience had brought him back in order to return them to their disrupted lives. "Why have you returned?"

"Surely you didn't think I'd disappeared forever. Not after such a night. I have to say I was most impressed. I never would have thought a gently bred young woman would participate so enthusiastically with some of my more perverse habits."

"You told me you didn't touch me," she said, trying to keep the uncertainty out of her voice.

"Oh, I never said that. How do you think your clothes came off?" He cocked his head, surveying her out of those mesmerizing eyes. "It's up to you to decide what happened in that bed last night."

"Why don't you tell me?" She tried to keep her voice caustic, but there was an unexpected roiling deep inside her. She'd assumed she could simply shrug off her ruination, thanks to her complete lack of memory. Confronted by the large, disturbing presence of the man himself, she wasn't nearly so sanguine.

"Because it's so much fun to see you try to figure it out. Your forehead creases so adorably."

She gave him a distrustful glare. No one had ever called her adorable. "I want your word as a gentleman that nothing happened."

He moved closer, and she stumbled back a step. "One, I am no gentleman, apart from an accident of birth. Two—I lie all the time. It's up to you to figure out when I'm telling the truth." He put one long finger under her chin, tilting her face up to his, and for a moment, she was breathless with the sheer ruined beauty of him. "So you tell me."

She was having trouble breathing, and she stepped back out of his reach. "You said I participated in perverse activities. What were they?"

He was watching her with a wicked glint in those strange, amber eyes, and he still hadn't answered, so she steeled herself. "Exactly what did you do to me last night?"

&

He KNEW when he was pushing someone to the edge of madness, and the honorable Miss Bryony Marton had a strained note in her voice. He had no intention of clarifying a damned thing—soon enough, she'd realize exactly what being ruined entailed, and he intended to make it very enjoyable for her. It would have been a shame to waste the effort on a comatose female.

"I'm afraid gentlemanly restraint keeps me from putting last night's activities into words. Cheer up—I have every intention of clearing the matter up as soon as I can get you naked, but in the meantime, you'll have to live with your uncertainty and anticipation. But I promise you that from now on, when you touch yourself intimately you'll always think of me." He pitched his voice low and seductive.

The dazed expression on her face was a small triumph, but he would take it. She was in for a great many surprises in the next twenty-four hours, and he intended on making them memorable indeed. He smiled sweetly at her. "And I am so looking forward to tonight," he purred.

❧ 10 ❧

PETER BARNES CAUGHT Cecilia before she'd gotten two steps away from him.

"Let me go!" she shrieked at him.

"Not on your life. I'm taking you back to the house to get your things, and then we're taking the next mail coach south to your loving family."

She despised him. His big hand was an iron grip on her slender wrist, inexorable but not painful, and he wasn't letting go. She had no choice but to let him pull her along the rutted dirt road, her wet clothes flapping around her legs, her hair straggling down in front of her face, while she fumed.

He walked on in absolute silence, holding on to her, not even looking back, and she wanted to kick him. It didn't matter that he was the handsomest man she'd ever seen, ever touched...

No, that wasn't quite true. Baron Kithbridge was almost celestially beautiful, and Mr. Villairs as enough to make any girl's heart flutter. By comparison *this man* was merely good-looking in a rough-hewn way. Not that it mattered—he was far beneath her in station and lineage, and really, she shouldn't be thinking of him at all, of the warm strength of his body...

That was it, she realized with sudden relief. She'd never been touched, held, carried by a man, and the feel of him, his strong arms, his chest, his shoulders...

She shook herself. What in the world was she doing, daydreaming about this brute? She found men boring, easily manipulated, and she hadn't met anyone who'd made her change her mind. She longed for all sorts of sinful things she barely understood, but everyone thought she was a silly, pretty ornament, and she was happy enough to play the role. Just not today.

She'd kissed absolutely every man who tempted her. Although she and Sylvia weren't completely out yet, her choices had been surprisingly varied, and she'd been kissed by the beautiful Baron Kithbridge and the handsome Mr. Villairs. She'd kissed her toady cousin Edward, the second groom, an Irish lad with sparkling green eyes, she'd kissed men she couldn't remember. They were all in love with her, they said, but they knew nothing about her.

And their kisses—fumbling, practiced, shallow, deep, hadn't touched the deep core of longing inside her. She was still looking for someone who could. Why she was thinking about this when Peter Barnes was dragging her down a country road was a total mystery. Of course it was.

Despite the thick, unnatural heat, she was starting to feel chilled in her damp dress, now liberally covered with mud, and for just a moment, she grinned. She was a perfect little ragamuffin, more at home in the woods than a drawing room. It had been too long since she'd felt that freedom.

Her bare feet were beginning to hurt, and she slowed down a bit, dragging at him, and he finally broke his dignified silence with a nice long tirade.

Oh, she was a terrible, useless female, determined to get herself killed by her foolishness, out of one scrape and into another, she was lucky the wolves didn't eat her, she shouldn't be allowed out without a keeper, was she all right, no it didn't matter, she deserved anything she got, oh, Christ, there was blood on her dress...

"There are no wolves in England, you dolt," she said calmly. "And I scratched my arm on a branch—it's nothing. You're just lucky I didn't get away from you—you'd never have caught me, and it would serve you right after putting your hands on me...."

"I'm about to put my hands on you again," he snapped. "Unless you fancy walking the rest of the way back to wherever you came from without shoes, and I'd think your feet would be hurting enough by now."

They both looked down at her feet, exposed by the too short dress she'd found in a chest, and she immediately bent her knees to cover them. Unfortunately, her heavy skirts pulled at her, and she began to topple, only to be caught in the man's arms, saving her from an ignominious tumble.

Though this had its own ignominity. He was distractingly strong, distractingly warm against her damp flesh. She would have thought nothing could have cooled her off during this heat wave, but the soggy dress had begun to make her shiver.

"Jesus Christ, you're like ice," he muttered, pulling her closer, and she let out a yelp of pain. At the same time, there was a sudden crackle of lightning, startling them both, and he almost released her. Almost.

He did what had gotten him into trouble in the first place—he picked her up. At least this time, he didn't toss her over his shoulder like a sack of grain—he settled her into his arms like a noble knight rescuing a damsel in distress, when she knew perfectly well he wasn't noble and she wasn't in distress. At least not much.

She decided not to bite him again.

"That's better," he said, hoisting her up a bit for a better grip, and the sack of grain returned to mind.

"You needn't act as if I'm that much of a burden," she said grumpily. "My cousin weighs at least a stone more than I do, and we're the same height...."

"What is your problem with your cousin? Is she some sort of ogre?" He was already moving, moving back down the road, and she pondered his deep, rich voice. It wasn't exactly Cockney—there were street vendors who were practically unintelligible—but he didn't have the sculptured tones of her class.

"I have no problem with my cousin—I love her very much. But she's definitely a bit on the plump side, and..."

"I think you're jealous."

"Of Bryony? Don't be absurd—she has...freckles. All over her."

"That's no kiss of death. My family's Irish—freckles go with Irish like they go with red hair. Is your cousin Irish?"

"God, I hope not," Cecilia said, and for a breathless moment, felt his grip on her slip. It tightened just before she landed on her bottom in the grass, and then he hoisted her up again.

"You have the good sense of a duck," he snapped. "I just told you I was Irish, and then you go ahead and insult the entire nation."

"I did not! I just said..." Words failed her, and she stammered to find some excuse. Finally, "Well, if you're Irish, then you know the difficulties the Irish face in this country. I just want the best for Bryony."

The sound he made was unencouraging as he trudged onward. They were closer to the house than she'd realized, and she heard another distant rumble of thunder. She half expected him to drop her onto her bruised feet once they'd reached a relatively smooth surface, but he didn't, and she snuggled a little closer in unspoken relief. Her feet were a mess, and she didn't fancy limping through dried horse-droppings and scattered pebbles. Besides, being carried by a strong man, being pressed up against his body, was a shockingly new experience, a not entirely unpleasant one, and she had every intention of savoring it until she was finally back and able to change into dry clothes. She'd been a fool and a half to go for a hike on her own, she thought, absorbing his delicious heat. If she'd been more sensible, she never would have landed in this awkward, distasteful position. She sighed with pure contentment.

The small manor house was set back, hidden by a thick copse of trees and surrounded by what amounted to a moat. Bryony had blathered on about something like a motte and bayley castle, which Cecilia had never heard of. The house didn't look the slightest bit like any castle she'd ever seen, but since she was singularly uninterested in architecture, she hadn't asked for further elucidation, and it still didn't look that interesting. It was a pretty house if you didn't know how dusty it was, built on a slight ridge.

The day was unexpectedly growing darker, far ahead of the late sunsets of spring. "I'm not going anywhere with you," she made herself announce as clearly as she could with her face tucked comfortably against his shoulder.

"You are," he said evenly, "but you can come up with all sorts of arguments once we get out of this storm. I might even bring your cousin back, though your parents weren't interested in her return. I imagine they put a higher price on you."

She stiffened. "My parents would never put a price on me!" she snapped, outraged.

"Wouldn't they, now? I was told to leave you be if you were ruined to the point that it couldn't be covered up, so as not to devalue your sister's future marriageability. That seems fairly mercenary to me."

"They want the best for Sylvia," she said stoutly, refusing to acknowledge the doubts that were creeping in. "But none of this was my fault! My parents would never blame me for something I couldn't help."

"You're as naïve as you look," he said in disparaging tones. Another crack of thunder, closer now, and she jerked in his arms, startled, only to have those strong arms tighten their hold.

She wasn't tempted to argue with him. Her parents loved her; she was absolutely certain of it. Reasonably certain of it. Wasn't it a given that parents loved their children? Just because they weren't particularly demonstrative didn't mean that their hearts were misplaced. They had a portrait of her and her sister painted and displayed prominently in the drawing room, an expense that her penny-pinching father declared to be a worthy investment, though she was never certain what they were investing in.

Of course, they expected her to marry well—what parent wouldn't—but that was neither here nor there. They'd rejected any suitors who weren't extremely wealthy—simply well-to-do applicants for their daughters' hands were not to be considered. Again, who wouldn't want the best for their children? And Sir James Elliston and his wife had seen to it that only the wealthiest men in England were in the running for either of them.

As he tromped up the driveway, Peter Barnes's temper seemed to increase along with the darkening sky. Cecilia decided to be social. "I wonder if it will finally rain and break this wretched heat."

"Yes, let's talk about the weather," he said in unpromising tones. "You'll be glad of this wretched heat come next winter." There was another distant rumble of thunder, which he summarily ignored.

"Well, you're not suffering from it."

"That's because I have a wet female dripping all over me. You shouldn't be hot either."

"I'm not," she said stiffly. So much for pleasantries.

He marched directly up to the massive front door, but of course, no footman was standing by, ready to open it to visitors. He kicked it, and it opened of its own accord, revealing the dusty front hall. "Nice place for an elopement," he said. "I'm not convinced I believe your tale about Adderley and your cousin—it seems a bit farfetched. In fact, I'm not convinced the Earl of Adderley has anything to do with your early-morning bunk."

"Then you'd be wrong," came a silken voice from the shadowy hallway.

Peter had just been in the act of setting her down when her arms tightened reflexively around him, as her entire body froze in...well, she didn't like to call it fear. He paused, turning to the sound of that dark, mocking voice, to look into the shadows.

But Cecilia had her pluck back, and she slid out of his hold, her bare feet landing on the cold slate floor, her dress lamentably soggy, clinging to her. "What are *you* doing back here?" she demanded in tones of deep loathing. "I thought you'd had your wicked way with Bryony and then abandoned us!"

"My wicked way?" Adderley repeated, his drawl rich with amusement. "What a delightful way to put it, my dear. And I was under the misapprehension that you two were wishing to be abandoned as quickly as possible—have I misread the situation? I do realize I never got around to debauching you—your cousin, alas, is far too enticing, but I'm willing to make the sacrifice and fuck you as well."

She retreated until she came up against Peter's immovable body. She didn't know what the word meant, but from his tone and Peter's stiffening reaction it was a bad word for what he'd done to Bryony.

Peter's hands came to rest on her shoulders in a reassuring gesture, and she didn't stop to question why it calmed her. It simply did. Almost as much as his words. "Use that language in front of her again, and I'll make you sorry you ever insulted the lady."

"You may try," Adderley said graciously, unmoved by the threat. "But in truth, your damsel in distress is safe from me. I've had my fill of the blandly pretty. Her cousin is far more interesting."

For a moment, Cecilia was seriously stricken. If she didn't have her beauty, then of what possible value was she? "You're being deliberately perverse," she said before she could think better of it.

"I am extremely perverse, as your cousin has cause to know," he murmured, and she shivered, telling herself it was the wet clothes clinging to her body. He ran his bored gaze over her and sighed. "Give me directions to your bedroom and I'll come take care of it when I have the chance. Will your belligerent young man take part or will he simply watch? Oh, watch, I suppose, since he hasn't managed to...er...pluck the rose by now." He turned his attention to Peter. "Is that polite enough for you?"

Those strong hands on her arms tightened and moved her back, carefully, putting her behind him, so that she had to peek over his shoulder, no mean feat since she was short and he was quite tall, almost as tall as the man taunting him.

But the menace emanating from the man in black was palpable, and for some irrational reason, Cecilia wanted to reach out and pull Barnes behind *her*. She could see how his broad shoulders tensed, his hands flexed, and the last thing she wanted was a battle. Odd, because she'd always thought the idea of two men fighting over her to be deliciously romantic. Not in this case, probably because neither man was the slightest bit interested in her. Bryony could explain their combative behavior—she'd lived such a strange, foreign life. But Cecilia had been raised to be the perfect, docile wife and daughter, and she knew what to do.

She slid in front of Barnes before he realized what she was doing, and she willed her body to be relaxed and natural. She couldn't bring herself to get much closer to the dark menace in front of her, but surely she could carry this off.

"Such ridiculous bantering, gentlemen," she trilled in an artificial voice she particularly disliked, the one she used when she had to be charming to some revolting old peer. She could hear the rumble of thunder, a counterpoint to the danger in the hallway, and she pushed on. "I'm sure our cook could be persuaded to bring us all some tea and biscuits—you both are probably peckish this late in the day."

Another rumble of thunder, this one louder. She needed to check on Bryony, as soon as possible. She was freezing, she needed to get out of these icy clothes, but she didn't dare leave the two men alone. Peter hadn't said much, but she was completely aware that silence didn't signify acceptance. If she believed Barnes could beat Adderley into a bloody pulp, she'd tell him to have at it, but she had no such assurance, and she needed Barnes in one piece, a buffer between Bryony and her and the incarnate evil of the Inconstant.

Except, of course, for the perplexing realization that the evil man didn't seem the slightest bit interested in her innocence, a fact that was both a relief and an insult.

Of course, neither man replied to her suggestion, still eyeing each other like a pair of rabid dogs. Cecilia went for another tack. "And where's my cousin?" she demanded. "What have you done with her?"

His strange golden eyes were devilish. "Nothing at all," he said, and with anyone else, she might have believed him. "When last I saw her, she was in the back garden playing at being a laundry maid." His dulcet smile made chills run down her back. "She was no more pleased with my return than you appear to be. I'm wounded."

"I'll see to—" Barnes started with a growl, and Cecilia kicked back, trying to stomp on his toes. Since she was barefoot and he was wearing thick boots, it barely made a difference, but he had the good sense to swallow the rest of his threat. He didn't like Adderley any more than she did, which was a point in his favor.

"And why don't you introduce me to your pet bulldog?" Adderley murmured, his voice a silken threat. "Pardon me, but I've forgotten your name. One ought to remember the names of the women one abducts, but I've never been good about minutia." His charming smile was chilling. "Clearly, your friend is longing to throttle me, and I like to know the names of the men I kill as well as my hostages."

There were just so many things wrong with that statement that Cecilia was flabbergasted, floundering for words, when Bryony appeared, her face flushed, her hair awry.

"Don't let him goad you, Cecilia," she said calmly, moving past him into the hall. "I doubt he can help himself—apparently, he lives to be offensive. First off, my lord, you may not call my cousin by her given name. She is Miss Elliston, though, since you haven't been properly introduced, you shouldn't be speaking to her at all."

"I would think that kidnapping the two of you would make that bit of etiquette unnecessary," he returned.

"Etiquette is never unnecessary. It is required to make the world of social conventions run smoothly. As for our newcomer wanting to strangle you, that should come as no surprise. Everyone you come in contact with wants to strangle you, even, I suspect, my erstwhile fiancé."

"Erstwhile?" Adderley had turned all his attention to Bryony, seeming to forget that Cecilia was even there, a highly singular experience. What was wrong with the man?

"I rather think kidnapping me breaks a certain bond of trust, don't you?" she said sweetly. "If a husband orders his best friend to kidnap his wife, then that hardly bodes well for a happy marriage."

"*Orders?* It was my idea, precious. I'm the one who kidnapped you—Latherby was simply along for the ride. And you don't have a choice in the matter. You've spent almost two days in the company of men, unchaperoned. You ought to accept the best offer you can hope for."

"He *was* the best offer I could hope for," she snapped. "At this point, after I've been indisputably ruined, I consider myself doomed to spinsterhood."

"Indisputably?" he echoed, an odd tone in his voice. "I thought that was still under doubt. Though you strike me as a woman who would greet spinsterhood with enthusiasm."

"If you were the only option, then I most certainly would!"

"Surely you can't be harboring even the faintest hope that I'd make an honest woman of you." His eyes were watching her closely, the other people in the great hallway long forgotten.

"I am an honest woman!" she snapped. "And I'd just as soon shed petty conventions. If your depraved behavior from last night renders me unmarriageable, then I do rejoice!"

"And if you can't remember anything, then why do you think I was so depraved?"

"Because you told me so!" Bryony said, her voice rising. Her cousin was losing her temper, Cecilia thought, marveling. She'd never seen anyone able to ruffle Bryony's immense calm no matter how great the provocation. Clearly Adderley was an exceptionally provoking man.

But Cecilia was not used to being ignored, and the man behind her was growling again, rather like a wolf, and it was time to bring the focus back to her.

"None of that matters!" she announced grandly. "Bryony, this is Mr. Peter Barnes of the Bow Street Runners. He's been sent after us, and he'll be bringing us safely back to Harlowe Street."

"I think not," Adderley drawled, never taking his eyes off Bryony. "Not until I'm ready to let you go."

The growl deepened, and this time, Cecilia felt herself shoved out of the way. "Am I to understand, my lord, that you willfully kidnapped these two young women, and you compromised that young lady?" Peter Barnes gestured toward Bryony.

"Her name is Miss Bryony Marton, and she will assure you that I did," he said mildly. "And I fail to see why my sexual excesses are the business of the Bow Street Runners. Don't you have something better to do? Anarchists to arrest, murderers to capture, thievery to halt? Tsk, tsk. Go somewhere else and rescue women—these two are mine."

Cecilia couldn't help it, she shrieked in horror, and Barnes took a step closer. "You touch one hair on her head, and I'll gut you."

"As I said before, you can but try." He dismissed Barnes like an annoying puppy and focused that strange, terrible gaze on Cecilia. She was freezing to death—despite the sultry weather, the hallway was large and drafty, and the damp dress clung to her most unpleasantly. She needed a hot bath if she had to drag the buckets upstairs herself, she needed clean, dry clothes, and she needed food. If Adderley was going to toy with her, she was going to scream.

But after a measured glance he turned his attention back to Bryony, who was watching all this with no expression at all, having regained her calm. "Tell me, my love," he murmured, "have you given the servants a menu for dinner tonight? By default, you're the lady of the manor, and it's up to you to arrange such things. I, for one, require a great deal of food and a long nap, once I see this distempered puppy off the premises. Your little cousin may join us if she must." He sounded so bored that it took Cecilia a moment to realize what he was saying, and another moment to react.

Before she could say a word, the man behind her erupted, leaping for Adderley, and Cecilia threw her arms around him, trying to stop him. Instead, she threw him off balance, and the two of them went tumbling to the floor and the threadbare carpets, her sopping clothes clinging to him as he tried to push her off.

Another crack of thunder, this one so powerful that the darkening world outside the open door turned an eerie silver, and the world was suddenly awash, the torrent of rain obliterating everything beyond the wide front door. They all froze, Cecilia in her undignified position entangled with Peter Barnes, Bryony, silent and staring at the rain, and even Adderley gave the torrential downpour its due, mesmerized as the rest of them were.

Bryony was the first to move, making her way across the already rain-soaked floor to the massive door, wrestling it into place and shutting out the worst of the rain, though the weather still roared outside. She turned in place and leaned her back against the oak door, looking at them all with her usual imperturbable expression, her momentary emotion vanished.

"I believe that no one will be going anywhere as long as this Armageddon continues. I suggest we retire to our respective rooms. Cecilia, you remember that lovely room we found on the third floor, in the front of the building? While you were gone, I managed to persuade the servants to clean it thoroughly, as well as put in a brief effort on the rest of the bedrooms. Mr....Barnes, is it? You can use the bedroom at the back of the building."

Cecilia heard his slightly bitter laugh, and she belatedly managed to crawl off him, though her wet clothes clung to him with greedy fingers, and they both scrambled to their feet, eyeing each other warily.

"Servants' quarters, Miss Marton?" Barnes said wryly.

Bryony actually rolled her eyes. "No, Mr. Barnes. Bachelor quarters, well out of reach of young females."

"And where are you sending me, my poppet?" Adderley inquired in silky tones, but Bryony didn't flinch. For some odd reason, she wasn't afraid of him, Cecilia realized, astonished.

"You've already claimed the best room, my lord," she said smoothly. "You even left your clothes behind."

"I could scarcely wear them when I bedded you, my precious. And exactly where do you mistakenly think you'll be?"

"There's a nice, small room next to Cecilia's—" she began, but he interrupted her.

"I'm certain there is, but that is neither here nor there. I find I'm reluctant to sleep without you by my side, and I am in dire need of a nap."

"You won't touch her again!" Cecilia cried out, ready to immolate herself on the funeral pyre of Bryony's lost virginity.

It was a mistake. He turned, slowly, and focused his amber gaze on Cecilia's face, then swept down her body with slow, deliberate insult. "I'll touch anyone and anything I please. Including you. If you have any sense, you'll stop annoying me with your melodramatic chatter and remove yourself. I find you boring in the extreme, but the longer your nipples poke out, the more likely I might decide to lower my standards and fuck you senseless."

Shocked silence greeted that appalling statement, and he nodded slightly, as if he considered his work completed. He took Bryony's lifeless arm, threading it through his, and pulled her along with him. "Come along, my love. Your sister and her terrier will do for themselves."

A moment later, they were gone.

❧ 11 ❧

THERE WERE at least half a dozen things Bryony wanted to say to the man who was ushering her down the hallway, and she turned each one over in her mind, eventually rejecting all of them. The storm was thunderous overhead, even through the thick walls. Her skin felt tingly, her heart was racing, and truth be told, she had no real desire to pull herself away from his casual hand, knowing it could tighten painfully if she even made an attempt. It was nothing he hadn't done to her already, though she'd had the blessing of not remembering the whole, horrid act. But her mind was of a scientific bent, and horrific or not, the whole thing held a certain amount of interest for her. After all, women survived its occurrence, and no one seemed to mind terribly.

Really, this entire situation was absurd. Here the man was, trapped with her gloriously beautiful cousin, and he didn't seem to have a moment to spare for Cecilia's remarkable charms, for which Bryony was truly grateful and oddly flattered. He truly was a perverse creature.

And as such, his lovemaking, if you could call it that, must be quite singular. Women flocked to him, those who didn't have stern husbands or fathers getting in their way, and she had no reason to suspect he treated them with any kindness, flattery, or respect. If she had to be ruined, it might as well be by a master in the field, and if she was already a fallen woman, then there was the possibility of conducting a scientific analysis of his actions.

She'd always enjoyed taking things apart, examining them to see how they worked, whether physically, in the case of clocks and machinery, or intellectually, when it came to wars or criminal behavior or great art. Cecilia always decried it—she thought the only way to appreciate something was with mindless adoration, and looking too closely ruined it. Bryony knew that understanding the details, for her, only increased her enjoyment.

Not that she expected to enjoy Adderley's repeated depravity, but if she concentrated on analyzing it, then she'd be able to endure it with a little more equanimity. After all, in the past, she'd deliberately bled herself, practicing with a cupping bowl, her arm resting in the curved opening as she made careful tiny slices to observe where the blood flowed the quickest, and she'd applied leeches to her arms and observed their actions, and she'd survived all that with perfect equanimity.

Suddenly, Adderley pulled to a stop, turning her to face him in the shadowy corridor. He was so tall, looming over her in the semi-darkness, that she knew she ought to feel afraid. For some reason, she couldn't.

"Now what has been going through your pretty little head, my pet?" he said lazily. "Every time I look at you, there's some odd expression on your face that makes me fair tremble in my boots."

"Nothing would make you tremble," she said. "And I was thinking about leeches."

He didn't blink, or move, just looked at her. "Leeches," he repeated finally. "I would say, my dear, that you unman me, but I'm afraid it's the exact opposite. And would you mind telling me why you were thinking about leeches?"

There was no reason not to. "Well, first I was thinking that you were probably going to repeat your actions from the night before, though why you'd want to do it so soon again was beyond my comprehension. From the fairly regular occurrence of offspring, I surmise that people copulate at least once a year, perhaps more often, since fornication doesn't always lead to pregnancy. But as you've assured me, you're perverse, so I doubt you really need me to be able to sleep."

"Fascinating," he murmured. "And trust me, I fornicate a great more regularly than that, though I blush to inform you of the details of my sexual prowess. But where do the leeches come in?"

"Oh, I decided that since you were doubtless going to assault me again, it would be good to take scientific notes, at least in my head. I expect the experience will be quite singular and, in retrospect, worthy of study. Unfortunately, I missed the first time, so I won't have any basis of comparison, but it still should prove moderately interesting."

"I would hope so," he said faintly. "But I have yet to hear about the leeches. They're not usually part of my seductive arsenal, but I'm willing to adapt if that's what excites you."

She gave him a withering glance. "It doesn't. I was merely comparing the upcoming assault with the time I deliberately bled myself to see what effect it might have. I tried cupping, but cutting myself was unpleasant, even for science, so I resorted to leeches." She narrowed her eyes, viewing him speculatively. "I don't think I'd have any problem wielding a scalpel against you, however."

He didn't even blink. "And which part of my anatomy were you thinking of hacking off?"

She couldn't help it, she blanched, the very thought of removing one particular appendage making her seriously ill. He'd outplayed her again, but she wasn't going to let his victory last. "I have no wish to deprive you of your manhood, my lord. I just wish you'd apply it elsewhere."

"On your pretty cousin?"

"I could, perhaps, use a very dull knife..." she replied instantly, and his laugh was no comfort.

"I'll make certain any knives in your possession are exceedingly sharp. If I am to undergo surgery, then I'd like it to be swift. I wonder if I'd enjoy being a woman."

"Cutting off your...your thing won't make you a woman. Castrati aren't women. Surely you realize that."

His smile was silken smooth. "But you weren't talking about removing my bollocks, my pet, you were alluding to slicing off my John Thomas, a different thing all together. I must say this conversation is having an unexpected effect on that state of my earthly desires."

She hid her smile of triumph. "I'm sorry—I expect the thought of being...unmanned...would make you quite ill."

"Didn't I warn you I was a perverse creature? I find it completely stimulating. I'd truly been thinking of a chaste nap, but now I find myself stirring, if you understand my meaning."

She looked before she could stop herself, right where the body part discussed was prominently displayed, even behind his midnight black clothes. They were fitted by a master, and they outlined everything, every muscle and bulge...everything. He caught her glance, a bland smile on his face, and her long-controlled anger began to stir as well.

"But I find the entire discussion boring, and I wish to sleep. Are you going to stop me?" she demanded.

"I wouldn't think of it, my pet. I'll simply lie beside you and pleasure myself. It should be quite—stimulating." There was an odd note in his voice, but she had no choice but to ignore it. Everything he said was loaded with meaning.

She hadn't realized how far they'd come—he had held open the door, and the huge bedroom, the largest in the manor house, awaited them. She paused at the entrance, her courage flagging for a moment, but his ungentle push took care of that problem. She stumbled in, he followed and closed the door, and they were met with a sizzle of white lightning and the loudest explosion of thunder she'd ever heard. Her ears were ringing, her skin prickled, and her entire body felt pummeled.

With her last ounce of common sense, she realized she was about to faint, and the word came from her mouth.

"Damn," she said, and slid bonelessly to the floor.

ADDERLEY DIDN'T MOVE, looking down at his insensible plaything, and let out a long-suffering sigh. His wicked, lascivious plans kept being subjugated by the poppet's propensity for collapse, and while he might have doubted it, he too had felt the powerful lightning strike sizzle through his body.

He'd relished it, half tempted to go out in the rain, hold his arms up and dare the lightning to strike him. It would be a glorious way to die.

Ignoring the unconscious woman, he turned back to the door and then halted. The time wasn't right, and there was no way he could avoid that truth. Even though he had the perfect means to go out in a literal blaze of glory, he couldn't do it. Not yet, his body told him, and he listened to his body far more than his brain. Turning back, he stepped over Bryony's form again to go to the window, watching the lightning spear down with almost constant regularity. The rain was coating the windows, obscuring everything but the bright silver flash of the lightning, and the thunder overhead was loud and constant.

But the room was quiet, shadowed, and an oddly safe haven for a short while, and he accepted it. He glanced down at the still unconscious woman, wondering if she was dead. No, her gorgeous breasts were rising and falling quite steadily. She'd simply been shocked. And he thought she'd been made of sterner stuff than that.

He was going to step back over her and find something else to entertain him, when he thought better of it. In truth, he was weary, and an uninterrupted sleep would do wonders for him. It wasn't a total lie that he wanted her beside him so that he would sleep. He'd had every intention of demonstrating the truth to her before he fell asleep, but all his plans seemed to be going to hell nowadays.

He scooped her up. She seemed lighter than before, and he frowned. He liked her plump curves, and he wanted her to eat, to give in to her basest desires, to find the savage that resided inside her, just as it did with him. In his case, that savage had taken over, and he was glad of it. He wanted to see just what Miss Bryony Marton was made of when she lost that calm, quick-tongued demeanor.

Setting her on the mattress, he climbed in beside her, pushing her away to make room. Once he began to settle, she automatically rolled back up against him, thanks to the soft, ancient mattress. He pushed her away again with a muttered curse.

He would never sleep. He was a fool to even attempt it, and he ought to get up and find mischief elsewhere, when she rolled up against him once more.

She was warm in the cool room. She was soft, and accepting, and she even smelled like flowers. With a resigned sigh he put his arm around her, pulling her closer, and her body melded to his as if that was what it was meant to do. Her heartbeat, her breathing, were both steady; there was nothing for him to worry about. Not that he'd worry, of course. He simply didn't care. He never did.

Nevertheless, her softness had an enervating effect, and her hushed, instinctive sigh of comfort echoed in his bones. When he returned to the city, he was going to have to invest in hiring someone peaceful to sleep with him.

Maybe then at last he'd sleep, which he wasn't going to do now, certainly not, with the warm creature wrapped in his arms, the light shadowed by the pounding rain, the soft mattress beneath his backside, the sweet, sweet feel of Bryony...

He was gone.

***Peter watched them disappear down the shadowed hallway, Adderley with his long stride, his hand on Miss Marton's wrist. He wasn't precisely dragging her, and she was making no protest, but he couldn't rid himself of the feeling that he ought to go after them.

Then again, it appeared that Adderley had already ruined her, and he'd been making threats toward the sodden creature who was staring at him with such impatience. Those threats may have sounded facetious, but Peter had no doubt Adderley meant every one of them, and sooner or later, he'd take Cecilia as well. He could scarcely imagine anyone being able to resist her, despite her sharp tongue.

"Well?" she said caustically.

"Well, what?" He had to raise his voice over the pounding rain, and he thought he heard a rumble of thunder in the distance.

"Aren't you going to go after them?"

"Why? According to the both of them, she's already been ruined, and she didn't appear to be particularly averse to the notion of repeating the experience. This way, he's less likely to turn his attention to you."

That managed to startle her. "He doesn't want me," she said flatly, and damned if there wasn't a disconsolate tone to her voice.

"Don't be ridiculous. There's no man alive who wouldn't want you," he said before he could think it through. She looked like a drowned kitten. She also looked more delectable than any woman he could remember, and he had a very good memory. Oh, she wasn't for the likes of him—he was a simple man when it came to desire. A financial transaction kept him free of entanglements, and Moll at the inn served his purposes very well. Cheerful, energetic, always up for a laugh or a shag. Whereas this woman...no, girl...was looking at him as if he were a snake.

Wait, that wasn't quite true. She had a speculative expression on her face, one he couldn't fathom, but it made him uneasy. It was gone a moment later, back to her usual disapproval. "So you're not going after them?"

"No."

"Then I am." She started forward, leaving a trail of water on the floor, and he caught her in two strides. He should have known she'd fight him. Slaps, kicks, imprecations, as he struggled to catch her flailing arms and ridiculous soft kicks. She even tried to knee his groin, momentarily shocking him, and he did the first thing he thought of, sweeping a leg behind hers. With any other female he would have boxed her ears in annoyance, but he was feeling alarmingly protective of the virago he'd plucked from a swamp.

They went down again in a tangle of limbs, and he covered her, catching her wrists between them, holding her legs down with his, so that he ended up between them, pressed right against that most precious part of a woman, and he wanted to groan. He could feel her warmth through the layers of wet fabric, and he knew he was growing steadily harder. Chances were, she'd have no idea what was going on with him, thank God. He needed to convince her to trust him, and she hardly would if she realized he was more of a threat to her chastity than Adderley was.

She stilled her struggles. "Get off me, you oaf," she spat at him.

He responded with a polite smile. "Not until you agree to do what I tell you. I'm not putting you in danger as well."

Again, that unexpected softening in her body. And then he realized just how cold she was, her chin trembling slightly from controlled shivers, her skin tinged with blue.

"You're freezing," he said shortly, leaning back between her legs, and he allowed himself only a slight regret for the lovely, passive sight she presented, lying pliant beneath him.

"I'm fine." Those stout words were belied by a slight quiver in her lower lip, and he cursed, rising to his feet and looking down at her. There was a real chill emanating from the old stone walls, and a sudden crash of thunder seemed to shake them.

Cecilia, whom he had already realized was a fearless soul, trembled, and enough was enough. He scooped her up easily enough, letting the damp fabric of her dress flap against his legs. "We're finding you a hot bath and warm clothes," he said in the voice that made hardened criminals cower.

"In this hhhhh…house?" she scoffed, unmoved. "The servants are useless. And I don't need a bath—the stream accomplished that, thank you very much. I just need some warm clothes." She was doing her best to keep her teeth from chattering, but every now and then, a shudder ran through her slender body.

He lifted his head with a subtle, *why me, lord,* and then looked down at her. He'd once tracked a murderer into a bog in Dartmoor, navigating the perilous terrain that could suck a man down in moments, and the memory came flooding back. One wrong step with Miss Cecilia, and he'd be a goner—if he had any sense, he'd turn and walk straight out into the pouring rain and take his chances with the lightning.

Scooping her up in his arms was easy enough for a man of his strength, and her body already felt familiar in his arms, damn it. "Where's your room?"

She shrieked and slapped at him. "Who do you think you are—

Adderley? I'm not taking you to my room."

He withstood the abuse stoically enough. "I don't care what room—I just need a bed to get you warm."

"I...I...I'm sure you do." Her shivers were getting worse, and even the fire in her eyes didn't help. "I'll scream for help."

"Please do," he said cordially. "I doubt Adderley will bestir himself, but it might prompt the appearance of your nonexistent servants."

"They aren't my servants, and they exist. They just don't do anything."

"Then scream."

She looked at him, startled.

"You heard me," he said grimly. "Scream." She was still silent, so he simply moved his supporting hand and pinched her delicious bum.

The scream that followed that was enough to deafen him in the huge hall, though it was swallowed up in another powerful crash of thunder. But it had done the trick—a very young maid appeared in the doorway, looking worried. She was about to turn and dart away, but he stopped her.

"You, there." This time his decisive tone had the effect he wanted, freezing her in place. "Miss Elliston has taken a strong chill, and she needs warming up. See that a bath is brought to her room immediately, have a fire laid, and then come help me bathe her."

Another slap at him, and he shifted her enough so that he could trap her nasty hands between their bodies. This was getting tedious.

"She doesn't have a room. That is, she was being kept in the housekeeper's old room, but that's been stripped. Miss Marton had us ready a new room on the third floor."

Cecilia was a slender creature, but the thought of three floors made him want to groan. "Where?"

"Third room on the right, the yellow room. Miss Marton thought it would be pretty for Miss Elliston."

Pretty, he thought with disgust. "I want the bath immediately," he said. "Get everyone on it."

"Me and Jimmy are the only ones I can find. I couldn't ask cook to haul water."

Cecilia was growing heavier by the minute. "Get anyone you can," he said grimly. "Where are the stairs?"

"You're...you're not going to just carry me off ..." Cecilia began, the tremors in her body turning to outright shaking.

"Quiet!" he thundered. "I intend to make sure you don't freeze to death, but that doesn't mean I might not strangle you if you annoy me enough."

She was not intimidated. "You and what army?"

He was tempted to throw her over his shoulder again, but he was already damp from their previous journey and he didn't want those wet skirts slapping about him again. He ignored her.

"Where are the stairs?" he demanded again, and the young girl pointed to the hallway on the right. Adderley had gone to the left.

He'd settle that once he dealt with this tiresome creature in his arms. She was squirming, and he glowered at her. "Do you want to go over my shoulder again?"

"No," she replied promptly, sounding subdued. "I...I'm just c...c...cold."

"Right," he said, and marched into the shadowed anteroom.

He'd dreaded the three flights of stairs, but in the end he barely noticed them. She was shivering so violently he had to clasp her even tighter against him, and his alarm was growing. Another few minutes in those icy clothes and she'd take an ague and die. He didn't want her to die, even if he wanted to kill her.

The yellow room was easy enough to find, the cheerful color muted in the eerie light of the storm. The windows were plastered with rain, though lightning sizzled in the distance, and there was no sign of the maid.

"Hell's bells," he said succinctly, setting her on her feet by the bed. Or at least he tried to set her down—she swayed against him, starting to crumple onto the floor, and he caught her.

"I'm fine." The foolish girl was trying to stand up on her own. "I'm utterly f...f...fine." She swayed again. "I'm just sooooo cold," she wailed.

The last thing he was going to do was put her wet clothes in the bed, so he did the only thing he could. He began to strip her in the chilly room.

She batted at him ineffectually, but he ignored it. "Close your eyes and think of Jesus," he suggested. He turned her around. The laces on her gown were loose enough, but with the water they'd become as strong as iron, and he pulled out a knife, causing Cecilia to shriek.

"Don't hurt me!"

"Christ, woman, I'm trying to help you." He cut through the laces, the busk parted, and it was the work of a moment to haul it down her arms and onto the floor. The skirt ties were likewise dealt with, then the three petticoats, and she was standing in her shift, the thin lawn plastered against her body, against her breasts.

He had time to notice they were possibly the best breasts he'd ever seen, and then he yanked off the chemise, scooped up her naked, shaking body and dumped her in the bed, covering her with every bit of clothing he could find.

She closed her eyes, shaking so hard the bed rattled, and he glanced at the fireplace. At least a fire had been laid, if not set.

"Don't move," he said to her, and was rewarded with a faint laugh.

"Sorry, but I c...c...can't stop moving," she said, shaking beneath the layer of blankets.

"Do your best," he snapped. Of course, the tinder proved to be stubborn, and it was several minutes before he could coax a good blaze out of the wood. The wind was howling, sending back billowy gusts of smoke into the room, and when he turned to look at Cecilia, he was hoping she'd fallen asleep.

She hadn't. The bed was creaking from the shakes racking her body, her face was dead white, and though her eyes were closed, he knew she was far from asleep.

He removed his boots as quickly as he could. The best thing he could do was strip down completely and warm her, flesh to flesh, but that would undoubtedly lead to other things that she wouldn't like, so he simply climbed on top of the covers, clad in shirt, breeches, and stockings, and pulled her into his arms.

She came willingly enough, sweetly, but it was a good while before her shivers began to lessen, and her body began to relax.

It gave him enough time to fully berate himself. It had been his stupid fault—he'd deliberately dropped her in the water, though, given the unnaturally sweltering heat, it should have been refreshing. And she'd been perfectly fine until this hellacious storm had exploded—there was no other word for it—over the countryside, but she could have died, might still, all because of his stupid pride and temper. The dismal truth was, he'd dropped her in the stream because he'd wanted her, and cold water seemed the best way to forestall any possible... He couldn't even think about it, though his body was doing its best.

He kept his hold tight, pulling her against him so that her head rested back against his shoulder, letting her nestle against him, and gradually, his own tension began to recede as the fire warmed the room. She was going to be all right. He'd seen enough people die from the fever that he knew how dangerous such a bone-deep chill could be. But Miss Cecilia Elliston, bless her sharp-tongued soul, was going to be all right, no thanks to him.

The fire had caught, though the wind still sent occasional gusts of black smoke into the room, and suddenly he was bone-weary. Cecilia should have smelled like the pond, but instead, her silky hair made him think of sex and flowers. Ridiculous. He pushed his face into it, breathing deeply, and fell asleep.

§.

DESPITE THE RAGING STORM, a gentle stillness settled over the manor house. Cook was dozing at the kitchen table, her wayward husband and the erstwhile lady's maid were naked in the laundry, having just romped their way through vigorous sex. Betsey leaned against the wall with broom in one hand, exhausted, and even Jimmy the boots slept in the corner by the fire. It was Sleeping Beauty's castle, under the thrall of some fairy godmother, but there was one problem.

Sleeping Beauty was wide awake.

ৠ 1 2 ৠ

BRYONY LAY in the huge bed, the one that had seemed so massive only this morning, with Adderley sound asleep beside her. It was much smaller now, with his body touching hers, and if she tried to move away from him, she'd end up on the floor. It wasn't as if she minded his touch—there was something oddly soothing in the feel of his strong body lying up against hers. He lay on his back, and he didn't snore. Of course not. The damned man was perfect.

Well, perfect in his imperfection, she thought fairly. His sinful beauty was an affront to God, though Bryony couldn't help but think her personal deity was seldom affronted by what He saw. Since He made everything, including Adderley, He must have had a reason.

She was lying on her back beside him, and there was something oddly peaceful about it. Like an ancient knight and his lady atop a marble bier, though Adderley's hands were not crossed chastely over his chest. She looked at that chest. It was broad, with clear strength in his shoulders, and lying beside him made her realize what a very big man he was. She was not a tall women, and she'd secretly disliked large men making her feel tiny and ineffectual. For some reason, that wasn't the case with Adderley. His strength made her feel stronger, safer, and she wanted to put her arms around him, have him press his large, strong body around hers, wanted it with dizzying force.

He wasn't going to do a thing. He'd taken his pleasure, he wouldn't do it again. He would leave once more, and they would somehow find their way back to London. The stranger who'd brought Cecilia back would help them, and she waited for her customary panic to fill her. She should try to escape, to go make certain Cecilia was safe, but for some reason, she couldn't move. Adderley wasn't constraining her—at least, not at the moment—but his body was like a magnet, and she was a raw metal.

And she was being a fanciful twit! Cecilia was her responsibility, she needed to make sure—

"Move one more inch away from me and I suspect you will regret it," came Adderley's calm voice. He didn't open his eyes, didn't alter his breathing, but he was indisputably awake, and Bryony wasn't sure if that was a relief or a disappointment.

"I need to check on Cecilia," she said. "There was a strange man with her..."

"That strange man was a Bow Street Runner. He'd be hardly likely to despoil her." He laughed, his low, cynical laugh. "What am I saying? He's a man, of course he'll despoil such a choice morsel."

Emotions swamped Bryony. Fear for Cecilia should have come first, but in truth, it was a great ways after her sudden surge of inexplicable jealousy. No one had ever called her a choice morsel. Not with her spotted skin and flaming hair. Which was a Good Thing, she reminded herself. Her life was complicated enough.

"You, on the other hand," Adderley continued as if he'd read her mind, "are hardly a morsel."

"You don't need to tell me." She couldn't manage to hide the disconsolate tone in her voice.

"It appears that I do. You, poppet, are a feast." His voice was lazy, and he still hadn't opened his eyes.

"You're mocking me."

"Hardly. You're the one who's lying beside me, your uncomfortable squirming putting me in mind of succulent flesh and vigorous rutting. I would so much like to taste you again. You were quite delicious."

"You did that? Oh, you mean when you kissed me."

"I did kiss you, my pet, and I intend to kiss you a great many more times, but that wasn't what I was referring to. I want to taste between your legs—I'm sure you're delicious."

Her response was utter horror, and she could think of nothing to say. Instead, she started to slide toward the side of the bed. "I really should check on Cecilia."

His hand shot out so fast it was like a snake striking. An adder. "You need to check on no one but me. If Cecilia doesn't have the wit to protect herself, then she deserves what she gets."

"Of course, you'd say that. You're a man, plain and simple."

There was a sudden, charged silence, and then, to her shock, Adderley laughed. Actually laughed, not that mocking half amusement. "I'm afraid you've got the right of it. I'm most definitely a man, with every single vice inherent in the species. I am not, however, plain and simple. Your life would be a great deal easier if I were." He turned his head, his amber gaze on hers, and she couldn't begin to read what was swirling there in his implacable look, but she suspected it wasn't going to be anything good for her. "As it is, I'm here to complicate your life beyond reparation."

"Why?" It was a simple question, one that should have discomfited him, but he didn't even blink.

"Because I can. I'm very spoiled, you know. If I want something I take it, and right now..." his voice trailed off, and she wasn't quite sure why.

"Right now you want me," she finished for him. "I can't imagine why."

"Neither can I. You're hardly my usual sort of bed partner, but then, as I may have mentioned, I've been bored recently. You may be clumsy and untutored, but at least you're not boring."

"I'm so gratified to hear it," she said in dulcet tones.

"And that's another thing I like about you. That sharp little tongue you use so effectively in your attempts to depress my more outrageous tendencies. Not that it does any good, but it's most definitely amusing. The thing is, you have the reputation for being a shy, biddable young thing, crushed by the pain of your unsightly appearance."

It caused a pang, when she should have been inured to it by now. Her hideous freckles had already made her an antidote, and Adderley had done everything he could to make her feel unsightly. Except when he touched her. Kissed her. Looked out her out of those hypnotic eyes. "If I'm that ugly, then why are you bothering with me?"

He sat up in the bed, looking down at her through the murky shadows. The storm still raged outside, but a greater storm was brewing in their room. "Don't fish for compliments—it's tedious. I do find your golden freckles to be quite enticing. I'm going to stretch you out on this bed in broad daylight and inspect every single one of your freckles, perhaps follow them with my tongue. I do hope they lead to interesting places."

If only it were humanly possible to control one's blushes. No matter how hard she fought back, she couldn't manage more than a feeble defense. She managed to pull herself up, though not out of his reach. "I'll do my best to be boring and uninteresting."

"Too late. Your secret is out. You'd love to be ordinary, but anyone with perception can tell that you're quite original, and that, quite simply, fascinates me."

She met his gaze steadily. She was still blushing, she could feel it, but it no longer mattered. "You're wrong," she said, and there was no disguising the faint note of triumph in her voice. "You suffer from an excess of self-assurance, but in this case, you're totally wrong, which I must say cuts you down to size. You've been trying to convince me that you're the bogey man, and your supposed omnipotence has added to that, but in truth, you've made a couple of wild guesses that have fortuitously struck home and then assumed you knew everything about me, when in fact you know nothing, you smug, degenerate swine." She was breathless when she finished, her heart beating hard, her breath coming quickly. She'd never been so impossibly rude to anyone in her life, and it both terrified and exhilarated her as she waited for his reaction.

But, of course, Adderley didn't give her the outrage she wanted so badly. "Degenerate is accurate," he said, leaning back, "and swine is an insult to pigs, but I rather hate to think I'm smug. It's simply that so little surprises me nowadays. In fact, the only one who's managed to stir my interest in the last year is you, my little termagant. Insult me some more—I'd love to hear just how outrageous my sober little nun can be."

She was having second thoughts, and she ground her teeth in annoyance. She never lost her temper, and yet this man had driven her to it. "I beg your pardon," she began stiffly. "You do have a tendency to rattle me, and I deeply regret my words."

"Oh, lord, don't!" he pleaded. "I like you much better when you're fighting me."

"But I have absolutely no desire to have you like me," she snapped back before she could help herself. She was about to mutter another apology but then closed her mouth abruptly.

"Too late, poppet," he said, his voice uncharacteristically soft. "I already do."

For a moment, she was struck dumb. He sounded almost sincere, and a sudden rush of warmth spread over her, one that her common sense couldn't halt. She pulled together her best version of a haughty glare. "You know just the right things to say to make a woman weak, don't you? It doesn't work on me!"

Why did such a devil of a man have such an angelic smile. "Doesn't it? You look like you need to be kissed."

Alarm spread through her, but she refused to retreat further. She would end up against the wall, trapped. "No one *needs* to be kissed, my lord."

"You do. Just to remind you I'm serious in my overwhelming lust." And before she could move out of the way, he did just that.

She knew about kissing. People kissed all the time—they clinked cheeks and kissed the air, they kissed their children, and they kissed hands. Mouths were closed when people kissed—it was the polite thing. Not with Adderley. He simply claimed her mouth with his, and while she raised her arms to shove him away, she could still feel her body begin that treacherous softening. He ran the tip of his tongue over her lips, teasing at them, and she knew she ought to bite him. She didn't want to.

She'd already accepted the fact that she was unlikely to be kissed much in her life. Marriage to a speckled antidote was not a sure thing, and if anyone took pity on her, he would be unlikely to want to shower affection on such a bran-faced creature. But Adderley seemed to want to kiss her, and she'd always been someone who longed for adventure.

This wasn't sailing along the Nile or scrambling over Etruscan ruins; it was more arcane and captivating, and as he caught her lower lip between his teeth, tugging at it, she no longer wanted to push him away. She wanted to draw him closer.

He lifted his mouth from hers. "Open up, poppet," he said, devilment in his eyes. "It's time you learned to kiss properly."

"I know about proper kisses," she said somewhat breathlessly.

"I stand corrected—let me show you about improper kisses." He dropped his mouth to hers once more, and his tongue touched hers with a slow, languorous stroke.

She didn't even notice when he pushed her down on the bed, her head in the cradle of his arms as he bent to his task. Adderley knew everything there was to know about kissing—he was touching her everywhere, with leisurely strokes, with hungry pressure and gentle bites, and no matter how her mind struggled, Bryony couldn't concentrate on anything but the pressure, the taste, the possession of his mouth on hers.

Was that what sexual congress was like, this kind of dreamy madness that made unmentionable parts of her heat and grow restive? She couldn't understand why her breasts were...were wanting something. The loose, old-fashioned dress rubbed against her untrammeled chest, usually protected by corset and chemise. He'd moved over her, and the fabric rubbed against her, and she needed something, something calming.

But still he kissed her, lifting his head to let her breathe, then kissing her again. It was no wonder she felt light-headed. No wonder her skin prickled. She needed some kind of ease from the mouth, the kisses that were luring her to a dark, dangerous place that she no longer wanted to resist. If this was what seduction felt like, it was no wonder there were so many fallen women in the world.

"You looked dazed, my pet." The soft shake of laughter in his voice should have outraged her, but she was too far gone. She would have given anything to have pushed him back, clambered off the bed, and stalked out of there. But then, he wouldn't be kissing her and she wanted more.

"You're a rat bastard," she whispered weakly.

"I am," he agreed, taking small nips from the column of her neck, moving down, and she wondered where he was going. While she missed the all-encompassing wonder of his mouth on hers, draining her of intelligent life, the tiny nips only fired her up further. He was moving toward her breasts, and for some reason, she wanted him to touch her there. If he just accidentally rubbed across her, it would be a blessed relief to the tight restlessness that seemed to emanate from deep inside her, and she shifted.

"Please stop," she gasped, knowing it was useless, but to her amazement, his mouth left her skin as he lifted his head to look down at her. If he'd looked at her with any tenderness, even passion, she would have reached up and brought his mouth back to her, back to her breasts, but she should have known better. There was calculation in those black-rimmed, golden eyes, curiosity, and a good dose of cunning. She wanted to cry.

She pulled herself together, reaching for calm. "Thank you for desisting," she said coolly. "You shouldn't have any desire to do this again, and I'm fairly certain your...loins were fruitful."

He stared at her for a long, frozen moment. And then he collapsed beside her, roaring with laughter, so uproarious that he shook the bed with it. There were tears of mirth in his eyes, and he seemed to have lost all interest in seduction. Thank God, she thought piously, ignoring that restless, longing feeling in her breasts and between her legs. How could she long for something she couldn't even remember?

She glowered at him as his laughter finally died out. "I don't see what's so humorous about it," she said defensively. "Isn't that what happens when two people...er...when they have sexual congress?"

"You mean when they fuck? Not usually, or there'd be a great many more people in this world."

"Well, then, why do it?" she demanded irritably.

"I'd show you, but you told me to stop." He propped himself up, watching her. "Can't imagine why I listened—some errant strain of decency that I haven't yet managed to eradicate. People fuck, my precious, because they *burn*." The word was low, sonorous, and it seemed to seep into her bones.

"I don't."

"Everybody does, sooner or later, as soon as they find the right person. Quite often, it's the most outrageously unsuitable partner imaginable. That's where bastards come from."

All heat left her, as if she'd been doused with cold water. "How many bastards have you sired?" She hated that word.

"None that I know of. I take precautions."

She didn't know which was the more shocking—that he had no other bastards from a lifetime of debauchery, or that one really could avoid it. "So my child will be your first?"

He no longer looked so amused. "You're not pregnant," he said flatly.

"How would you know? I know what my body feels like—I feel utterly different than I ever have before."

"Oh, really? Describe these symptoms."

"They're personal." She was hardly going to be describing her aching breasts, the strange feelings between her legs, the longing for...

"Not if you're carrying my child. But you're not. Assuming I actually did ravish you, it takes weeks for someone to discover whether they're pregnant or not, and it usually starts with spewing."

"How do you know? You said you had no bastards."

"I had one, long ago. He died." He glanced idly at his fingernails, and she wondered if he had someone to tend to them. They were simply part of his beautiful hands, hands that had touched her, held her.

"I'm so sorry!" she said impulsively. "That must have been dreadful."

The man shrugged, as if they were talking about a bad patch of weather. "He had the misfortune to have wretched parents."

As would hers, at least on the father's side. "Who was his mother?"

He gave her a bored glance. "Christ, women love melodrama. His mother was an opera dancer, French, and slightly unhinged. Marriage was out of the question, so when Christian was less than a year, she filled her apron with stones and walked into the sea with him. There wasn't much left of him by the time they found him."

She stared at him in utter horror. He was relating it like it was the latest *on-dit* from Paris, not a gruesome tragedy, and she had no idea what to say. She wanted to touch him, but she didn't dare. As far as anyone could tell, he was totally unconcerned by the story, but Briony didn't believe it. In fact, she was starting to disbelieve a great many of Adderley's excesses.

"I'm sorry," she said again, such inadequate words.

He shrugged. "It's of no particular consequence. Since then, women have tried to foist off a child on me, but I've been extremely careful to make certain I'm not the parent. If there seems an outside chance that I am, I then provide money for an apothecary to take care of things, and a little extra for their trouble. So I'm informing you that there's no way you could know you're carrying a child this soon, and if you were, I have an excellent sawbones who'll take care of the problem."

She couldn't help it, she *was* horrified. "You kill your children?"

The brief look in his eyes was dangerous, and then he shrugged. "They're not children at that point, and won't be for months. When you think what kind of life they'd have, you'd agree they were better off never to have existed in the first place."

"And how many children have you lost in that way?" she asked shakily.

"Just one. Since then, I've been more careful, as I was with you. I didn't spill my seed inside your unconscious body and you don't get pregnant through skin."

"But..."

"I'm tired of this conversation. Either end it or I'll end it for you, and you won't like my form of distraction. Or maybe you would—you're very unpredictable. That's one of the things that fascinate me about you." He glanced around him in the shadowed room, and the sound of rain lashing against the stone walls was oddly soothing. "Lie down."

She jerked, startled. Those odd feelings had vanished, leaving her with an overwhelming sorrow, but fortunately, Adderley's wicked spirit seemed to have vanished as well, leaving him bored and disinterested. He closed his eyes. "You don't have to sleep if you don't want to, but I recommend you don't disturb me. I don't like raking up my sordid past—my sordid present is much more entertaining."

"Then why did you tell me?" she asked.

He didn't open his eyes, but a cool smile crossed his firm, beautiful mouth. "To horrify you, my pet. And it worked."

She sat watching him for long minutes. As far as she could tell, he was sound asleep, but she knew if she tried to move off the bed, one of his hands would snake out and capture her. She was trapped.

She slid down on the bed beside him. He was asleep—she could tell by his breathing, but something made her move her hand along the counterpane, slowly, just close enough to brush against his arm. His face remained expressionless, his body still in sleep, but his arm turned, and he caught her hand in his much larger one, and it made her think of her current situation, a small bird trapped by a dark predator. But his hand was warm, strong, and for that moment, it was all that she needed.

❧ 13 ❧

WHY THE HELL had he told her about Christian? Kit thought. He'd made the decision years ago that he would never think of him again, and when the temptation had come, he'd always been able to drown it in brandy. There was no brandy near at hand, there was only the far more enticing female by his side, her hand in his, as trusting as a child....

He released her, but she didn't wake, she simply sighed and curled up against him, and he wanted to shove her out of the bed in his sudden rage. Didn't she know what he was? Hadn't he done his best to demonstrate it on every possible occasion? Was the female irredeemably stupid? Why didn't she tremble in fear as most women did? Why didn't she kick and fight and refuse to go anywhere with him? Why did she reach out and hold his hand, rest her body against his, kiss him back when he kissed her?

Perhaps he was losing his touch. On top of everything else, perhaps he'd become simply a bogey man rather than a man to terrorize virgins. Then again, the little idiot didn't realize she was still a virgin, and therefore had something left to lose. Not much, of course. The very fact that she'd spent the night, unchaperoned, under the same roof made her a trollop. The fact that she'd been naked in his bed ensured it, and no one would believe he wouldn't have taken her.

He turned his head to look at her. Her eyelashes were a burnished red, resting against her freckled cheek. No, he could assure himself he was still relatively perverse. Most men would look at the splashes of gold against her skin and draw back in horror. He looked at them and wanted to lick them.

His depravity assured, he looked at her mouth. It was a generous one, with full red lips in a faint pout, as if puckering for a kiss. That wasn't the kind of kiss he usually wanted, of course—he seldom kissed females on the mouth. Still, there was something about her mouth that aroused more thoughts than his cock in its warm depths.

The erotic fantasies were strong now, playing through his mind, bringing his body to full attention, and he contemplated waking her up in the rudest possible way. He reached down and resettled his rampant cock, then glanced at her consideringly. The smartest thing he could do was get away from her, and his maudlin lapse was the deciding factor. She was...weakening him. Sapping his nasty soul, and if that was gone, what would be left? An empty shell of a man of no use to anyone, particularly himself.

He gave a silent, mirthless laugh, but she slept on. He already was a useless shell, and there was no longer anything that could arouse his interest, apart from the maddening creature curled up beside him.

Maybe he ought to debauch his little virgin so thoroughly, with such extravagant dedication, that she was shocked and disbelieving, and then he could abandon her, forget about her. They were less than a day's ride from his favorite hunting lodge, a tumbledown pile of rocks known as Waycross. Only crows lived there now, but no one would bother him, and he could decide whether he wanted to end his weary, tiresome life or not.

But first he'd have her. He'd destroy her, her innocence, her totally misplaced faith, and maybe then his ridiculous obsession with her would stop.

❦

SIR GEORGE LATHERBY woke with a startled snuffle, staring around him blearily, wondering where the devil he was. It was dark, dank, and cold, when the last thing he remembered was that it had been damned hot. He shifted, reaching about him in the dark until he found what he needed—the silver flask of brandy he carried with him.

It was almost empty, and he let out a loud moan of despair before tipping the last drops down his throat. It had been full when they'd left the inn, and he'd already been half shot to begin with. Damme, he was impressed with himself. He always could drink anyone under the table, with the exception of Kit Adderley.

And where the deuce was he? Sir George's eyes were growing accustomed to the dark, and he came to the unhappy conclusion that he was still in the carriage. He shifted his generous weight, but there was no answering reaction from the front of the carriage. Clearly someone had tended to the horses. They just hadn't tended to him.

He sat up, straightened his neckcloth, and belched, the sound wet and satisfying. Why the hell had Kit insisted they return—he couldn't remember, but at the time it had seemed like a good idea. It could hardly be for his future wife—Kit had much better taste than to waste his time with a freckled, red-haired gorgon. Not that her nature was a problem—the girl was ridiculously acquiescent, accepting his token proposal of marriage with good grace. Perhaps she hadn't even realized she'd been trapped into it. But lord, it was a crime to let that large an inheritance go begging when he had such a dire need for money.

Of course, he had no need for a wife, but women were easily dispensed with if you knew who to hire. He needn't be troubled by his wife for long.

What had Kit said? Something about taking her for himself? Why he should want to was a mystery to George, but he'd learned long ago never to question Adderley's more bizarre impulses. He'd already bedded her, saving George the trouble of popping her cherry, and indeed, he didn't have any particular interest in enjoying that pale, freckled flesh. He'd insist she pleasure him with his mouth and punish her if she was hesitant. His two favorite things, punishment and fellatio, preferably at the same time.

No, he wasn't going to sit back and let a moneypot like his fiancée be stolen by his best friend, particularly since Kit would have no particular interest in her dowry. The man was an absolute nabob, with more money than the King, and no matter what he did to bankrupt himself, he always failed, amassing more and more wealth. If Kit was feeling like ruining someone, he could turn his attentions to his fiancée's pretty little cousin. Cecilia, wasn't it? Even George himself was more sentimental than Adderley—his friend would have lost interest before he'd even pulled out.

Speaking of which, had he pulled out? As far as George knew, Adderley had no bastards, not since that brat whose mother had drowned him. Adderley wouldn't give a damn whether he left someone pregnant, but he'd had the luck of the devil since his bastard died.

It would be an interesting situation if his seed had taken last night. His blushing bride would already have a bun in the oven, and George would already have an heir, saving him the necessity of begetting one. George didn't care who inherited his mortgaged estate and gambling bills when, decades from now, he shuffled off this mortal coil, and there'd be gambling bills and mortgages no matter when he died. He just wasn't made for sober economy, making Bryony Marton's place in his life of paramount importance.

Pushing open the carriage door, he lumbered down on the iron step which had fortunately been lowered, and landed on the hard-packed floor of the stable with only a slight stumble. He could smell horseflesh and manure, and he knew Coombs must be somewhere. George had been put out when Kit had insisted on taking his carriage, but now it was proving fortuitous if he were going to end this little outing to his best advantage. The coachman to the Marquis of Adderley might not take orders from his lordship's friend, but his own carefully chosen servant would do anything he requested, up to and including cold-blooded murder. Coombs had proven his worth time and time again, and he'd continue to serve faithfully.

He heard the rain then, with the distant rumble of thunder, and shivered in the dampness. He knew his horses—they spooked at bad weather. He shrugged—he was in no particular hurry to drag his bride to the border. No one was going to give him any trouble, certainly not Kit. He might as well enjoy a good night's sleep in a warm bed before he took to the road again.

No one had left so much as a lantern in the stable, and he had no choice but to stumble through the darkness, trying to guess exactly where he was. All he could do was thrash about until he found a door that led toward the main house, and then partake of Pevensey's fine cellar. At least the man had died before he'd managed to ruin the Pevensey collection of wines. Would have been a demmed shame.

No, his mind was set. He would spend a comfortable night, well-lubricated by the wine cellar, and first thing in the morning, he'd haul his ruined fiancée off to Scotland. After all, she should be grateful he was still willing to take her.

He couldn't imagine Kit would object—he'd be grateful, too. In fact, George was being the ultimate of good friends, dispensing with a messy little problem quite neatly, though the thought of being trapped in a carriage with his bride was a bit daunting. She hadn't viewed him with any charity since she'd been kidnapped.

Still, it wasn't up to her, nor Kit if it came to that. He would marry the wench, take her money, and when it ran out, she could conveniently die in childbed or carriage accident or a fever could carry her off. These things were simple enough to arrange, and he considered himself a very clever man. A night of careful imbibing—enough to enjoy himself but not render him senseless—and he'd be off on the last bit of his wedding trip. He could teach his blushing bride about using her mouth on him during the long trip.

With a satisfied huff, he blundered into the door, and he pushed it open. For once, life was going his way.

❧

CECILIA BEGAN TO STRETCH LUXURIOUSLY, awash in well-being, when her arm collided with an object. A very solid, male object, one that was as deeply asleep as she had been, and she froze beneath the heavy covers and the heavy arm that was embracing her. The man snored slightly, and settled back into sleep, and her initial panic began to fade.

Only to start up again when she realized she was completely naked beneath the fine linen sheet, clasped in a man's arms with only the bedding between their embrace. She didn't dare move, to wake him again, so she lay very still and took stock of her situation.

The room was dark, with only the glow from the fire illuminating it. She could hear it pop and crackle, and the sound was reassuring, further chasing her fear away. Even through the thick walls of the manor house, she could hear the rain pounding against the walls and windows, but at least the deafening thunder had ceased.

And she was in bed with a Bow Street Runner.

She surveyed the room as best she could without moving her head and startling him awake. His boots were in a damp puddle, his coat and vest a pile on the floor as was her fine clothing. The sight was depressing. Anyone, anyone else would have draped her clothes to dry, not left them in a crumpled heap. Therefore, she could only assume that she'd been undressed by Peter's rough hands.

Though not always rough, she remembered with frustrating vagueness. She'd been so cold, so desperately, bone-deep cold, and he'd held her, his warm hands on her, stroking her face as he whispered to her. What in the world had he said? She could only remember the sound of his voice, the rumble in his chest, but she couldn't remember the actual words, just the comforting warmth of him, the sense of well-being that had flooded her.

Ooooh, men were the very devil! No wonder it was so easy to ruin oneself, no wonder Bryony seemed so calm and matter-of-fact after the horror of her ruination. Though Cecilia had to admit that it didn't appear to be much of a horror. But still, she'd done nothing but fight with the man who now lay beside her, and yet she'd taken his comfort without a single demur.

This was bad, this was very bad. There was no way she could slip out of bed—Peter lay between her and the room, curse it. There was no avoiding it—she would have to wake him.

She shoved, he rolled, and ended up on the cold stone floor, cursing with such colorful invective that Cecilia was impressed. She would have liked to remember some of his expletives but she was far too nervous.

"What the hell?" he roared, and then his eyes narrowed as he looked at her. "Oh." It was an inadequate noise, inflaming Cecilia's temper further.

"Oh, indeed," she snapped, pulling the covers around her as she struggled to sit up. It was a difficult task with both hands holding the coverings around her body, but she wasn't going to have a conversation with the man while she was lying down. "How dare you!"

Peter Barnes's temper had faded as hers rose, and he arranged his long limbs comfortably on the floor, leaving Cecilia with no choice but to take stock.

He was a good-looking man in a rough-hewn way, his brown hair too long and curling over his forehead. His eyes were brown, a deep, warm color, his jaw strong, his cheekbones delineated. The only flaw Cecilia could find, if one could call it a flaw, was an aggressive nose, and that kept him from being too pretty, doubtless a disadvantage in his line of work.

She couldn't help but notice his body as well—she'd already learned he was too tall and too strong for her liking. She preferred men to be closer to her height, and harmless. That was what bothered her about Peter Barnes, she realized belatedly. Not his rude behavior, but that underlying streak of danger. She couldn't remember ever running into that before with a man. Oh, Adderley was the viper his name suggested, a monster in every way, but that was different from Barnes. Adderley would destroy without noticing or caring. Peter Barnes would bring about destruction in a focused, ruthless manner.

At least, unlike Adderley, he'd have a reason for it. And Cecilia knew she should be worried about Bryony, but right now, the man sprawled casually beside her bed wearing nothing but breeches and a loose shirt was taking all her attention.

"Sorry, your highness, but you were shaking apart with cold, and even the fire and the covers weren't making a dent."

"Being divested of my clothing wouldn't have helped! I assume that Betsey took care of that." *Please, let it be Betsey.*

"You're forgetting that you were sopping wet. And I'm afraid I was your lady's maid. Trust me, it's nothing I hadn't seen before—nothing special."

She could feel the heat rise in her cheeks, and to her consternation, she could feel the sting of tears start in her eyes. Tears of rage, embarrassment, and pride she told herself. No one had ever dismissed her so easily, and no one, apart from her maid, had seen her without clothes. She wanted to scream.

"Get out." Her voice was deadly calm, thank God, and a few good blinks got rid of the tears so quickly that they would go unnoticed.

"For God's sake, why are you crying?" Peter demanded, clearly more observant than a normal human being. "You must have legions of men falling at your feet. Must you really have me as another besotted fool? Stop it right now!"

Of course, it was the worst thing to say. The tears returned with a rush, she let out a choked sob, and flung herself back on the bed, her face pressed into the pillow. "Go away!"

She heard a long-suffering sigh as he got to his feet. "Stop crying," he said, but his voice was surprisingly gentle. "You're tired, you're hungry, you've been carried off by a stranger, and now you're at sixes and sevens. You know I'm not going to hurt you, and I'm damned well not going to let anyone else touch you. You're safe."

Her tears were slowing as the truth dawned on her. She was everything he said, but most important, she truly believed she was safe in the most fundamental of ways, and for some reason, that made her want to cry some more. Her parents saw her more as a commodity than a child, and they were auctioning her off to the highest bidder. But every man she'd met revolted her, with the possible exception of the big, mean oaf looming over her....

She felt his hand on her shoulder, her bare shoulder, and it was large and warm and strong and she knew she should throw it off. She didn't move, her tears dissolving into a few stray hiccups.

"That's the girl," he said, and his voice was low and calm. "I'll go find the damned maid and send her up with some food and hot tea. That'll set you to rights. And soon, you'll be safely back in the bosom of your family and you'll never have to think about me again."

The fact that she didn't immediately wail was a triumph. He squeezed her shoulder gently, almost a caress, and a moment later, he was gone.

As soon as the door closed behind him, she rolled over in the bed, the covers clutched around her. "Oh, no," she said. "Oh, good God, no. I can't."

But she knew she could, she had, she did. After a lifetime of manipulating love-struck gentleman, she had finally fallen prey to the dread disease. She had fallen in love with Peter Barnes, the most unsuitable, irritating man on earth. And there wasn't a thing she could do about it but pray it would go away.

❧ 14 ❧

THE KITCHENS at Pevensey Hall were warm and welcoming, full of wonderful aromas. Bryony had managed to slip away from Adderley's bed to arrange something for dinner, though she half expected he'd willingly let her go. The man seemed to be able to see everything, even when he was asleep, and if he hadn't been willing for her to leave, she'd still be there.

By the time Bryony made her way back down to the kitchens, Mrs. Seeley was already at work roasting a solid haunch of beef, with a brace of pheasants ready to go as well as a wonderful-smelling sole bisque. "I told young Jimmy to bring back supplies," the cook said cheerily, "since I was thinking there wasn't a carriage to let in town. You'll be spending another night here, miss, but at least you'll be well fed."

Bryony greeted that news with equanimity. "Since the rains still seem to be coming down like Noah's flood, I had assumed as much. Are you in need of any help?"

"Miss Bryony!" Mrs. Seeley was clearly scandalized. "The day I would ask the quality for help is a day I would never wish to see. Betsey's a good girl, and she's a fine helper. You'll be pleased to know she and I have gone through the cupboards and found proper clothing for you and the young miss. Years out of date, they are, but Betsey has already washed and pressed them, and they'll do well enough until you get where you're going."

It was a tactful way to put it, and there was no censure in Mrs. Seeley's face. "That's very thoughtful," Bryony said. "I shall have to thank her." She glanced around the kitchen.

"Oh, she's setting the table with Miss Blench right now, but she'll be back to help me with the pudding."

"I'm surprised Miss Blench could be persuaded to offer her services."

"Oh, I gave her no choice," Mrs. Seeley said grimly. "She's been here since the old mistress died—the young master let everything go to rack and ruin and he probably didn't even realize she was here. I pointed out that being agreeable was her best option, and she was wise enough to recognize the truth of it. Besides, she won't do any of the work; she'll just make sure Betsey gets her forks and knives in the right order. Girl was supposed to be a scullery maid, and I've done me best to train her, but there's still a ways to go." She eyed Bryony thoughtfully. "And what would you have us do with Sir George?"

Mercy, she'd forgotten all about him! "He's here?" she said faintly.

"In the study, going through the best bottles of Mr. Pevensey's wine cellar. Or so he thinks."

"I beg your pardon?"

For a moment, the cheerful Mrs. Seeley looked uncertain. "I thought his Lordship wouldn't want that man to be drinking the very best the cellars had to offer, so I'm having Seeley bring him...oh, mebbe the third best. We've a lot of that, which is a good thing, because Sir George seems to go through it like water. Should I have given him the canary?"

"You did exactly right, Mrs. Seeley." She ought to go find the man. He was a useless, amoral sot, and if she never saw him again, she would be more than happy, but there were things left to settle. She should return the ostentatious engagement ring that Cecilia still had on her finger, and she should make it clear their connection was irrevocably severed, but at the moment she wasn't quite up to it without fortification. "Could I bother you for a cup of tea?"

"Merciful heavens, it's half daft I am, not to have provided for you, miss! It's been so long since we've had a lady in the house that I never thought...still, that's no excuse. I'll have Betsey bring you tea in the pink drawing room, shall I?"

Bryony was about to agree, when a shocking idea popped into her head. "I'd like to drink it here, Mrs. Seeley," she said steadily. "I have...er...questions I'd like to ask you, if I'm not being too impertinent."

Mrs. Seeley looked at her in amazement. "Anything you want to know, miss. I'm here to serve you in any way I can." With a great economy of manner, she brought down the big brown teapot used for the servants' hardy brew and threw a handful of tea leaves in. In moments, the heady scent was overlaying the roast beef.

Pouring Bryony a cup, she stepped back, still at attention, and Bryony's stomach began its familiar roiling. She couldn't really do this, could she? How shocking was she willing to be?

"Please join me, Mrs. Seeley," she said. "I'm afraid there are no simple answers to what I wish to know."

"I'd be honored." Pouring herself a cup, she took a seat across from Bryony. "Now what is it you wish to know, lass? I've got the linens all marked down, and the silver, and..."

"It...it doesn't have to do with the household. Indeed, that's none of my business. I'm here as a...guest." She could think of no more accurate word for it—one could hardly lay claim to being a hostage. Cecilia had announced to the servants that they were there against their will, but none of them had reacted with particular surprise or outrage.

"That's all right, dearie. I've been on this earth a sight longer than you have, and I've seen a lot of things. If I have the answers you're looking for, they're yours."

Bryony didn't dare hesitate for fear she'd chicken out altogether. She was a great believer in plain speaking, but there were some subjects that were simply too impossible to be spoken out loud. "I wanted to ask you about..." Christ, she couldn't even think of the proper word for it! "...the marriage bed." She let out her pent-up breath.

Mrs. Seeley, bless her heart, didn't bat an eye. "Certainly. Were you wanting to know about me and Seeley or about the subject in general?"

"Oh, heavens no! I mean, general knowledge. I would hardly ask you such personal questions...." Except she just had.

Mrs. Seeley's smile was warm and motherly. "Did you want to know the mechanics, then? Your mother should have explained this all...."

"My mother died when I was born," Bryony said in a small voice. "I could hardly ask my father."

"No, I suppose not, though there's nothing shameful about it, for all that people like to make it so. The man's got a member, different between the legs than we have. He has a sword, you have the sheath, as me mother used to tell me. Except it's much nicer than a sword, bless you."

"Nicer?" That was hardly the word Bryony would have used when it came to the sexual act.

There was just the hint of a grin on the cook's placid face. "Ever so nice," she said firmly. "The man gets hard and he puts it into the woman. He pushes for a while..."

"For a while?" Bryony's voice was faint.

"For a while, and they both like the feel of it, if he's doing it right."

"Really?" She took leave to doubt it. "How long does this go on?"

"Why, it's anyone's guess. The longer the better, I say. It goes on until he comes, and then he's done, whether the woman is or not."

Bryony understood ancient Greek, Aramaic, Latin, and advanced mathematical reasoning, and she couldn't understand a word of what Mrs. Seeley was saying in her thankfully matter-of-fact tone. She shook her head, her forehead wrinkled, and Mrs. Seeley patted her hand before she poured her a second cup of the devilishly strong tea.

"The man pumps away at the woman until he spills his seed. Usually inside her—that's how babies are made. If he's not wanting to get the lass pregnant, then he might pull out and spill on the bed or on her stomach."

Bryony made an unconscious clutching motion at the top of her gown. "It sounds...messy."

"Oh, it is. Wet, and messy. The sheets I've had to clean over the years! When you live in a small house like this, you end up doing whatever work they hand you." She shrugged her massive shoulders. "And of course, the first time with a man is always different."

"I've been told it hurts."

"It does, more or less. There's blood as well, but if the man knows what he's doing, he can still bring the girl pleasure." A worried look came into her eyes. "You mean his lordship hasn't bedded you? We all assumed—well, since you clearly shared a bed, and there was a bit of a mess on the sheets."

What had he said to her? *I didn't spill my seed inside your body.* At least that much was true. Bryony could feel her cheeks turn pink, but she pushed onward.

But Mrs. Seeley wasn't looking happy. "Were you thinking of bedding down with his lordship? If you've managed to avoid it so far, then I'd think twice about it if I were you—I've heard from that sly coachman that he's the worst man in all of England."

She could no longer summon up a blush. "I...I..."

Mrs. Seeley was looking quite fierce now. "He's not going to take you to his bed if you don't want to go, I'll tell you that right now. I don't hold with rape, and my man will stop him. My man will do whatever I tell him to do."

The thought of Adderley facing off against the burly Seeley was distracting. Seeley was much heavier, and his fists were like small hams, and she suspected Adderley would make mincemeat of him.

She needed to set Mrs. Seeley straight. "I already spent last night with him," she said in not much more than a whisper. "Naked, in bed."

The cook sighed. "Well, good for you, but I'm sorry to see it happen to a man like him. Anyone who's that handsome ought to be able to make babies."

Again Bryony thought of the ancient Greeks. "What's that got to do with making babies?"

"If you spent the night naked in his bed, then the only reason he didn't have you was a soft willy."

"A what?" She wasn't sure she wanted to know.

"A soft willy. A member that doesn't get hard enough to get inside you."

All right, now the blushes were coming, but they'd come too far for her to back down. "It looked very big and hard."

"Well, did he bed you or not? There was no blood on the sheets, but if you weren't a virgin..."

"I was!" Bryony protested, as the truth dawned on her. "I am," she added in a quieter voice.

"So he didn't put his thing inside you?"

"I don't know. I was asleep."

Mrs. Seeley snorted. "No one sleeps that soundly."

"I do."

"No, you don't. Are you sore? Do you hurt between your legs? Was there wetness there?"

"No," she said in a slightly strangled voice.

"Then you're still untouched," Mrs. Seeley said firmly. "And while his Lordship is quite the handsomest man I've seen in a long time, you'd be wise to keep your distance. Unless, of course, things simply don't work down there. But you said he was big, so he must be all right."

She didn't want to think about it, about the stiff part of his body so prominently displayed. The one he hadn't used on her.

"Thank you, Mrs. Seeley." She tried to keep her voice serene and unemotional, and came close to succeeding. "You've answered all my questions, and I appreciate your frankness. It appears that you have dinner well in hand, so I think I'll go have a bit of a rest before we eat."

"Are you all right, miss? You look upset." Mrs. Seeley sounded so motherly that for a moment Bryony wanted to throw herself on her massive bosom and weep. Which was ridiculous—what did she have to weep for? She should be celebrating.

She put on her best smile. "I'm much relieved, Mrs. Seeley. I thank you for your frankness and your honesty." Indeed, she couldn't imagine anyone else who would have spoken that clearly about the unmentionable subject.

And because it was unmentionable, she'd made the very grave mistake of thinking Adderley had had his wicked way with her, when in truth he hadn't touched her. Couldn't bear to touch her. He'd told her so, hadn't he, and in all her puffed-up vanity, she hadn't believed him.

The halls were empty as she made her way up to the third floor, not to Adderley's bedroom but to the small dressing room at the end of the hallway across from Cecilia's room. The results of Betsey's labors lay starched and pressed and waiting for her, including prettily-embroidered chemises and plain shifts and clocked stockings.

Slowly, Bryony crossed the room to the large mirror that hung over the dressing table. She looked, at the tangled mane of red hair, at the green eyes that seemed to have water in them, at the horrible layer of unsightly spots that covered her skin.

Her father had called them sunshine's kisses. But her father loved her, and love was blind. Even in the most flagrant of circumstances, the worst man in England couldn't bring himself to touch her, the man who'd boasted of his perversities, and she knew there was no possibility that it could have been his better nature that had stopped him. He had no better nature.

She crossed her arms and rested them on the dressing table. Slowly, slowly she dropped her head upon them, pressing her face against her hands. And very quietly, she began to weep.

❧ 15 ❧

BY THE TIME Cecilia sailed into the dressing room, Bryony was dressed in a dull, bottle-green gown, her hair plaited and pinned to her head with painful precision, a fichu tucked up high, covering every expanse of the skin between her chin and the neckline of the modest gown. Her arms were unpleasantly bare, and there were no long gloves to cover them, so she made do with a silk shawl wrapped tightly around her. The unceasing rain had cooled the house a bit, but it was still unseasonably warm, and she clutched it over her like a blanket.

"I hear we have new clothes!" Cecilia announced cheerfully. "I can't wait to get out of these rags." She made a beeline straight for the pile of dresses, snatching up a bright yellow one dappled with pink flowers and holding it up against her shapely figure. "This one is gorgeous," she announced, twirling around, and then she came to an abrupt stop. "What's wrong?"

Unlike the rest of Cecilia's family, Bryony had seldom made the mistake of underestimating her intelligence, but she certainly wasn't going to expose her shameful secret. Not that Adderley had left her untouched, but that she minded. Minded most terribly.

"Not a thing," she said calmly.

But Cecilia wasn't fooled. "Then why are you looking like someone drowned your cat, and why are you wearing that incredibly ugly gown when there are so many better choices? And why are you wrapped up like an Egyptian mummy?"

"I'm cold," she lied, pulling the shawl closer. "Tell me about that man you brought back here."

It was the right thing to say. The frown left Cecilia's celestially beautiful face and she began to strip off her wrinkled clothes with a complete lack of modesty, exposing her pale, perfect skin. "Isn't he divine? Completely infuriating, of course, but he's..." For some reason, Cecilia's milky skin turned pink, and Cecilia never blushed. "He's a Bow Street Runner, sent by my parents to bring me back before I'm ruined." She frowned again, in the midst of putting an exquisitely embroidered shift over her head. "You'll come with me, of course. I don't know how they'll deal with the fact that Adderley assaulted you, but you're family, after all."

Bryony shut off that incipient surge of emotion. "Adderley didn't assault me," she said in a tight voice.

Cecilia reached for the fine silk chemise. "All right, all right. Adderley took advantage of you."

"He didn't."

"Well, for heaven's sake, what do you want to call it? He ruined you...."

"He didn't. He didn't touch me." She sounded blessedly sanguine, her shame hidden beneath many, smothering layers.

Cecilia froze in the midst of fastening the voluminous skirts at her tiny waist. "What do you mean?"

"Exactly what I said. Lord Adderley did not deflower me, debauch me, or in any way ruin me. I'm as virginal and innocent as the day I was born." Well, not completely, she thought, remembering the resplendent glory of Adderley in broad daylight, completely nude.

Cecilia looked nonplussed. "Why not? You were naked, he was naked. Why didn't he?"

"Apparently he has a revulsion for freckles." Another calm statement. She was doing an excellent job, she congratulated herself.

"Impossible. The man has no standards at all."

"Why, thank you, Cecilia."

"You know what I mean. He wouldn't let freckles stop him, and you know perfectly well that they're not that bad. One might almost say they're pretty, as I'm certain any discerning man would tell you."

This was definitely not helping. "The good news is, I don't need to worry about being pregnant after all, and once I get back to London..." She stopped as she saw the expression on Cecilia's face. "Your parents won't have me back, will they?" She tried to keep the excitement out of her voice. There was a good possibility escape had fallen into her lap.

"I don't even know for sure if they want *me* back," Cecilia replied, putting her arms through the bodice and presenting her back for lacing.

"Of course they will. You're their daughter," Bryony protested.

"I am. But they were counting on me for a good marriage, and given this little sojourn, I doubt I'll interest many peers of the realm."

"That's not fair. This wasn't our fault, and no one even touched you...."

"You said Adderley didn't touch you."

Unbidden, Bryony remembered his mouth on hers, the strange, drugging wonder of his kiss. "Not much," she qualified. "He may have...kissed me."

"He kissed you, got naked with you and didn't dishonor you! Is the man mad?"

Bryony was unable to hide her small smile at Cecilia's vigorous defense. "Freckles, remember," she said lightly, lacing up the back of Cecilia's bodice. "I may as well have the pox."

Cecilia was honest enough not to argue. "Well, I think they're lovely!" she said stoutly. "Once you get over the surprise of them, they look like...like...very pretty spots."

To Bryony's surprise, she could laugh at Cecilia's faint praise. "Indeed," she said. "But you still haven't told me how you came across your runner, and why he was carrying you, and how you managed to get soaking wet...."

She watched with a sinking feeling as Cecilia's exquisite porcelain skin turned pink. Cecilia was a hoyden—she didn't blush, and yet she was certainly blushing at that moment. Oh, dear.

"Oh, it was nothing. I was caught in the woods on this little spit of land amid torrents of water, and he heard me calling for help."

"Cecilia, you could have drowned!"

"Well, it wasn't that deep," she admitted sheepishly. "But I didn't fancy getting my feet wet, so I called for help and Peter showed up like a *deus ex machina*..."

"Peter?"

"Mr. Barnes," Cecilia amended hastily.

"If he rescued you, then how did you come be so wet?"

"He dropped me," Cecilia said in a dreamy voice. "I bit him, and he dropped me in the water."

"Oh," Bryony said blankly. "I'll look forward to making his acquaintance." Her ridiculously irrational hurt had fled in the face of this new information. Cecilia was never dreamy about anyone. Men adored her, scrambled all over themselves to do her bidding, and she had evinced no more concern than if they'd been chess pieces to move on a board.

And now she was looking starry-eyed because a man dropped her in a stream, all the while Bryony had been nursing a very fortuitous slight. This rearranged her priorities—Adderley was the least of her worries. Once again, she had to save Cecilia from herself.

The door opened suddenly and Betsey stumbled in, obviously never having learned the niceties of a maid's duties. "Mrs. Seeley says to tell you that dinner's almost ready, but that the new gentleman has gone out in the storm, and she can't hold it back or the roast will be ruined and the soufflé will fall and..."

"Slow down, Betsey. Which gentleman?"

"The runner, miss. He said he was going to find a way out of this hellhole, begging your pardon, miss, and he went out in the rain an hour ago, and hasn't been back since."

"He's out there in the storm?" Cecilia said shrilly, and Bryony's heart sank further. Cecilia didn't care about her flirtations; she mostly didn't care about anyone but her own well-being unless she realized that someone she loved was in need.

"I'm sure he'll be fine, dearest," Bryony said calmly, straightening her back. She was needed, and that was the best thing possible. If Cee Cee needed her, then Adderley could be ignored. "Come along —aren't you hungry?"

It did the trick—Cecilia was always hungry. "There's a roast for dinner?" she said, momentarily distracted.

"Mrs. Seeley's got a right feast laid up for you, and she's wanting to know if she should wait."

"And ruin the roast?" Bryony said. "Never. Come along, Cecilia. Your prince charming will return, safe and sound." She waited for Cecilia's laughing denial.

"No, he'll be fine," Cecilia said instead. "He's very big and very strong—a little bad weather won't be a problem for him." She straightened her ivory shoulders and smiled her dazzling smile. Catching a filmy fichu from the stack of clothing, she tucked it into the low neckline of her dress so that her assets were still prominently displayed, checked herself in the mirror, and grinned at the reflection. "Yes, let's go eat."

᠗

HIS DAPPLED PRINCESS was angry with him, and Kit had no idea why. Normally it would scarcely matter—he strolled into the large dining room to find the long table sparsely populated. George was at the head, with the ravishingly beautiful and totally uninteresting child on one side and Bryony on his right. He managed to hide his surprise at the sight of her—she was muffled to her ears in swathes of fabric, her hair was pulled back against her head so tightly that he assumed her scowl was the result of a headache, and she refused to look at him or acknowledge his presence.

There was a place setting at the foot of the table, much too far away to torment his plaything, but he took it anyway, sinking into it lazily. "No one informed me that dinner was served," he said in cool voice.

"Why would you care, Adder?" George slurred, using the name Kit hated even more than "the Inconstant." "The day you care about food is the day I give up the ghost."

"You will be appropriately mourned," he replied, his words halted as Bryony rang the tiny silver bell by her side. She might be ignoring him, but not her duties as the default lady of the manor. A moment later, the beefy manservant came in, his uniform threadbare and gaping a bit in front, followed by the simple-minded maid. Though she might not be that simple-minded—she ran any time she saw him, which showed a certain amount of good sense.

George was snickering into his glass of wine. "That's a good one," he said. "You'll mourn me. Ha! You might be the only one who would."

"I'm definitely the only one who would," he replied. "And where is our intrepid Bow Street Runner? There's no place set for him. Has he been banished to the kitchen?"

For a long time, no one answered him. Too long. "Well!" he snapped, and everyone jumped. Still, Bryony kept her face averted.

"Damned if I know," George said, draining his wine glass. "Where'd a Bow Street Runner come from?"

"Apparently, someone objected to our carrying off two nubile young damsels."

There was a noise from the one muffled damsel, the only one he was interested in, and it sounded rather like a snort of disbelief. He turned to her. "Do you doubt you were missed?"

She would have liked to ignore him—he knew it—but good manners were bred in her bones, so she simply turned an icy gaze in his direction. "My cousin was missed, my lord," she said. "Apparently, I'm disposable."

"Ah, poor little orphan," he said lightly. "Are you trying to incite my pity? I believe I'm fresh out of it."

"I want absolutely nothing from you." The words were clipped, sharp. Interesting, since she must be sweltering in that get-up. The oppressive heat had returned, despite the unceasing rain, and there were faint beads of sweat on her high forehead. He wanted to lick her.

"I don't like it," George said. "Damme, it's indecent! Can't a man elope without them sending the whole metropolitan force after him?"

"Only one runner, I believe," Kit said lazily. "As Miss Marton pointed out, we're not that important."

"Just one? Well, we can make short work of him. Even so, I believe we should leave in the morning for Scotland before anyone else throws a spanner in the works."

Both women made fiercely protesting noises at that statement, but the silly one...Cecilia...spoke first. "I believe you'll find Mr. Barnes a little more difficult to manage."

"Who the hell is Mr. Barnes?" George cried petulantly.

"That's the name of our stalwart officer of the law. Where is he, by the way?" Kit drawled.

"Looking for a way out of here," Cecilia shot back, then subsided after a look from her cousin.

"And I wasn't thinking of managing the creature," George went on heedlessly. "Disposing of him, more likely. What's one policeman, more or less?" He was already quite drunk, Kit realized with no surprise.

"I'd like to see you try," Cecilia shot back, but Kit wasn't looking at her. He was watching Bryony's expressive eyes, reading the concern and uncertainty in their green depths.

"Sir George is making a joke," he said firmly.

"Sir George isn't doing any such thing." George drained his refilled wine glass, and the ruby liquid splashed on his pale gray coat, joining the gravy that resided there. "I'm not going to let anyone interfere with my upcoming nuptials. Can't disappoint my little bride." He leered at Bryony, and Kit felt an inexplicable stirring of...what? He couldn't pinpoint it. He only knew he didn't like it.

"Sir George," Bryony said in that calm voice that simultaneously amused him and drove him mad, "You are the very last person in the world I would agree to marry."

George took this with good grace. "Don't know that you will have any choice in the matter, m'dear. And such hyperbole! I know for a fact that you would marry me before Adderley, so I'm hardly the last one."

Dead silence followed that artless statement, with the only sound in the room the rustling of clothing. "I stand corrected," Bryony said finally. "But I have no intention of marrying either one of you. I have no intention of marrying at all."

"We shall see," George blabbered on. "I know for a fact that Adder can procure enough opium to render you completely acquiescent. You've brought some with you, haven't you?"

He addressed this to Kit, who easily covered his annoyance. It was past time he severed his connection with Sir George Latherby. The man was a witless boor, even if he was able to keep up with Kit's most depraved vices, and he had no sense at all when to keep his mouth shut.

"Of course," he replied politely. He didn't need to glance at Bryony to see her reaction—she was busy ignoring him and sending off such waves of anger one would have thought he'd raped her mother. Perhaps she'd decided her imagined ruination was the depraved thing it would have been—she'd been oddly sanguine about the whole thing so far.

In fact, he wondered what she'd be like with a taste of the poppy. He used it sparingly—he'd observed that if one became overfond of it, then it lost its pleasant effects—and he'd certainly combined it with sex to pleasant results. He could picture those green eyes hazy with the drug, unwilling and unable to stop him from doing anything he damned well pleased with her.

"I thought we agreed that marriage with Miss Marton was no longer a goal," he said lazily, not wanting to bestir himself, but the girl didn't deserve the kind of life George would doubtless deliver. He owed her some gratitude for delivering him from boredom.

George shrugged. "I'd forgotten about her fortune, and my pockets, if you remember, are very much to let. Besides, it would be absurd to have kidnapped my fiancée and never managed to marry her."

"I have a great fondness for absurdity."

"And I have a great fondness for money," George shot back, alert despite the amount he had drunk. "Besides, she's not that bad. In the dark, I won't even see the damn freckles."

"Ah, but the freckles are the best part."

Bryony overturned her wine. She hadn't been drinking it—he was able to observe her quite closely even as he conversed with George, and he saw her jerk at his statement. What the hell was wrong with the girl? Did she have some problem with her delicious freckles?

"I forgot you had her first," George said genially. "Tell me, was she worth it...?"

"Gentlemen! If you will not cease your coarse conversation for my sake, then will you please do so for my cousin's?" Bryony's voice was strained and the pink color on her cheeks only made the freckles more delightful. Her cousin, however, was looking both furious and terrified, which would have been amusing if she held the slightest bit of interest for him.

But at least Bryony's concern for her cousin had forced her to look at him, one clear advantage. Never taking his eyes off Bryony's, he said, "Are we offending you, Miss Elliston?"

"Yes." The answer wasn't much more than a whisper, and he smiled like a serpent. The more he poked the brainless one, the more Bryony would object, and he had every intention of pushing her far enough to find out what was behind the rage simmering in her eyes.

But then it seemed as if something had shut down around her. She blinked, and turned her gaze away from him, dismissing him like an insignificant cockroach, and he was charmed. One could love a woman who was so impervious to his baiting.

He was about to try again when there was a sudden commotion, and the door to the dining room was flung open, exhibiting a tall, broad figure dripping water. Oh, yes, the Bow Street Runner.

He didn't miss the girl's...what was her name? Celeste? Cellendra? Cecilia!...reaction, and his amusement deepened. That certainly hadn't taken long.

"And who the bloody hell are you?" George demanded irritably from his spot at the head of the table, apparently thinking that placement made him the lord of the manor.

"Our Bow Street Runner," Kit murmured, "and rescuer of fair damsels."

"Well, go 'round to the kitchens, man, and someone will give you something to eat. You don't go interrupting your betters in the midst of a meal."

It was a wonder steam didn't billow off the man's soaked clothing. Cecilia was looking at him like he was some noble knight come to rescue her, and Bryony seemed far too interested. He might have to do something about that.

Bryony rose, going straight to the interloper. "Nonsense. We'll have them bring a place setting here so he may tell us what he's discovered."

Kit didn't like the way the man looked down at Bryony either, but his furtive glances at the other girl set his mind at ease. He might not have to kill him after all.

"I doubt my stomach could take the company," the runner said in a low voice. "I took a look around, and right now this place is a virtual island. There's water everywhere—overflowing the river-banks, filling the fields. No one's going anywhere until the rain stops and some of the water subsides."

George's pout made him look like a distempered, extremely slovenly child. "Don't be ridiculous! I have a bride to claim."

"Claim anything you want," the runner said rudely, "but no one's getting out of here for the near future."

"Let me find a servant to assist you, Mr. Barnes," Bryony said briskly. "I'm certain you'd like some dry clothes and more pleasant company than this room provides. Come along." She started toward the door, but Barnes didn't move, his eyes on Cecilia's.

God, young love was so tedious. The girl threw her serviette down on her plate and rushed to join her cousin without a backward glance at the two men remaining at the table. She tried to take his arm, but he avoided it, quite deftly, in fact, as he walked out of the room, and Kit decided to let them go. He would wait until a better time to find out exactly what Barnes wanted. And more importantly, who. Because if he were here to rescue Miss Bryony Marton, he was going to come up against a brick wall in the shape of the Earl of

Adderley. He could take the silly one anywhere—Bryony stayed with him.

And if George thought he was putting his poxed hands on her, then he'd be forced to teach him a lesson. He had no intention of discerning why it mattered—he assumed it was just his legendary stubbornness. But Bryony was his, freckles and all, and no one else was going to touch her.

✤ 16 ✤

"I NEED NO HELP," the drenched man said grumpily, and Cecilia kept her smile to herself. Of course he would say that, and she'd learned from Bryony that the best way to deal with obstreperous males was simply to ignore their bluster. Her cousin had gone off to arrange a warm bath and clean clothes, and Peter was looking as if he wished she were anywhere else, but she wasn't leaving his side. She'd seen the flash of darkness in Adderley's eyes, and she knew the man's reputation. If it came to a fair fight, then her money would be on Peter, but Adderley would undoubtedly cheat.

They were standing by the grand staircase, and Cecilia was not about to let him stomp off without her. "I'm sure you don't," she said soothingly, "but you're drenched and chilled to the bone. You looked after me—it only makes sense that I return the favor."

He raised an eyebrow. "You're going to strip me and get in bed with me?"

Cecilia could feel her cheeks warm, but she didn't falter. "I don't think that will be necessary. In fact, I doubt it was necessary earlier, but I believe your motives were noble."

His laugh surprised her, and she realized she hadn't heard him laugh before. "You believe in fairy tales and unicorns as well, Miss

Elliston?" Before she could answer, he started up the stairs, and she rushed to keep up with him. "Where are you going?" he demanded.

"I'm coming with you. I intend to make sure you have everything you need. We certainly can't have you dying of a putrid fever."

"It would take a great deal more than a fever to carry me off. And if you think you're following me to my bedroom and watching me while I bathe, then I'm afraid you're in for a disappointment."

Her flirtatious nature kicked in automatically, and she gave him a bewitching smile. "I could scrub your back?" she suggested.

He stopped abruptly halfway up the stairs, and rounded on her, just a few steps behind, his move so abrupt she almost tumbled down. Instead, she caught his arm to steady herself, his strong, muscled arm, and he didn't shake her off. "I need to remind you, Miss Elliston," he said, his voice a low growl, "that I'm not one of your tame society dandies. I don't play games, I don't flirt, and you can take those pretty smiles and give them to someone else."

That pretty smile faded as irritation filled her. She knew men, and she knew when a man wanted to kiss her. She'd sampled all sorts of kisses, but she suspected this man's might be very different. "Should I bestow my smiles on Lord Adderley?"

It worked. A dark storm filled his eyes. "You'd do so at your own peril. And don't expect me to rescue you from your folly."

"Why not? Isn't that precisely why you're here?"

He opened his mouth to refute it, then shut it again in frustration. "You're an idiot," he said finally before turning and continuing up the stairs with a heavy tread.

"That's what you think." Cecilia scampered after him, unabashed by his criticism. "I spend a great deal of time trying to convince men that I'm completely brainless, and most of them happily believe it. I would have thought you had more perception."

He didn't stop or look back. "Why would any sensible girl pretend to be an idiot?" he snapped.

"Because one has a great deal more power when people underestimate you. You can make them do anything you want if you're clever enough. I can enjoy kisses and not have to promise anything if I'm a scatterwit."

They'd reached the landing on the third floor, and at the end of the hallway Cecilia could see Betsey struggling with a bucket of steaming water, presumably for his bath. "Go away, Miss Elliston," he snarled. "I don't need these artless confidences, and I can't imagine why you've chosen to share them with me." He started down the hallway in the direction Betsey had been heading, and she had to skip to catch up with his long stride.

"Because I don't want to have power over you," she said breathlessly.

He halted, so suddenly she almost slammed into him, and turned to look down at her. "And you don't want me to kiss you?" His voice was still a growl, but there was something else beneath the harsh tone, something that was making her melt a little inside.

"I didn't say that." Her voice was small, nervous, but he heard her clearly.

"You want me to kiss you?"

"I didn't say that!" This time her voice was stronger, and she tried to back up a pace or two.

Because he was advancing. "And you say you're not an idiot. It appears to me, Miss Elliston, that you don't know what you want. One would suppose it was Adderley, since you were mad enough to elope with him, and yet now you're making moon eyes at me...."

"I am not!" she protested weakly. "And I didn't elope with Adderley, he kidnapped us."

"Why? Another of your besotted admirers? You'll find Adderley is not as easy to manipulate as I am."

"You're not easy to manipulate."

"Exactly."

This conversation wasn't going the way she wanted it to. He was supposed to sense her shy attraction, he was supposed to respond passionately, and...and...

"Never let it be said I disappointed a lady," he muttered, and before she realized it, he'd crossed the safe distance that had remained between them, slid his hands through the loose curls on the back of her head and crushed his mouth down on hers.

Cecilia Elliston had kissed seventeen men and boys, and she

ANNE STUART

considered herself a reasonable expert in the matter, but she'd never, ever been kissed like Peter Barnes kissed her. He'd turned her around, pressing her up against the wall, and his mouth slanted across hers, hot and hard and wet. With a stroke of his thumb, he had her opening her mouth, and when she tasted his tongue, she was so shocked she should have pushed him away. She pressed closer to him. In the darkened hallway there was no one but Peter, shutting out the light, shutting out the second thoughts, shutting out any last bit of common sense. She tilted her head back, giving him fuller access, and his mouth left hers to move down her cheek, the edge of her jaw, the soft, sensitive skin on her neck. She felt the sharp nip of his teeth, followed by the benediction of his tongue soothing the bite, and she heard her own little whimper of pleasure. In a moment, he would stop, and she would die if he did, but he moved back to her mouth, and there was no longer anger, there was a sweet longing tenderness as his ran his tongue over her lips, taking soft little nips of her trembling mouth. She felt lost, dreaming, floating away into something wonderful, and she pressed her body to him, feeling the hard, warm strength of him, the muscles, the power in him. Feeling the—

She pushed away from him in sudden panic, but the gentleness vanished, and he didn't let her go. He moved back to her mouth with a raw, hungry sound, and he moved closer again, sliding one strong hand up her back, another along her hip as he caught her hand in his, holding it, moving it, until he placed it on that unmistakable bulge in his breeches and she froze in sudden shock.

She tried to yank her hand back, as if scalded, but he held her in place, lifting his head. "That's what you're playing with, you little idiot. You've never been around a real man in your life, just other idiots who have to play your games. Well, that's not me." He pressed her hand harder, and his body surged beneath her touch. "Before you start playing with fire, you'd better make sure you have a way of the putting out the flames, or you wouldn't like the consequences."

With that, he abruptly released her, so that she fell back against the paneled wall, and he walked away from her without a backward glance.

৯৯

DAMN THE GIRL! What the devil had she been up to, flirting with him like that? And why, in God's name, had he kissed her? He should have spanked her instead. She was a spoiled brat with no sense of consequences, even if he'd just demonstrated one of the very real consequences her thoughtless actions could bring about. And the damnable thing was, he still wanted to kiss her, hard and longing, sweet and seeking, he wanted to put his mouth all over that delicate white skin and make her cry out...

And now he had an erection that he hoped would escape his ostensible hostess's eyes. Since women of that class kept their gazes firmly above the waist, he could be fairly safe on that account, though what the hell she was doing with someone like Adderley beggared his imagination. Unless, as Cecilia said, they'd really been kidnapped.

Miss Elliston, he reminded himself sharply. He had no call to think of her by her given name. He'd done a decent job of scaring her off, and from now on, she'd watch her step around him.

And he was right pleased about that. It was what he wanted, wasn't it? Except...why had she tasted so damned sweet?

৯৯

CECILIA'S RUNNER, as Bryony thought of him, came in the door looking calm and unruffled despite his sodden clothes and tousled hair, but Bryony wasn't sure she quite believed it. Something was going on between Cecilia and Peter Barnes, something Bryony couldn't quite identify. He was hardly Cecilia's type—she liked shallow, pretty young men she could wrap around her finger. Barnes was a man, not a callow boy, and the word pretty could never be applied to his rough face. He had a scar under one eye, and his features were strong and forceful, his gaze direct and no-nonsense, while Cecilia reveled in nonsense. Nevertheless.

"I've brought fresh clothes for you, Mr. Barnes. I'm afraid most of the clothing in this household is decades out of fashion..."

"I have no use for fashion," he said grimly. "Begging your pardon, Miss Marton."

"And Betsey has brought you bath water. If you'd like to join us after you've changed you'd be welcome...."

"You might be welcome, miss. I doubt your companions would be as open-minded. Miss Elliston informs me that neither she nor you eloped with the gentlemen in question, that you were kidnapped. Is that true?"

Like a bull terrier with a rat, Bryony thought resignedly. "Indeed. But pressing charges against them would be a waste of time—what's most important is to return Cecilia before word gets out or she'll be ruined, regardless of what happened here."

"Those are my orders," he said grimly.

"And what, precisely, are your orders about me?"

She was surprised the man could look so uncomfortable. "I was told to bring Miss Cecilia back."

"And not me?"

He didn't say anything, and Bryony accepted it with her usual equanimity. Indeed, this made things easier. If she had to wait until Peter Barnes decreed it was safe to leave, then she might run into real trouble. At this point, no one had any use for her except Sir George and his pocketbook, and Bryony would rather sell herself in the streets than marry the man. There was nothing keeping her here.

She straightened her back. "I can trust you to take good care of my cousin. See that she's returned home in the same pristine condition that she left?"

Oh, dear. An imperceptible flush appeared on those hard cheekbones. Wasn't life complicated enough? "Of course, Miss Marton. Bow Street holds itself to the highest of standards."

"But most Bow Street Runners don't run afoul of my little cousin. She appears to be quite taken with you."

The flush darkened. "Miss Elliston enjoys playing games," he said in a noncommittal voice.

"You know that much about her already? Very observant, and it fails to set my heart to rest. It might be better if I kept you company when you return her."

"Certainly, Miss Marton," he said, not missing a beat, but if he was perceptive, she was even more so, and she saw that momentary flicker in his deep brown eyes. Maryanne and James wouldn't look kindly on her resurrection.

The man had to be years older than Cecilia, and decades older in terms of life experience. He would have too much sense to be sucked in by a pair of china-blue eyes. But then, he wouldn't know that her guileless demeanor hid the heart of a ruthless general. If she really, truly had set her sights on Peter Barnes, then resistance would be futile.

But it was absurd to think so. Cecilia had sailed through the season heart-whole, and she valued her status and creature comforts. She was hardly going to throw everything away on a Bow Street Runner.

"I think we'll have Betsey accompany you, just to keep everything proper. When do you expect to be able to leave?"

"It depends on how long it takes for the water to go down, and it'll need to stop raining first. At this point, it would be too hard to find solid footing with all the standing water."

"But you could find footholds?"

"I could," he said. "But I don't fancy dragging Miss Elliston through the muck."

So it was possible, Bryony thought with relief. If she were careful, she could get away from the place before anyone realized she was gone, leaving Cecilia in Peter Barnes's safe hands. At least, she hoped they were safe. Barnes would do what he could to keep Cecilia at bay, and Cecilia had a wonderful sense of self-preservation.

But Bryony hadn't liked that look in her eyes, the unconscious sigh. She'd never seen Cecilia so taken with anyone.

She brought herself back to the business at hand. "I'll have cook send up a tray then, shall I? You must be famished."

"I'll bring you back with us," he said suddenly. "Your family can't refuse to take you in."

Bryony took leave to doubt that, but she merely smiled. "I've made other arrangements, Mr. Barnes, that will suit me far better. Just promise to protect Cecilia, and I can rest easy."

"With my life." The moment the words were out of his mouth, he looked like he regretted them. "That is, the Bow Street Runners accomplish their assignments—we always get our man."

"Or woman, in this case," Bryony said lightly. She had a bad feeling about this. Cecilia was too stubborn, and Peter Barnes, for all his disapproval, was clearly smitten. She simply had to hope he was equally stubborn and determined to return her to her family.

As for her, she had one choice and one choice only. It was time to escape.

❧ 17 ❧

"I THOUGHT THEY'D NEVER LEAVE," George said cheerfully, pouring himself another glass of wine and spilling half in the process. "Women are such tedious creatures. I'd sew up their mouths if I could, but then I prefer face fucking, so I suppose I have to put up with their attempts at intelligent conversation." He belched loudly, and Kit surveyed him as if from a distance. He really was a revolting specimen, and the thought of him putting his pudgy hands on Bryony...on someone like Bryony was a travesty.

Kit poured himself a glass as well, albeit more neatly. He'd had a great deal to drink already while he'd been trying not to watch Bryony, and retiring to the library with a fresh bottle sounded like just what he needed, as long as George didn't tag along.

"Got nothing to say to that, eh?" George demanded, slurring slightly. "Don't know what's gotten into you nowadays. You've already availed yourself of my fiancée—either do her again or let us continue on our trip."

"I'm not going to Scotland."

"Well, that's a fine thing, I must say. I didn't want you along in the first place, but you insisted. You can stay here while I drag my intended north, maybe diddle the younger one if that dratted runner

167

doesn't get in your way. You wouldn't think he'd dare, but the working classes are becoming alarmingly bold nowadays."

"Bryony isn't going to Scotland either," Kit said flatly.

"Who? Oh, you mean my wife? Forget her blasted name—I just think of her as the freckled one. She most certainly is, if you want any chance of being paid back for our last night of gaming."

"I don't."

"Oh," he said blankly. "That's well enough, but I've got other creditors, you know, and after this debacle, no one's going to look too kindly on my suit. No, the girl's going with me to Gretna Green, all right. Things are getting downright unpleasant with my bills."

"Things will get a great deal more unpleasant if you try."

George was not so drunk that he didn't recognize the look in Kit's eyes, but his lower lip jutted out like a baby's. "Listen, you had her already, what the hell do you care what I do with her? She won't get in the way of our carousing if that's what you're thinking—I plan to tuck her away in the country. She might even like that—she's a strange girl. Gotta get a brat on her first, but then we needn't think of her again."

Kit looked at him with wonder. How had he ever thought such a dunderhead to be a worthwhile drinking companion? "As a matter of fact, I haven't had her already," he said.

George knocked over his wine glass in shock. "I thought you said you had. Not that I blame you—it's those spots of hers. Enough to turn a man's stomach. I intend to insist on a darkened room so I don't have to look at them."

"I like her freckles," Kit drawled.

George let out a bark of laughter. "You would. So what's the problem? She's been yours for the taking since the moment we got her in the carriage, and you know I would have enjoyed watching. I know you're not interested in the cousin, which is the outside of foolishness, but if you want the girl, why haven't you taken her?"

It was not a question Kit was in the mood to consider. The Honorable Miss Bryony Marton was a boil on his backside, and if it were up to him, she'd be long gone, back to her miserable cousins. "I haven't decided what I'm going to do with her," he replied in a frosty voice that would have put the fear of God into most men. George was drunk enough to be impervious.

"I don't give a damn what you do with her, but tomorrow, I'm taking her to Gretna Green. Once I get back here, she'll probably stay close to her room, and I can find someone else to take her to my estate in Hampshire. Damme, I might even leave her here. The place is big enough, and she won't bother anyone."

"You're going to keep your filthy hands off her." Kit's tone was so deadly he regretted it; he only knew that the thought of George touching Bryony made him mad with rage.

George blinked, looking at him owlishly. "I don't know what's come over you, but this ain't like you, Adder. The girl's managed to get inside your head somehow, and you need to get her out of it. If you haven't had her yet, then there's the problem. Abstinence brings about all sorts of bad humors. Take the girl to bed, vent all of that energy on her, and you'll be right as rain the next morning."

For a moment, Kit was silent, considering. It was uncharacteristic of him to leave her be, particularly since he seemed to be obsessed with her. George was probably right—good, hearty sex would take care of the problem. She'd become simply another anonymous quim, not a conundrum he had to solve.

"Unless, of course, you're afraid to," George added with a crafty expression in his milky eyes. "Don't tell me you think you're in love with the chit—I wouldn't believe it. You're a bad man, Kit, a very bad man, and there's no room in your life for a well-bred young virgin, no matter how bizarre-looking she is."

"Go to hell," Kit snapped, then could have bitten his tongue. What the hell was his problem? It had nothing to do with George's mad conjectures, but there was no denying that the advent of Bryony Marton into his life seemed to have thrown everything for a loop.

"You don't..." George began, then had the wit to stop in the face of Kit's ferocious glare.

"I don't give a damn what you think, and never have," he said coolly. "I don't bed women according to your timeline, and there are some I don't bed at all."

"You can't tell me you don't fancy Bryony," George said. "You already admitted as much."

Kit pushed back from the table and rose. He'd had too much to drink, and he'd let George goad him, but there was no turning back. George was right, she'd gotten into his head, and there was only one way to exorcise her.

"Where are you going?" George asked blearily.

"To bed your fiancée."

"That's the ticket," George said, laying his head down on the table in the middle of the spilled wine. He was snoring before Kit even left the room.

᠅

IT WAS ASTONISHING HOW A SMALL, infuriatingly calm female could disrupt his life of dedicated depravity, Kit thought, striding through the halls. He ate young women like Bryony for breakfast—he had not a care or even a thought to spare for marriageable females. George, on the other hand, needed one with the appropriate income, and Bryony fit the bill. He should wash his hands of the whole thing, send George and his bride on their way, and return to town to raise more hell.

He'd raise more hell, certainly, but George was going to keep his goddamned hands off her. He ought to do the same, but he prided himself on a total lack of conscience. He did what he wanted, the devil take the consequences, and he wanted Bryony.

The coldest, smartest thing he could do was see her safely back home, and then he could forget all about her. Her and her captivating freckles. But he wasn't going to.

She'd be breathtaking in some sunny clime like Italy, skimpily dressed, the sun blazing down on that gorgeous skin of hers. If he were a different man, he'd take her there, and make love to her in the vineyards with the glorious sky all around them. But he was the worst man in England, and there was no room for sunlit afternoons and lazy lovemaking and dappled skin that looked splashed in gold.

He heard the noise in the distance, and his never even temper rose. He was not in the mood for more of George's drunken ramblings.

But no, the footsteps behind him were steady, and for a moment, he thought it might be Bryony. Every sense became alert, until he realized the step was too heavy. It must be the runner.

"Mr. Barnes," he said in an even voice he knew would carry as he turned to face the man.

The formerly sodden man appeared, looking not at all surprised by his presence, and Kit suspected he'd been looking for him. Barnes was dressed in some of the ancient clothes that had hung in the cupboards, and he clearly hated them. Kit's mood improved.

"Yes?" Barnes stopped a few feet away, looking at Kit with acute dislike.

"I have need of your good offices," he said lazily, leaning against the wall. "You have information I need, and I have a task for you."

Barnes was not a man who showed reactions. A worthy adversary, in fact. "What exactly did you want from me, Lord Adderley?"

"A better report on the weather conditions. Just how bad is the flooding? Could a horse make it through?"

"One could do," Barnes said carefully. "I wouldn't push it if I were you—you never know what's beneath the water. I can certainly understand why you and everyone else is desperate to leave here, but it makes more sense to simply give it a day."

Kit looked up from his perusal of his fingernails.

"That brings me to the second part of this conversation. You're to take Miss Marton back with her cousin."

"I had orders not to," Barnes said.

"My orders supersede those. Return her to the bosom of her family and they wouldn't dare kick her out."

Barnes raised an eyebrow. "Have you met the Ellistons, my lord? They're a nip-farthing, cold-hearted pair, and I wouldn't put anything past them. She's better off here than abandoned in the streets of London."

Damn. She was going to have to rely on George after all; that, or he'd have to leave first and pay a little call on the cousins. He could put the fear of God into them, but then, where would Bryony be?

No longer his responsibility. He was a man who refused responsibility, and Bryony's future was of absolutely no interest to him. But still...

"Who else asked you about the roads?" he asked suddenly.

"Miss Marton. She wanted to know when I would be able to leave."

"I don't think so," said Kit slowly. "I think she wanted to know when *she* would be able to leave. The little idiot."

"She wouldn't be so foolish as to go out into this weather."

"Miss Marton is fearless. It's possible she's showed some sense, but..." He pushed past the runner, just missing Cecilia by a hair.

"I'm looking for Mr. Barnes," she said coldly, a little hiccup in her voice.

She'd clearly been crying, but Kit didn't give a damn, and he pushed past her with a total disregard for manners. "You've found him." He was about to move on when her words stopped him in his place.

"Oh, Peter, I can't find Bryony!" she wailed.

"I knew it!" Kit said grimly, turning back and grabbing Cecilia's shoulders, ignoring her shriek of protest. "When did you last see her? Where?"

"I...I don't know," Cecilia said shakily. "She was telling me not to worry about her, that she knew how to take care of herself, and then when I went to check on her, she wasn't in the little room she'd chosen, and I can't find her anywhere."

"If you don't take your hands off her," Barnes said in an icy voice, "I'll break your neck."

Kit's response was so harsh and obscene that Cecilia let out a little squeal of shock, but he not only released her, he pushed her back into Barnes's waiting arms. "Just take care of this one," he snapped. "I'll see to Bryony."

"She's Miss Marton to you!" Cecilia rallied for a moment, and Kit repeated his shocking response, this time directing it at her, and then he was gone.

PETER'S BODY was warm and strong against her, and some of Cecilia's panic began to recede. He'd automatically caught her, and his big hands were warm and soothing on her upper arms, unlike Adderley's furious grip. He was stroking her, she realized dazedly, his thumbs gently brushing against her skin in a soothing motion. She would have given anything to simply sink against him, but for once, something was more important than her own wishes. "Someone should go after her," she said in a husky voice.

"I believe that's what Adderley is about to do. That doesn't mean he won't throttle her when he finds her, but he strikes me as a man who gets the job done if he decides to bestir himself."

She pulled back, out of his comforting hold, to look at him incredulously. "He's a degenerate and a care-for-nothing. I can't imagine he ever bestirs himself."

Peter had a thoughtful expression on his face. "I suspect your cousin managed to inspire him to heights of minimal decency. Go back to bed, Miss Elliston. All will be well. Don't worry your pretty little head about it."

Cecilia had two reactions to his dismissive words—one, that he thought her pretty, two, that he thought she was shallow and silly. She was sorely tempted to kick him in the shins again, but she remembered the pain her previous attempt had caused her. She did the next logical thing—grabbing the oversized white shirt in her hands, she yanked him down to her and kissed him.

It was the smartest thing she'd ever done, and the greatest mistake. His response was electric—he caught her up in his arms, pulling her tight against his body, and he was so big, so strong, that she felt dwarfed, overpowered, protected. Before she could pull back from her impulsive kiss, his hand came behind her neck, cupping it, and he deepened the kiss, holding her still as his mouth answered hers—a slow, sensual bite, followed by his tongue as it wet her lips, and then she found herself opening her mouth to him, welcoming him inside.

Geoffrey Parkhurst had tried to kiss her this way, telling her it was all the rage in Paris, and Cecilia had shoved him away in total disgust. With Peter, she simply moved closer, pressing her breasts against his chest, wrapping her arms around his waist and holding on while he plundered her willing mouth. She loved the taste of him, the feel of him, the knowledge that this was like another, deeper possession, and she could feel the heat in the tips of her breasts, in the place between her legs, and she wanted him.

She, who had told Bryony that she intended to have sexual congress with her husband exactly twice, in order to produce and heir and a spare, and possibly once more if an inconvenient daughter appeared, she wanted to lie beneath this man and take him inside her. She wanted to drown in him, she wanted to revel in the touch and feel of him, and his tongue was the most mesmerizing—

He released her, and she fell back, breathless, staring up at him with dazed eyes. "You want me," she said with a shaky note of triumph.

"Of course I want you—I'd be a fool not to. I'd also be a fool to take what you seem to be offering, so go up to your room and lock your door."

"You love me," she said, undaunted.

Peter Barnes looked horrified. "I want to tup you, not marry you!" he protested.

But her enthusiasm was undaunted. He was hers, whether he realized it or not. She would have to learn to be patient. Men were such finicky creatures.

"Nonsense," she said graciously. "You love me."

He had dark brown eyes and he rolled them at her words. She'd have to break him of that habit, but first things first. She reached up on her toes, kissed him on one warm cheek and then scampered away before he could reach for her again. Oh, yes, he was most definitely hers.

If he rolled his eyes again, she was going to kick him in the shins, but he simply nodded, walking past her, skirting her widely in case she decided to touch him again. She watched him go, her eyes taking in his tall, strong body, and when the door closed behind him she let out a tiny, satisfied giggle.

🖈 18 🖈

BRYONY HAD to get out of there. There was no way she was going to marry George Latherby—the more she saw of him, the more revolted she was, and yet Adderley sat by with a cat that ate the canary smile and said nothing. Why should she be surprised—did she really think the man would rescue her when he was the one who'd taken her in the first place? She was a joke to him, the speckled antidote who thought she could lure a beautiful fallen angel, and she knew they'd laughed together, George and Adderley, about her pathetic presumption that she'd been deflowered.

That a man had wanted her, much less a connoisseur of women like the worst man in England, was a joke. She was a fool, and everyone knew she was a fool, and she wanted to run and hide and cry. She wanted to hit someone, hard, but Adderley would hit her back, most likely, and besides, she never wanted to see him again. Her only choice was to escape, now, before anyone could try to stop her.

There was a worn pair of clogs in the deserted kitchen, and several layers of shawls to ward off the pouring rain. She was going to get soaked anyway, she might even drown, but it didn't matter, as long as she was out of this house and never had to see Adderley again.

Because the miserable truth was, as much as she hated him, she...cared about him as well. He was an impeccably evil bastard, but there was something about the way he looked at her, the touch of his hands, the touch of his mouth...

Which was all a complete lie, she reminded herself furiously, leaving the servants' quarters with as much stealth as possible. Mrs. Seeley or Betsey might have offered her some help, but in the end, they'd side with the man who would pay their salaries, and they'd give her up in a trice. She was on her own.

By the time she reached the deserted servants' hall, her resolve had hardened. The clogs were too noisy, so she slipped them off as she headed for the oaken door that led to the stable yard. She had no idea where Adderley was—off drinking with George, no doubt, but she didn't want anyone to hear her and try to stop her. She tiptoed to the door, set the clogs down and began unfastening the many locks. Once the final one gave way, she pried it open with a sigh of relief, reaching for the shoes, when the door was slammed shut again, and she was trapped against it by Adderley's body.

She looked up, and she knew she should be frightened. He was far more furious than the storm raging outside, but instead of cowering back away from him, she straightened her back and looked him coldly in the eyes. "What do you want?"

"What the bloody hell do you think you're doing. Going for a midnight stroll?" His anger was tightly controlled, but formidable, nonetheless.

"I'm leaving." Her voice didn't quaver, though she realized her legs were unsteady beneath her. "Get out of my way."

"The hell you are. You'll die out there."

"What do you care? Haven't I lost my entertainment value by now? There are just so many times you can laugh at me for my foolishness."

"The idea of you venturing out in this storm is the most addlepated thing you've done so far, and I find it tiresome. You're coming to bed."

She scoffed. "Of course I am. You don't scare me, Lord Adderley. I know perfectly well you're not going to touch me, so don't bother."

A thoughtful expression tempered some of his anger. "And just why aren't I going to touch you? I've touched you any number of times already. I like touching you."

"Stop it!" All right, now she was sounding strained, but there was a limit to how much provocation woman could stand. "I know perfectly well that I'm still...a...a...virgin." The word was hard to say out loud.

"I never said otherwise." He was calmer now, as she was growing more agitated. "And why do you think that is? Surely you have a theory."

"It certainly has nothing to do with finer feelings or any ideas about honor. You don't care about anyone or anything. Up to now, you've found my idiocy amusing, and I don't blame you, but I know exactly what...what *that* entails, and exactly what you think of me, and I'm not going to play your games anymore. Now let me go."

He didn't move. He'd backed her against the door, and she could feel the storm battering against the other side. If he let her go, she would probably get only a few steps before being knocked down by the wind.

"And exactly what do I think of you?" he asked mildly enough.

"I'm an antidote, in your words. I'm so hideous that you couldn't bring yourself to touch me, when I have it on the best authority that men can't be around women without a chaperone simply because they can't control their animal passions, so I can only assume that I don't inspire even mild interest in your case, or I would hardly have passed the night in the same pristine state I started it."

He was looking at her in complete fascination. "So you now have this absolute abundance of sexual knowledge, and what drives men, and you think you've figured everything out."

"Do not try to tell me that it was a latent gentlemanly instinct that kept you from...from deflowering me."

"Such a delicate term," he mused. He was so close, she could feel the heat of his body through her clothes. "You've got only part of this, a very small part, right. I was enchanted that you thought you could sleep through my fiendish depredations on your fair flesh."

"It's not funny!" she snapped.

"It's very funny. When I take you, you'll know you were taken. There won't be any doubt in the matter, no matter how untutored you are."

"Stop it!" she cried, almost in tears. "Stop lying to me, stop trying to make a fool out of me."

"You're the foolish one, my pet. Your sudden, vast knowledge of intimacies somehow managed to miss the point that tupping an unconscious body is not only uncomfortable, but boring. Don't ask me how I know. I had every intention of having my way with you when you woke up, and I'm afraid I did pleasure myself while I watched you sleep."

She blushed then but said nothing.

"In truth, I find you a little too enticing—I prefer my women to be anonymous. You're distracting, and my wiser self wishes you would just go away so I could feel more like myself again."

"Then let me leave."

"That's my wiser self. I never listen. I think you need to demonstrate all your newfound knowledge so I can judge the accuracy of your information."

A part of her wanted to shrink back against the door, but she stood her ground. "I know the mechanics. That's enough."

"Oh, hardly. And I wonder who told you—your little cousin would certainly have no idea, or she wouldn't be playing around with Mr. Barnes the way she has been. It must have been the estimable cook. It's a great deal too bad you left the table—you missed an excellent meal. I might even transfer her to my London house."

"I'm sure that's a good idea. In the meantime—"

"In the meantime you're being tedious. Clearly your education needs broadening." He stepped back and reached out his hand for hers. "Come along, my dear. I'm taking you to bed."

She wanted to kick him, but he was wearing boots and she was barefoot, and slipping on the clogs just to attack him seemed a pathetic idea. "I don't want to," she said stubbornly.

He gave her an angelic smile. "Then you don't have to. Rape is even more tedious than unconscious women. But it wouldn't be rape, would it? You're feeling sorry for yourself, convinced that I find you a troll, when actually I find you uncomfortably entrancing, and you're going to want hard, physical proof of that. I'm here to offer it. Come along."

She eyed his hand silently. The hall was suddenly very quiet beyond the noise of the storm, but there was a hum beneath it, a dark energy that called to her. She would tell him no, and he would let her be. She could find an empty bedroom and sleep, alone and safe. And empty.

He was terrifying. He was mesmerizing. She should run as fast and as far as she could.

She reached out and took his hand.

❧

SHE FOLLOWED HIM, his hand insistent on hers, and Kit moved quickly, not allowing her time to change her mind, pulling her up the staircase, and she briefly wondered what would happen if someone met them on the stairs. Would anyone dare to interfere? She followed, Persephone into hell, with Hades in front of her, dark and implacable. Was she out of her mind?

Yes, most definitely. Did she regret it? She knew she should, but she kept going, up the flights of stairs to the bedroom she'd shared with him. They were in a different wing of the house, no one would see them or hear them, and it added to the otherworldly feel to the night. Overhead, the thunder rumbled, and still she climbed, knowing if she pulled back, he'd let her go.

It was unfair. She wouldn't be able to blame him tomorrow when she was disgraced and numb with horror; at least, she fully expected to be. Mrs. Seeley's description of the mechanics was shocking, even though Bryony knew that most people, short of nuns, did it at least once or twice. She'd survive, knowing a great deal more about the world by tomorrow. And then she need never think about it again.

They reached the room too quickly, and Adderley dropped her

hand, opening the door for her, leaving the choice up to her. She couldn't meet his gaze, but she hesitated, one last frisson of uncertainty spiking through her. She was mad to do this. She glanced up at him, about to tell him that she'd changed her mind, when she looked into his eyes, those golden eyes with the strange black ring around them. She expected to see triumph, contempt, amusement, but there were none of those emotions in his unreadable gaze. Simply patience.

And that was enough. She walked through the door, and he closed it behind him. All she could see was the massive bed, but she told herself to be sensible. She'd slept in that bed with him, twice, and she hadn't gone up in flames. It wasn't the bed she had to fear, it was Adderley. It was the way she felt about him.

He locked the door. That quiet, clicking sound sent a shiver of uncertainty through her body, and she whirled around to look at him. "Why did you lock it?"

"I locked the others out. Unless you preferred an audience?" He slipped out of his jacket with surprising ease, given how well-tailored it was, and began unfastening his neckcloth. She swallowed. "I thought not."

She wondered if he was going to strip down completely while she watched—he'd certainly had no modesty before, and she wasn't expecting a tender and gentle lover. Adderley was not a gentle man. "Could we blow out the candles?"

"We cannot. I want to see you."

"What if I don't want to be seen?"

"The key is on the inside of the door." He moved across the room with his stalking grace, dropping down into the wooden chair that looked as if it had once belonged in a medieval castle. A bottle of wine stood on the table beside it, between the chair and the bed, and there were two glasses. He filled both, then leaned back to survey her as she stood in the middle of the room, feeling like an idiot.

"Two glasses?" she finally said. "You must have been expecting me."

"Yes. I've waited long enough."

He said she could leave. As long as she remembered that, she wouldn't panic. She could do this, she wanted to do this....

"Why?" His voice was a silken drawl, and it was as if he'd been reading her mind. She jumped slightly—she was as nervous as a cat.

"Why what?"

"Why are you here?" He looked entirely at ease, lounging in the chair, but she wasn't fooled. He was as tense as she was.

"I'm calling your bluff," she said defiantly.

"I don't think so. Try again."

"I have a scientific mind and I'm curious. It's a part of life no one talks about..."

"Except for Mrs. Seeley," he interrupted, and she was surprised he even knew the cook's name.

"As I said, I was curious."

"Liar. You're not a meek, curious little creature, you've got the heart of a lioness hidden deep inside all the impeccably demure behavior, and you want to know what life is really like. You want to know what it's like to be bad, to be selfish, to be free, and you want me to show you."

"No." Her voice was strained. "I don't want to be bad, and I don't want to be selfish."

His smile was wolfish. "But you want to be free."

"Yes." Her answer was immediate.

"And you want me to show you."

It was a statement more than a question, and her answer was slower. "Yes."

"And maybe you want to be just a little bit bad?"

She bit her lip. The room was warm, with rain lashing at the windows, and she wanted darkness, she wanted him to do things to her that she couldn't admit to. In truth, she wanted to be very bad.

He nodded, not expecting an answer. "Then take off your clothes."

"What?" Her voice was a squeak.

"You didn't think I was going to lift your skirts in the dark in a business-like fashion, did you? I want to see every inch of your glorious skin, I want to count every freckle on your body—"

"Don't!" she said, shame washing over her.

"You're going to have to get used to it. I find your freckles the most enticing thing I've seen in years. Start with those shawls you have wrapped around you. You must be steaming inside of them."

In fact, she was cold. She unwound them, one by one, with the unbidden memory of Salome and the dance of the seven veils coming to mind. She only had three, plus a lighter evening wrap, and she certainly wasn't going to dance around the room. She looked around for some place to put them when Adderley spoke.

"Just drop them on the floor. Now the fichu that's practically strangling you."

She remembered tucking the filmy lace into her dress, determined to cover every bit of her speckled skin, and she pulled it out slowly, uneasily, dropping it on the floor with the shawls.

"Now for the dress. Do you need me to unfasten it for you?"

She wasn't ready for him to touch her. Shaking her head, she took an instinctive step back. "I can do it. I got myself into it, and the laces aren't tight."

Again that wolfish smile. "I'm delighted to hear it. Take it off."

It was far easier said than done. At least she knew she wasn't providing much of an erotic spectacle as she shrugged and wriggled her way out of the various pieces of the dress, but Adderley was watching her with a calm intensity that made her heart skip. When she finally stepped out of it, she kicked it out of her way in frustration, then looked up at him.

"The petticoats?" she asked.

"All of them." Another pile at her feet, and then she was standing in her chemise, the plain shift underneath it.

She couldn't meet his gaze. Up to now, she hadn't really thought about what she was doing, but dressed only in her most intimate of undergarments, she was suddenly acutely aware of his eyes on her, roaming the length of her exposed arms, the swell of her breasts above the chemise, the countless freckles that danced on her skin.

"Take off the chemise," he said, and his voice was suddenly tight. "You may leave the shift on if you wish."

That small relief made removing the chemise easier, until she realized the thin batiste was almost transparent as she stood there amidst the pile of her clothes. "I don't think..." she began.

"Very good. Don't think. It will only confuse you. Tonight isn't for thinking. Now, come here."

He'd poured her a glass of wine, and she edged closer, reaching for it eagerly when he moved it out of her way. "Now sit on my lap."

The wine would make her relax, but he wasn't letting her have it. "Why?" she said, looking at him askance.

"If you're going to question everything I ask you to do, then the night will become very tiresome."

This was what she had feared. That he'd find some excuse, that this had all been another of his extravagant bits of cruelty, that he would tell her he didn't want her....

Before she realized what he was doing, he'd caught her wrist and pulled her forward, onto his lap, arranging her stiff limbs as if she were a nervous child. He shook his head with a soft laugh. "This is going to be a very great deal of trouble," he murmured, tucking her back against his chest.

"Then maybe you don't want to bother," she said, her voice high-strung and nervous.

"Oh, you're definitely worth the bother," he murmured. "Try this." He handed her the wine glass. "You're shaking."

"I am not," she said, taking the glass in one trembling hand and draining it. She gave herself a brisk shake. "What next? Should I lie down and pull up my gown?"

His half smile told her nothing. "I think I'd better explain things to quiet your scientific mind. There are many ways to make love, and I have every intention of showing them all to you."

"Many ways?" It was a choked gasp. "Mrs. Seeley..."

"I expect I know a great deal more of the matter than she does. I've travelled in exotic lands, and I know all sorts of...shall we say, different aspects to the art of coupling. By the time the night ends, you'll have received a thorough education."

"Such as what?" Was it too late to run away? She was feeling half drunk with his nearness, dizzy and dreamy and yes, a little bit afraid.

"I think you'll be better off just agreeing. If you question me on every move, I'll have to keep you locked up for another night, and I'm not sure you can handle that, my sweet little termagant."

"I'm not a termagant."

"Perhaps not. In fact, I'm not entirely sure how sweet you are beneath your calm exterior. I have every intention of finding out." Before she could sense what he was doing, he'd slid one hand behind her neck and drawn her face to his, his open mouth covering hers.

She'd thought he was calm, poised, playing games with her, but his kiss wiped out any pretense of self-control. With a low growl, he turned her in his arms, so that she was straddling him on the wooden chair, and she could feel him between her legs, that hard part of him that fascinated and frightened her. He used his tongue, kissing her with such a ferocity that she could do nothing but let herself be kissed, as slowly he moved her, back and forth over that solid ridge of flesh beneath his breeches. He lifted his head, his eyes blazing into hers. "Take your hair down."

Dazed, she reached behind her, pulling out pin after pin that she'd used to plaster her hair to her scalp. She felt dizzy, hot and cold, as strange feelings bubbled inside her. She'd pulled half of it down when she looked at him accusingly. "You drugged the wine," she accused him.

His smile of amusement was annoying. "I didn't. That's lust you're feeling, poppet. Sheer, animal lust. And it's only the beginning. By the time the night is done, you'll be begging for me."

"I won't," she said, dropping the handful of pins onto the table and pressing herself harder against him. "I won't beg."

He cocked his head to one side, surveying her. "You're probably right. I'd respond to the merest hint."

And suddenly, it was all too much. Before he could stop her, she pulled away, stumbling backward as her wild tangle of hair came loose. "I've changed my mind," she panted.

She'd expected him to rise up, to take her in his arms and kiss away her doubts, but he didn't move, merely pouring himself another glass of wine. "No, you haven't. All you have to do is walk to the door. You could even lock me in if you're that frightened of me."

"I'm terrified of you," she said.

"Perhaps. You're also fascinated. Come back here and undress me."

She stared at him in disbelief. "You're mad."

"Indisputably. Come back here."

If he was mad, so was she. Slowly, slowly, she approached him, her heart hammering inside her breast. He was so beautiful, with that leonine mane of hair, the stark lines of his face, his cynical mouth that kissed her into foolishness, and she couldn't resist him. She was a fool to even try.

"Get on your knees in front of me," he said in a low voice, and she did so, waiting, waiting for what?

"You can start by pulling off my boots," he suggested, and the mundane nature of it calmed her. They came off with surprising ease, and of course he had long, beautiful feet in his clocked stockings. She dumped them on her pile of discarded clothes, deliberately, then turned back to him.

"Kneel," he repeated, and she did so, eyeing him warily when she saw the knife he held. "Don't look so terrified. You'll be pleasuring me with your mouth, but you'll want to. In the meantime, cut off my shirt."

She took the knife, and then met his eyes. He was absolutely fearless, and he didn't move when she took the loose hem of his shirt and sliced upward, tearing it in half. "Now push it off my shoulders."

Lord, he had beautiful shoulders. Strong, slightly bony, and, oh my God, he had freckles across the tops of them. She froze, and he shrugged off the rest of the shirt, leaving her to stare at his chest.

He had hair. Not much, just a golden patch between his nipples, arrowing down to his breeches, and she stared with wonder. When he'd been naked before, she'd been too distracted by that hard part of him, his cock, to pay attention to his chest, but it was fascinating, the muscles delineated, the stomach flat. She wanted to touch his skin, feel the texture of that hair, she wanted to feel it against her body.

And he seemed to know it. Taking the knife from her nerveless hand, he smiled down at her with peculiar sweetness. And then he ripped the shift in half, pulling it off her, so that she knelt in front of him, naked and vulnerable.

She made half an attempt to cover herself with her arms, but he caught them and held them apart as he surveyed her body. "You're just as delicious as I remembered," he said, and there was a hoarse note in his voice. "I don't suppose you lost your virginity to a lusty stable lad years ago? It would make things so much simpler."

This made no sense to her. "I thought you wanted to deflower me."

"Christ, I couldn't care less about your reputation. I want to fuck you. I thought I made that clear. If I haven't..." He took her hand away from her body and placed it between his legs. "There's your proof. If you want to swear this night never happened, then be my guest. Most men wouldn't notice whether you were a virgin or not."

She tried to pull her hand back, but he held it there. "Night?" she echoed doubtfully.

"All night long," he confirmed. "Now come here."

"I am here," she said stubbornly, trying to ignore the fear and desire that were building anew within her.

"Closer." Obediently, she crossed the tiny distance so that she knelt between his long legs. "Now kiss me. Kiss me the way I kissed you."

This was the point of no return, her last chance to say no. She leaned forward and put her mouth against his, and her uncovered breasts pressed against his chest. She tried to retreat, but he put his arm around her, pulling her closer, and he deepened the kiss, his tongue meeting her shy one, coaxing it, teasing it, so that she forgot to think, so lost in sensation that she felt drugged with it. With lust, he said. She closed her eyes, sinking into the wonder of it, vaguely aware that his hand skimmed her side, his long fingers stroking the flesh of her back, her hip, slipping between their bodies to brush across her stomach. It wasn't until his hand slipped lower that sanity returned, and she stiffened, trying to pull away.

But his arm held her secure, and he slid his fingers down between her legs, touching her where no one had ever touched her, and she jerked, then stilled. "What are you doing?" she demanded hoarsely. "This isn't right."

His soft laugh floated on the night air. "Oh, this is very right indeed," he murmured, and she felt him touch her, enter her, circle against her. She'd lost the ability to protest, and the arm behind her back was pushing her closer, into his shocking invasion, and she knew there was no escape, no retreat. She didn't want to escape.

"Relax," he whispered in her ear, and he moved the hand from her back up to her head, pushing it against his shoulder as his long fingers pushed into her. "Just let it happen."

She had no idea what he was talking about, but a strange lassitude had spread over her, and she closed her eyes as her body was suffused with the sheer physicality of what he was doing to her. She felt odd, restless, eager, frightened, and still he circled his thumb on her, his fingers pushing, pushing, until her body suddenly convulsed as she let out a muffled cry, shoving her face against his skin as she felt the sensation race through every part of her body. It didn't stop, it went on, and on, as he touched her, stroked her, and she wanted to weep with fear and joy and completion.

When he finally released her, she felt as if she were boneless, ready to drop on the floor beside her discarded clothes, but he hauled her up onto his lap again, and she shivered as she felt her body brush his. Everything felt strange down there, as if some electric shock had gone through her and still lingered. He brushed the tangle of hair away from her face, and she could smell her scent on his fingers.

"So what am I going to do with you now?" he murmured, his lips grazing her jaw, moving upward. "I can think of half a dozen things I'd like to try, but perhaps we ought to get rid of that pesky maidenhead first."

He rose, seemingly effortlessly from the chair, still holding her, which was a good thing. She wasn't sure her legs would support her. Carrying her across the room, he set her down on the bed that had once been familiar but now felt akin to some pagan altar. "I could suggest you use the knife on my breeches but that might be a bit dangerous," he said lightly. "I'll simply have to undress myself." He made quick work of it, and she closed her eyes, waiting.

The bed sank beneath his weight, but he didn't touch her. Slowly, reluctantly, she opened her eyes to meet his amused ones. "You've seen it before," he chided.

Before she could help it, she glanced down at him, then closed her eyes again. "This is impossible," she whispered.

"I specialize in the impossible," he replied. "I'm certain this would be easier if I were on the small side, but then, if you were deflowered by a tiny willy, it wouldn't be mine. I'm a tall man, built upon big lines."

"Yes," she said in a strangled voice.

"You'd best get used to it. The two of you are going to be intimately acquainted by the end of the night."

How could words be arousing and worrisome at the same time? She looked down and told herself it was nothing to fear. It was simply a part of his body. She tried to think of the David, so resplendent, but he'd looked very different down there, and if she didn't have Mrs. Seeley's word for it, she'd think Adderley was deformed.

Very gently, he took her hand in his, very gently he placed it on his cock, and she was shocked by the feel of it—warm, silken flesh covering hardness, and it pulsed with life. She relaxed her clumsy grip, exploring him with her fingertips, moving over him as he lay perfectly still, but despite his relaxed attitude, all his muscles seemed tense and straining, and finally he took her hand and placed it firmly around his girth, tightly.

"This is what you do to arouse me," he said, moving her hand up and down as he tightened her grip.

"I thought you were already aroused?" Bryony replied warily. "Do you get bigger than this?" The thought was horrifying.

"Sometimes. Keep doing that." He rolled onto his back and closed his eyes with a soft groan of pleasure.

There was a strange, mysterious beauty to the thing, and she wanted to see if it would taste different from the rest of his flesh. In fact, she didn't know what he'd taste like at all, so she leaned forward and licked his shoulder.

He shuddered in pleasure, and she nuzzled her nose against him, loving the smell of him, the taste and the feel of his skin. It tasted of rain and soap and clean sweat, it tasted of whiskey and lust, it tasted of despair. She licked him again, and his cock jerked in her hand.

"I'm going to come all over you if you don't stop that," he said in a raw voice.

"Isn't that the point?" She'd gathered that much from Mrs. Seeley.

"The point is to move inside you, and give you pleasure at the same time."

"Why should it give me pleasure?"

He closed his eyes in exasperation. "Just trust me." Carefully he moved her hand from his shaft. "Lie back and spread your legs."

Now he was going to do it, she told herself. He was going to put himself inside of her and spill his seed. It would all be over, but at least she would understand the arcane things he was saying to her.

Obediently enough, she lay back, clutching the bedsheet beneath her as she braced herself, and she heard his quiet laugh. "It's not going to be *that* bad," he whispered, and then, to her shock, he put his mouth between her legs.

She gave a little cry, trying to push him away, but his big shoulders were too strong, his long fingers holding her hips in place, and she screwed her eyes closed, telling herself she could bear it, she could bear anything he did to her, no matter how disgraceful....

He was licking her. Slowly, deliberately, as if he loved the taste of her, there, and she took deep, calming breaths, determined to let him do what he wanted with her.

The first, tiny wash of pleasure was a shock, and she let out a little gasp as it hit her. He lifted his head, breathing on her tender parts. "You liked that, didn't you? Stop fighting me and you'll like it a lot more." He licked again, and then slid two long fingers inside her.

The sudden invasion shocked her, and she squirmed, but it only seemed to bring her closer to his mouth, as he explored, licked, and sucked with seemingly all the time in the world, and his fingers pumped into her slowly, readying her, and this was all too much...

The sudden convulsion hit her, so fast and so hard that she cried out, but instead of drawing back, he redoubled his efforts, and she felt the nip of his teeth. It was the last thing she remembered, as darkness shut around her, her entire body seemed to explode in tiny pinpricks of reaction, and no sooner had one wave crashed them another rose, and she was crying, thrashing, caught in the maelstrom.

She wasn't even aware when his mouth left her—she just knew that he was covering her, his body between her legs, his mouth on hers, tasting of her, and she was shocked, aroused, confused, as he caught her earlobe in his teeth and bit, hard, sending another white-hot streak of pleasure through her.

"I should do more," he whispered in the darkness. "I want to suck on those hard nipples and make you come that way, because I know I could, but I've waited too long for you, and I never wait for anyone." She felt him spread her legs farther apart, but she was too spent to stiffen, to feel anything but this glorious, edgy kind of lassitude that made no sense and yet it consumed her.

"This will hurt," he said. "And for some perverse reason, it brings me no pleasure to hurt you, but give me time. The night is young."

She could feel him, feel that hard part of him against her, and then he was pushing into her, a slow advance and retreat, and he was huge. This wouldn't work, he would never fit....

"Bite my shoulder," he whispered, and she did, just as he thrust through, pushing the entire, impossible length of him inside of her.

She wanted to cry, wanted to scream, but she did neither, clamping onto his smooth skin with her teeth, silencing her distress.

He didn't move, holding himself just slightly above her so that his full weight wasn't crushing her, and his eyes were closed, his face cold and hard in the moonlight. Slowly, her body relaxed, beginning to accept his presence so deep inside her, and she wanted what she'd felt before, that glorious, unsettling crash of feelings that had now left her completely. She tried to shift, but his voice came, hard and strained.

"Don't move."

She stayed still, wondering when this would be over. Though

admittedly, there was a certain...pleasure in being covered by him, surrounded and invaded by all that strength.

"Are we done?" she whispered, uncertain.

His laugh was the last thing she expected, and she could feel it all through her body, everywhere his skin touched her. "We've only begun."

It wasn't the most cheerful news, but the initial pain had faded, and it was simply uncomfortable. "I don't mind," she said bravely, and was rewarded with another laugh.

"By the time I've finished with you, you won't be minding anything. Now close your eyes, sweetheart, and think pure thoughts while I ravish you. Even better, think impure thoughts and tell me all about them. I'll endeavor to make them all come true."

How could he sound lighthearted at such a dark moment? This was...this was...

He began to move. Slowly, sinuously, he was withdrawing, then pushing in again, and though she braced herself, the pain had gone, leaving only a memory, and she wanted this, she wanted him. He was inside her, and it felt strange, filling...wonderful. The tiny edge of pain was simply one more arousal, and she put her arms around his neck, and buried her face against his shoulder as he thrust into her, steady, even thrusts that were beginning to stir strange feelings again once again. She wanted to move her hips, and he caught them in his hands, moving her in rhythm with his steady strokes, tilting her to receive him.

Her nipples were very hard against him, and she was aching inside, not from pain but something else, and she pushed up, suddenly needing more of him, nothing but him, taking her, owning her, wanting her.

There was a purr of approval from his chest. He was hot, she was burning, and she needed...

"More," she whispered helplessly.

"Holy hell, you'll kill me," he whispered, laughter and despair in his voice. Without slowing his pace, he dropped his head down and caught one hard nipple in his mouth, sucking it in deep, and a bolt of pure pleasure went from her breast to between her legs. He sucked and pulled at her, and the two warring sensations were making her head swirl, her breath come in desperate pants, and she still needed something, something...

He bit her breast, and reaction slammed down on her, that mindless, blinding delight, multiplied by a thousand candle flames, and he was moving fast now, deep, powerful thrusts that only made her needier. She wanted to tell him, but she'd lost the power of speech, and he was moving so fast, slamming into her, and their bodies were slick with sweat, and she needed...

And she was gone, lost in a storm of sensation that she simply shattered in his arms, holding tightly, as if she were drowning, and he was the only port in the storm. She was vaguely aware that he suddenly pulled out of her, and she felt the heat and wetness on her stomach, and she wanted to cry out. She needed him inside her, she needed everything....

And then he rose up and kissed her, hot and sweaty and breathless, catching her in his arms and rolling her with him, so that she lay sprawled across his big body. He was sleek with sweat, and they slid together. "More," he whispered hoarsely, and before she realized what he was doing he'd pulled her down onto him, still hard, and she let out a little cry of distress and satisfaction, as she felt him grow within her. "Your turn," he said in a rough voice, hard hands at her hips, moving her.

She pushed against his shoulders, straightening up, and the sensation was strange, different, wonderful, and he was moving her, in small increments, up and down his shaft, rubbing inside her. Fresh need filled her, and she was the one who needed more, needed more of him, all of him. She didn't need his hands guiding the rhythm, she'd caught it on her own, and she moved, sure and certain, pulling up high and then sinking down again with a cry of pure satisfaction. She needed this, so badly, she needed him, and she arched, tossing her head back so that she could feel her hair ripple down her back, the impossible possession that was not hers, not his, and then everything went sideways. She lost the rhythm, and he caught her and pulled her under him, slamming into her so hard she could hear the slap of their bodies together, his muffled grunt of pure animal need, and then he was done, pulling out of her. She could feel the wet heat of his release, and then he was inside her again, still hard, pushing her farther, until she broke apart with a choked scream.

She was messy, dirty, sticky, and unaccountably near tears as he withdrew once more and pulled her into his arms.

For the first time, he wasn't the angry, wicked creature he pretended to be. For now, he was just a man, sated and relaxed, with no ghosts haunting him, no wickedness to prove. He was falling asleep, holding her tightly in his arms, and he was hers.

She felt the same, drugging lassitude, tucked against his strong shoulder, and she gave in, pressing her mouth against his hot, damp skin. She felt strange, changed in some way, filled with the same kind of peace. She simply didn't know whether to laugh or weep. Instead, she slept.

❧ 19 ❧

SHE WAS ASLEEP, curled up in his arms, her breath soft on his chest, and he lay very still, willing his heartbeat to slow, willing his body to relax completely. He could surrender to sleep so easily, the sleep that often eluded him, but he didn't want to. He wanted to lie there and feel her, small and soft, tucked up against him.

It should have been enough. He'd brought her earth-shaking pleasure, enough so that no man would ever measure up to him—at least, he hoped not. He was a selfish bastard, and he wanted to be the only one, so that when she was a little old lady with her grand-children around her, she'd remember her demon lover with a wistful sigh.

He was a monster, and he knew it. A good man, a halfway decent man, would want the best for her. He wanted sorrow and longing. Because it would match his own.

Not that it would be longing for her. He'd forget all about her soon enough. As long as he lay naked in bed with her, she was bound to be foremost on his mind, bound to feel as if his life had shifted in some unalterable way. Once he left her and dressed, he could happily forget all about her. He'd exorcised her power over him.

He hadn't done as thorough a job as he'd planned—he was

obsessed with feeling her mouth on his cock, he wanted to take her from the back, in a chair, up against a wall, in a bath. He wanted to try other things that society frowned upon, things that would require her active participation, and he wanted to spend hours teaching her how to kiss.

But he'd done enough. He could get those other things from any other female, and there were always countless women available, even virgins if he decided he liked them. But he didn't want another virgin, another untried lover, and innocent to initiate. He wanted Bryony.

His disgust was enough to make him move, to slip away from her. She made a soft sound of protest, and his cock began to harden once more. Of course it did, he reassured himself. Naked man plus naked woman equaled erection. It was simple arithmetic, and had nothing to do with her.

She had freckles across her belly—he'd seen them when he'd used his mouth on her, licked them. He'd promised to lick every freckle on her, and he'd only gotten to a handful. He could spend a lifetime discovering those beguiling splashes of color.

It was enough. He slid out of bed, silently, looking down at her. He supposed he ought to feel sorry for her, so small and vulnerable in the middle of the big bed. He wouldn't have thought there was any pity left within him, so why did he want to return to that bed, to that warm, clinging body, and take her again, and again, and again?

The rain had stopped, he realized with sudden surprise. They would be able to leave before long. The question was, who would go with whom.

He was half dressed when he heard it, the soft, seeking sound of the female in his bed, of Bryony in his bed, and he turned to look at her. Her eyes were wide open, and he wanted her, so damned much.

"Where are you going?" Her voice was low and husky, as if she'd been crying. He hoped she had.

He managed an extravagant yawn. "I've had enough of you," he said. "You've a great deal more to learn, but I find I'm tired of it, and I'm seeking my rest elsewhere. I never sleep with women." Why was he telling her all this? He had no need to answer her questions, particularly when his words were an arrant lie. He'd slept with her already.

Her expression didn't change, but her eyes did, the color darkening as she struggled to sit up. Her sweet breasts were perfect, and he'd scarcely given them the attention they deserved. He should at least...

He slammed out of the room without another word.

§●

BRYONY WATCHED HIM GO, darkness falling around her. How could so many feelings sweep over her in such a brief time? She'd gone from celestial heights to utter despair, and she hated it. She wanted her books and her cottage in the country and she even wanted her chickens, and she never wanted to think about that...that bastard again.

But she could still feel him inside her. She didn't need to touch herself, she knew she was a mess. No wonder he'd found her misapprehension so funny. The very thought that she could have slept through it, even with her ability to block out everything when she did sleep, was absurd, and her entire body felt battered. But whether she liked it or not, it felt delicious, even though she wanted Adderley roasting in hell.

If he thought she was staying here in a bed that smelled of him, smelled of them, with the tumbled sheets and the remembered feelings, his mouth between her legs, his cock thrusting into her body, his fingers touching her...

With a sound not unlike a moan, she crawled out of bed, bringing one soiled bedsheet with her. She had no idea where she was going, but she would find a place, somewhere small and safe, where she could banish this night to long-forgotten nightmares. She would forget, soon enough. Her body would feel like its own before long, and she would never, ever think of Adderley again. Wrapped tight, she reached the door and turned the handle.

It was locked.

BRYONY WAS WOKEN by Betsey's cheerful voice and the scent of hot, soapy water. She still had the sheet wrapped round her like a mummy, and she quickly rubbed at her eyes, hoping there was no sign of last night's weakness after Adderley had abandoned her.

"His lordship told me as how I was to bring you a hot bath, miss. He told me to let you sleep, but it's past noon, and every time I looked in you were sound asleep. You look like you had a right miserable night, miss, but a nice hot bath will set you to rights." She yanked opened the curtains, and sunlight flooded the room, in contrast to her dark mood.

"Such a goings-on we've had this morning, miss," Betsey continued in a chatty voice, pouring the bucket of water into the hip bath she'd pulled from the cupboard. "It's been such an uproar, young Jimmy sent to find a carriage two towns over just as Seeley wanted him, as well as letters arriving and his lordship leaving and that Sir George going through the wine cellars like it was ale. I don't like him much, I can tell you that. He's a bad 'un, for sure."

"Lord Adderley?" she asked dazedly, not quite following all this information.

"No, miss. Sir George. He says to tell you that as soon as you're ready, you'll continue on your trip north." Betsey looked around her questioningly, but whether she recognized what had gone on in this bedroom last night or not was not clear.

"And Lord Adderley?" She could pride herself on how calm she sounded.

"Gone, miss. Left as soon as Jimmy did."

"Did he say anything?" she demanded, sitting up as reality began to sink in. "Did he leave a note, perhaps?" Something, anything, she silently begged.

"No, miss." Betsey retrieved another bucket of hot water from the hallway and poured it into the bath. "There was a letter from London, but it was for Mr. Barnes, and how they found him here is beyond my poor brain, but word must have reached them..."

"Reached whom?" she demanded faintly.

"Dunno, miss. Mr. Barnes read the note and then put it in his pocket. He wasn't best pleased with it, I can tell you that, and he told me I wasn't to say a word to Miss Cecilia and so I won't, but he didn't tell me I wasn't to tell you about it." Betsey finally ran out of breath. She turned to survey Bryony's sheet-wrapped, bedraggled appearance, and her sunny smile faltered for a moment. "I'm happy to help you with your bath, miss. Wash your back for you."

"No, thank you," she said too quickly. The last thing she was going to do was expose her body to anyone else's curious eyes. "I can do it on my own."

"I'll just go and bring you some fresh clothes then, shall I? Mrs. Seeley found a cupboard of day dresses belonging to an old governess that should fit you. She said you were wrapped up so tight last night that you surely must be uncomfortable in those low-cut dresses we found. They're awfully plain, though," she added doubtfully.

Bryony stood up, wavering only slightly on unsteady feet. "They'll be perfect for me," she said truthfully. Back to a governess's wardrobe, back to a governess's life. In truth, she felt pale and drab and disheartened, except that her heart had absolutely nothing to do with it, just a very bad man and a very stupid choice on her part.

Betsey was still standing there. "If you could go retrieve them," Bryony suggested helpfully.

Betsey bobbed a clumsy curtsey. "Yes, miss." And finally left her, closing the door behind her sturdy figure.

She half expected to hear the sound of the lock turning, but of course she didn't. Adderley was the one who'd locked her in, and Adderley was gone, run like a coward. Except there was nothing and no one to be running from—she meant nothing to him. It was as he said, he'd grown bored before the night was even at an end, and gone in search of new distraction.

She hesitated for one moment at the side of the tub, dropping the sheet on the floor. She was a mess, sticky and tender and bruised in strange places, a purplish mark above her breast, sore between her thighs, which should be no wonder, and then she quickly slid into the tub, determined to scrub every last trace of him from her body. The water stung a bit, but it was blissfully hot, the soap smelled like wild roses, and she washed every bit of her, refusing to think about why, refusing to think about him, she simply scrubbed until the cake of soap was a tiny sliver and then she washed some more.

And still she could feel him inside her, that insistent, thrusting possession, and she put her head down on her knees. She would never have to feel that again, thank God. And she was not going to shed one more tear, even if she knew her heart, the heart that hadn't been involved, was breaking.

Of course, Cecilia swirled into the room just as Bryony rose from the bath, and no matter how fast she grabbed for the sheet of toweling, it wasn't fast enough.

"Bryony..." she began breathlessly, and then stopped, eyes wide. "What happened to you?"

"Nothing," Bryony said. "I may have tripped, but it's nothing." She should stop saying "nothing" before Cecilia got even more curious.

Suspicion was not the problem. "Those aren't bruises," Cecilia said narrowly. "At least, most of them aren't. I had a mark like those on my neck once, after indulging in a few kisses with Mr. Appleby. Those are love marks."

Love marks? Love had had nothing to do with it, at least, not on his side. "You're imagining things," she said briskly, wrapping the towel under her arms.

"I know what I saw. What did that monster do to you?"

Bryony took a deep breath. "Don't worry about me, Cecilia. I'm perfectly fine. And Lord Adderley has left."

"I know. He was talking with Peter when I came down this morning. You're to come back to Harlowe Street with me, Peter will see to it."

"I somehow doubt your parents will be overjoyed to see me," Bryony said wryly.

"Well, keep your clothes on and they'll have no reason to guess what you did last night."

Bryony could feel her cheeks warm. "What do you think I did last night?"

Now it was Cecilia's turn to blush. "Whatever it was, Lord

Adderley didn't enjoy it. He was in a foul mood this morning."

It felt like a blow to the heart, entirely unexpected and dealt with unerring accuracy. She'd never considered that she'd been found wanting, but he'd abandoned her in disgust, and she was—

"Don't look like that!" Cecilia said. "I didn't mean it that way. If I didn't know it was a complete impossibility, I would have said the man felt guilty."

"Adderley? Guilty? I doubt it," Bryony said. She needed to drop the towel and pull a shift over her head, but she was entirely unwilling to give Cecilia another view of her body. "And despite what may or may not have happened last night, your parents wouldn't have wanted me back on any terms."

"Apparently your lover is going to see to that. I imagine he could make anyone do anything, even my parents."

"Don't call him that!" she snapped. "He's not my lover; he's a stranger, and he's gone."

Cecilia moved farther into the room, caught up the shift that Betsey had laid across the bed, and handed it to her. "Get dressed. Peter wants to leave as soon as possible. We'll have to make do with two horses and that heavy coach, but it's not to be helped. In the meantime, you need to get ready. My parents will welcome you with open arms—Lord Adderley will see to it."

They would, too, Bryony had no doubt of it. He'd left her without a word, but he'd see to her well-being. There would be no babies from their illicit night—he'd been sure to withdraw and spend against her stomach—and she'd probably never have to see him again. Hallelujah. But despite his total lack of mercy and honor, he would see that she was safe, she knew it.

But if she went back to Harlowe Street, she'd be back where she'd been before, imprisoned under the watchful eyes of her cousin. She would rather starve.

She was about to say so when she thought twice. Her own reputation meant very little—Cecilia's meant everything. As long as her older cousin had been present, there would be no doubt cast on Cecilia's purity.

And going back would give her time to plan. She had a small

cache of jewelry from her father tied up in a kerchief among her clean clothes back in London. She could take them to a reputable jeweler and realize what money she could from them. It might be enough to support her for a couple of months, or it might be enough for a cottage and a future—she had no practical idea of what she needed. She knew the price of a healthy young camel trained as a pack vehicle, but she doubted she'd be in the market for one at any time in the near future.

She really had no choice in the matter, even if her heart cried out to run. In the end, what did she have to run from? If Maryanne and James seemed inclined to hold onto her in hope of her eventual inheritance, she had only to tell them about the night she spent with—

No, she wouldn't do that. That was private, for her alone, and she wouldn't give in to Cecilia's eventual blandishments either. All she had to say was that she spent the first night in Adderley's bed, and that would suffice, no matter how chaste it had been. That would suffice.

"I'll be ready," she said in a voice that strived for steady but merely sounded listless. And Cecilia, single-minded as ever, left her to go in search of her runner.

❧

PETER BARNES WASN'T in the breakfast room, the library, the front courtyard, or the stable, though the carriage had already been put to with the horses restive in their traces. Cecilia eyed it dubiously—her previous sojourn in that vehicle had been torture, and if she wasn't assured that Peter Barnes would be with them, she might have refused.

She finally tracked him down in the kitchens, seated at the scrubbed oak table with steak and eggs and gammon in front of him. The cook—she couldn't remember the name Bryony had called her —must surely approve of him. He had coffee by his side, not the more usual tankard of ale. Coffee wasn't for the working folk, but Peter must rate a little bit higher.

He eyed her warily when she stormed into the room, starting to rise, and then he clearly thought better of it, sitting back down again and reaching for his coffee.

Cecilia got it first. "Just so you know, I prefer tea," she told him, draining half the cup and pausing reflectively. "Though I could get used to coffee." She reached out and snatched a thick sausage from his plate and bit into it with her sharp teeth. "I told Bryony we'd be leaving soon."

He grunted in response, and the moment she set the coffee down, he took it and drained the rest, leaving nothing behind just as she was learning to enjoy the taste of it. She took another bite of the spicy sausage, letting it roll around on her tongue, and surveyed his plate. Cook had already fed her quite well, with kippers, eggs, sausages, and barley cakes, and she'd thought she'd eaten her fill until she saw Peter's loaded plate. Finishing off the sausage, she reached for a piece of his toast.

He slammed his fork into it to hold it in place, but she simply ripped it in half and crammed it in her mouth. He glowered at her, and she beamed back at him. "How long do you think it will take us to get back to London?" she asked cheerily, taking the seat beside him, too close. Or not close enough. He smelled delicious—soap and leather and fresh rain, and she wanted his arms around her. Instead, he concentrated on his beef like any good Englishman. Except that he was Irish, wasn't he?

And she, who'd always been so conscious of minor social distinctions, didn't give a fig.

For a moment, she didn't think he was going to answer her—he seemed too devoted to protecting his food from her rapacious ways, and then he sighed, handing her the second half of the piece of toast.

Cecilia knew when she was being bribed, and she persevered through a mouthful of toast. "How long?"

"Two days if we're lucky. It'll be slower going with only two horses, but if the roads aren't too bad, we could be back by Wednesday, Thursday at the latest." He popped the last piece of ham into his mouth, and she watched it disappear with sorrow.

"I've lost track—what's today?"

"Monday. You ran away—"

"Were taken," she interrupted, wishing she had some hot tea to spill in his lap.

"You were taken Saturday morning," he amended grudgingly. "You've been gone two nights, which is two nights too many, but with your cousin as chaperone, you should manage to scrape through this, whether you deserve to or not."

"Exactly what do you mean by that?" she demanded.

"That you're a born troublemaker, I can see it in those pretty blue eyes, and you probably thought of this as a kind of lark."

Very hot tea, she thought wistfully, followed by a plate of runny eggs on his head. "And just who do you think aided and abetted me? Does my cousin strike you as having a flighty disposition? And you think I waltzed up to someone like the Inconstant and suggested he carry us off? The man terrifies me. As for Sir George Latherby, I find him revolting. But perhaps I was able to convince everyone to aid me in this endeavor. Then why would I let you stop me?"

"I'm not giving you a choice."

"You're a mutton-headed oaf."

"And you're a ramshackle hoyden. I pity your parents."

"Have you met my parents?" she countered.

He paused, considering it. "Point taken. If they were my parents, I'd want to run too."

"I didn't run," she said with exceptional calm, even as she was grinding her teeth. "Nor did Bryony. We were kidnapped by that odious man, and now he's taken off and he'll never be held accountable for all the things he's done."

"Wealthy peers are never held accountable, Miss Elliston. Only innocent young girls pay the price."

"That's better," she said, beaming as Cook set a plate of eggs, sausage, and toast in front of her without comment. "At least you realize we're innocent young girls." She promptly ate another sausage.

"Miss Marton is innocent," Peter replied, and to Cecilia's absolute shock, he reached over and pinched one of her sausages, biting into it. "You were born trouble."

The food was soothing some of Cecilia's ire. "You like trouble. Why else would you be a Bow Street Runner?"

"We don't call ourselves runners. We're officers of Bow Street, if you must, but never runners. It's demeaning."

"And your confidence is so easily shattered?"

He glared at her. He was so handsome when he glared, she thought, wondering if she would stab him if he tried to steal another sausage. "All right, Mr. Officer of Bow Street. Admit you like danger and excitement."

"I like peace and tranquility even more."

"Liar. You like me."

He cast her a brief, frustrated glance. "That's neither here nor there. The sooner I get rid of you, the better. I just have to convince the dratted coachman to get the carriage ready, which he absolutely refuses to do without order from his master."

"But Adderley is gone, thank God."

"He's actually Sir George's servant, driving Adderley's coach. We aren't going anywhere until we get Sir George's approval, and chances are, he'll want to come along."

"No," she said flatly. "I refuse to share a carriage with that man, and I know Bryony would agree with me."

"Can't say that I blame you."

"Besides, the coachman must have changed his mind. While I was looking for you, I went into the stable and the carriage is all set to go."

To her surprise, Peter Barnes froze, as if she'd given him the worst possible news, and then he rose abruptly, pushing back from the table.

Naturally, she abandoned her food with only a passing sigh, jumping up as well. "What's wrong?"

"That coachman wouldn't change his mind. He's Latherby's man. Sir George must be planning to do a bunk, and I doubt he wants to bring us with him."

He headed out the door, Cecilia close on his heels, but by the time they reached the stables, it was already too late. The carriage, the driver, and Sir George Latherby were gone.

Peter let out an impressive string of oaths. "How long ago did you see the carriage?"

"Almost an hour ago. They've had plenty of time to get on the road."

He looked around him furiously. The one horse remained, but there was no sign of a reasonable conveyance among the dusty and broken carriages in the abandoned stable, not even a pony cart.

"Hell and damnation," he said, not bothering to apologize for his language, and Cecilia felt a little thrill go through her. There was something so manly about his anger—in fact, everything about him was delicious.

"What are you going to do?" she asked. Presumably they were trapped together in this house, which suited her just fine. After having almost anyone she wanted fall at her feet, she was finding that Peter Barnes wasn't so easily enchanted. Oh, he was interested in her —there was no question of that, particularly after last night's kiss. But his sense of duty and honor was distressingly strong, and she was going to need some time to break through his iron resistance or she'd end up, alone and bereft, back in her parents' house on Harlowe Street.

"For the time being, we aren't going anywhere," he said grimly, clearly not as thrilled with the idea of deepening their acquaintance. "I'll look through the stables and see if there's anything we could use to take us far enough to find more traditional transportation. Even a farm cart would do, though there's a limit to what one horse can pull. In the meantime, you may as well break the news to your cousin that we'll be staying longer. At least Adderley has left us."

"I'm not convinced that's much of a comfort for her," Cecilia said carefully. Peter cast her a quick glance but didn't respond, and for a moment, both of them stood in the middle of the stable, too close, too far away, as their eyes met.

Cecilia's breath caught in her throat, and her entire body warmed suddenly, beneath his steady perusal. Was he judging her, finding her wanting? But no gentlemen found her wanting, except that stupid Adderley, a fact she could celebrate despite the blow to her vanity.

She didn't want a dark, romantic, dangerous man—life would be too unsettling. And she'd changed her mind about a boring titled husband who asked nothing of her but an heir and a spare. She wanted a real, solid, honorable man with brown eyes and broad shoulders and a wonderful mouth; she wanted to walk away from everything she'd ever known and follow him. Her parents would disown her, her so-called friends would snub her, and she didn't care. She was tired of lordlings and stableboys and earnest students and elderly widowers. She wanted this man, and she was going to have him.

She had no idea whether he could read her mind or not; she only knew the connection between them was intense, and he took one step toward her. She knew he was going to kiss her, and she wanted it —she wanted his kisses, she wanted him to lay her down on the fresh straw they'd brought in for the horses, she wanted his hands on her body.

But he pulled himself up short. "Go find your cousin," he said roughly, as if they hadn't just shared a moment of sheer...was it lust? "I'll see what I can do down here."

She was dismissed, and there wasn't much she could do about it. Peter Barnes was proving to be particularly difficult, she thought, climbing the first flight of stairs toward the bedrooms. But then, most things worth having were seldom easy. Bryony would know what to do—Cecilia could always count on her for excellent advice.

Bryony would tell her to leave Peter alone, that her parents would lock her up, that they'd do what they could to ruin Peter. She'd tell her that she was fickle, and she needed to show some sense. And then Bryony would look in her eyes, sigh, and promise to help her any way she could.

Because Bryony was wise about the strangest things, and she would recognize that this was no arrant flirt on Cecilia's part. It was ridiculous, irrational, to fall in love this quickly, and Cecilia knew it.

It was also solid and strong and unchanging, even if Cecilia wanted to change it. In fact, it was inconvenient in every sense of the word, both for her family and for her own particular love of comfort. But there was nothing for it—the more she was around him, the stronger his draw, and turning her back on him would do nothing so much as break her heart.

Bryony's door was still closed, but Cecilia didn't hesitate. It wouldn't do to brood—Adderley had disappeared, and it was time to learn how to survive without him. Helping Cecilia trap a Bow Street Runner...er, officer...would be just the thing to distract Bryony from her dismals.

"Bryony," she began as she pushed open the door. "I need to talk to..."

Her voice trailed off as she surveyed the empty bedroom. The cupboard door was open, clothes were strewn on the floor, a chair was knocked over as well as Bryony's breakfast tray, and for the first time Cecilia wasn't interested in rescuing an errant sausage or piece of toast. Bryony was gone, and someone had taken her!

໒

PETER WATCHED HER GO, no longer hiding his troubled expression. He could feel the letter in his pocket, burning a hole. It was no surprise it had found him so quickly—those who worked at Bow Street were adept at finding what they needed to know, and they'd somehow managed to track him down.

He was to return to Bow Street, alone. The Ellistons had withdrawn their request for the errant daughter, and henceforth, she'd no longer be a member of their august family. Pretty harsh sentence for the victim of a kidnapping, but Peter had no intention of paying any heed to it. His money was on Adderley taking care of things. The worst man in England seemed to have his own code, and if he was going to persuade the Ellistons to welcome Miss Marton back into the bosom of their family, they would have to take their own daughter as well. Adderley struck him as a man who always got his way.

His plan was unaltered. He would take the two women back to London and wash his hands of them, particular Cecilia Elliston. Assuming he could.

❧ 20 ❧

THE HORSES WERE GOING at breakneck pace on the muddy, rutted road, the stench in the carriage of unwashed flesh and ancient liquor was overpowering, and Bryony's hands and ankles were tied, with some sort of cloth tight around her mouth. If she threw up, she would choke to death, and the man opposite her was in an alcoholic stupor.

Sir George Latherby snored wetly as Bryony squirmed. Her hands were tied in front of her, but the more she tried to wriggle out of the bonds, the tighter they seemed to grow. They'd threaded the rope through her arms and around her back and she couldn't raise them enough to pull the gag free, but she kept at it despite the agonizing pain in her arms. There was a ball of something stuffed into her mouth, and a long piece of cloth securing it, and every time the carriage went over a bump, her stomach went too.

She'd been foolish to be so trusting. Latherby had already announced he intended to carry through with the wedding, but she'd assumed he had no help, and she couldn't imagine the portly man carrying her off against her will. She hadn't counted on the villainous-looking coachman, or the obviously well-paid Seeley. She'd fought, and fought hard, but the coachman clipped her across her face, rendering her unconscious for just long enough for them to truss her up and carry her out of the manor house without anyone else noticing.

Seeley was going to be in a world of trouble once Mrs. Seeley discovered what he'd done, and in any other circumstances, she would feel sympathy for the man. The kindly Mrs. Seeley had a will of iron, and Seeley himself was well under her rule. She was going to make him very unhappy, but it would be too late to make any difference to her.

She struggled to lift her hands, tears of pain starting in her eyes. The side of her head was pounding, and she felt dizzy as well as nauseated. At least she needed to be able to breathe the fetid air without the gag, or she'd die.

One more try, and she managed to get the very edge of the gag with the tips of her fingers. It hadn't been enough to get a purchase on it, but she steeled herself and tried again, letting out a low moan of pain as the rope dug into her. Something ripped, and then she had it, tugging the cloth down to her chin and spitting out the rag that had been shoved in her mouth. She refused to look at it, or her stomach really would give up its contents, but at least she could breathe better, and if she did throw up, it wouldn't be trapped in her mouth.

Apart from that, it did her no good at all. She could hardly scream for help—the coachman was the one who'd hit her. Latherby was dead to the world, and even her rasped demands couldn't rouse him. She had no choice but to sink back in the carriage seat and consider her situation.

No one was coming to her rescue. Adderley was long gone, and he didn't care. For all she knew, he'd told Latherby to finish the job, but even if Latherby acted on his own, it wouldn't matter to the Inconstant. He was done with her, on to new distractions, more enticing ones.

Peter Barnes and Cecilia wouldn't come after her either—he'd been hired to do a job and clearly that job hadn't involved her. Besides, there would be only one horse left at Pevensey Hall, and she really couldn't see them riding tandem to her rescue, though Cecilia would certainly try.

No, Bryony was reaping the result of her own folly. If she hadn't agreed to marry the odious Sir George in the first place, he never would have kidnapped her. She'd had a strong suspicion he was no good, but in her desire to escape her cousins, she'd gone along with it anyway.

Escape was going to be a lot more difficult now. She was being carted off to Scotland, there was no doubt as to their final destination, and he'd find someone, anyone to marry them, someone who didn't listen to the bride's panicked objections.

If she were lucky, he'd simply abandon her once the deed was done. After all, he had no use for her, only her money, and as long as he had his legal marriage lines, he could spin any kind of tale as to what happened to her. If she followed him back to London, it would do her no good—her money would be his money, and he had the legal right to do anything he wanted with her, short of killing her.

George was not going to trifle with niceties. A man widowed on his honeymoon would be the object of solicitude, not suspicion, and maybe she was getting hysterical, but she had the very strong feeling she wasn't going to have a forced marriage of any longevity. There would be any number of ways to rid oneself of an inconvenient wife, and she would be surprised if Latherby didn't know most of them.

Her companion let out a loud, squelching sort of sound, one she didn't want to identify, and slid lower in his seat, his belly protruding, his mouth open, his wig askew, but at least he slept on, and, given the case of Pevensey Hall's best wine by his side, he would continue to do so. That gave her just so much time to figure her way out of this before they reached Scotland, and she had no idea how far north they were.

She wasn't going down without a fight. Bright, hot anger suffused her, the emotion that she'd always avoided so carefully, but the rage wasn't for the abominable creature who'd kidnapped her once again. It was for the man who'd promised he'd keep her away from Latherby and then vanished, wishing her a happy marriage.

It was the man who'd taken her to bed, showed her things she'd never imagined existed, and then abandoned her to her fate without a backward glance.

She was going to get away from Latherby. And then she was going after Christopher Constant, the Earl of Adderley, and she was going to make him sorry he'd ever even heard of her. A lifetime of proper behavior had finally shattered, and she was a vengeful goddess, out for blood.

She had every intention of dancing in it.

❦

AT ONE POINT in its life, Waycross was every gentleman's perfect hunting lodge. It was small—only a dozen bedrooms, decorated in masculine fare such as stuffed animal heads that were now molting, a wall of antique fighting weapons on display, and paintings of dead animals in the dining salon. Kit doubted a female had ever entered its sanctioned halls. It had been years since he'd come this far north, and the building had not fared well under the skeleton crew he kept in residence—the shrubbery surrounding the place was overgrown, shooting through the cobbles in the stable yard, and the entire place had an unused, dusty feel, making Pevensey Hall, in comparison, a warm, welcoming household.

The carriage horse had performed surprisingly well with a rider on his back, and Kit took the trouble to brush him down and water him, though he could find no feed in the deserted stables that could accommodate a great many more livestock. There'd be something in the house to feed him. Kit might be the worst man in all of England, Scotland and Wales, but he took care of his horses. They were more reliable than human beings.

The house wasn't quite as bad as the outside suggested, but he could find no trace of old Ferriday and his wife who were supposed to look after the estate. The entire place had a closed-up air, and he wondered how long they'd been gone.

There were dried apples in the larder, as well as sacks of grain and flour, and he simply picked up the satchel of oats and carried it them back out to the stable, ensuring the horse had a decent meal and a good rest after all his hard work. It was more than he expected for himself.

Waycross was built along a bluff, the cliffs providing defense from Scottish border raids, but no one had attacked the deserted place in decades, maybe centuries, and at least Kit expected to have a quiet time of it.

It was what he needed, craved, and he was just as glad the caretakers were gone. He didn't want anyone fussing over him; he simply wanted a couple of bottles from his excellent cellars and the time to make sense of the last few days. He hadn't felt this unsettled since he was young and vulnerable, a lifetime ago.

The building was designed around a great hall, with the bedrooms on an upper floor surrounding it and the wide staircase off to one side. A fire was already laid in the massive fireplace, and he lit it, dragging a high-backed chair closer and propping his feet on a stool. He would sit and think, and common sense would return.

He wouldn't see Bryony's pale, stricken face when he lied and told her he was done with her. He wouldn't see her face when he'd made her come, and her green eyes had filled with helpless tears and she'd clung to him.

He despised women who clung. So why had it felt so good with Bryony?

At least he'd gotten away from her in good time. He'd ordered George to leave Bryony alone, and George was much too great a coward to disobey. Peter Barnes would take her back home, and she would find someone boring to marry, and he would never have to think of her again.

If only he could stop thinking of her right now.

He still wanted her, quite fiercely. He'd been painfully hard when he'd left her, determined not to touch her again. The whole thing had blown up in his face. He'd assumed that once he had her, he'd lose interest—that was what happened with every other female in his memory.

But Bryony was staying front and center in his consciousness, and the more he tried to dismiss her, the more stubbornly she clung.

Normally, he would have simply fucked her out of his system. Not this time. The closer he got to her, the tighter her hold on him.

So he'd run like a coward, and he had no regrets. He was the worst man in England—there was no room for a clinging innocent looking at him with those calm green eyes that couldn't hide what she was feeling.

She thought she was halfway in love with him. Most women had too much sense—they knew the monster he was, and they were guarded against him.

But the peculiar, dangerous truth was that Bryony didn't see him as a monster, no matter how badly he treated her, no matter how shocking his behavior. He'd seen her eyes when he'd stripped her of all her defenses, and he'd recognized the love there.

Odd, because he didn't remember anyone else looking into his eyes with love. Lust, perhaps. Hatred, certainly. Even his harridan mother had despised him, but then, she'd despised everyone, particularly his equally belligerent father. He'd been a quiet witness to their rages, and consequently, he seldom lost his temper and never raised his voice. No one and nothing would have that much power over him.

But still he thought of Bryony, stripping off her clothes for him, her lovely, round breasts, the soft cries she had made, her final cry the last time he'd made her come.

Maybe he'd been a fool. There were so many things he wanted to do with her, to her. He wanted her to take him in her mouth, and wanted...he wanted...

He smashed his wineglass into the fireplace. It didn't matter what he wanted. He'd walked away from overwhelming temptation, wisely. He would find someone, anyone, to play out his fantasies with. Surely there were women with freckles in London.

He reached out for the wine bottle, tipping it back and drinking from it. He was tempted to throw that after the shattered glass and thought better of it. Not that he didn't have wine and glasses enough to keep him satisfied. Except nothing but Bryony would satisfy him, and he'd left her with the job half done, run away in fear that she would somehow reach beneath his monstrous exterior. In fact, she already had, and that was why he'd run.

A wise man would continue to run. A fool would re-saddle his horse and head back to Pevensey Hall before the new carriage and driver arrived. And do what?

No, one carriage would take Latherby on his way, the new one would bring the runner and the two women back to Harlowe Street. And he would go nowhere at all, simply stay right here and drink. If no one showed up to cook for him, so be it. There was plenty of wine and there was solitude. What more could he want?

Bryony.

❧

"You HAVE TO GO AFTER THEM!"

Peter Barnes didn't even bother to look at her from his spot on the rain-washed terrace. It was covered with puddles, stray branches, and other detritus from the powerful storm, but at least the sun was shining. "I've got more important things on my mind, such as how to get you and a chaperone back to London when we have one horse and no carriage."

"So we might as well take the horse and head after them," she said.

"It's a carriage horse, not a riding hack, and he's going to have a hard enough time with just me on his back. If I tried to put you up as well, we'd end up in the mud."

Cecilia bit her lip. This wasn't going quite the way she wanted, but she could be reasonable. "All right, then you can go after her alone, but you must bring her straight back to me. We might be able to keep word of Lord Adderley's involvement in this debacle from the public, but if she keeps going off with gentlemen, it's bound to get out. I don't know what my parents would say, but I don't intend to let Bryony be married off to that sodden lecher who kidnapped her...!"

"You forget, I'm not a gentleman," he said, unmoved by the thought. "And I thought Adderley kidnapped her."

She let out an exasperated sigh. "She is engaged to Sir George," she said. "Or, at least, she was. As far as I could tell, this was all to speed up the marriage to enable that cretinous pig to get his hands on Bryony's money."

"Cretinous pig?" he echoed, momentarily diverted.

"What else would you call him?"

"My lord," Peter said calmly. "And I'm not going after them—there's nothing I can do. You think anyone would take the word of a Bow Street officer against a peer of the realm? Accept it, it's a lost cause. I'm going to ride to the first town I can find that has a carriage and horses for hire, and then I'll get you back to town before you drive me mad."

She glared at him mulishly. "No, you're not."

He made the very great mistake of laughing at her. "Yes, I am, Miss Elliston, and there's not a thing you can do to stop me. You'll be safe enough here with the servants while I go find transport."

"No!"

"Mrs. Seeley is making up something for me to eat, and I'll be off in the next hour. You just behave yourself until I come back."

"You're a pig!" she shot back.

"But not a cretinous one."

"You're worse. You know better than to abandon a woman to a monster like Latherby, and yet you have every intention of doing so."

"I've learned long ago not to interfere in the affairs of the upper classes. You're making a great fuss over nothing—she's simply going to marry someone she doesn't care for, not going to the scaffold. Do you know how many women have to marry men they barely know? The same will come to you." There was an odd note in his voice, but Cecilia was too furious to consider it.

"Sir George has lost two wives in the last five years," she said in a grim voice.

"Women often die in childbed. He's had a run of bad luck."

"Or he's helped them along their way."

He spun around to face her, his irritation in full view. "Stop trying to make a fuss over nothing. I very much doubt that Sir George Latherby is some kind of Bluebeard, and frankly, after meeting your cousin, I'd back her against almost anyone short of Adderley himself."

"She could best him as well!" Cecilia said loyally.

"Then Latherby should be child's play. Stop fussing. You have enough on your mind as it is."

He was too close to her, and he seemed to be hesitating, as if there was something he wanted to say, something he wanted to do, and for a brief moment, Bryony went out of her mind as she breathed him in, so big, so warm, so strong. He was going to kiss her again, she knew it, and she could either continue to berate him or lift her mouth for him, and, wretched cousin that she was, she wanted that kiss, just one more taste.

He lowered his head, and she closed her eyes, breathless, waiting, until she felt the soft brush of his lips against her forehead, like she was a misbehaving child, and then he was gone.

The word she uttered out loud would have shocked a sailor, and she took great pleasure in it. "Be damned to you," she added in a low voice. He was headed to the kitchen; the stables were in the opposite direction. She had a head start.

She wasn't the best rider in the world, particularly in a loose dress and slippers, no hat, no gloves, no boots. It didn't matter—everyone else might abandon Bryony, but she'd be damned if she would. There was a plethora of old, dusty saddles in the abandoned tack room, and after only a moment of contemplation, she ignored the ladies' sidesaddles in favor of the more traditional astride version favored by gentlemen, hoping she'd feel more secure with her legs clasped tight around the horse's belly. He was a stolid, stocky bay, and she had to drag the mounting block over to get the saddle on his back. It was a good thing that Bryony had insisted she learn how to saddle and bridle her horse, otherwise she would have been doomed to abide by Peter's arrogant decision.

Tightening the girths as much as she dared, she swung herself off the mounting block and into the saddle, holding on as the horse sidled nervously, clearly unused to having a human being on his back. He'd simply have to get used to her, because she had no intention of letting Peter stop her. Bryony needed a rescue, and she was going to be the one to do it or die trying.

She pushed out into the sunlit courtyard, and as her mount moved restlessly, she tightened her grip on the reins, just in time to see Peter emerge from the front entrance, shouting at her.

She didn't wait. She kneed the bay with all her might, the two of them leaped ahead, and a moment later, they were racing down the rutted, puddled road, faster than she'd ever ridden before.

She had no choice but to lean forward, clinging to the horse's strong neck, and pray. He would run out of energy soon enough, and they could subside to a sedate trot, but in the meantime, the faster and farther he went, the better. She couldn't let Peter stop her with some piffle about her reputation and chaperones and getting back to her family. To hell with all of them. Cecilia was a heroine, racing to the rescue, and no one and nothing could stop her.

Apart from the puddle so deep and wide it might as well be a pond, and the bay came to an abrupt halt, stopping so quickly that Cecilia kept going, flying over his neck like a bird. *I'm going to die*, she thought dazedly, before she ever learned what passion was, and it wasn't fair, and if Peter were there she'd make him admit—

She might have been better if she landed in the water. As it was, she came down on the ground, shaken by her hard landing, the breath knocked out of her, her vision blurred, her heart in a panic. *I'm going to die*, she thought again, and everything went black.

❧ 21 ❧

SHE WOKE up with his hands under her skirts, and she immediately sat up and slapped him. Peter Barnes sat back on his heels, and the red mark of her hand bloomed on his dark face. "You were supposed to be unconscious," he grumbled.

With a groan, Cecilia sank back down again. "You were being indecent."

"I was trying to see if you had any broken bones, you little witch. I should have just let you be and taken the horse—it would serve you right. What in the devil's name made you think you could ride a carriage horse?"

"Adderley did. You were going to. I'm an excellent rider." That was an arrant lie, but how hard could riding astride be? Hard enough, she thought, feeling the ground beneath her, and she groaned again.

"You're a selfish, foolish child who doesn't care who she hurts. You're just lucky you were thrown close enough to the house for me to find you—otherwise you'd be lying in a ditch somewhere with no one to help."

He was yelling at her, and she didn't understand why. She ought to yell right back, but for some reason, her throat tightened and tears pricked her eyes, when the last thing she wanted to do was cry in front of him. "I just wanted to help Bryony," she wailed.

"You can't help someone when you can't even help yourself," he said sternly. He was touching her again, but now it was her arms and shoulders, checking her for injury. "You seem to be in one piece. Do you think you can stand? I need to get you home."

"That place isn't home," she grumbled, pushing herself up. He helped her rise, and she wanted to slap his hands away, but she wasn't quite able to stand by herself. "And you can go to hell. I'm going after Bryony."

His initial fury seemed to have faded, and he turned her to face him. "You're not," he said. "You're going back to the house and have some tea and a warm bath to soothe your aches while I go secure us a carriage."

"They don't have one at the local inn," she said triumphantly.

"I wouldn't take the servants' word for it. I'm good at getting what I want." For a brief moment, his eyes dropped down over her bedraggled body, and she wanted to slap him again. Clearly, she was the very last thing he could ever want, and she wasn't sure whether to weep or to run. Running was out of the question—her body was too shaken to summon up the energy, and he wasn't going to see her cry, damn it. She was pathetic enough.

Think of Bryony, she told herself, straightening her shoulders. Bryony didn't whine, didn't cry, didn't fuss, and neither should she. "I'm not going to argue," she said, starting forward with a resolute expression.

"You're going the wrong way," Peter said, not moving.

"How do you know which way I intend to go?" she shot back, a weak demand, but all she could manage at the moment. Her head ached like the very devil, and she wanted nothing more than to curl up in a ball and comfort herself. No, that wasn't true. She wanted to curl up in Peter Barnes's arms, have him tell her everything would be all right, that she was smart and pretty and perfect instead of the drab, spoiled creature he clearly thought her. Still, he'd kissed her. He wouldn't have kissed her if he found her repulsive, would he? And what a kiss! She'd considered herself a connoisseur of kisses, and yet nothing had ever come close to the bone-shaking power of that long, deep, seductive mating of their mouths, because that's what it had been, a mating.

Clearly it was the only mating she was going to get from him, which was a good thing, all considered. Her parents would never let her marry a Bow Street Runner...er, officer. Her parents would marry her off to the highest bidder, and even though there would now be a blot on her reputation, it wouldn't be enough to render her worthless on the marriage mart.

For the first time, she realized Peter wasn't alone—he'd brought back her runaway horse. Cecilia eyed the bay with acute dislike. "I hope you're not expecting me to get back up on that demon horse," she said finally.

"Of course not. I'll ride, and you'll trail along behind me like a good girl."

Her temper flared for a moment, but before she could say anything, he'd simply picked her up and thrown her onto the wide back of the horse. It was so unexpected, she had to scramble not to fall off, and she cast him a withering glance before settling herself on the horse's back, hiding her winces as her sore muscles settled around the unfamiliar saddle. "Are we going after Bryony?" she demanded in an icy voice.

"We're taking you home."

She didn't even stop to think, she merely dug her heels into the broad sides of the carriage horse and took off, leaving Peter Barnes in a fury.

Of course there was no way he could catch a runaway horse, and her mount seemed just as displeased to have her on his back as he had been before. Once again, she clung to his neck, terrified, as she tried a soothing litany of sounds to calm the maddened creature. The horse was even angrier than the abandoned Peter Barnes, and she had no choice but to hope he'd tire of his mad dash before he sent her flying once more.

It was endless, every stride jarring her body, and within moments, she was cursing herself for being so headstrong. What the hell did she think she was going to do whenever this beast from hell decided he'd had enough of trying to kill his unwanted rider? And what was Peter going to do, abandoned in the middle of the woods, God knew how far from Pevensey Hall? He was going to be so mad....

The bay began to slow his maddened pace, and Cecilia dared to sit up, clenching the reins tightly in her blistered hands. God might not know how far from Pevensey Hall they were, but the blasted horse clearly did. Instead of carrying her farther north, the wretched bay had simply returned home to the stable yard, coming to an abrupt stop as if well-pleased with himself.

"You ill-favored bastard," she said, enunciating clearly. Slowly, painfully she slid off the horse, and in response, the bay tossed his head and whickered his disapproval. "I suppose you think you're going to get fed after all this?"

The horse ignored her. His coat was wet with sweat, and he was puffing noisily, and she began to unfasten the heavy saddle. "I should leave you like this," she scolded. "It would serve you right." Dumping the saddle on the ground with a grand disregard for propriety, she took the reins and led her equine foe into the stable and the nearby stall that she'd taken him from. He stood perfectly still and well-behaved as she brushed him down, removing the tack and even, at the last minute, giving him a bucket of oats. "You don't deserve my kindness," she grumbled. "I'll think twice before I trust a horse again."

The bay lifted his head from the water trough to look at her, liberally sprinkling her with water, and she managed a weak laugh. "It's too late to apologize," she said sternly. "I'm just glad Peter has to walk."

Though in fact, she might have preferred walking to the jarring race back to the stable. Every bone and muscle in her body hurt, her head was pounding, and her room and soft bed were up two very long flights of stairs. Enough was enough. Sinking down into the pile of soft hay, she lay back in it, groaning in relief. She'd just lie here a minute and try to compose herself before she faced the challenge of all those stairs. In the meantime...

❦

BY THE TIME he reached the front gates, he was limping—he was made for city streets, not hikes through the country—fraying his temper even more effectively, and he had every intention of taking Miss Cecilia Elliston across his knee and give her the waling she deserved. That was, until he found her.

He saw the horse, and he breathed a sigh of relief. He'd seen the discarded saddle first, and the bay had been brushed and watered and fed, something that he'd been doing the last twenty-four hours, so he knew she was back.

"You belong in a stew," he told the bay, who simply cast him a baleful eye. "Where'd you leave the girl?"

No answer, of course, and Peter was about to head into the house in search of her, determined to give her a very loud piece of his mind, when he heard something from the adjoining stall. He peeked over the side to see Cecilia curled up on a bed of straw, sound asleep, and some hard part of him melted a little bit. He should scoop her up, carry her up to her bedroom, but that would be an extremely dangerous thing to do. He didn't want to think of her and bedrooms, particularly since there was no one there to distract him. He couldn't touch her—duty and honor were important to him, and he wasn't going to betray both for the sake of the prettiest girl he'd ever seen.

He never should have kissed her last night, but she'd been driving him mad. One thing was sure, he'd never give in to temptation again, and holding her in his arms was likely to lead to exactly that. He was going to watch over her, wait until she woke up, and then tell her exactly what he thought of her behavior while he herded her into the house.

It was cool in the stable, and he searched around until he found a horse blanket that wasn't too odorous. Draping it carefully over her sleeping form, he moved across from her, sliding down against the stable wall to sit in the clean straw. The bay was eating quietly, the soft sound of him munching his oats adding to the peacefulness of the afternoon. Crossing his long legs in front of him, he let his eyes roam over Cecilia's sleeping face, and contemplated what an unforgiveable mess his life had become.

෴

THE MOMENT SIR George Latherby opened his eyes, Bryony closed hers. The horses were slowing to a stop, and she could hear the sound of voices, sense the light behind her eyes. It was almost dusk, darker in the shadowed carriage, but light flowed into the confines when the door was opened. She kept completely still, feigning sleep, but through the tiny slit of her eyes, she could see Latherby's nasty coachman, the one who'd threatened her and Cecilia during their mad dash from London. If he'd managed to keep the two of them from escaping, then she was unlikely to do better on her own, but she still had every intention of trying.

The coach rocked beneath Latherby's bulk as he descended, but his voice came back clear. "I intend to have me an excellent dinner and a couple of bottles of wine. Now that we've got her, there's no particular hurry—it's not as if anyone else wants her. She won't give you any trouble—she's still asleep, and even if she wakes, she'll do what you tell her to."

"What if she needs to piss?" the coachman said, and Bryony wanted to wince at the crudeness.

"I'll send someone out with a pot and something to eat. I'll send food and ale for you too. We've got a long night ahead of us."

"You aren't wanting to spend the night here, then?"

"I don't want to have to deal with a difficult woman in a busy public inn like this one. You never know who might listen to a hysterical female, and I abhor scenes."

"Yes, my lord."

"And Coombs?"

"Yes, my lord."

"I'll send a pretty girl out with the food. I shouldn't have all the fun."

"Your lordship's always done right by me."

"Just keep an eye on the girl. She's always seemed docile enough, but there's that red hair of hers."

The door slammed behind him, and she could hear Latherby's unsteady footsteps move away. She had just opened her eyes when she felt the weight on the carriage again, as someone opened the door, and she quickly shut them as a man lumbered into the carriage and pulled the door behind him.

"You asleep, miss?" he inquired in his oily voice. "Because I don't think you really are. In fact, I'd be right shocked if you didn't know I've got a knife right in front of those bubbies of yours."

Slowly she opened her eyes to focus on the knife pointing at her breasts. It was still shadowed in the carriage, so she didn't get a good look at the coachman, but she could smell him, his fetid breath and unwashed body, and she stiffened.

"You ain't half bad-looking in the dark. The shadows hide those freckles, and besides, I ain't picky. I don't think you're near as ugly as everyone says you are."

Was she supposed to thank the man? She kept her mouth shut, watching him carefully.

"You got a mouth like anyone else, and I was thinking you might take care of me while we're waiting for his lordship. He won't mind —he already let his best friend have you, and just between you and me, he's having trouble with his old willy. Servants know everything, and he hasn't been able to get a cockstand in months, so you don't have to worry none about him. You can give me wet whistle 'stead of him, and we'll keep it to ourselves, just you and me."

She was trying so hard to keep her face inexpressive, but her disgust must have shown through. Coombs laughed. "And if you don't want to, well, then, that's no problem."

Somewhere she found her voice. "I would rather not," she said icily.

"You'd rather not?" he mimicked her. "Fraid you misunderstood. I'm not giving you a choice. I just said it was no problem if you didn't want it. I likes a woman with fight in her."

He was reaching beneath his grease-stained leather waistcoat, clearly about to unfasten his breeches, when there was a knock on the carriage door. "Go away," he snarled, momentarily pulling the knife away.

"I've brought dinner for the lady," came a young female voice. "And his lordship told me as how I was to entertain you too."

Coombs let his knife drop. "There'll be time," he muttered underneath his breath, and he moved to the carriage door, kicking it open.

He was the one to dump the tray of food on the floor of the carriage, followed by the heavy china pot, and he slammed the door afterward. Looking down at the food, Bryony wasn't sure whether she was going to eat everything in sight or throw up—she was wagering on the latter. She needed to use the necessary, but something stopped her. She had no weapon, nothing to fight back with but the chamber pot, and while she didn't mind dousing Coombs with her bodily fluids, she knew she'd have a better chance of hitting him with an empty pot.

And she needed to eat, whether she wanted to or not. If she were to have any chance of getting away, she needed to be at her best, so she methodically ate the thick mutton stew, dipping the coarse bread into it to sop up every last bit.

The time seemed endless as she waited for Coombs to reappear, and she most definitely did not want to sort out the various sloshing sounds she was hearing. Curling up into the corner of the carriage, she waited, the chamber pot in her hands.

She was almost unprepared when the door was suddenly jerked open, and Coombs stuck his head in. "Having fun, miss?" he began in a mocking voice, starting to clamber in, when she swung the heavy porcelain pot with all her strength and hit him squarely on the jaw. He went down in an immediate lump, not a sound coming from him, and she scrambled down the steps, half afraid he'd come after her, half afraid she'd killed him, but she didn't have time to fret. There was no sign from the inn—they were alone in the courtyard, and she expected Latherby wouldn't be in much of a hurry to leave his bottle and join her in the coach. She glanced up at the box, wondering if she had the ability to drive the thing, then decided that was hopeless. She'd driven a small pony cart and a donkey in her adventurous life, but never two animals at the same time, or such a huge conveyance. The one thing she could do was ride—anything, from a camel to an elephant to a carriage horse.

It only took her moments to unbridle the horses. They were a matched set, but she chose the more placid one—no need to look for trouble. She needed to get as far away as she could, as quickly as possible, and she led the big horse to the mounting block and managed to scramble onto its bare back.

The horse pulled, unused to a passenger, but she managed to control him with her knees and the bridle, and in another moment, she was off, the abandoned carriage behind her, the body of the coachman half in and half out of the door. She was around a bend in the road when she realized the second horse was keeping up with her quick canter, and she didn't know whether to be annoyed or amused. Two animals to feed, but one to sell when she needed money. For now, all she needed was to put as many miles between her and her dedicated kidnapper as she possibly could.

❧ 22 ❧

CECILIA WOKE SLOWLY, lazily, the smell of spring all around her. Sweet timothy, green earth, horse droppings...

Her eyes opened in the shadows, and it took her a panicked moment to remember where she was. The stables, lying on a bed of straw, where she'd curled up when she'd escaped from Peter Barnes.

Who sat across from her in the stall, watching her out of calm, brown eyes.

"What are you doing here?" she demanded in what should have been a disdainful voice, but instead simply sounded sulky.

"Watching over the sleeping beauty. If you'd woken up alone, you probably would have tried to mount that behemoth again, and I've gotten quite enough exercise running after you."

She tried to sit up, but the pain in her backside made her moan and flop back down. "Go away! Don't worry, I'm never getting on a horse again in my life, I promise you. Just leave me alone."

"I've never met a woman so in need of a spanking," he replied in a deceptively calm voice. "Do you have any idea how much trouble you've caused?"

"I don't care. And don't bother spanking me—that part of my

anatomy has already suffered enough indignity. Just go away. Go back to London and tell my parents I'm a lost cause."

He hesitated for a moment. "And then I'd be out the reward money."

For some reason, that felt like a stab to the heart. "I forgot," she said, pulling herself into a sitting position a little more carefully. "This is all a financial transaction for you, isn't it?"

"What else did you think it was? I don't come running after runaway virgins for the love of it."

"I'm not..." Her voice trailed off, discouraged. It was a waste of time to argue with him.

"Not a virgin?" He sounded no more than curious.

"Not a runaway!" she snapped.

"That's not my concern. As long as you're still untouched, I'll return you to the bosom of your family and wish you luck."

"And if I had managed to get ruined somewhere along the way?" she shot back.

She was astonished at the sudden dark flare in his eyes, a glimpse of pure male hunger that she had never seen before, and everything inside her flared to life, responding to that need. "Then I'd take you home with me and never let you go," he said, his voice tense, his expression fierce, and for a moment...for a moment...

"But you're not ruined, your parents will welcome you with loving arms..."

"You're certain of that?" Cecilia interrupted.

"They're no worse and no better than many," he said. "You'll have a comfortable enough life."

"What if I don't want a comfortable life?" she said in a very small voice. "What if I want something more?"

He didn't pretend to misunderstand her, but that moment of hot desire had passed, leaving a cold, dutiful man in its wake. "You'll learn to count your blessings. You'll go to balls and house parties and soirees, you'll never have to soil your hands a day in your life. Your nanny will raise your children, your husband will worship the ground you walk on, and you'll be content indeed."

It sounded like hell to her. "What makes you think my husband will adore me?"

"How could he not?" he said simply, and the warmth in her heart returned.

"And what kind of life will your wife lead?" she demanded, no longer caring if she sounded pathetic.

"She'll nurse her own children, she'll work alongside me, and she'll be managing a home, not spending her life on frivolities."

"She sounds very admirable," Cecilia said caustically. Better to be caustic than cry. "And will you worship the ground she walks on?"

"No," he said flatly.

"Why not?"

"Because I already gave my heart to a foolish wench who's busy going to balls and soirees and houseparties."

For a moment she couldn't breathe. "Peter," she said in a whisper.

"And he'll always think of her," Peter went barreling on ahead as if she hadn't spoken, "but he knows his place and he knows hers, and he'll never regret his choice."

"Never?" The one word was undeniably plaintive.

"Never," he said firmly. Pushing against the side of the stall, he rose to his full height, towering over her, and she recognized the determined expression on his face, recognized the hopeless longing in his eyes, and she wanted to weep.

She wouldn't, of course. She was just a silly runaway virgin, someone who lived in a social whirl and had no deep emotions, even if it felt like her heart was crumpling inside her. She could feel tears stinging her eyes, but she blinked them away, giving him a brave smile.

"It sounds as if you've worked it all out very well," she said. "I bow to your superior wisdom. And now, if you don't mind, I think I'll go to my room."

"I'll tell Mrs. Seeley you'd like a bath. You must be aching after that ride."

"As you wish." Hot water would do wonders for her painful body, but it would do nothing for her heart. "And then?"

"And then tomorrow we'll leave for London and I'll return you to the bosom of your family as quickly as I possibly can. All you have to do is throw yourself on your parents' mercy and beg forgiveness."

Her eyes narrowed. "Why should I have to do that? Didn't they send you after me? Why would I have to beg for anything?"

His mouth closed in a stubborn line. "Just behave yourself and everything will be fine. Before long, this will seem like a faraway dream."

He was wrong about that one—it already felt like a dream. A nightmare. But she wasn't going to talk to him about that. "I look forward to it," she said in a leaden voice, turning her face away, missing the instant darkness in his.

❦

BRYONY WOULD HAVE BEEN fine if she hadn't stopped. Clinging to an oversized carriage horse without a saddle was far more trouble than she would have expected, and despite her full skirts, she had a hard time gripping the bay's wide girth and keep up a decent pace. Somewhere along the way the second horse fell behind, no longer interested in following his partner, and Bryony rode on into the darkness. There was only a quarter moon that night, providing marginal light on the narrow, muddy roads, and she knew she ought to leave the main thoroughfare, but the thought of wandering through the menacing woods with an uncertain mount beneath her was just too much to contemplate. Now that she was away from her captors, she had time to think, and those thoughts were not encouraging. She needed to reach another town, but how in the world did you get a job and a bed for the night? Did you walk into an inn and simply ask? It was a reassuring thought, but she had her doubts that it would be that easy.

She hadn't actually made use of the chamber pot before slamming it into the coachman's jaw, and her body was reminding her of a basic biological need, one that each jarring step of the horse brought closer to an absolute necessity. When she could wait no longer, she led the horse into a thicket, just off the side of the road, and dismounted, vaguely wondering if she would be able to clamber back up on the beast again when she was done. There was a definite limit to her resilience. Perhaps she could tie the horse to a tree and simply bed down in the bushes for the rest of the night. Daylight would be more encouraging.

She had just finished when she heard the sound of the carriage far in the distance, and she froze for a moment. They couldn't have come after her—she'd taken the horses, and she'd had a head start. With luck, the coachman had a broken jaw or even a broken head, and she could hardly imagine Latherby managing a coach by himself. No, it had to be some other north-bound traveler on the king's high-way, intent on a fast journey.

Which didn't mean she was about to show herself. There would be questions, possibly even danger. Taking the horse's reins, she moved deeper into the thicket, dropping down on her knees in the damp earth and waiting.

She had no idea what made the coach stop where she had—she'd hardly left a trail of breadcrumbs in the road, but nevertheless, the huge carriage pulled to a stop, the horses restive and prancing, and she heard a mumble of voices. It was too dark to know if it was the same coach—it was huge, as Latherby's had been, but the horses were equally dark, and as one man dismounted, she quickly flattened herself, holding her breath.

"Why the hell do you think she's here, Coombs?" Latherby's voice came suddenly close, and panic sliced through her.

"Them horses knew," was the mumbled response, and Bryony knew a quiet thrill of triumph. She might not have broken his jaw, but his voice was barely intelligible. "She's around here, all right, or I miss my bet."

"Then find her, goddamn it!" Latherby snapped peevishly. "I'm tired of all this. How you could let a slip of a girl blindside you like that is a disgrace."

Coombs's response was muffled and possibly obscene, but clearly Latherby wasn't meant to understand it. She could see him fairly well, his portly figure staring up at the sky as if searching for answers, and he went on.

"You should have known she was a wily one—otherwise why

would I have been forced to carry her off? A sensible female would do as she was told. She agreed to marry me, and I mean to see that she does. That's simply too ripe a purse to pass up, and if I tup her in the dark, I won't have to see those damned freckles. Might even get an heir on her, though I don't know that I'd care for the expense. Her jointure isn't endless, and the last thing I'd want is to be tied to a speckled virago and a squalling brat."

He seemed to be directing his discourse to that thin sliver of moon, which seemed extremely odd, but he continued, going on at great length about what he'd rather be doing with her money, none of which involved her, thank God, and she wondered where Coombs was during all this, when a heavy hand clamped down around her shoulder and she felt herself hauled upright to face the furious coachman.

He had a grimy white bandage around his head, madness in his eyes. Grabbing her by the hair, he yanked her forward. "Got her!" he shouted in garbled triumph, twisting her arm painfully.

"Don't hurt her!" Latherby called, closer than she would have thought. "It's your own damned fault she got the better of you. If anyone's going to administer punishment, it's going to be me."

With a muttered imprecation, he dragged her from the woods and then simply threw her at Latherby's feet as he stood still in the middle of the road, the huge coach behind him.

"There you are, m'dear," he said mildly enough. "What a great deal of trouble you've put us to. I doubt Coombs is going to forgive you, and I must admit to being a bit miffed myself. After all, you gave your word that we'd marry. Why the sudden fuss?"

She lay in the mud, every part of her body aching. Slowly, she tried to pull herself to a sitting position, rising on her knees and finally standing to face Latherby. He was shorter than she was, she realized, swaying slightly in an exhausted haze.

"You don't want to marry me," she whispered.

"Of course I don't. But I want your money, and it's the only way I'll get it. Don't be naïve, dear girl—this is the way things work. Now get in the carriage."

She glanced at the open door, the steps let down for her to mount, then back at her former fiancé. "No," she said mutinously.

She didn't even see it coming. He slammed his hand across her face, so hard that her head whipped back and she lost her balance once more, falling back against the coach. The horses shifted restlessly, and when she looked back at Latherby, there was a spark of pure madness in his mottled face, one that frightened her. "Get in the coach, m'dear," he repeated silkily, and she was all out of fight for the moment. Climbing upward, she sank into the corner, closing her eyes.

All she could think of was Adderley, with that mocking, almost tender smile, and she didn't know if the thought of him weakened her further or gave her the will to fight. He was gone, and that was far worse than a couple of criminals dragging her to an unwanted marriage. She would survive, she had no doubt about it, and if survival involved putting a knife in Sir George's wattled throat, then so much the better. She was bloodthirsty in her rage, exhausted in her pain. Keeping her eyes closed as the carriage sagged beneath her former fiancé's weight, she gave in to exhaustion and slept.

❧ 23 ❧

CECILIA SAT IN HER BED, her borrowed nightclothes around her. She was swathed in Mechelin lace, mostly transparent, and it was a good thing the heat wave hadn't abandoned them completely, because the clothing would have provided no warmth at all. It was finely made, just the thing for a man to appreciate his lover's body beneath the almost transparent stitchery, and Cecilia would have preferred sackcloth and ashes. Somewhere in this house lay Peter Barnes, his big, strong body probably wearing nothing at all, his arms, that could curl around her so protectively, were empty, when she needed to be held.

At least, they'd better be empty, she thought with sudden irritation. If he succumbed to the innocent Betsey's wiles, she'd kill him.

No, he'd hardly seduce a maid when she was there for the taking. It was only his damned honor that stopped him from coming to her, his damned honor that was going to make him fulfil his duty and return her to the bosom of her family when she was feeling like a dyspeptic asp. And nothing she could say or do would change him mind.

Unless... What if he could be persuaded to take her virtue? Wouldn't that debt of honor outweigh all the others? He would hardly refuse to take responsibility for a ruined virgin, particularly when she knew full well that he wanted her as much as she wanted him.

And there was the answer to her conundrum, to her restlessness, to her need. She would find where he slept and wake him by climbing into bed with him. Nature would take care of the rest.

There were no slippers for her bare feet, and they were icy cold. There was no wrapper to go around her diaphanous nightgown, but she didn't care. Leaving her room, she flitted through the halls like a ghost, looking for her lost lover.

It would have been a great deal simpler if the doors to the unused rooms were open, but in fact, she had to quietly open each one and peer into the darkness to see if the beds were occupied. The manor house was of a modest size, but even so, there were too many bedrooms, and she ground her teeth in frustration as she moved from the second floor to the third. She wanted him. She could remember the weight of his body on top of hers, and she wanted that again; she wanted things she was only half aware of, indecent, glorious things. And if, in the end, he still refused to marry her, then she could be content in the fact that once, long ago, she'd known love.

The back end of the third floor was in rough shape, the wallpaper soiled and stained; the rug that ran along the hallway was ripped in some places, shredded in others, but it was beginning to look familiar. She started down the corridor, her candle in her hands, as she listened to some uproar from the faraway kitchen. The servants must be having a party, she thought. All the better for her plan.

She knew it was the right door before she even opened it, and she blew out the candle before reaching for the doorknob, plunging everything into darkness.

The door was mercifully silent when she opened it, just as quiet when she closed it behind her. Her eyes were growing accustomed to the darkness, and there was the barest trace of moonlight from the open window, enough to show the outline of the bed.

Setting the candlestick down on the floor, she glided forward, standing over him. He looked so peaceful lying there, she just wanted to—

"Jesus Bloody Christ!" he exploded, rearing up in bed, one hand on his heart. He wore no shirt. "What the hell are you doing, Cecilia? I thought you were a ghost!"

Not exactly the welcome she was looking for, but she could adapt. Pulling the nightgown over her head, she picked up the edge of the covers and slid beneath them, right up next to him, and oh, blessings, he was naked. How absolutely splendid!

"What are you doing here?" he repeated, his voice dangerous.

"Isn't it obvious?" She tried very hard to sound arch, but her voice wobbled nervously. "I'm here to seduce you."

There was dead silence in the room, but Cecilia was not discouraged. He moved then, as far away as he could in the narrow bed, but she didn't make the mistake of thinking he was making room for her. He was trying to get away. "Go back to your room," he said flatly.

Cecilia wasn't easily cowed. "It's too far away, and I'm cold. Can't you warm me up?"

He groaned, a heartfelt sound. "You need to go back to your own bed and forget this foolishness."

She followed him across the small expanse of mattress that lay between them and twined her arms around his neck. Her breasts pressed up against his hot, sleek skin, and a frisson of delight danced through her. Yes, she thought. *I want this.* Placing her mouth against his, she kissed him, delighting in the feel of his lips, until she realized they weren't moving, they were locked tight, and he was holding himself away from her. She looked up at him from beneath her tousled hair. "Aren't you going to kiss me back?"

"No," he said, but she took advantage and pressed her mouth back against his, and he seemed to have no choice but to respond, his mouth seeking hers for just a moment before he pulled back again. She needed his warm hands on her arms, she needed his body wrapped around hers.

And the most terrifying doubt assailed her. She was naked, she was beautiful, and she was in bed with a naked man who didn't want to touch her. "Don't...don't you want me?" She couldn't help it, it sounded entirely pathetic, but she had no defenses left.

"Oh, Christ," he groaned, and this time he pulled her into his arms, skin to skin, and there was a great deal more to him than she expected. "I'm not an idiot. Of course I want you. I'd die for you. Which is why," he said, "I'm not doing this."

Before she realized what had happened, he'd pushed her out of the bed, so that she landed hard on her backside, right on top of her discarded nightgown. "Go away," he growled, and she could hear the anguish in his voice.

She was going to cry, and she desperately didn't want to. Tears spilled hotly down her face, and she yanked the nightgown from beneath her, trying to pull it over her with shaking fingers. "I will," she said, hiccupping slightly and no longer caring. "You're an idiot, and you deserve a lifetime of loneliness and misery. I love you, and you're just throwing me away as if I were a...a...an old shoe." She got to her knees, still struggling with the diaphanous lace, and realized she had it on upside down. Swallowing her instinctive wail, she ripped it off and put it on again, just as a little sob escaped her. "And you're a stupid, selfish clod who doesn't realize what a gift I am, and you're going to end up married to someone horrible and it will serve you right and..." She dissolved into tears.

He climbed out of bed as she knelt there and wept, her shoulders shaking, her throat raw and painful, and then a moment later, he picked her up in his arms and sat down on the bed again. He'd put on pants, she realized with regret, and then she didn't think at all as she wept against his strong, bare shoulder, his hand entwined in her hair as he murmured soft, comforting things. He smelled so good— of woodsmoke and skin and just a hint of brandy, and she wanted to bury herself against him, in him, she wanted to breathe him in and kiss him and—

He gently pushed her head up to meet his gaze, and his own expression was both tight and rueful. "I can't do that to you, sweetheart. You're made for better things than the likes of me, and I love you too much to let you throw yourself away on a Bow Street Runner."

"I thought you didn't like to be called a runner," she said amidst hiccups.

His small smile warmed her. "Only for you, sweetheart. You can call me anything you want. But you have to go back to your room. If your parents are going to welcome you home, you need to be above reproach."

Ice swept through her as she began to understand his words. "Why wouldn't they welcome me back home? Is there something you're not telling me?"

Ignoring the question, he rose, setting her on her feet. "I'm not going to touch you," he said again. "My job is to return you to London in the same condition you left it."

"Return me to where? My parents' home? You make it sound as if they don't want me."

"Of course they want you," he said. "How could anyone not want you?"

He was so close she could feel him, and she wanted to sway toward him, so that she was back in his arms. But it would do no good; he'd simply set her away again, and she wanted to howl with pain and frustration.

"You're a...you're a..." Words failed her, and she glared up at him in the darkness. "If you think I'll offer myself to you again, then you're greatly mistaken. This is your last chance."

"I don't want you."

It didn't matter that they both knew that was a lie—the pain of those words sliced through her. "You change your mind awfully fast," she managed to say, drawing her flimsy nightdress around her.

He said nothing, and the shadowy room was too dark to read the expression in his eyes, but she knew what she'd see there. The truth, the need, the longing.

But he loved his twisted sense of honor more. "Go to the devil," she snapped, and slammed the door behind her.

❦ 24 ❦

The next day

CECILIA ELLISTON WAS FURIOUS. So angry, in fact, that she said not one word from her spot in the corner of the small travelling coach that Peter Barnes had hired, along with four strong horses. He hadn't listened to her protests, her demands, her pleas. He hadn't gone after her when she'd run from his room; he'd simply ordered her dressed and packed the next morning and then walked away amid her rants.

It was raining—otherwise he would be riding outside the coach, not cramming his big body into it so that he seemed to take all the space and air. He'd climbed in and shed his wet overcoat, leaning back and closing his eyes. He was doubtless hoping to shut her out.

But she'd already decided not to grace him with one word of conversation, a punishment he was taking far too well. He'd kept as far away from her as possible, seemingly ignorant of the fact that she was fighting back with silence, and his own quiet, thoughtful mood was an additional affront. How dare he punish her with silence when he was the one who was clearly in the wrong?

She'd seen just how effective silence was as a weapon, seen it wielded by her mother and sister to devastating effect. Peter Barnes seemed immune, and if he didn't say something soon, she was going to scream.

The one thing she wasn't going to do was break the silence herself. She would go to her grave with her lips tight together, and nothing he said or did would get her to open them again. She was made of sterner stuff than that, blast it. Bryony wouldn't give in, and neither would she.

Which reminded her—where in the world was Bryony? The worst man in England had already left, which was some reassurance. Even if Sir George had eloped with her, she might have gone willingly enough. After all, she'd already agreed to marry him, and their little detour to Pevensey Hall shouldn't derail the eventual ceremony, particularly if they wed in Scotland. Bryony was probably perfectly well. Cecilia just wished she could believe it.

But that left her with the second worst man in all of England, a pigheaded, narrow-minded, moralistic Bow Street officer who cared more for honor than the gift of love she was offering him. But she wasn't going to tell him so—she was going to keep on with her dignified silence until she was dumped back at her parents' house, and maybe well beyond that, since she'd be mourning her lost love and her parents were likely to harangue her day and night.

She refused to believe they might not want her back—they'd always made such a fuss of their pretty daughters and their excellent prospects on the marriage mart. Her own chances had dwindled a bit, to be sure, but that would hardly make her parents abandon her on the streets of London. They couldn't.

Most probably, they'd quickly accept one of the lesser offers for her hand, no longer holding out for a duke or even a minor earl— she'd be lucky if she ended up with a baron, though Maryanne and James Elliston desperately wanted a title. In fact, she might stay silent, sad, and mournful for the rest of her life, like some beautiful wraith, dressed in flowing lavender garments and dreaming her life away in voiceless misery. She would never speak again.

"You're a mutton-headed bully." It popped out before she could stop herself, and she couldn't regret it. "Do you have any idea what you're throwing away? I love you!"

Peter sighed. "You don't even know me. I'm some stranger who came into your life a few days ago, and will be out of it even sooner. You've got a silly girlish crush on me, and I can't imagine why, but if you think I'm going to let you ruin your life by throwing yourself at me, then you're dead wrong. You're going back to your parents in the same condition you left, to make a good marriage and be a good mother and live out your life in pampered luxury. You'd never survive on a Bow Street salary."

Well, at least he'd thought about it that much. "I have money of my own," she said. "From third cousin Cecily who thought I was named for her. It's not much, but I imagine we could make do."

"I'm not taking your money," he growled, affronted.

Cecilia remembered a few facts from Bryony's quiet rants up in the schoolroom. "It won't be my money—the moment we marry, it will be entirely yours."

"We're not getting married!" he snapped. "And what kind of man would I be, to live off his wife's inheritance?"

"Just like everybody else in society."

"There's the problem in a nutshell. I'm not in society, Miss Elliston, and never will be. In my world, a man lives off the sweat of his brow, not his woman."

"You don't need to live off me. We'd be partners—that's what the best marriages are."

"Will you get it out of your silly little head that I'm not marrying you? After tonight, I won't even see you again."

She tried to ignore the pain in her heart at the thought. "What if someone comes after me again? Would you rescue me?"

"No one's coming after you, Miss Elliston. According to Adderley, they didn't even want you in the first place."

"No, they didn't," she said quietly. "No one wants me."

Peter made an exasperated noise. "Everyone wants you, you silly twit, and you know it."

"Everyone but you," she said, sounding properly forlorn. It wasn't working, but at least she could try.

He looked heavenward, as if for strength. "I have no room in my life for a spoiled aristocrat."

"I'm not spoiled!" she shot back, then honesty required her to amend that. "At least, not very. And I'm not an aristocrat. My grandfather owned coal mines in Cornwall."

"Then why are you required to marry well?"

"Because my uncle gambled it all away before conveniently dying and leaving the title to my father." The moment the words were out of her mouth she regretted them. "That is, I'm not..."

"I know more about you than you think. Your parents were looking for a title and a fat settlement, not a penniless Bow Street Runner."

"You don't like the word 'runner,'" she reminded him.

"Sod the word! I've told you, I'm not the man for you," he snapped, and for one dark, dreadful moment she believed him.

"You don't love me?" she asked in a tiny voice. "Not even a little?"

"No."

"You don't want me?"

He hissed out a breath. "I'm not entirely mad, woman. Of course I want you. I'm just having none of you. I'm out of your class, and you'd come to your senses in a week."

"No, I wouldn't," she said eagerly. "I told you—"

"Yes, you told me you were in love with me. And I told you that you're a complete idiot who'll forget all about me the moment you rejoin society, and I'm tired of this argument. I'm going to sleep." With that, he crossed his arms across his broad chest, stretched out his long legs, closed his eyes, and prepared to ignore her.

Cecilia sat very still. Of course he ignored her. She was everything he said, a silly, stupid girl who got everything she wanted thanks to her pretty face and charming manners, neither of which were of any use with a man like Peter Barnes. He wasn't going to budge.

She loved him. For so many reasons, apart from his truly impressive appearance, his warm brown eyes, his strong shoulders, his wonderful mouth. She loved his decency and his honor, no matter how inconvenient, and she had the horrible certainty that this excess of affection wasn't about to disappear. Her great-aunt Cecily had suffered a similar fate—she'd fallen in love with a farmer, someone lower than a runner, and she'd longed for him the rest of her solitary life. Elliston women loved once and loved truly, and Cecilia was doomed. At least Cecily's farmer had loved her back, even if he'd taken the huge settlement her grandfather had given him to make him go away.

Peter didn't even need a settlement. He didn't care, even though she'd been desperately sure he did beneath all that starched-up honor. He really didn't love her.

She felt the tears well up in her eyes and she did nothing to stop them. She could cry in silence, and the man opposite her wouldn't even notice. She was an ugly crier—her nose turned red, her eyes grew swollen, her face blotchy, but none of that mattered. All her vaunted beauty had no effect on this stubborn man who really didn't love her. She would cry because she couldn't not cry, but when he sent her away, she would be stone-faced. This would be the last time she cried in front of anybody.

❧

EVEN THE PELTING rain was better than this, Peter thought, doing his best to appear relaxed and on the verge of sleeping. Every moment he was with her was torture, and all the stern lectures he'd given himself hadn't done a bit of good. She was driving him crazy, pulling him to pieces, and clearly he wasn't nearly as strong as he thought he was. A better man would be tempted—hell, he was more than tempted. He was being torn apart, and it was all he could do to present his calm, implacable face to the woman he... To this woman, with her silly claims of love and her beautiful face filled with longing. It was ridiculous, and he knew it.

He wasn't even sure if he believed in love—he certainly knew it wasn't for the likes of a practical person like him. Silly society wenches could moon about a pair of broad shoulders, but men like him were practical. If he ever married, it would be some stout, level-headed woman who wouldn't make demands or even conversation, whereas Cecilia had trouble shutting her pretty mouth. He wanted to kiss that mouth again, so badly. He wasn't going to touch her.

It didn't help that her fancifulness had rubbed off. He'd actually considered what life would be like if things had been different between the two of them, if her father had been a shopkeeper or a tradesman. She had a laugh like a silver bell, she was feisty and funny and so beautiful it made his eyes ache, and she was off-limits, not for his sake, but for hers. He was saving her, and she didn't know it. He was denying everything he had ever wanted, and if that wasn't love, then maybe it didn't exist. The answer was no.

He'd known a moment of hope when he'd first received that letter. If her parents had turned her off, then he was a better option that the streets of London. But common sense had reared its ugly head—she would never end up on the streets. Those miserable, skin-flint parents of hers would take one look at her sweet, beautiful face and open their arms. They simply had to.

He heard the noise then, a soft, surreptitious little snuffle, and his eyes flew open despite his best interests. She was leaning against the window of the carriage, her eyes closed, her skin blotchy, her face drenched in tears. And something snapped.

A moment later, he hauled her into his arms, cradling her against his chest. She'd fought for just a moment, sobbing. "No," she'd said. "You don't..." But he hadn't let her finish that sentence, putting his mouth over hers, tasting the salt of her tears, and then pulling her close, stroking her hair as she shook in misery.

"Yes," he said. "I do." And leaning down, he kissed her again.

"I love my parents," she announced a great deal later, curled up in his arms, and he knew a sudden sinking feeling.

"I'm certain they could be persuaded..." he began, when she squirmed delightfully on his lap to look up at him.

"No, I mean I love that they've cast me out. I think otherwise you would have just kept fighting me." A sudden darkness crossed her sunny expression. "That is...you aren't just feeling sorry for me, are you? You really want me?"

His kiss should have left her no question as to the intensity of his longing, and she curled up against him happily. "And now I won't even have to feel bad about not seeing them. They would have cut me off the moment we were married anyway, so this makes life a great deal simpler."

He decided not to mention that he never would have given in if her parents were still willing to take her back. He knew far better than she did how sparse his life was, and he would still let her go to anyone who would provide her the kind of life she was born to. Assuming he approved of their character, manners, fortune, and adoration of this beautiful creature.

All she needed to do was pack on a few more pounds and she'd be celestial, and given the way she ate, that happy day would be soon approaching.

"Then I suppose this might be a good time to mention that we aren't headed to London at the moment."

She pushed away, looking up at him with a hopeful expression on her face. "Are you taking me to Gretna Green?"

"No. At least, not if I can help it. I've changed my mind. We're going to rescue your cousin. Consider it a wedding gift."

"Oh, Peter! I knew you would!" she breathed in delight, then looked slightly doubtful. "But how will we find them?"

"You forget, I'm a Bow Street *Runner*." He put an ironic stress on the word. "This is what I do. We'll find them, all right."

"And what if they're already married?"

"Then it will be up to Lord Adderley to take care of that inconvenience."

Her adorable forehead wrinkled. "But why would he? He's long gone."

"I suspect he's not as far away as one might think. And he's far from indifferent, whether he realizes it or not. He's not going to stand by while someone like Latherby marries her."

"But Adderley is the Worst Man in England!" she cried.

"I'm not sure your cousin agrees with you." Peter tugged her closer again, and she went with a sigh of pure happiness. "She might just be the making of him."

"Or he'll be the unmaking of her," Cecilia shot back, worried.

Peter simply shrugged, unconcerned. "I didn't want you to

suddenly decide to rescue her without me around to get you out of trouble."

Cecilia was unoffended. "Well, if we end up in Gretna Green, we may as well get married. I'm already ruined, and it would simplify a great many things."

"You'll marry me in a church with a proper Church of England rector," he said sternly.

Her smile was so bright it dazzled him more than he was already dazzled. "Yes, Mr. Barnes," she said, tucking herself into his side. "I thought you'd never ask."

❧ 25 ❧

THE HEAT WAVE had finally broken. A chill crept down Bryony's backbone, and Latherby sat swaddled in soft woolen robes as the carriage continued its endless, bone-rattling pace on the night-shrouded roads, and there was nothing she could do but huddle in on herself and try to stay warm. Would this miserable coach ride ever end? No matter how this misadventure ended, she was never getting in a coach again.

She almost wept when the carriage pulled up to an inn, and Latherby reluctantly bestirred himself when Coombs opened the door.

"Horses are about done in," he announced. "They're going to need to rest before we push on much farther."

"We ain't even in Scotland yet!" Latherby fretted.

"No, sir, and we won't get there until tomorrow. The landlord says he has no fresh cattle, and no private rooms left. We're stuck here."

Latherby's unattractively mottled face settled into a pout. "Exactly where is here?"

"Town called Underhill-Upon-Avon, the landlord tells me. You could sleep in the carriage, I 'spose...."

Latherby ignored his ruminations. "Why is it that towns all over England are called 'upon-Avon'? The damned river's not that big."

"Dunno, sir."

"I wasn't expecting an answer," Latherby snapped. "And I'm not spending the night in this carriage with m'bride. Can't imagine anything more uncomfortable. Feed and water the horses and then we'll move on."

"I told you, them horses don't have much left to give," said Coombs, clearly liking horses more than humans.

"They won't need much. If I remember correctly, Adderley has an old hunting lodge in this area. It was dreadfully rustic the one time I visited, but it's got beds and a roof and that's all I care about right now. I fancy my bride won't like it overmuch, but she's got to come to terms with the fact that Kit abandoned her to me."

Bryony stared straight ahead, her expression stony. Adderley was the last thing she wanted to be reminded of right then, but life wasn't paying much attention to her choices. If spending a night in one of his abandoned houses was the closest she ever had to come to him again, so much the better. George was absolutely right—Adderley had handed her over to him without a backward glance. The sooner she stopped thinking of him the better. Before long, the revolting George would wipe out any physical remainder of their night together, and there would be nothing holding her to the worst man in England.

The sooner the better, she told herself in her anger and misery. This was her new life, and there was no escape. She needed to let go of any trace of her former life. Any trace that mattered, and Adderley had mattered a great deal.

George and Coombs were still talking. "Ask the landlord for directions—he'd know how to get there. I don't believe it's too far away, not over five miles, and the horses should survive. All you'd have to do is follow the damned river and we'll find it. Great, ramshackle place called Waycross. I think they used to burn heretics and witches nearby."

A fitting place for Adderley to thrive, Bryony thought bitterly. Maybe someone would decide to burn him at the stake.

But no one would. He was a man, and he was the aristocracy, with a very great deal of money. No one would interfere with him. No one could interfere with him, no matter how much they tried.

"We might just anticipate our wedding vows if I can bestir myself," George said, staring at her blearily. "It's colder than a witch's tit tonight, and I might need something to warm my bed. You aren't the prettiest thing in the world, but you're better looking than Coombs."

"But probably less agreeable," she muttered with a weak trace of defiance. To her surprise, George laughed.

"True enough, my pet. Coombs does what I tell him, and so will you, even if I have to beat you to break you. Can't abide troublesome women."

"Then you'd be wise not to marry me," she said, her voice stronger. "I can be a very great deal of trouble."

He gave her an unfriendly glare. "So you can. Never would have thought it—you seemed like such a quiet, biddable thing. Not to worry though—once we're married, I won't have to see you over-much. I'll just take you away someplace where you won't be any bother."

"My heart rejoices," she said, her tones dripping ice.

George's puffy eyes narrowed. "That, or I might hand you over to Adderley to see if he wants another taste."

"He wouldn't," she said. "I bored him."

"Well, I could count on him to come up with some unpleasant way to punish you. Never been so deceived by a woman in all my life."

"You'd be wise just to let me go. I'm more trouble than I'm worth."

"No, you ain't. I need your money, and I can put up with a little discomfort to get it. Just don't annoy me," George said. "Or you really won't like your wedding night."

She sank back against the squabs, momentarily giving up. There was no way she could escape from the coach again—the two were watching her far too closely. An abandoned hunting lodge was a different matter altogether.

She almost slept the final five miles of their endless journey, but George's noisy snores kept her alert and ready for her chance. It was close to a full moon shining down brightly as they pulled into the carriage yard, and she looked out at the building, looking for ways to escape.

It was big for a hunting lodge, and signs of decay and disrepair surrounded it. No one had trimmed the overgrown shrubbery in years, and the roof looked in need of mending. At least it set her mind to ease on one count—this was clearly the last place that interested Adderley. He'd let it go to rack and ruin—he'd hardly decide that it suddenly needed help.

Coombs had pulled the coach up to the front door, and George scrambled down ungainfully, the carriage rocking beneath his weight, before turning and holding out his hand for her. Bryony didn't move.

"Don't be tiresome, girl," he snapped. "I can always have Coombs drag you out of there, and he doesn't have my gentle touch."

Bryony's cheek throbbed in memory of that gentleness, and she reluctantly pushed herself up from the seat, crossing the carriage to climb down the iron steps. At least she didn't have to use George's proffered hand.

"I can have Coombs train you," he muttered, disgruntled. "He's very good with a whip, is Coombs, and he's tamed more restive fillies than you."

Wisdom had her keeping her head down, and she followed George as he mounted the front steps. There were decorative flower pots flanking the door, now filled with weeds, and she wondered how heavy they were. The chamber pot had done a good job on Coombs's thick head, perhaps this might serve for Latherby and she could escape.

Before she could make an attempt, Latherby grabbed her wrist and dragged her up the steps and through the open door, pulling so hard she tripped. They were in a large hall, but to her horror, it wasn't abandoned as the outside had led her to believe. A fire was roaring in the fireplace, though no one was in sight.

"At least there are servants," George said, releasing her wrist to shove her down on a high-backed bench. He let out a bellow. "You there," he shouted. "We're friends of Lord Adderley's, seeking shelter for the night. Show yourself."

"You don't have to be so loud, George," came a familiar, silken voice. "I saw my long-lost carriage come down the drive."

George's bulk was blocking her, but it didn't matter. She'd know that voice anywhere, and it almost took the last bit of fight from her. Latherby was bad enough, but his partner in crime could devastate her more than Sir George could ever hope to manage.

"To what do I owe the honor of your unexpected visit?" Adderley continued, moving farther into the room and dropping a pile of logs beside the fireplace before brushing his hands clean. "I would have thought you'd returned to London by now."

"As I expected you would. You forgot I've got a bride to claim." George reached down and hauled her upright, and pushed her into the room, his hand cruelly tight.

If Adderley was surprised to see her, he didn't show it. "I thought you'd changed your mind about marrying Miss Marton," he said. "What's she doing here without a chaperone?"

"Took her," George said flatly. "I mean to get the thing done tomorrow. Hoped for today, but the horses were knackered."

"So you decided to avail yourself of my hospitality. Take your hands off her, would you?" It was a mild request, but to Bryony's surprise, he released her, and she surreptitiously rubbed her bruised wrist. "A good thing you haven't been to Scotland yet. I might have been obliged to kill you." He turned to survey them. "I'm afraid my hospitality is very poor right now—my caretakers are nowhere in sight, and the larder's empty. There is, of course, an excellent wine cellar still untouched."

"That's all we need," George said jovially. "That and a pack of playing cards. Er...did you say you'd have to kill me?"

Adderley's smile was dulcet. "I don't believe Miss Marton wishes to be married to you, George."

"Doesn't have any say in the matter," George replied. "Neither do you. Can't imagine why you'd care, one way or another."

"I can't imagine why either," he said blandly. "But I seem to have a perverse interest in her fate. Why don't we play cards for her?"

"You cheat."

"So do you," Adderley replied.

"I ain't giving her up," George said stubbornly. "But I'll put her up for the night. Can't imagine why you'd want her, but you seem to. A hand of piquet should settle it."

Adderley smiled like the snake he was. "I don't think so. I find I don't want her to marry you."

"That don't signify. She's marrying me. You can have her for the night, or simply not bother—it's up to you."

"We'll start with the night," Adderley said coolly. "I'll get the cards."

❧

KIT WAS MORE than adept at hiding the few emotions that troubled him, but his rage at the moment was so monumental that he wanted to skewer George with a red-hot poker. Bryony, his fierce, argumentative Bryony, was broken, her wrist bruised, the mark on the side of her face could only come from a fist. He could rip George's spine from his body quite happily, and then kill Coombs as well. He'd do whatever it took to bring a light back to Bryony's dull eyes, strength back to her hunched shoulders. He was going to murder them all.

But she wasn't looking to him for safety, for protection. She expected nothing from him, which should be exactly the way he wanted things. He'd get her away from George—he owed her that much, and then he'd decide what to do with her.

He didn't believe in signs or omens. He didn't believe in anything at all. But she was here, and that had to mean something. Maybe he could redeem himself, if he had any interest in doing so. He never did. But she looked so lost.

By the time he returned with the cards, she was sitting on the high-backed settle once more, far away from the fire, while George had managed to drag a table and two chairs over to take full advantage of the warmth.

"Two bottles of wine, Adder? That will hardly give us a start. I mean for you to match me, glass for glass, you know. No sense in giving you an unfair advantage."

"I can drink you under the table, George," he pointed out coolly, setting the bottles and glasses onto the table. "And there's plenty more where this came from. Even you couldn't drink my cellars dry."

"I can try," George said, dropping down into his seat and reaching for a bottle. "Who's the third glass for?"

Kit took the bottle and filled it. "For the bride."

"Don't waste it on her—nothing would warm her up."

"Nevertheless." He crossed the room to the settle, and she looked up at him, her eyes meeting his.

The rage in those green depths was remarkable, and he wanted to smile. Not broken after all. His Bryony was made of sterner stuff. Not his Bryony, of course. He didn't want her to be. Nevertheless, he placed the glass of wine in her passive hand, pressing her fingers closed around it.

"Drink it," he ordered, his voice implacable.

For a moment, he wondered whether she would fling it in his face. It would have been entertaining—clearly, she held a deep grudge over his summary dismissal of her—but instead, she took a small sip of the stuff, his very best, and he could see some small trace of tension leave her.

"Good girl," he said softly, so that George couldn't hear him, and then turned to join his enemy at the card table, settling in for a long night.

They were too well-matched to make fast work of it, and they traded leads back and forth. Kit did his best to ply George with all the wine he could possibly want, but the drunker George got, the craftier he was. His cheating might be a bit sloppy, but neither of them ever called the other on it. Skill in cheating was as important as skill at cards.

He took Bryony a second glass of wine the moment she finished the first one—he'd been watching her covertly as George shuffled and dealt the cards from the top and bottom of the deck. George complained loudly that he shouldn't waste it on her, and Bryony had looked at him with daggers in her eyes, and Kit was content. He much preferred her enraged than defeated.

He had no idea of the time when the last hand was played, his mastery over George undeniable. His own cheating was indiscernible, giving George no clue when the play would be fair or not, and when Kit laid down his final hand George sank back in his chair with a groan of defeat.

"Take her—you've won her fair and square. Well, you cheated, but we know each other. Don't know why you'd want her—you already tupped her and then took off in a pet. Can't imagine what interest she could hold for you."

"You never were very good at seeing possibilities, George."

"But you had her!" George protested.

"I want more." Bryony's head jerked up at that, and her angry eyes burned into him. She'd been paying attention all night long—she'd known that she was the stakes for their game, but once it had been decided, her anger had blossomed.

There was another bottle and a half on the table, just the right amount to finish off George for the night, and Kit rose gracefully, strolling across the hall to Bryony's side. He held out his hand. "Come."

She had a mulish expression on her face, one he found particularly entertaining. She wasn't going to be easy tonight, and he looked forward to the challenge. "No," she said clearly.

But not clear enough for George to hear. "Would you rather bed down with your fiancé? I should warn you, he not only has the pox but a few unsavory habits as well."

"And your habits are so wholesome," she shot back.

"Oh, good God, no. I just prefer not to injure my partners. George has a special interest in pain."

She blinked, and he congratulated himself.

She still hadn't taken his hand, so he simply reached down and took hers. She tried to pull away, but he held her tight, and she hissed. "I thought it was George who liked pain, not you."

"Oh, I like everything. I just prefer not to hurt someone who doesn't wish it."

"I don't wish you to hold my hand so tightly."

"Then come along without an argument." He loosened his grip marginally, knowing he could tighten it again at a moment's notice.

She rose obediently enough, but he wasn't fooled. He was in for a battle tonight. He looked forward to it.

❧ 26 ❧

SHE WAS GOING to kill him. Bryony didn't know how, or when, but surely something would appear that she could use as a lethal weapon. He was carrying one bottle of wine in his other hand as well as two glasses, and she could always steal the bottle and crash it down over his head. George looked on the verge of passing out, Coombs would be bedded down somewhere, and as soon as she knocked Adderley on his thick head, he'd be out of commission as well. She could escape, and this time no one would catch her.

"You can dream about it all you want," he murmured, "but I wouldn't suggest trying."

"Try what?" she said innocently.

"Whatever bloodthirsty thoughts you're having. You really don't want to rouse my temper."

"I don't give a fig for your temper." Her voice was tight with suppressed rage.

"And I don't give a damn about yours. In truth, I find it endearing."

"Stop it!" she spat at him, as he drew her up the wide stairs above George's nodding head. "I won't be mocked."

"Oh, dear," he murmured. "I'm afraid that's quite out of your control."

She'd smash the bottle open and cut his throat with the shards, she thought furiously. She would dance on his grave, she would laugh at his pain. Her one attempt at yanking her hand free only succeeded in him tightening his grip, and she wanted to bite him. Dignity, she reminded herself, straightening her spine. He could do anything he wanted with her, and she would react like the lady she was brought up to be.

"We'll take my bedroom, shall we?" he purred, but she had the sudden odd feeling that he wasn't as sanguine as he appeared to be. She glanced up at him, but met only his usual saturnine smile, and she knew she should be frightened. She wasn't.

They'd reached the first landing on the broad stairs, but when she glanced back, she saw that George was still alert, staring up at them. He was too far away for her to read the expression on his face, but a shiver of uneasiness ran up her spine.

And she must have lost her mind. She was being taken to bed by a notorious rake, and yet for some reason, she was more worried about a useless man on the verge of passing out.

And then she remembered his wicked blow across her face, the bruise hidden by her tumbled-down hair. Was it really possible that there was more to fear from George than from the worst man in England?

"Come along, poppet," he said, pulling at her. "I promise it won't hurt." They reached the top of the stairs. "Unless, of course, you want it to."

That was enough to stir her out of her dignified silence. "Why in the world would anyone desire pain?"

"Oh, George is very fond of it. It's a variation I've never particularly enjoyed, but it has its occasional uses."

She pulled her gaze away from his. "I prefer to do without," she said stiffly. "You'll simply have to do your worst without resorting to tricks."

He laughed then, and she felt an infinitesimal softening in his edgy mood. "Tricks are half the fun, precious. And I plan to do my very, very best."

"Have at it," she said carelessly. "I intend to ignore the whole messy business."

"At least you've learned enough to know it's a messy, sticky, wicked business," he said, his voice caressing the word "wicked." "So you've decided to be a martyr?"

They'd reached the top of the stairs, and he started moving her down the hallway, out of sight of George's peculiar regard. "I intend to remain dignified in the face of your assault on my person."

Before she realized what he was doing, he'd whirled her around and pushed her up against the wall, and his long fingers cradled her cheek. "Oh, sweetheart, there's no dignity in fucking."

She blinked at the word, trying to ignore the treacherous warmth his voice engendered inside her. "Do what you want," she said coldly. "I really don't care."

Reaching behind her, he pushed open a door, and a moment later, she was inside, the door shut behind them. He was going to kiss her, she thought, reading the light in his eyes, and strip off her clothes, and there was nothing she could do but let him, and she didn't want to fight him; she wanted to feel his tall body hard against her, she wanted him to keep his promise and lick between every freckle on her body. He loomed over her, and she held her breath, waiting.

And then, suddenly, he released her, moving over to the table and setting down the wine glasses. It was dark in the room, though a fire burned low in the fireplace, but a moment later, a light flared as Adderley lit candles from the smoldering coals.

He only lit two, and the room was still shrouded in a dangerous darkness. It was warm up there, a soft, cushiony warmth, a treacherous, seductive warmth.

"Could you please put out the candles," she said with icy courtesy. She knew it was a vain wish—he'd left them burning the first night he'd spent with her.

"I was thinking of lighting more. I want to see your freckles. I want to memorize them."

"Why?"

"Because they're pretty," he replied.

"Stop it! I don't even know why I'm here—I couldn't sustain your interest for more than a few hours. I can't imagine why you'd want to revisit something that was patently unsatisfactory."

"That was unkind of me, wasn't it?" he mused. "The problem is, I am never kind, and I wanted to give you a disgust of me."

"You succeeded admirably."

"Ah, there's the dignified martyr again," he marveled. "This is going to be fascinating. Will you be reciting grammar lessons when I'm inside you? Say please and thank you when I use my mouth on you? The proper phrase in those circumstances is 'thank you', but then, perhaps I'm the one who should thank you. You taste delicious."

Dignity be damned, she could feel color rise in her face. "Do you have to keep talking? Can't we just get this over with? This is getting tiresome." At least her tone was even despite the betrayal of her color. Perhaps he couldn't see it in the dim candlelight.

"You do blush so delightfully," he murmured, pouring wine into the two glasses. "I've never bedded anyone who blushed."

"Given your behavior, that's hard to believe," she shot back before she could stop herself.

"Perhaps I simply wasn't paying attention," he said, holding out one of the glasses to her.

She didn't move. "No, thank you."

"Don't make me force you," he warned her.

"Isn't that what you're planning to do?"

His smile was peculiarly sweet. "Of course not. There's no way you could want me as much as I want you—I doubt that's humanly possible—but you do want me. I know the signs."

"You flatter yourself."

"There's no need—everyone else flatters me. I can read you very well. You wouldn't have responded the way you did if you didn't like it."

"That was disgust."

"Hardly. You either want me or are afraid of me." He looked at her for a long moment. "Probably both."

He was damnably right. She was afraid of him, of his long, beautiful hands, of his wicked mouth, of his strong, hard body, and she needed him to touch her, hold her, wipe out her uncertainty and fear...

It wasn't uncertainty, she reminded herself. He'd made it very clear he had no real interest in her, and why he was continuing his little joke was beyond her comprehension. He lied when he said he found no particular pleasure in pain. He clearly found a great deal of enjoyment in tormenting her. Even if he carried through with it, he'd most likely end up laughing at her pitiful need, handing her back to George as he mocked her ineptitude.

He was still holding the glass of wine for her, and she took it, draining it in one swallow. "All right," she said. "Let's get this over and done with. Shall I remove my clothes again or would you just like to lift my skirts and have at it?"

"Tempting," he said, "But there are, of course, your delicious freckles."

"Stop it!" she cried, goaded. "You know you hate my freckles."

"Stop being tiresome," he countered. "You know they enchant me."

Enough was enough. She flung the empty glass at him, but it simply bounced off him, smashing on the floor near the fireplace. She looked for something, anything else she might throw at him, preferably something lethal, but a lit candle would do no harm, and there was nothing else in reach. Lacking a weapon, she threw herself at him, all fists and feet, hitting him, kicking him, biting him.

She might as well have attacked the statue of David itself. He was impervious to her rage, catching her hands as they flailed at him, imprisoning her kicking legs with his. A moment later, she was on her back on the bed, and he was on top of her, pinning her down as she struggled furiously, trying to hit his head with hers.

"Enough!" he roared when she'd landed a blow that doubtless hurt her more than it did him. "This is a waste of time," he added in a calmer voice.

"Not if it convinces you that I want nothing to do with you," she spat back.

He froze, and his sudden stillness startled her. And then, just as quickly, he released her. "All right," he said in a mild voice.

She didn't move. "All right, what?"

"All right, go back to Latherby. He's passed out by now—he won't give you any trouble. Tomorrow I'll send you back to London in the carriage he absconded with and you need never think of me again."

She lay still beneath him. "I have nowhere to go in London."

She fully expected him to come back with "go to the devil, I don't care" but he surprised her. "Your cousins will take you in—I'll see to it. Failing that, I expect you could go live with your idiot cousin and her Bow Street Runner."

"My...what? You must be mad—Cecilia isn't going to marry the Bow Street Runner."

"And you must be blind. Of course she is. Like you, she has nowhere else to go, though I could arrange it for either of you. The Ellistons simply need enough money to overlook the slight shadow of impropriety. You can go back to your comfortable life and never have to see me again."

"I don't want to go back," she said before she could think better of it.

He rolled onto his back on the bed, looking up at her, and he looked glorious in the moonlight with his lion's mane of blond hair and his dark, cynical face. "Of course you don't," he said mildly enough. "But as long as you won't admit what you do want, then you're caught between a rock and a hard place."

"And which are you?"

That glimmer of a dark smile danced in his eyes. "Oh, most definitely the hard place. Have you made up your mind?"

"I didn't know I had a choice."

"Of course you did," he scoffed. "So what will it be? Latherby, your cousins, or me?"

She wanted to rail at him. The choices were far from equal, though none of them were permanent. With Adderley it was be less than a night—no safe choice at all.

"You," she said meekly. It was a dreadful decision, against all her common sense. And yet it felt right. "You," she said again, her voice stronger. "I'll take you."

KIT LET out his breath at her words. He hadn't even realized he'd been holding it—he only knew that that had been the last chance he was giving her, and if she'd said no, he would have left her, never to see her again.

But astonishingly enough, she chose him over marriage, no matter how troubled that marriage would probably prove to be; she chose him over safety. She chose him, when he was nothing but wrong for her. She chose him.

He pulled her underneath him, pressing her into the soft mattress, and cupped her face. "I'm not a very kind man."

She actually laughed. "That's putting it mildly. You're the worst man in England, and probably Scotland and Wales as well. Are you warning me away?" Her wary face fell, and then she managed a bitter smile. "Oh, of course, this was all a joke, a kind of test, to see if I would be fool enough to believe that you could want..."

He stopped her mouth with his, and he tasted tears on her lips. She was a silly, confused mess, was his Bryony, and he told her so, between soft, clinging kisses, and could feel her longing, feel her reluctance. He rolled, pulling her with him, so that they lay on their sides, his leg between hers. "Save your thinking for Herodotus, not the bed, poppet. You get too confused."

He was very adept at undressing women—he'd made it a lifetime's work, and Bryony's clothes were simple, made for a woman without a maid to assist her. He unwrapped her like a present, layer after layer, his mouth following.

He was led astray by her breasts—they were beautiful, rosy-tipped, and blissfully hard. Taking the nub of one into his mouth, he sucked hard, and she jerked involuntarily beneath him, letting out a soft sound that could have been distress or pleasure. He licked the peak, and she made the sound again. Definitely pleasure. He was going to make her come so hard she'd be unable to summon a single doubt. He moved to the other breast, sucking, as his finger played with the first nipple. So hard, so delicious, and he hummed his approval against her, making her jerk slightly, and he knew he was winning.

He wanted to taste her again; he needed to see if she was damp between her legs, and he got a little clumsy, ripping the ties of her lone petticoat as he pulled it away from her legs. He slid one hand over her stomach, down between her curls, but there was only a trace of dampness there. Instinctively, he bit down on her breast, just a small bite, and he felt the liquid flood her. "You see," he said, lifting his head, "sometimes there's a place for a little pain."

She said nothing, her eyes huge in the darkness, and he could wait no longer, sliding down to cup her rounded hips in his big hands and put his mouth on her, drinking in the taste of her, the scent of her, centering on her small nub. He felt her fingers in his hair, holding him there, and he smiled against her as he slid a finger inside her.

She arched off the bed so fast it might have been electricity that touched her, and he could hear the soft sounds of pleasure she was making. She still sounded worried, and he didn't know how to wipe out that lingering trace short of pushing inside her, and he wasn't ready for that. He redoubled his efforts, using his tongue like a cock, and was rewarded with the shimmer and jerk as a small orgasm shook her body, but it was far from enough. Reaching down, he released his cramped cock into the warm night air, stroking himself while he licked her delicious juices.

She came again, harder this time, and the little shriek was music to his ears, but when he went back for more, she pushed him away. "Wait," she said in a hoarse voice. "Wait."

"I don't feel like waiting," he growled, so close to the taste of her that it was driving him mad.

"Get over it," she said, and he fell back with a laugh. She was standing up to him. No one ever stood up to him, particularly in bed, and his cock grew unimaginably harder.

She got to her knees on the mattress, looking down at him, and she looked like a hoyden, an angel, and something in between. She looked like a woman without fear, and he wanted to celebrate it, but instead, she pushed him down on the bed and followed with her kiss.

She didn't know how to kiss, which was endearing in itself. Catching her chin, he used his tongue, knowing she tasted herself on his mouth, and he taught her the moves, burying himself in her mouth as he wanted to bury his cock between her legs.

He let out a moan of protest when she pulled away, but her mouth followed the path his had travelled, down his chest, dancing across his flat nipples, and he wanted to hold her there, but she was exploring, and he wasn't going to risk stopping her. She kissed his stomach, and he trembled, wanting, needing, knowing she would never...

"What do I do next?" she whispered, her breath on him, and he almost came right there and then.

"Put your mouth on me." His voice was harsh in the darkness, almost unrecognizable, and he was rewarded with the softest, lightest kiss on his iron-hard shaft.

"Take it inside your mouth," he said. "Suck on it. Please."

If she was unpracticed at kissing, she was helpless at fellatio, and he almost came at the shy touch of her lips, as she took him inside the warm, wet darkness of her mouth, the pressure, pulling at him, sucking at him, and he gasped. Taking her hand, he put it on the base of his cock, tightening it, showing her the movement he needed as she sucked at him, and she moved up to kneel over him, her cloud of crazy hair surrounding his hips. He pushed it out of the way, wanting, needing to see his cock disappear into her now-eager mouth, and he realized she was developing a taste for it, and he groaned.

She jerked away. "Did I hurt you?"

"No," he said shortly, pushing her head back down. He needed this, so badly, needed her to do this for him; he needed to come down her throat, empty inside her, and he was so close, so close...

But at the last minute, something stopped him, and he pulled her away just as he was about to erupt, a rare moment of sanity intruding on his erotic haze, and she let out a cry of protest that almost made him spurt. But not like this. Not without her.

With ungentle hands, he pushed her down on the bed, moving

between her legs, but she was still fighting him. "I want to..." she began, but his mouth silenced hers, and she was as voracious with his mouth as she'd been with his cock. He shoved into her with one hard push, and she took him with a soft groan that was part discomfort, part completion. He was better than this; he could fuck for hours on an erection, but she affected him as no other woman could, and after a few hard strokes, she was whimpering, trembling, and he knew she was close.

He pulled out, and she let out of cry of desolation. "No!" she moaned, but he simply flipped her over beneath him, so that her face was in the disordered sheets.

"Yes," he said, pulling her hips up. "This way." And he pushed inside her from the back, feeling her quim tighten around him once more, rippling in reaction, and finally he was released, let go. He thrust into her like a madman, over and over, until she suddenly shrieked, clamping down around him, and he exploded inside her, filling her with his seed, collapsing over her, holding her beneath him as he spurted, and at the last minute, he latched his teeth onto her neck and bit her like a big cat marking his mate.

They tumbled down on the bed, and he didn't want to leave her, he wanted to stay inside her still-clutching warmth, so tight, so perfect. She was trembling underneath him, and he suspected she was crying. He hated women who cried. He wanted to drink her tears.

Rolling onto his back, he took her with him, and she went easily, curling up against him, her last defense banished. He could get rid of her now, he realized. He could mock her, pull away, and she'd be so shattered she'd never let him come near her again.

It would be the smart thing to do. She was his destruction. He'd tried to do that once, and he'd already been on the verge of going back for her when George fortuitously showed up on his doorstep. Instead, he pulled her into his arms, kissed her sweat-damp forehead, and let her fall into a deep, exhausted sleep.

He'd come inside her. There'd been no sanity left in him—he never thought once of pulling out, when that was all he had ever done, since the debacle with Christine. He'd sworn never to allow himself into that heartbreaking position again, and he'd never made a mistake.

He had no heart, he reminded himself. And pregnancy wasn't that easy to achieve, or there'd be a great many more bastards in the world. He was safe.

He tightened his arms around the fragile bundle beside him. He hadn't been safe since he'd set eyes on Bryony Marton, and he wasn't fool enough to think there was anything he could do about it. He'd lived long enough to know when life had the upper hand, as it did right now. He could retain the vague hope that time would weaken the powerful bond he felt for his red-headed virago, but he wasn't counting on it. He was tied to her, body and soul, and he had no idea what to do about it.

❦ 27 ❦

"I MOST CERTAINLY WILL NOT," Cecilia announced, crossing her arms over her chest. She knew she looked like a recalcitrant child, and that was what she felt like, but on this one matter she was determined.

"You will," said Peter Barnes, surely the most stubborn man in all of England. "I don't know what we're going to find at Wayside, and I intend to keep you out of danger, no matter what the cost."

She eyed him from her seat across the carriage, the one she'd decamped to when he'd first come up with this foolish notion. "No," she said flatly. "I'm not going to cower at some inn while you go off to rescue Bryony. She'll be distraught—she'll need me for support and comfort."

"Are we talking about the same woman? As far as I can tell, your cousin has nerves of steel," Peter countered. "Not even Adderley could upset her."

"Shows how little you know. He absolutely crushed her. She's in love with him, you silly gudgeon, and that makes every woman vulnerable."

"You don't seem the slightest bit vulnerable to me," he grumbled.

She gave him her blinding smile. "That's because you aren't the worst man in England, and you're man enough to realize you love me back. Adderley isn't quite so wise."

"And you're such an expert at recognizing the bonds of true love? Where did you get your expertise from?"

"I've read a lot," she announced sternly.

"Ha!"

"And I have first-hand knowledge of what it's like to be in love," she added, and she could see him softening for a minute.

"True enough," he conceded, that deliciously familiar glint in his warm brown eyes. "But you're still not coming with me to Waycross. Not only is Latherby there, but Adderley as well, and I have the impression their friendship has fallen apart. Women will do that."

"Which just goes to show he cares about her!" Cecilia said triumphantly.

"What if he does? What do you expect me to do about it?"

She gave a frustrated sigh. "I won't know until I ask her. I just know that she wouldn't have gone with Latherby of her own free will. Maybe you're right and Adderley is an undeserving lunkhead, but I can't leave her alone with three men trying to decide what she should do with her life. I'm coming with you."

He looked equally frustrated. "I want you safe."

"Then keep me safe. But if you try to leave me at the nearest inn, I swear I will follow after you, on foot if need be."

"Not if I tie you to a bed."

Cecilia was momentarily distracted by such an interesting notion. "We can do that after we're married," she said innocently.

Peter Barnes blinked. And then he reached for her, hauling her across the distance between the two seats and back into his arms. "You're a witch," he groaned before he kissed her.

Cecilia put her arms around him and kissed him back with great enthusiasm. They were going to have a lovely marriage.

❧

BRYONY DIDN'T WANT to leave the bed. She didn't want to leave the long, strong body that lay curved around hers, and she wondered at the depth of her longing for him. How could something, someone so foreign to the first twenty-five years of her life suddenly feel so indispensable? She wanted to burrow against his hard chest, she wanted his hands on her body, his mouth on hers, she wanted...

She wanted Christopher St. James Constant, the Earl of Adderley, and he didn't want her at all.

Well, that hadn't been strictly true. His body had wanted her, as it had before. But she knew what would happen when he woke up and found her there. The ice would be back, and she would be bereft once more, and she didn't think she could stand it. She needed to sneak away from him before he could send her, but as long as he held her, she couldn't let go. Her heart, her soul, no longer felt as if they belonged to her—she'd lost them somewhere in the night and she wasn't going to get them back. All she could salvage was her pride, and even that seemed a paltry possession.

She just didn't want him to hurt her again.

Slowly, carefully, she began to pull away from him when his arms tightened. "Where do you think you're going?" he demanded, his voice husky with sleep.

"It's almost dawn. I thought I might..."

"No." It was one word, simple and concise, and it ended all conversation as efficiently as his body pulled tightly against hers, all that warm, hard flesh touching her everywhere, and he was hard again, she could feel it, feel him, wanting her. She turned in his arms, opening to him, and pride was lost as well.

※

ADDERLEY FELT the loss even before he was completely awake. The emptiness, when that had always been what he preferred, what he insisted on. He opened his eyes to survey the place in the bed behind him, and he sat up. She'd be downstairs eating a healthy breakfast— he'd worked her hard last night, and she'd be hungry. George would be passed out somewhere in the ramshackle old lodge—he wouldn't be anywhere around to hurt her.

But he'd seen that strange, queer expression in George's eyes, and all bets were off. Throwing on his discarded clothes, he headed downstairs, trying to ignore his misgivings.

At first, everything looked peaceful enough. Bryony sat at the end of the long table, a plate of food in front of her, but she didn't lift her head when he descended the stairs. And George was to her left, leaning back in his chair, looking well-pleased with himself.

That was when Kit saw the pistol.

It lay on the table, by George's hand, and he realized belatedly that Bryony's face was white beneath her mass of red hair, and there was a bruise on her check that he hadn't noticed in the darkness. A surge of violent rage swept through him, but he displayed none of it, continuing his lazy descent and moving into the room.

"There you are, sleepyhead," George said in a fond voice. "We wondered what was taking you so long. Didn't we, darling?" he inquired of Bryony.

She didn't move, didn't answer, and George reached out and grasped her hand. "Didn't we?" he repeated.

Bryony let out a quiet gasp of pain. "Yes," she said in not much more than a whisper.

"Yes, my love," George prompted her, still squeezing her hand.

"Yes, my love."

He released her, bare moments before Kit would have torn his head off, and instead picked up the gun, surveying it casually. "Can we offer you some breakfast, Adder? My man Coombs has managed to concoct a rough meal for us, but my fiancée doesn't seem to have much appetite. Come and join us, won't you?"

Kit surveyed him warily. That unfamiliar light was still playing in George's protuberant eyes, and something felt very, very wrong.

He didn't bother plastering an affable smile on his face—George would see through it. Instead, he merely did his best to look bored as he strolled over to the table, taking the seat on the other side of Bryony's still figure.

"There, now," said George. "This is very cozy, just the three of us. I felt I should, perhaps, clarify a few matters, based on our long and cherished friendship. I intend to marry Miss Marton, and I can't have you interfering with that plan."

"Why would I?" Kit said, his lazy voice hiding his tension. "Your marriage plans are none of my concern."

"So one would hope," George said. "But I fear your interest in my wife-to-be is a little more than one could hope for. I do realize my own attractions are less obvious than yours, but I can at least congratulate myself on the fact that I'm far from the worst man in England."

"Not far enough," Kit said pleasantly.

George's high-pitched laughter was unnerving. "Very funny. I was hoping you weren't going to be a problem. You screwed the girl; time to let her go."

"Have you ever known me to give a damn about some random female I've taken to bed?" he replied, and for some reason he couldn't begin to comprehend, he moved his leg over under the table until it touched Bryony's.

It seemed to galvanize her. Her back straightened, and she cast him a quick, cold glance before returning to her perusal of her gelatinous eggs.

"Never," George said. "But this time feels different. I want your word of honor, as a gentleman, that you're not going to interfere when I take Miss Marton over the border this afternoon."

Kit leaned back. "My dear George, you should know as well as anyone that my word is worthless. And I don't believe I'll let you carry her off. I'm not finished with her yet."

"Don't be difficult," George whined. "You can have her after we're married. Just give me time to get a child on her and then you can do what you want with her. Though God knows why you'd want to bother."

"I don't think so." His tone was amiable iron.

George blinked. "How are you going to stop me? I have the gun."

"Are you going to shoot me, George?"

George picked up the pistol and waved it in his direction. His hold was shaky, and it wavered dangerously. "I would hate to have to do that," he said with the deliberate care of the inebriated.

"Then why don't we be civilized about it? Let me have her first. If you're still interested when I tire of her, you can marry her then."

Bryony's head jerked up, and the shock in her green eyes was a testament to his acting skills. George was never going to put a finger on her.

"I'd rather marry George," she said bitterly.

George hooted with laughter. "Well, then, that solves the problem. No need for bloodshed."

"I disagree. I don't care what she wants, or what you want, you should know that by now. I want what I want, and I intend to have it." He gave George a dulcet smile. "I'm willing to fight you for her."

George scoffed. "You'd kill me."

"Did you put that bruise on her face?"

George peered at her blearily. "I suppose I did."

"Then, yes, I'll kill you."

Again, he felt Bryony's start. Poor child, he was confusing her.

And then she pushed back from the table and rose, quivering in fury. "To hell with both of you!" she bit out, and before he realized what she was doing she'd grabbed the pistol from George's slack hand and was pointing it at some spot between the two of them.

"Put it away, poppet," he drawled. "You don't know how to shoot."

"My father taught me," she snapped. "I just have to decide who I want to kill more." She swung the pistol his way. "And that would be you."

He gave her his most charming smile. Her response was a low growl, but she hadn't counted on Latherby making a lunge for her. They both went tumbling onto the hard floor, and Kit moved fast, trying to secure the pistol, but it was too late. George had Bryony clasped tightly in his arms, and the pistol was pointed at her head.

Kit froze where he was. "What do you think you're doing, George? You have no reason to hurt Bryony."

"Oh, don't I?" There was the edge of hysteria in his voice. "I don't think even her money will be enough to get me out of the hole I'm in, and I don't care. My life has been cursed since I met her."

"Then let her go."

"No!" he screeched. "You want her, and that's enough reason to kill her."

272

Kit took a deep breath. "Dear me, such anger, George. I never knew you harbored such animosity. Why not get straight to the point and shoot me instead?"

The gun moved shakily in his direction, and Kit held very still. George had an arm across Bryony's neck, and if she struggled, George would shoot her. He'd always been a terrible shot, but the way the gun was waving in the air could prove surprisingly lethal.

"Kill me, George," he said, his voice soft and beguiling. "You know that's what you want to do. I'm useless, a monster, no good to anyone. Let her go and shoot me instead."

"You're confusing me!" George cried, tightening his arm across Bryony's throat, as he moved the gun back to her head. It was shaking so hard, Kit was afraid it might go off by itself and he was paralyzed with fear.

"Don't, George," he said softly. "Kill me. Please. Kill me."

George didn't move the gun, but a crafty expression crossed his face. "That's what you want, isn't it? I think I'll put a bullet in Miss Marton's brain so you know what real suffering is like."

Kit tensed, ready to leap on him if there was no other choice, when there was a sudden scraping of the front door, and the idiot cousin's voice came loud and clear.

"I don't know why you had to tie up the coachman—"

It was enough of a distraction. George whirled to face them in surprise, temporarily loosening his hold, and Bryony tore herself out of his grip. Time seemed to move with aching slowness—the pair at the door suddenly realizing something was very wrong, and George knew he'd lost his prey. With a vicious look at Kit, he pointed the pistol at Bryony and fired.

𝕊 28 𝕊

KIT LEAPT JUST IN TIME, throwing himself in front of Bryony, and he felt the fiery pain in his arm as he landed, covering her.

"No!" George was screaming. "No, no, no!" His hysterical voice was suddenly silenced, and Kit looked up to see Peter Barnes shaking his bruised hand as he stood over George's limp body. Kit didn't give a damn—he pulled back and turned Bryony over.

"Are you hurt?" he cried hoarsely. "Damn it, answer me! Were you hit?"

And then the annoying cousin pushed him out of the way, taking Bryony's dazed body into her arms and weeping so noisily it penetrated the temporary deafness caused by the explosion of the gun.

"I'm fine," he heard her say, and his relief made him lightheaded. They would take care of her, George was stopped. He could leave; all he wanted to do was get away from everything and he rose, pushing himself up from the floor, and glanced down at his blood-soaked arm.

"Damn," he said softly, and passed out.

𝕊

BRYONY LET out a shriek as she saw him fall, tearing herself out of Cecilia's arms. She crawled over to him, pulling his head against her breast and sobbing, the tears that had been in abeyance tumbling down her cheeks. "Oh, God, no!" she wailed, rocking him.

Peter Barnes knelt down beside them, trying to loosen her clutching grip, as he surveyed Kit's bloody arm. A moment later, he'd sliced open the sleeve of Kit's loose white shirt with a knife and surveyed the bloody wound.

"Is he going to die?" Bryony sobbed.

"Not likely. It's just a graze. Wake up, old man!" He had the indecency to slap Adderley across the face, and Bryony would have slapped him in turn if Adderley hadn't started to come around, shaking his head.

"What...?" he said dazedly.

"Well, I must say you're a great disappointment," Cecilia announced with a frown on her lovely face. "One little scratch and you fall over in a dead faint. What idiot said you were the worst man in England, tell me that!"

"Be quiet," Bryony snapped, holding his head to her breast and stroking his brow. "He's had a shock."

"Don't like...my own blood," he said thickly, then cast a fulminating glance at Cecilia. "I wouldn't mind yours."

"Cecilia, see to your cousin," Barnes ordered, carefully prying Bryony's hands away. "I've got to bandage this mess before he loses any more blood...."

"Is he going to die?" Bryony wailed again.

"No, it will simply make a bigger mess to clean up. Take her somewhere and let me get on with this."

She hated to leave him. His beautiful face was so pale, the blood so dark as it saturated his torn sleeve. He was going to die, she was sure of it.

It would serve him right! When he got tired of her...how dare he, the pickle-livered bastard. Where was her Shakespeare when she needed it—he had the very best insults, and Adderley deserved every one of them.

Except. He'd jumped in front of Adderley's gun. He'd taken a bullet for her. Why would he do that when he cared for nothing and no one? It made no sense.

"Come along, dearest," Cecilia was saying, sounding oddly mature. "Peter will see to him, and if Peter says he'll be all right, then you may be sure he will be."

Wearily, she allowed herself to be pulled to her feet, realizing belatedly that she was covered with his blood. She tried to go back to him, but Cecilia stopped her. "The sooner he's bandaged, the sooner he'll be back to his old, wicked self."

"He's not old," Bryony protested. "Wicked, I'll grant you." She took one last look at him as Cecilia pulled her from the room, but Barnes's bulk was hiding him from her eyes.

"Now, where is the kitchen in this place?" Cecilia demanded crossly, heading down a shadowy hallway. "You need to wash off all that blood."

"It doesn't matter. I have nothing else to wear." She put protective arms around herself. If he was dying, if he was dead, his blood would be the last thing she had of him, and she wasn't going to give up her stained dress without a fight.

"I brought some dresses along," Cecilia said. "I'll see to it."

Slowly, common sense began to sneak in beneath her panic. "What in the world are you doing here? How did you find us?"

"Peter's a Bow Street Runner," she said proudly. "He can find anyone."

"And why are you calling him Peter?"

"Because I think calling my future husband Mr. Barnes would be excessively silly," she announced.

Bryony looked at her in shock. "You can't marry him. Your parents will disown you."

"My parents have already disowned me. Which is just as well—he probably would have refused my offer if they hadn't."

"*Your* offer?"

"You've always told me to go after what I wanted, really wanted. I want Peter."

"That doesn't always work," Bryony said in a hopeless voice.

"You don't know until you try."

It took her a long time to get washed and changed. First, she had to deal with her belated reaction to her near death, then listen to the loud curses that echoed from the front room that assured her that Adderley was not only very much alive but in no charity with the man trying to bandage him. Good, she thought. She hoped it hurt.

Then she had to cry for a solid ten minutes, then listen to Cecilia's raptures over Peter Barnes, and then, finally, she was ready to face her nemesis, because that was what he was. The worst thing that had ever happened to her, and she loved him so much it ached.

The main room of the lodge had been put back in a semblance of order. There was no sign of George, and Kit was sitting in a chair by the dead fire, leaning back, his eyes closed, the bulk of a bandage wrapped around his upper arm beneath the fresh shirt.

"I've got Latherby and Coombs tied up in the gatehouse, and I'll leave them to the local magistrate to deal with," Peter said as he righted another chair. "Though I doubt there's much can be done with Sir George in the long run. He'll be dead soon—I've seen enough of the pox to know when someone's reached the end, and he's just about drunk himself to death as well. He won't be giving anyone more trouble. As for Coombs, he'll get transportation, and serves him right."

"We don't have to take them up in the carriage, do we?" Cecilia asked anxiously.

"No, my dear, we don't. We'll just have your cousin join us." Adderley didn't move, and Peter continued doggedly.

"The coach that brought Latherby is his lordship's—it's got his crest on it. Do you want me to find a coachman from the town, Adderley? The magistrate probably knows one."

"I'm perfectly capable of driving a coach," Adderley said irritably, his eyes still closed. "What about your coachman?"

"I'm not giving him up." Peter looked at his still figure, then back at Bryony's. "Don't you have something to say?" he demanded irritably.

"Such as what?" Adderley was equally fractious. "Thank you for bandaging me? If you hadn't come barging in, Latherby wouldn't have gotten a shot off in the first place."

"And didn't I hear you begging him to kill you instead? What was that all about?"

Adderley's beautiful mouth closed in a thin, hard line. "Go away, all of you. Leave me in peace."

All of you, Bryony thought, dying a little inside and determined not to show it. Nodding at Peter, she took Cecilia's arm and swept from the building.

The bright sunlight and warm air were a shock after the gloomy darkness of the great hall, and Bryony blinked, momentarily dazed. No, she reminded herself. She wasn't going to cry over him again. She wasn't going to cry over anyone.

"I'm so glad you're being sensible for once," Cecilia observed, paying no attention to her own rash behavior. "That man is absolutely impossible, and you deserve so much better. We simply have to convince Peter that we continue to the border so that we may be married and then you can come and live with us. He assures me he has enough room, and sooner or later, we'll find someone absolutely splendid for you...."

"I'm never going to get married."

"Oh, don't say that. I'm sure you'll find someone."

"I don't want to," Bryony said grimly.

"Well, there's only one worst man in all of England, Scotland, and Wales. Everyone else has to be better."

Bryony cast her a quelling glance, but Cecilia was undaunted. "I suppose it's not your fault that you fell in love with such a selfish cad. He's very, very handsome in a devilish kind of way, and I expected he was very adept in the marriage bed."

"There was no marriage. It was just a bed." And a chair, she thought. And the floor. And up against the wall that last time.

"I'm sure you'll find someone equally adept and much nicer. A sweet, kind gentleman who'll put you first. Wouldn't that be perfect?"

"No!" Bryony snapped. There was a light of amusement in Cecilia's blue eyes, but Bryony was in no mood to see humor in anything.

"Just be happy you're free of that monster," Cecilia continued.

"He's not a monster!" Bryony shot back. "He's just...he's just..."

"A very bad man," Cecilia supplied.

Bryony's eyes met hers and all her rage was gone. "Yes," she said. "But he's *my* man."

A moment later, she was out of the carriage, running across the stable yard to the massive front door. She passed Peter Barnes on the way, but he made no move to stop her.

⚜

THE COACH ROCKED as he climbed in and gathered his fiancé into his arms. "Took you long enough," he said. "I was afraid Adderley was going to come out and shoot me."

"He wouldn't dare. Let's get going before he can stop us."

"You're certain this is a good idea?" Peter asked, his forehead creased.

"The very best," said Cecilia.

He nodded, and kissed her upturned face. "Then on to Scotland."

❦ 29 ❧

ADDERLEY HADN'T MOVED from his seat by the fireplace. He had to have heard the door open again, but he said nothing, didn't even turn his head, and Bryony froze there, uncertain what to do. And then her temper, the one she had always tried so hard to control, burst free.

"You were just going to let me go?" she demanded, giving full vent to her anger.

"It seemed a good idea. Why did you come back?" he sounded no more than curious, and her hands curled into fists.

"I have a few things to say to you before I left." She came into the room, still keeping her distance from him.

"Fine. Go ahead and tell me what a wretched human being I am. Curse me for an unfeeling monster. Tell me all about how I destroyed your life."

"You're not a monster."

"Tell me about... What do you mean, I'm not a monster?" He finally opened his eyes to look at her, his fake ennui disappearing. "I'll have you know I've spent years building up a very solid reputation as the worst kind of man. Never tell me my efforts have been for naught."

"You're not a monster."

"I suggest you stop saying that, or I'll be forced to come over there and prove to you just how monstrous I can be."

"Stop threatening me when you don't mean a word of it," she shot back.

"Are you really so naïve as to underestimate me? I do assure you, my reputation is earned. I care about nothing and no one. I'm a—"

"Oh, stop it!" she said crossly. "Your protestations of evil are tiresome. I'm sure you've done many wicked things in your life and will happily continue your profligate ways. But we both know you're not going to touch me again, so stop threatening me."

He rose from the chair, but he kept his back toward her, staring into the cold fireplace. "I believe I've touched you quite thoroughly already."

"You were being deliberately perverse."

"I am perverse," he agreed gravely, "but I would put my actions with you down to hedonism rather than perversity. I have a very strong sexual appetite."

"You said you were going to educate me on all sexual matters. You have. There's no reason to continue the charade."

"Hardly a charade," he said, moving closer, and she wanted to back away, but she stood her ground, strong in her outrage. "Though I'm afraid we've barely scratched the surface—you still have a great deal left to learn. For instance, did you know there's a book from ancient India that describes sixty-four different ways of having intercourse? For that matter, there are certain Arabian customs that might be worth investigating, and I haven't even gotten around to simply tying you up."

"Tying me up?" She was momentarily diverted. "Why would anyone like that?"

"Oh, you would, my dear, under the right circumstances. You most definitely would. In fact, I think you would probably enjoy anything I did to you, almost as much as I'd enjoy it."

"There are times when I hate you," she said bitterly. He was moving toward her and she found herself backing up.

The frown stayed on her face. "You left me for George. He told me."

"I did not leave you for George. I'd made all the arrangements— you were to go back to London with your cousin and Barnes, and I was going to make certain your family would take you in. I didn't get that far. But don't worry, I'll make arrangements."

"You will, will you? So what's going to happen to me now?" she said.

"You can do anything you want."

"No, I can't." She took a step toward him, suddenly very sure.

"Don't do that!" he snapped. "I'm a monster, and you know it. I have no feelings, no tenderness, no mitigating circumstances, so stop looking at me like some Drury Lane actress playing Juliet. You don't love me. You don't know me. I've done my best to make sure that nobody can."

Poor baby, she thought, as her uncertainty and hurt drained away. "I know you," she said, calm and steady. "And I'm in your hands. So what are you planning to do with me now?"

"The easiest answer would be to toss you out the window," he said bitterly. "Then at least I wouldn't have to bother with you anymore."

"You aren't going to do that." She moved closer, and he had the look of a trapped fox. "You love me."

"Don't be absurd. I don't even believe in love."

"It must be very confusing then," she said sympathetically, close enough to touch him.

"I can still return you to your family," he suggested. "Or I could give you enough money to make you go away so that I never have to see you again."

"You could," she agreed, and she was starting to feel very smug. "But then you'd just have to kidnap me again, and you know how tiresome carriages can be."

He growled. "Or I could set you up in a townhouse as my mistress until I grow tired of you. I usually do after two months, but you're contrary enough that I might keep you for three."

"You might," she agreed placidly. "But I think you'll keep me for a lot longer."

"Hell's teeth," he said defiantly, glaring at her. "I think I'll marry you."

"I think you will," she said, and went into his arms. "And I promise, it won't hurt a bit," she whispered, just before her mouth met his.

EPILOGUE

"And that's my I-don't-know-how-many greats grandfather Christopher," Mary Adderley said to the man by her side, looking up at the huge, fearsome painting of a very beautiful man. "He looks quite ferocious, doesn't he? Apparently, he was considered the worst man in England until he met his wife, and even then no one liked him but her."

"It doesn't sound like a match made in heaven," Richard, her very proper boyfriend remarked.

"Oh, but it was," Mary said, moving on to the next painting in the vast portrait hall. "She's the magnificent redhead there, with all those glorious freckles. Apparently, she was as sweet as can be, gave him seven children, and they all survived, and the two of them died within hours of each other. They're even buried together like some old crusader and his wife."

"I never would have thought you'd be such a romantic, Mary," Richard said. "You're forgetting the lice and the disease of Georgian England, and if he was considered to be the worst man, he probably beat her."

"I don't think so. Family legend had it that he was absolutely devoted to her, and I prefer to believe that."

Richard sniffed in the way she absolutely hated. "Well, these two portraits will have to go with the others. They're worth a fortune." He moved down the row. "Who's this?"

"Oh, that was Bryony's cousin, Mrs. Barnes. She created almost as big as scandal when she ran off with a Bow Street Runner."

"And you're going to tell me they were blissfully happy as well," he said cynically, and Mary wondered exactly why she'd agreed to have him come with her as the paintings were inventoried. Richard was a good man, but he was absolutely devoid of imagination.

"In fact, I believe they fought a great deal, but they were happy as well, with four children. You've met my cousin Ginny—she's their descendent."

"Yes, dear, you have a glorious, romantic family who belong in one of those dreadful bodice-rippers," he said in a condescending voice. "Can we go home now?"

Mary took one last look at the portraits and sighed with satisfaction. "Yes, Richard."

And Richard Latherby took her arm and drew her away from the portraits. Perhaps they weren't as well-suited as she'd thought, Mary pondered as she followed him out to his practical Fiat. But where in this life was she going to find the modern worst man in all of England?

ABOUT THE AUTHOR

Anne Stuart is a grandmaster of the genre, winner of Romance Writers of America's prestigious Lifetime Achievement Award, survivor of more than forty-five years in the romance business, and still just keeps getting better.

She's won numerous awards, appeared on most bestseller lists, and speaks all over the country. Her general outrageousness has gotten her on *Entertainment Tonight*, as well as in *Vogue*, *People*, *USA Today*, *Women's Day* and countless other national newspapers and magazines.

When she's not traveling, she's at home in Northern Vermont with her luscious husband of forty-five years, an empty nest, and five sewing machines. When she's not working, she's watching movies, listening to rock and roll and spending far too much time quilting and making doll clothes because she has no intention of ever growing up.

Follow her on her website at Anne-Stuart.com social media at:

 facebook.com/author.annestuart
twitter.com/TheAnneStuart
instagram.com/Annestuartwriter

Darkness before Dawn

At the Edge of the Sun

HISTORICAL ROMANCES

The Devil's Waltz

Hidden Honor

Lady Fortune

Prince of Magic

Lord of Danger

Prince of Swords

To Love a Dark Lord

Shadow Dance

A Rose at Midnight

The Houseparty

The Demon Count Novels

The Spinster and the Rake

Lord Satan's Bride

Angels Wings

Demonwood

Cameron's Landing

Barrett's Hill

The Absolutely, Positively Worst Man in England, Scotland and Wales

WOMEN'S FICTION

When the Stars Fall Down

Return to Christmas

ROMANTIC SUSPENSE

Into the Fire

The Widow

Silver Falls

Rafe's Revenge

Heat Lightning

Chasing Trouble -

Lazarus Rising

Rancho Diablo

Crazy Like a Fox

Glass Houses

Cry for the Moon

Partners in Crime

Bewitching Hour

Rocky Road

Museum Piece

Heart's Ease

Chain of Love

Against the Wind

COLLABORATIONS

Dogs & Goddesses – with Jennifer Crusie and Lani Diane Rich

The Unfortunate Miss Fortunes with Jennifer Crusie and Lani Diane Rich

NOVELLAS

Blind Date from Hell

Night and Day

A Midnight Clear

Burning Bright

Dark Journey

Date with the Devil

MANGA

A Dark and Stormy Night

Night

Manufactured by Amazon.ca
Bolton, ON